NEITHER SAFE NOR PROPER

Leaning against the side of the wagon, Luke hooked his thumbs into his gun belt. "I've made you and Tommie a bed out here. Don't sleep in there. Whoever ransacked the place might come back. I can keep watch so you'll be safe."

"I don't think it would be prop—"

"Proper?" Luke finished for her. A bitter laugh echoed into the night. "Then it won't be proper every night you're on the trail with any male guide. What do you want, Tess, safety or propriety?"

Perhaps she had lived so long with her own secrets, she now suspected everyone else of harboring them. "Can I trust you?" she asked aloud, unaware her suspicion had taken voice. Though innocent, the question needed an answer for so much more.

"That's for you to decide." His voice was low, evasive in its huskiness. Clouds drifted over the moon, cloaking his expression.

THE BEHOLDING

DIA HUNTER

LEISURE BOOKS   NEW YORK CITY

A LEISURE BOOK®

November 1997

Published by

Dorchester Publishing Co., Inc.
276 Fifth Avenue
New York, NY 10001

ISBN 0-8439-4321-1

The name "Leisure Books" and the stylized "L" with design are trademarks of Dorchester Publishing Co., Inc.

Printed in the United States of America.

This book is dedicated to
Tom Koumalats
—friend, historian, Texan

Your support of my writing has always been
as reliable as a spur jingle.
With deepest appreciation.

Prologue

"You shouldn't be out here alone . . . in the dark."

The deep male voice nearly startled Tess out of next year's growth, making her stumble as she gathered the last sheet from the clothesline. She swung around to face the man only to discover his chest pressed dangerously near.

"Don't!" she cried almost hysterically, twisting her body away as if she'd been stung.

"I was only trying to stop you from falling, Miss Mitchell." The man backed up and put his palms up in mock surrender. "No harm intended."

"Oh, it's you." Tess exhaled slowly, relieved to discover it was only Clifton Harper, the soldier from Fort Smith. For one long, terrifying moment, she had feared that the man who had turned her life into a living hell two days ago had returned.

As a friend of her parents, every time Clifton Harper had business to tend to in Hot Springs, he made a point of paying a visit to the bathhouse they managed. But those visits had become more frequent lately. "I-I'm sorry, Mr. Harper. I'm afraid it's been a difficult week."

She pointed toward the right wing of the bathhouse which provided living quarters for the current manager. "Father and

Mother have retired for the evening, but I'm sure they wouldn't mind being awakened if you need them.''

He took off his hat and twisted it in his hands. "I didn't come to see them, Miss Mitchell. I hoped I might have a word with you.''

"Me?'' She eyed him curiously. Suspicion crept into her thoughts, forcing her to gauge his height and weight. Could he be the one? She could remember very little about the attack two nights ago. It seemed her mind only wanted to block out the horror of it all.

"And why tonight? Can't it wait till morning?''

"No, it can't.'' With a good deal of effort he finally allowed his gaze to meet hers directly. "You see, Miss Mitchell . . . Tess . . . the law knows about your daddy's and mother's schemes. That last fella—Webster Krugg—he had fifty dollars stolen while he was bathing in your pa's bathhouse. Said you lured him in with all that talk about you being forty years old and the waters offering a fountain of youth of sorts. He told the marshal that you lured him in and your parents robbed him while he bathed.''

"I had no part in it!'' Tess defended herself, thrusting the sheet into the basket with the other linen.

"But you knew they did, didn't you?''

His tone wasn't accusing and his expression offered sympathy. Tess couldn't deny her knowledge. "I suspected my father for a long time, but didn't find out the truth until a few days ago.''

"Yet you continued to let them use you to scam the bathers. You can't be a day over fourteen.''

"Fifteen, and I didn't *let* them use me. I had to or . . . or, well, it's none of your business.'' Tess refused to tell him that her father tended to make her mother suffer for any disobedience Tess showed him. Silent little bruises her mother had said were hidden where inquiring eyes couldn't question. Bruises, Tess had since learned, that never existed.

Clifton took a step closer. She grabbed the basket and held it in front of her, putting distance between her and the soldier.

"I know this isn't my concern, but if I don't speak my hopes tonight, I might not get another chance. And maybe you'll want to hear what I've got to say."

"Then say it, Mr. Harper. You seem intent upon doing so anyway."

"Tess, girl, I guess you've noticed how many times I've come around. And I know I ain't as young a man as you'd probably hoped to wed one day, but I won't beat you and you'll never go hungry—"

"Are you asking me to marry you, Mr. Harper?" Tess couldn't hide the astonishment in her voice. She started back up the path toward the bathhouse. "Why, you hardly even know me."

He fell in step beside her. "That's true. But I know I've wanted you for my wife ever since I seen you the first time. And I happen to know that if you don't get out of here this very night, Krugg and the law plan to pay you and your parents a visit in the morning. I can tell you the circuit judge don't take kindly to thieves. And it doesn't matter which of you did the stealing. He'll figure you were all in on it."

A giggle of hysteria erupted in Tess's throat as she halted. She started to stifle it, then didn't, shaking the voluptuous body that had proven her undoing.

"Are you all right, Tessa?" He reached out to steady her, patting her hand.

He wasn't much to look at, was probably near her father's age. And as a soldier, he would never be a rich man. But he had one quality she needed desperately: he was willing to love her despite her . . . imperfections. Perhaps devoting herself to making his home and life more comfortable would be enough to repay him for his timely offer.

"No, I'm not all right," she whispered, not shying away from his soothing touch, "but you seem to be willing to take me as I am. God forgive me for doing this to you; you probably don't deserve it. But yes, Mr. Harper, I'll marry you."

11

Chapter One

Fort Smith, Arkansas 1866

"Hell of a way for a man to make a living," Luke Reeves muttered disgustedly. He pulled up the collar of his black duster and tugged the brim of his slouch hat lower to shield his eyes from the downpour. After dismounting, he glanced briefly at the taller of the two bodies stretched over the extra mount taken on at Pencil Bluff. The dirty sidewinder deserved the bullet in his gut, but only time would tell if the other one had met his Maker too soon. Innocent or guilty, Clifton Harper was just as dead.

Telling Widow Harper had been put off long enough. Luke tied the reins to the hitching post outside the row of white-washed apartments assigned to officers with families. This wasn't the first time he'd changed a wife's name to "widow," and it wouldn't be the last.

An amber glow in a calico-curtained window drew him to the Harper home. Childish laughter challenged the rumbling thunder. The echoing mirth belonged to a woman, rich, melodious and compelling. A powerful thirst corded Luke's throat as his fist paused, then struck the door three times. He should have satisfied the urge for something fiery to drink before he finished this piece of business. Maybe if he had, whiskey could have melted the cool aloofness that had numbed his soul for more years than he cared to remember.

"Clifton? Is that you? Let me move the rags from below the door; the mud is leaking in again."

The voice sounded younger than Luke's investigation indicated. Clifton Harper was on the down side of forty, and the wife he married in Hot Springs was reportedly near the same age. He'd bet his next payroll she was less than twenty-five.

The door jerked open with a squeak of the hinges. Accustomed to being denied entry, Luke took a step forward, letting one boot nestle between the door and its jamb.

"Oh, I thought you were my husband." Tess Harper pressed her body against the door, closing off the warm welcome she'd intended.

"Ma'am." Luke tipped his hat and from beneath its broad brim, studied her. Eyes the shade of mountain mint revealed both her curiosity and the wariness he expected of someone running from the law.

Sweat rolled off him despite the cooling rain and trickled into his eyes. Flickering shadows cast by the oil lamp hinted at the lushness of the widow's mouth, full and shapely, almost pouty. Small wonder the report said she was so successful at swindling the bathers. With lips like that added to a figure Michelangelo would have considered perfection, a man could imagine all kinds of ways to show his appreciation for such beauty.

"Are you here to see my husband?"

Youth made her voice soft, expectant. Twenty, maybe. Not twenty-five as he'd earlier figured. That would have made her about fourteen at the time of the Hot Springs scam. Must've been quite a beauty early on.

"Name's Luke Reeves." Determination hardened his mouth into a grimace, deepening the curved lines that bracketed his face. "I've come to speak to you about Mr. Harper."

The lady leaned closer, trying to peer around his shoulders.

Though she was taller than most women, she stood a good five inches shorter than his own six-foot frame. Luke almost wished she would deny knowing Harper. From his brief glance at the soldier, he couldn't figure how such an older, barrel-shaped man could ever attract such a lovely, younger woman. But then, understanding women had never been one of his talents.

"What's wrong, Mr. Reeves?" Tess asked suddenly, her scalp tingling with premonition. Cold dread settled heavily in her stomach as she stared at his hard slash of a mouth. He had the look of a hunter—cold-eyed and with sinews carved from long days in the saddle. He bore the weight of the gun resting against his left thigh well, revealing the weapon as an inherent part of him and not something donned in a moment of irritation. Was he the one she long suspected would take her from Tommie?

Glancing at her son, she mentally wrapped him in a protective embrace and vowed she would fight to the death before she'd let anyone separate them. Tess's voice took on an edge of caution and hope that her fear was needless. "Tommie, get Mr. Reeves something to dry himself with while I pour him some coffee." After wiping her hands on her apron, she pretended to brush away nonexistent dirt from the folds of her linsey homespun.

At her son's departure, Tess Harper attempted to cloak the foreboding that coursed through her as she looked up quickly to meet the stranger's gaze. Taking a breath, she braced herself for the worst. "What is it that needs saying on such a soggy night, Mr. Reeves?"

Luke admired her control and was surprised that his hands felt clammy inside the dark cowhide gloves. "Like I said, it concerns your husband."

Instantly a new worry welled. "What has he done?"

"Nothing," Luke admitted. *That is, nothing I can prove yet,* he should have said. "It's what I've done."

Luke stepped into the light and awaited the startled gasp he knew would follow her first sight of his scars. To his surprise, none came. She was a lady, he'd give her that. Most women objected loudly. Hell, so had most men he'd faced. Luke once considered growing a beard and mustache to hide a portion of it, but the jagged white scars that had zigzagged his right cheek and brow from birth made his job easier. Many a man had backed down from Luke's fierce expression and the gun hand that backed it up.

"He's in trouble, then?"

Tess Harper did what few others attempted, studying Luke with a frankness he admired. He hoped like hell she wasn't guilty. The thought of taking her back to stand trial grated against his better judgment. His instinct for finding the truth had been honed to a fine edge over the past twenty-seven years. But truth traveled many side trails if a man was willing to be led down them.

Luke met her sea-green gaze directly, unsure if he honored her so because he was impressed with her or because something inside him wanted to hurt—wanted to feel, even if it was pain he inflicted on someone else. "Ma'am, there's no easy way to tell you this." He paused, searching for better words but found none. "Your husband's dead. Shot this morning about daybreak near Pencil Bluff."

"Shot?" Tess's body flinched as if she'd been struck. The word ricocheted through her mind and lodged in her heart with such force that her knees threatened to buckle beneath her. *Clifton's dead. The torment's finally over.*

Within her, turbulent emotions boiled anew, echoing the tumult rumbling in the Arkansas sky. Their marriage shouldn't have ended this way. Never *this* way. Finding her voice, she swallowed the painful loneliness of years threatening to close her throat. "How did it hap—" Her question stopped abruptly as her son returned.

"Here it is, Mommie. Gosh, Mista, you all wet!"

The tow-headed boy seemed to bounce as he walked across the room. The child's uneven gait revealed his limp to be the kind long endured, not of a recent injury. Embarrassed at the same ogling he had expected of Tess, Luke accepted the of-

15

fered towel and deliberately sought the boy's eyes. "Much obliged, Mr. Harper."

The small boy giggled and rocked back on his feet. "My daddy is Mista Harper. My name is Tommie, and I'm almost four years old."

"Pleased to meet you, Tommie. I'm Luke Reeves." Realizing he had just delivered devastating news to the boy's mother and now stood there chatting as if nothing had happened, Luke decided he needed to get the child busy so he could finish giving the details to the widow. "Do you know how to shine boots, Tommie?"

Tommie's head bobbed. "Gooder'n everybody! Papa taughted me. Don't you know how, Mista Yuke?"

"Not as well as you, I'll bet." Luke ruffled the boy's blond hair, surprised at the warm stirring that kindled in his heart. Would those eyes a shade darker than his mother's look up at him with such friendliness if the lad knew his reason for being there? "I only pay for the best. You want to earn a nickel?"

Tommie's emerald gaze narrowed into a mischievous slant. "How about two nickels?"

Enterprising as his mother, so it seemed. "You drive a hard bargain, Short Pants." Luke offered to shake on the agreement, and the boy clasped his palm warmly.

"It's a deal, sir."

While the stranger took off his boots, Tess looked for something to keep her trembling hands busy. A rush of guilt consumed her. In wishing for her own safety, had she brought harm to Clifton? Maybe if she had been the kind of wife he wanted and did not anger him so often that he felt compelled to stay away, Clifton would be alive.

Don't do this to yourself, Tess silently reprimanded and began to polish spoons she'd already dried once. She had promised she wouldn't condemn herself anymore about failings beyond her control. Clifton made his own choices. Just like her mother and father had. When would she quit being everybody's pawn? She didn't kill Clifton. It was time to think of Tommie. *I'm all he's got now.*

Tess felt Luke watching her, studying her, and suddenly she was all too aware of him as a man. Confused emotions too frightening to identify stirred deeply within her, and she was surprised at this attraction. She'd thought that part of her had died long ago.

"Got 'em!"

Luke's sudden declaration startled Tess. She dropped the utensils, causing them to clatter against the wooden floor. "My goodness," she muttered, bending to pick up the mess. Tears welled in her eyes and a great sob wrenched from her soul. With enormous effort, she attempted to appear composed. Why tears now, Tess wondered, when she had ached for their release so many times before? "This will n-never do," she stammered. "S-so clumsy."

As she gathered the spilled dinnerware, the stranger's hands gently rested over her own, halting the task. Tess trembled as the sympathy they offered warmed the cold that iced her heart. She looked up into eyes the dark blue of twilight in the Ozarks and was engulfed by the genuine concern found in the carved strength of his face.

Warm prickles raced down her neck and spine. Despite the rawhide glove he wore, she could feel the strength in his hand. The musky scent of leather, rain and man swamped her thoughts as his fingers touched her own, scorching her entire being with his heat. She shivered, as if staring into the approach of a dangerous wildfire.

"Tommie, do you have more rags where you found the first one?" Luke asked, never taking his gaze from hers.

His low voice rumbled in her ear, and Tess found the timbre compelling.

"Yessir. Mommie, you care if I get some more?"

"Go ahead, son." She squeezed her eyes closed. "Use what you need."

Tommie ran into the other room, leaving Luke wondering what to say next. Could he believe the innocence he saw in her eyes? Though soft, tender and almost shy, those beautiful green depths kindled a fierce desire within him. A desire that

17

had lured men into the baths only to be robbed and beaten? And her touch? Was this touch of hands capable of swindling men of their mining claims, as well?

Despite his life-long principle never to let emotion rule his decisions, Luke was surprised to discover that a little decency still lingered somewhere deep inside him. He didn't want to destroy her, and the fact amazed him. How long had it been since he wanted deliberately to be kind, or believe any woman?

Her hand slid away, and she reached for the blue-speckled pot on the stove. "Would you like some coffee, Mr. Reeves? I always have a pot waiting for Clifton when he comes back from—"

"There's no use wasting it." When Luke took the cup, her eyes revealed all the confusion and grief she must be feeling.

"It's kind of you to keep Tommie from hearing this," she whispered.

You might not be so friendly if you knew what I have to say, he warned silently.

Tess offered a high-backed chair. "Were you there when my husband died?"

Luke sank into the chair and took a sip from the imported china. Unconsciously he scraped an arm across his nose and mouth to clear away the foul taste of the words he was about to utter. "I shot him."

She stopped in mid-pour, then after only the briefest pause, filled her own cup to the brim.

"You?" Tess was amazed at the calmness in her voice. Alternating emotions raged within her in harsh discordance. She hated Luke Reeves more than she had ever hated anyone. He had taken Tommie's father away forever, and the boy loved Clifton so. Yet in that same taking, this stranger released her from the hell that had become her life. What manner of woman was she that she couldn't despise Luke Reeves for bringing Tommie such pain?

Tess took another look at Luke, this time setting his features to memory. Six foot. Black hair. Indigo eyes. Scars on his right cheek and brow. Broad shoulders and a leanness of physique that could have wrestled Clifton's bulkier frame easily to the ground. Why had the man needed to kill her husband?

Tess's gaze focused on the ivory-handled Colt resting in his left-handed holster. The pistol looked well-used, with grips yellowed from age. Was this man so accustomed to killing that he thought of no other alternative?

"I'm a bounty hunter of sorts, Mrs. Harper," he began. "I make my living tracking down wanted men and do some troubleshooting now and then for a financial concern." Luke inwardly berated himself for the word choice. "Your husband got into the line of fire when I attempted to capture three scoundrels who were selling rifles to a bunch of Comanche. Unfortunately, one got away."

He noted her surprise and knew, if nothing else, she lacked guilt in the rifle scheme. "I warned your husband repeatedly to stay out of the way. Wasn't sure it was my bullet that got him, but the one I pulled out of him was the same caliber as mine. Near as I can tell, I killed him."

What Luke saw in the emerald depths of her eyes nearly made him drop his cup. He had faced the steel-eyed glint of some of the fastest gunfighters in the territory and never blinked an eye. He had stared down the boldest look of pity ever offered a man with scars, but not once had he looked into genuine forgiveness. An unearned forgiveness. This woman knew how to stir a man to his core. Maybe she was guilty, at that.

Tess set the pot down and released the handle.

Here it comes, Luke thought, waiting for her to slap him. His jaw tightened in anticipation of the blow. Instead, Widow Harper gently pressed her palm against his scarred cheek, as if she understood his sincere regret at killing her husband.

"I know it was difficult for you to bring me the news, Mr. Reeves." Tess let her hand slide slowly back to her side. "Thank you for bringing him back to us."

She owed this man nothing, yet she couldn't allow him to leave her home without letting him know she understood. Tess wanted to strike him, hurt him for leaving Tommie fatherless. But that part of her that had once been unjusty accused of misdeeds reached out and offered comfort to this stranger. Offered a promise that if she faced up to her own past as Luke Reeves faced her now, she might one day forgive herself.

"Do you have any idea why your husband was at Pencil Bluff?"

Tess shook her head. What could she say? *I suspected Clifton of dealing with Hoot Hill. Wondered if Jim Daggert might be involved as well.* Surely her husband's best friend didn't know of Clifton's involvement or he would have already told her of the mishap.

If only she had stood up to Clifton when she confronted him with her suspicions months ago. When he told her to mind her own house and leave a man's business alone, she'd known her husband had shady dealings. Just as she never said no to her parents at Hot Springs, neither did she tell Clifton he was wrong. All she had ever done was live by someone else's demands, never her own choices. The day for her to trust herself had finally arrived. Tess knew it was the only way she and Tommie could remain together. Circumstances would never again frighten her into doing something against her principles. "My son and I would like to be alone now," she insisted, irritated that her voice trembled.

Luke recognized purpose in the widow and suspected she was gathering strength to meet the many hardships pressed upon a fatherless family. How well he knew the anger that nourished a mind and body after devastating blows to the emotions. It fueled the conscience when hard choices needed to be made and principles got in the way of common sense. When hurt seeped in so deep a man wept tears from his wounded heart.

Though she stood inches away now, Luke felt the imprint of her hand upon his cheek. Tess's simple touch chipped away at the fortress of indifference built around Luke's heart. The report must be wrong. His gut instinct told him there was more to the Hot Springs story than he had been told. An error had been made somewhere along the line. He meant to make quick work of Tess Harper's involvement in the mining and Hot Springs scams, then planned to journey on to Colorado and follow up on the lead he obtained concerning her husband's dealings. But sudden caring found a voice within Luke.

"Ma'am, I know it's policy for the widow to leave the post as soon as the funeral's over. I'd like to escort you and your son to wherever you mean to settle. I figure your husband deserves half the reward money I collect for bringing in Hoot Hill. I'll see you get it before you leave."

Offering her half seemed little enough reparation. Luke's thoughts surprised him. He didn't know whether or not she was guilty, and what he just offered went against the grain of his suspicious nature and profession. Soft inside. That seemed to be the only way to describe his feelings. Almost too human for a man who lived his life by the gun. Was this new bent toward neighborliness a result of her having a boy to care for, or did something else urge this recklessness?

Unable to endure any more, Tess wanted to scream as she hurried to the door and flung it open. "That's unnecessary, Mr. Reeves. Now if you'll excuse me, I have much to do."

Knowing he'd been dismissed, Luke strode past her and trudged out into the mud. Too late he realized he had sank up to his bare ankles. "Do you want me to take his body to the undertaker?" Luke motioned to the horses. "Two's no more trouble than one."

Tension began to pulse at Tess's temples, and all she could think of was her need for Luke to disappear. "Please, just go."

She had no idea how much money her husband had saved, if any. Affording the undertaker's fee might not be a possibility. In a friendlier tone, she stepped out into the rain and moved toward the horses. "I'd best see to him."

"You'll need help getting him inside."

Resentment curled in her stomach, not so much aimed at Luke's offer but at the way life threatened to challenge her resolve to prove herself capable even now. As she stepped closer to the horses, it seemed Heaven mourned with Tess. She was glad for the heavy drizzle. Grief surged through her, and a flood of relief streamed down her face. A part of her still loved Clifton and could mourn him, not for the man he was but for the husband and father he might have been to her and Tommie.

The bounty hunter looked at her and, despite the distinct odor of death, she nodded slowly, folding her arms protectively around her waist. When he pulled back the blanket, her hands shot to her mouth to stop the bile rising from the pit of her stomach. Tess averted her head from the horrifying sight which no amount of preparation could have made easier. "What am I going to tell Tommie?" she whispered behind her palm. "Dear God, you didn't think of Tommie."

Tess took a deep breath to steady herself, then stepped forward. She stumbled on the heavy dampness of her skirt hem. Luke's hands shot out and caught her at the shoulders to prevent the fall. The momentum propelled her against his hard warm body. Tess felt Luke's strength in the iron sinew of arms wrapped around her, pushing against the underside of her breasts. Anger compelled her to jerk away from the hands that had wielded the gun that had killed her husband. But the spell of human compassion filling Luke's dark blue gaze forced her to halt as heat kindled in her cheeks, the peaks of her breasts, then banked low within her abdomen.

A longing engulfed her, hitting like a blast of cold air. Shaken by the powerful emotion, it took all of Tess's effort to ignore his touch and the shameless possibility that she felt an attraction toward her husband's killer. "I shouldn't have been so clumsy," Tess muttered. "I really must get him inside."

"Here, let me." Luke exhaled a long, tense breath. What would she think if he hauled her up against him, grabbed a fistful of that sunshiny hair and kissed her? Would she be so forgiving if he invaded her mouth with his tongue and pressed his chest against her breasts, searing them with the heat that now coursed through his loins? Where was her anger?

The Beholding

Beware, pretty lady, he silently warned. *Be like the others. Hate me. Despise me. Pity me, but never offer anything I can turn against you. It's my job. To find your weakness. I'll hurt you before I'm hurt.*

Hefting the corpse on his shoulder, Luke found the exertion a welcome release to the tension spiraling through his body. The effort to keep his balance while sloshing through the mud blessedly drew his thoughts to less dangerous avenues. "Where do you want him?"

"On the kitchen table."

Luke followed her into the house, scraping his feet to keep from tracking up her floor. He swallowed back a curse as splinters jabbed his left sole.

"Papa?" Tommie ran toward the door, and his small face took on a look of confusion. The question turned into a shriek as his confusion whitened into fear. "Papa's sick! Wake up, Papa! Wake up!"

"Please, lay him there and go, Mr. Reeves." Tess enfolded Tommie in her arms and tried to quell the growing hysteria she felt soaring in her son and herself. "Shhh . . . son. It's all right. Everything will be all right."

While gently placing the body on the eating table, Luke made certain Clifton was situated so his wife wouldn't have to move him further. As he straightened, Luke ran a hand through his disheveled hair and the black strands fell down in his face. He had dropped his hat somewhere. Widow Harper bent and picked up the slouch hat, now caked with mud to its crown, then thrust it into his stomach. Her eyes insisted he leave even as Tommie clutched at her skirt, wailing.

Luke moved toward the door but something urged him to stay. The feeling made him uneasy. Steeling himself against the unaccustomed surge of emotion, Luke sought ease in setting the trap he had planned all along. "Remember my offer, Mrs. Harper. I'll take you wherever you need to go. Back to your folks, maybe?" He awaited her reaction.

"Get out of my house. Now!" Tess demanded. Anger at an unfair past and the cruelty of the present filled her with a

23

surge of strength. Letting go of Tommie, she shoved Luke backward, past the threshold, into the night. "Stay out of our lives, and don't involve me in yours!"

Though conviction gave her courage, she doubted that a planked wooden door would do very much to hold such a man back if Luke Reeves truly wanted to make a nuisance of himself.

Damned woman! Who would have thought a female like that could get under his skin? Luke cut out the remaining splinter from his bare feet and tossed it away. His gray dun wrestled some livery feed into its mouth, then nuzzled Luke's neck.

Luke stood, scratched behind Talon's ears and stowed the knife in his pack. He'd have to wait until tomorrow before he returned it to the hidden sheath in his boot where it belonged. Taking a cheroot from his pocket, he lit it and inhaled the tension-relieving tobacco.

The rain stopped, urging him out of the livery's confines and into the night. Stars rose over the Arkansas hills, bright and shining, and newly washed. Locating the North Star and its position in the heavens, he gauged the hour of the night. A couple of hours before dawn. The business at the undertaker had taken longer than expected. Guess he should be getting some rest. The widow would be up and making preparations soon. Just because he hadn't slept in close to three days didn't mean she would wait on him. He intended to escort her where she went, despite her anger. Probably for that reason alone. Though a rash offer, the idea seemed a perfect way to pursue his investigation.

Green eyes haunted him. Eyes clouded with grief and fear had also looked up at him with challenge and purpose. He hoped the fear was of him and not of the law he represented. She needed to fear the emotions she evoked within him. He wanted her. Burned for her like for no other woman who had lain beneath him in passion.

Flicking the cheroot into a puddle, he imagined stamping

out the flame as he wanted to rub out the memory of her breasts pressing hotly against his chest. Luke sauntered back to the stall and unbuckled the wide leather gun belt strapped low on his hip. Placing it alongside the saddle he used as a pillow, he stretched his body onto a bedroll next to the dun.

Served him right having to forgo a softer bed for the night, letting himself get pushed out of the Harper home without his boots. Pride kept him from purchasing a room, not wanting to walk in anywhere barefooted. Fortunately, the gravedigger wasn't the curious sort. Then again, Luke supposed a bootless man wasn't such an uncommon sight to an undertaker.

Linking his hands behind his head, Luke didn't see the livery's planked roofing any longer. Instead, green eyes seemed to be staring at him, trusting . . . asking something of him he didn't know how to give. Dammit, could he destroy the innocence he had seen for the sake of fulfilling a contract with the Denver Stock Exchange?

Determined to forget Tess Harper, Luke crossed his arms across his chest and closed his eyes. Instead of the numbing void of sleep, he envisioned a blond-haired beauty with forgiving green eyes and a small boy with equally trusting features. Luke cursed and sat, resting his arms on bent knees.

Talon snorted.

''When I find out what the hell's going on, fella,'' Luke grumbled, ''I'll let you know, too. Then maybe we'll both get some sleep.''

Chapter Two

The sweet scent of mountain honeysuckle drifted on the breeze that fluttered the black veil covering Tess's tear-streaked face. She kissed one petal of the white rose and gently placed it on the muddy earth now resting over Clifton's wooden coffin. Urging her son to do the same, she winced as he pricked his finger on a thorn while trying to place the offering near her own. The sight of her child's blood sent a shudder through Tess. Even death seemed to mar Tommie's love for his father.

A handful of Clifton's friends, Jim Daggert among them, remained at the top of the hill crowned with crooked wooden crosses and rough-hewn tombstones. The respect Tess sensed was given to her husband rather than herself. Let them harbor their false impressions; she no longer cared. She had lain awake all night wondering what else she could have done to be a better wife. Her only conclusion: it was not her fault.

When Tommie's small fingers reached up to thread her own, she gave a reassuring squeeze. "Are you ready to leave now, darling?" She stared at the quadrangle of buildings which had been his only home. How would he handle the move and giving up his friendship with the other camp children?

His small hand squeezed hers in return.

"I yove you, Mommie."

"And I love you, too, Tommie." Despite all the wrongs of her marriage, one great blessing Clifton Harper had given her was this wonderful little boy.

"Wait, please, Mrs. Harper."

Tess stopped her downhill trek, taking a deep breath and steeling herself against the interview with the general's wife. Mrs. Henry J. Hunt waddled to a halt, one gloved hand splaying across her throat as she huffed and puffed with exertion. How had she ever managed to walk up the brush-covered hill to the gravesite?

"Will you be ill?" Tess asked, trying to sound sincere in her concern. The woman could either help or hinder her plans.

"It's the altitude, Mrs. Harper, the uncommon altitude." Tugging at the shirtwaist riding up the swell of her nonexistent waist, the rotund woman flicked open her parasol to shield out the hot Arkansas sun rising over the hills. Silver brows arched over rheumy gray eyes. "Where do you intend to go?"

The question was *where,* not *if,* as Tess knew it would be. Hearing it struck a bitter finality to any hopes of staying on at the fort. As Luke Reeves had reminded her, Army regulations required a widow to leave upon completion of the burial. Regulations or no, Tess would never have been invited to remain. Too often she had spoken her opinion, one seldom corresponding with Mrs. Hunt's. The general's spouse allowed no mutiny among the company wives.

Tess took a certain pleasure in wiping the smug look from Mrs. Hunt's face. "My husband has holdings in Colorado . . . a place called Harper Hall."

Remembering the document she'd tucked away in the pocket of her skirt that morning, Tess wondered again about the warning written on the pouch she'd found among her husband's belongings. *Do not open until after my death.* The message scrawled in Clifton's handwriting had caught her attention while she searched through the carpetbags to look for his pocket watch. It had not been on his body. And, try as she might, Tess couldn't believe that a man who was honorable enough to face a widow whose husband he had killed would be the sort of man who stole from a corpse.

Unable to find the timepiece, she discovered the bag and record that listed the name of an estate Clifton owned in Georgetown, Colorado. It was odd, since he'd never mentioned such a possession.

Her gaze shifted to Jim Daggert's tall form among the gathering, and she wondered if he knew anything about the Colorado holdings. He seemed to know so much about what went on with Clifton.

"Then you'll be leaving promptly, I assume." Both of the matron's chins lifted, her voice offering false cordiality.

Tess gave Mrs. Hunt her full attention and realized the general's wife had taken note of her interest in Jim. "As soon as I've hired a man to take us across Indian territory."

"Injuns! Oh, boy!" Tommie squealed with delight, his hands pulling back an imaginary bow. "They can learn me to shoot arras."

The parasol twirled, and the matron's face assumed a stern look of disapproval. "I hardly think so, young man."

Quick defense rose to spur Tess's words. "Perhaps we should get to know them first, darling, before we decide what's best for us to teach them and they, us."

Suddenly the sympathizer-to-griever mask disappeared. The rheumy eyes sharpened and the shrewd manipulator emerged. "Well, yes, I'm sure. Across Indian territory, you say? It will be difficult to find anyone willing for such employment. Heaven knows Henry can't spare anyone to offer you escort."

Battle lines were drawn. Mrs. Hunt would make certain she had difficulty in finding a guide unless Tess found a way to persuade her otherwise. As the general's wife, the matron wielded a heavy saber of influence. Tess met the woman's aggressive gaze steadily. "I know General Hunt will help if he can. I'm sure I'll find someone."

The woman quirked a brow. "You do seem to land on your feet, my dear, when life gives you a tumble."

A catty remark raced to the tip of Tess's tongue, but she

decided not to bicker. An eye for an eye might work for men, but women went for the reputation. The general's wife was influential enough to damage what little reputation Tess had managed to salvage. Better to stroke the cat than yank its tail. "Thank you for your vote of confidence, Mrs. Hunt. I would appreciate it if you put in a word for me with the others. Perhaps as the gentler authority of this garrison, you might persuade someone to help me in this matter."

Beaming with the compliment, Mrs. Hunt nodded, bobbing her chignon and the blond-gray curls that framed her forehead. "Perhaps you need look no further, Mrs. Harper," she purred. "See that young man over there—Luke Reeves—the bounty hunter? He might attend you. He's obviously well accustomed to rough country and tough dealings with dangerous sorts. I'm told he's the man who brought in Sergeant Harper."

Swinging around in the direction of the woman's gaze, Tess felt the unvoiced thought setting Mrs. Hunt's lips into a satisfied smirk. The matron knew how hard it would be for Tess to accept help from the man who killed Clifton, whether or not the deed was an accident. Her gaze swept over the remainder of the mourners who visited the gravesite, noticing that the bounty hunter stood off from the others. Dressed in black, his hat gripped respectfully in his hand, Luke Reeves still wore the Colt that had taken Clifton's life.

A jolt of attraction coursed through Tess again, and she planted her black parasol into the muddy ground to steady herself. Dirt covered her husband's grave less than a few hours and all she could do was gawk at the man who'd put him there. Maybe those people back in Hot Springs were right. Maybe a thread of indecency ran through her and she would never be able to overcome those blood ties.

Despite the cover of a lace veil, Luke's dark gaze pierced hers as he became aware of her regard. Like an intangible touch, it traced a lingering path of appreciation to each swell and curve, kindling a not-so-unpleasant warmth in its wake. Was it the aching numbness inflicted by her husband's death which made Tess aware of how much more alive the bounty hunter seemed? Or did Clifton ever possess such raw, lethal masculinity? Her husband's memory dimmed before her eyes, and the unsettling comparison yanked her back to reality.

Tess willed herself to look away, but her will disobeyed. Drawn to the inexplicable power he exuded, she met his gaze. A slow grin lifted one corner of the bounty hunter's lips as he nodded once, nestled his hat on his head, then turned and disappeared into the woods. A pent-up sigh exhaled slowly from Tess's lips.

Movement among the crowd captured her attention. Jim Daggert's broad-shouldered form sliced through the mourners until he arrived at the same spot where Luke had stood. He took a few steps in the direction the bounty hunter had disappeared, then seemed to think better of it. Turning, Jim's dark brown gaze sifted through the throng, as if he felt Tess watching him. As his attention finally settled on Tess, his chestnut-colored brows veed together over a long-staring question she didn't understand.

Mrs. Hunt reached out and touched Tess's sleeve, making her realize she had been staring far too long. She smiled an apology to Jim, who tweaked one edge of his mustache, revealing irritation at the matron's interruption. How many times when he and Clifton made plans and Tommie begged to tag along, had she noticed the gesture? Though Jim never voiced his aggravation with the boy, she suspected he didn't care for children—particularly handicapped ones.

Turning away from her husband's best friend, she discovered a look of suspicion etching Mrs. Hunt's features.

"Purely a pity we won't have time to get to know each other better, Mrs. Harper." The older woman's gaze went to Jim, then back to Tess. "Please accept my condolences for your loss."

Tess preferred to think the woman meant the loss of Clifton rather than any designs Tess may have had in mind for Jim. At least the general's wife attended the funeral, more than she could say of others. For that one concession, Tess forgave the matron's snobbery. "Thank you. Tommie and I won't forget your kindness."

"Mommie, can I go pway with Zach?" Tommie tugged at her hand, impatient with big-people talk.

She let go. "About an hour, son. And thank Zachariah's mother for the corn dressing and turkey. I've some business to attend to, then we'll finish. . . ."

The three-year-old was a blur of blond hair and stubby legs wobbling down to the garrison. ". . . packing," she half chuckled. It felt good to laugh. Tess feared she might never do so again. If only her spirit could be as free as Tommie's. But then, it had never been. Ma and Pa saw to that.

"Would you pick wildflowers and place them on Clifton's grave for me each year, Mrs. Hunt?" Tess felt an urgent need to end the conversation and escape to the tasks ahead which might take her mind off the past. Despite all the problems awaiting her, Tess's heart quickened at the possibilities of the future. A future she would control.

The matron nodded. Tess thanked her, then lifted the hem of her skirt from the moist grass. Treading the rain-soaked path to the fort, she hurried past the laundry huts and stables, then sought the clerk at the camp supply. She posted a notice about the need of a guide and gave the clerk a list of essentials to gather for the journey. At the livery she stopped to purchase a wagon. Finding the cost much more than she expected, Tess visited the paymaster to receive the last of Clifton's earnings.

"Fifteen dollars?" Her voice rose despite an effort not to reveal her distress. Blood drained from her face as Tess realized how little pay Clifton made as sergeant. He lost more than that amount on one night's gambling. If she had any doubts before that he was involved in the rifle scheme that got him killed, she could no longer justify them. The grave on the hill held a stranger. A stranger and a thief.

The paymaster looked apologetic. "That's all I can give ye now, Mrs. Harper. Payroll's nigh two weeks late. Me and the boys got up a month's pay for ye and wee Tom. 'Tisn't much, but all we can muster among us."

"It's kind of you. Clifton would be grateful." With each drop of a coin into her reticule, Tess's hopes plunged. How could she afford a wagon now, much less an escort? She had intended to refuse the reward money the bounty hunter offered. But now, how could she without depriving her son of essentials for the journey? *Can I let pride stand in the way of common sense?*

Too exhausted for further thought, too tired to make decisions, Tess was too full of anger even to cry. Offering her hand to the Irishman, she berated herself for being so utterly gullible.

The paymaster ignored the handshake and, instead, gave her a big bear hug. After lingering a moment, he awkwardly let her go. Taken aback by his impulse, the giant of a man's cheeks flushed a deep crimson. "To the divil with Clifton Harper, lassie. 'Tis ye and the lad we be wanting to help. A happier life to ye both, and a better man to warm yer pillow and sweeten yer dreams. No offense to the departed."

She returned the embrace, unsure whether she did so out of anger at her late husband or from gratitude for the genuine regard for her and Tommie's future.

"'Tis alone he left ye long before now, lassie. We're betting ye'll make us all proud."

Had everyone known how lonely her life had become these final two years? Known how she'd fought to remember her wife's duty when Clifton bedded her, yet wouldn't touch her otherwise? No handholding. No affectionate hugs. No lingering looks of love or even guarded respect one might offer a stranger. Yet the worst of it was that she had remained with Clifton. Though she asked herself a thousand times *why,* only one answer surfaced. *Tommie was with someone he loved.* Other reasons whispered to her from places deep inside her soul, but she refused to listen. Could not listen even now.

Emotions of the morning mixed with the unhappiness of years added haste to Tess's farewell. A need to purge herself of the tidal wave of tears welling up inside made her put off the remaining tasks and head straight for officers' row so she could have a good, hard cry.

When she opened the door to her lodgings, she gasped in disbelief.

Stripped from their pleats at the windows, the calico curtains looked as if someone had taken a razor to them. Furniture had been piled in the center of the room as if in preparation for a bonfire. Tins of meal and sugar were dumped over, their contents spilled on the shelf and table. All her carefully folded clothing lay in crumpled disarray.

As she stepped cautiously into the room, feathers fell from perches in the rafters and joined the dozens of others near the slashes in the bed's tick mattress. Everything she owned had been riffled through, destroyed. Who would do such a thing? *Why?*

Touching the quilt which had taken months of handwork to piece together and seeing it fall in shreds to the planked floor sent anguish plunging to the pit of her stomach. Fury rose from those churning depths as Tess picked up what was left of the reading lamp she had purchased on her birthday the year Tommie had been born, bound and determined she would learn to read so she might have the honor of teaching the same to her son.

The sight of Clifton's carpetbag ripped from its handle was more than she could endure. Anger and desperation brewed in the cauldron of circumstances that had become her life and erupted into a wail of rage. Tess lifted the first thing her hands reached and threw the china with all her might. The saucer crashed against the wall, the sound somehow echoing her shattered life. Another and another struck the wall as she spent her outrage on the unseen person who had destroyed the last of what had been her home.

"Whoa there, lady!" a masculine voice shouted as she spun toward the door.

The cup had already left her hand. Luke Reeves dodged, but he was too tall and her aim too compelled by fury for her not to strike the mark.

"I'm glad I hit you!" she yelled, knowing she meant every word and needing to release the scream that careened through her. But one look at the bloody scratch she dealt his forehead made Tess burst into hiccuping sobs. "I d-didn't mean to h-hurt you. To hurt any-anyone."

He held out his arms to show she'd done little damage. "Look, it's nothing. Only a scratch."

Seeing the sympathy in his eyes proved Tess's undoing. She forgot all the man represented. Forgot his role in her current despair. All she saw was the man himself. His compassion. His strength. How she needed strength right now.

Tess flung herself into his arms, desperately in need of human comfort. The sobs strengthened until they shook her to the tips of her toes as she cried the heartache of a woman deprived of her home, a wife unloved by her husband, and a child abused by her parents.

Chapter Three

Tess's body heaved with another jerking sob. Luke placed his hands on her shoulders and let one hand slip to the middle of her back. "There, hush, now." He patted her, wondering what a man was supposed to say at a time like this. "Don't cry. Things will get better."

That set her off. Luke's pats increased awkwardly with the pitch of her wails. "It's gotta get better. Can't get much worse, can it?" Never one to talk much, Luke wished now he had kept his mouth closed. It was the most ignorant statement he had ever made.

After a while, the sobs slowed to a soft hiccup, then a painful silence ensued. Finally she raised her head to stare at him. The mourning veil blocked his view of her eyes, but he sensed the misery in them.

"Y-you haven't had much experience at comforting people, have you?"

He heard the jest in her voice and was glad for it. Maybe now she could garner the strength to face the days ahead since she shed the healing tears. Unconsciously, his hand slid up and down her back in one final touch of comfort. "Guilty of the opposite, I'm told, but I meant well."

Tess unwrapped her arms from his shoulders, took a step backward and lifted off her veil. Tossing it onto an overturned chair, she wiped at a remaining tear which trickled down her cheek. Embarrassed that she had thrown herself into his arms, she supposed he deserved an explanation. But the hurt ran too deep for words. How could she explain when she didn't understand it all herself? Why did she feel compelled to make him understand? Perhaps he would take a simple reassurance instead. "I feel much better now."

"That's because you have what it takes, Mrs. Harper."

She blushed more at the respect staring back at her than the compliment he offered.

Luke mean what he said. He watched as she went about the business necessary to move on. Tess Harper was very much capable of taking care of herself—a fact which made him both admire her and added to his suspicions.

The uncertainty of how to soothe her kept him from acknowledging the press of her woman's body against his chest. Now as she stood in front of him, wisps of disheveled hair cascaded to her breasts and her eyes blinked up at him as pretty as rain-washed emeralds, forever imprinting every feature in his mind. Nothing he'd imagined in the stable matched the reality of her touch. The slow burn which had kept him awake all night would be a banked fire for days to come.

Shaken by his blatant look of desire, Tess averted her gaze and waved toward the spilled tin. "I'd offer you some coffee, Mr. Reeves, but I'll have to restock first."

Luke found the motion tantalizing for it defined the swell of her cleavage. *Hell of a man you are, Luke Reeves,* he berated himself, *lusting after a woman you just put in mourning. But you'd have to be dead yourself,* he reminded, *if you didn't see how beautiful she is . . . how good she feels against you.* He'd known her less than twenty-four hours and already Contessa Harper touched him in ways no woman ever had.

Luke reminded himself she was a suspect and he should regard her as such. Inspecting the debris, he tried to dispel the reluctance to complete his assignment. "Do you have any idea who did this or what they're looking for?"

Tess shook her head, then stacked pieces of quilt on top of each other. If Clifton had been, indeed, guilty of the crimes she had suspected, there might be any number of things someone would want. "I have no idea."

Spying the cracked worn leather footwear he left behind, Luke joked, "Good thing it wasn't my boots." He turned over a chair and tested its sturdiness before offering it to her. In a more serious tone, he continued, "Anything particular missing?"

"Nothing except Clifton's pocket watch," she answered before taking time to gauge whether or not she should share the information with the bounty hunter. The thought of him delving too closely into her and Clifton's lives made Tess fidget with the buttons on her kid glove. He might learn too much. Yet Luke seemed the sort of man who would think her silence even more suspicious. "Who would go to this extreme for a watch?" she asked, deciding to listen to her intuition about the bounty hunter. "It makes no sense."

Luke began to separate the repairable from the irreparable. His nose for tracking hinted that a clue lay hidden in the rubble. Whoever did this thought that Contessa Harper had something to hide. If she did, then it was as much his business as hers to discover what they were after. "Anything special about the watch?"

"Nothing that I know of." Tess refused to sit, instead stripping off her gloves to join in the clean-up. "You needn't bother, Mr. Reeves."

"I'd like to. It doesn't look like the Ladies Auxiliary will be much help." She rewarded him with a smile, and he was glad he had inspired such a lovely sight.

"I don't suppose they will, Mr. Reeves."

"I insist you call me Luke. Lucas to my parents. Luke to my friends," he offered, knowing only two such people in his past.

"Friends?"

37

Though she appeared a bit reluctant, the widow held out her hand and Luke shook it like he would have any man's. The worth he found in her small grip was second only to the amazement he experienced at finding something so delicate and soft fitting perfectly into his own callused hand.

As they stood with hands grasped in a bond of acquaintance, their gazes locked in silent truce.

"Tess," she finally relented. "Call me Tess."

"Thumbody's in bi-i-i-g trouble," a small voice announced from the opened doorway.

Yeah, and it's me, Luke acknowledged as Tommie's blond head peeked around the door.

The boy carefully edged into the room with his palms raised, looking as if he were being held at gunpoint. "I promise, Mommie," Tommie whispered, "I di'n't do it."

Luke and Tess snatched away their hands as if they'd been caught stealing from a candy counter. Luke busied himself with clearing off the spilled flour and coffee while Tess crossed the distance and bent down on one knee to hug her son.

"I know you didn't do such a terrible thing, darling."

"Reckon they wanted the paper, Mommie?"

Tess stood and brushed folds from her skirt, trying to stop the racing of her pulse. But she felt the pressure of Luke's hand cupping her own as if he still held it.

"What paper?" Luke's investigative sixth sense prickled with premonition.

"Daddy's paper."

Tess delved into the pocket of her skirt and pulled out the pouch. "Tommie might be right, Luke. I found this in Clifton's things this morning. I didn't have time to read it all or I'd have been late for the burial. It's a bill of sale for someplace called Harper Hall. Tommie and I are going there to claim it since there's nothing left for us here."

She handed him the document and Luke scanned it carefully. The vagueness of details made him suspicious, but the fact that Harper Hall was located in Georgetown, Colorado, only increased his interest. Did the hall tie in with her husband's misdeeds? Was she really desperate enough to set out for the unknown on the slim chance this might make a difference in her and her son's life? Perhaps she purposely misled him about what awaited her in Colorado.

Either way, he had been assigned by the Denver Stock Exchange to learn the truth. The fact she was heading for Colorado was the first real clue that she could actually be involved with the mine scams. "When will we be leaving?" he asked, taking an estimating glance around the room. "Doesn't look like there will be much to pack now."

"We?"

"If you think this is all a joke, Mrs. Har—Tess, you're wrong. You have something someone wants. Or they think you have. Maybe it's this paper, then again maybe it isn't." Luke returned the document. "Even if all you have to worry about is the unfriendlies you're going to meet on the trail, you can't take the chance on leaving here without a gunman to protect you. You and I both know there isn't a man on the post who's going to agree to escort you across Indian territory."

"But I've posted an advertisement."

"Yeah, and a dozen men have already turned it down. Until the War Department quits shuffling military jurisdictions and can maintain surveillance, there isn't a soul who'll risk his life for you. I took down your notice. Consider the job filled."

Anger flashed through Tess. "Don't you think that's a bit presumptuous, Mr. Reeves? Do you really believe Tommie and I could travel with you anywhere?" She glanced at her son, careful with her choice of words since she hadn't revealed to him Luke's role in Clifton's death. "What gave you the right to take down my notice?"

"Let's just say I'm going that direction anyway. You'll keep me from having to eat my own grub, and I'll see to it you keep that comely head of hair. It'll make me sleep better at night knowing you're protected."

"I'm sorry, no. I'll find someone else, thank you."

"Aww, come on, Mommie. I yike Mista Yuke." Tommie tugged on her skirt. "Why ya wanna be so fussy?"

Luke had already checked at the livery and with the pay-master. He knew she didn't have enough money to purchase a wagon. Lending a ride might prove profitable in discovering her part in this mess. "I've kept a wagon outfitted to take back the stolen rifles. Since that fell through, why not plan on putting your belongings in with mine? We can be off in the morning."

How could she convince him he was the last person she wanted for a guide? "Look, Luke . . . Mr. Reeves . . . or whatever name will make you listen. I'm trying very hard not to be rude, but I can't make any decision at the moment until I clean up this mess and decide what's worth repairing."

"If the three of us work at it, it won't take as long." Luke walked over to the counter and grabbed a washbowl. "Tommie, will you fill this for your mother? Maybe she won't mind wrangling us up something to eat while you and I get started."

The bounty hunter was persistent if nothing else. And it did make sense to get the meal preparations out of the way. Nodding reluctant approval to Tommie, Tess made a silent vow to find someone besides Luke Reeves for a guide. *Anyone.*

Indecision kept the boy rooted for a moment until he decided he liked the idea better than he disliked it. "I gotta wash?"

Luke rolled up his sleeves. "Only whatever part we get dirty, partner. How's that?"

"No fair, I always git everthang dirty."

"Then I'll wash, too, and that'll make it no fair for both of us."

Two scrubbed gentlemen, one freckled-faced and the other ruggedly handsome, sat on the edge of the wagon bed with Tess.

She was far too aware of the clean smell of soap, leather and the man whose legs dangled on the other side of Tommie's. Luke Reeves's strong profile drew her attention to his

40

lips and the way he enjoyed the meal. Though her better sense warned her to be rid of him as soon as he completed helping her straighten the mess, hospitality ruled. The meal seemed small compensation for all the work he'd done.

As her gaze traveled upward to admire the dark sooty lashes foresting his eyes, Tess's heart thudded to a stop. A light sensation waved through her when Luke regarded her with lazy interest. Her heart pounded wildly, flooding her face with a blush that only caused more embarrassment.

"The food tastes better under the stars, don't you think?" he asked.

Tess nearly choked on a gulp of food. Luke thumped her on the back to relieve her distress.

"There are few indoor kitchens between here and Wichita," he informed her. "By the time we get to the overland stage, you'll be glad for a meal you won't have to cook. But I doubt any will be as good as this one, even then."

"How long will it take us . . ." Why did that single two-letter word seem suddenly so intimate? Tess meant she and Tommie and the guide she chose, but she could find no word which would clearly exclude Luke Reeves. ". . . to cross the territory? Is it really that dangerous?"

Glancing at the boy, Luke held out his tin. "Would you take mine and your mother's plates inside? Then I'll let you practice tossing my lariat, like I promised earlier."

"Sure will, Mista Yuke!" Tommie grabbed the utensils and made a beeline for the house.

Luke slid off the wagon bed and stood. "I didn't want the boy around when I answered you, Tess. Give me a minute to get him settled. And by the way, does he always mix up his L's?"

"If he slows down and thinks about what he's saying, he speaks well," Tess fiercely defended her son. Her hackles slowly lowered as she realized it was merely a question and not meant to degrade Tommie. "He just gets in too big a hurry and his speech doesn't keep up with his thoughts."

"Maybe we can work on that some," Luke said as they

strolled to the front of the wagon staked near the Harpers' living quarters. The bounty hunter set up three bottles. "I used to have the same trouble myself when I was a kid, but it was with R's."

Tommie joined him before Luke revealed any more of his past, and Tess felt mildly disappointed. It seemed difficult to imagine this man as anything but the rough-edged man standing before her.

When Luke explained how to form a lasso and toss the rope over a quarry, Tommie squealed with appreciation. The smile that darted across Tess's lips quickly faded. Had Clifton ever taught him the trick? She couldn't remember. Though she had many misgivings about Luke, appreciation for the man swept through her. He was thoughtful to her son, and that revealed a side of the bounty hunter worth knowing.

"Now you practice real hard," Luke instructed, "because it'll come in handy down the road."

As he joined her once again, Luke's voice lowered, offering an intimacy not shared with her son. "Now, back to your question. It will take us a couple of weeks at best, a month at worst. Depends on whether or not we run into hostiles."

"Indians?"

"Not necessarily."

Luke turned toward her, his gaze roaming over her as if estimating her worth in some way.

"With the war still fresh on folks' minds, we'll have to watch out for all kinds of raiders. God knows you're a lady, Tess, but a Southern lady. Some Northerners might think that will give them the right to harass you, if they take a notion. Then there's a few Blacks who will attempt to steal anything, horses, wagons, food, if we don't keep our eyes open for thieves. Most don't mean any harm, but the Proclamation left them a bit short of things they need. Indians are probably the least of your worries, but you can't discount them. As long as we don't violate any tribal hunting or burial grounds, we'll keep our scalps intact."

Tess suppressed a shudder. She'd heard of a few occasions

where women caught in a raid were killed, or worse. Boys Tommie's age usually ended up adopted into the tribe. With his limp, would his captors take time to discover his worth or consider him useless?

"But that means we've all got to work together," Luke continued. "Both of you must do as I say without question *when* I say do it."

Indignation stiffened Tess's lagging spirit as the demand echoed in her brain and conjured up memories of other such orders. Demands she had vowed never to cower to again. Luke was already assuming too much, and she needed to set things straight with him. "Tommie, time for bed!"

He ran toward her, whimpering, "I wanna stay out here with you and Yuke." His whine developed into a yawn.

Luke nudged him forward. "Run along now, son, and mind your mama. Tomorrow's a big day. You need your rest if you're going to help me scout for trouble."

"Really? Oh boy!"

"I'll be in soon to tuck you in," Tess added, finding it difficult to keep the anger from her voice. "Don't forget to wash your hands and say your prayers."

As Tommie limped into the house, Tess scooted off the edge of the wagon bed and threaded her arms below her breasts. She didn't want to sound ungrateful for his kindness, but she also needed to make certain Luke understood her feelings. "I think you presume too much, Mr. Reeves."

Luke stood, towering over her in the night shadows. "Presume what?"

Too angry to acknowledge the attraction which had inspired a level of tension between them since their first meeting, she said firmly, "First of all, I have not said my son and I will be traveling with you for certain; so you're making false promises to the boy. But more important, should I decide to purchase your services, I *will* question what you say and I won't necessarily do what you command when you command it. I'm no one's chess piece to move around at will. Whether you or anyone else guides us, or we go by ourselves, I'll take no more orders . . . from anybody.''

Circumstances would no longer rule her life. Tess vowed her life would be fought and won with choices. *Her* choices. She could almost feel the anger building in him.

"Please yourself. If you don't care to save your and your son's lives"—deadly menace made his tone compelling—"then I'll not consider it part of the job to save them for you." He loomed over her like a phantom of the night, silhouetting the violence he held in check. Moonlight highlighted the scarred planes of his face, the powerful pull of his eyes.

"Explain yourself."

"I won't order a lady to do anything unless I think she's in danger. If I say run, I mean run for your lives. If I tell you to shoot, then I mean shoot to kill. I don't bully folks, particularly women, no matter what you might think of bounty hunters. But if I demand you react, then you react or die."

"It doesn't matter what I think of you." Tess shook to her very bones, but she held her ground. "If I hire you, it will be because I decide you're the best man for the job, not because you bullied me into it."

She had spent her life taking orders from her father, then from a husband who loved the role of commander he was unable to acquire outside their home. Both had been wrong in their decisions, and Tess had known it. When she finally made up her mind to stand up to both father and husband, the damage had already been wrought. Could she even consider this forceful man as a guide and still maintain control over the journey?

"I'll make no demands unless you're in danger."

Luke stared directly at her, and she knew he uttered the truth.

"Agreeable enough?"

His face shifted in the shadows, and she sensed he drew away. He seemed disappointed, but disappointed in what? The puzzlement left her feeling restless. The day had been too long, and she feared that those upcoming would prove even longer.

"Good enough," she finally answered out of pure exhaustion, then hastily added, "should I hire you." Tomorrow beckoned her to stand on her own two feet for the first time in her life and do what she knew was right. Tess needed to prove to herself she could do it. "I'll give you my decision in the morning."

Luke reached out as if to touch her but halted within inches of her arm. "Contessa, wait. There were two names signed up to take you." He pulled the notice from his pocket and uncrumpled it, handing it to her.

Two? Why did he tell her now? Positioning the paper better in the moonlight, Tess squinted at the name listed above Luke's. *Jim Daggert?* A choice as difficult as the first, for she trusted neither man. Yet which was the safer—the man who'd killed her husband or the one who wanted to take Clifton's place in her bed?

"You don't want to go with him." Luke glared down at her with eyes that flashed dangerously. "There are things you don't know about this man."

What do you know of him? she wondered yet couldn't ask, for it would reveal her own suspicions. "An odd reason for me to deny his application," she declared, "when all I know about you is that you killed my husband. Jim Daggert was Clifton's best friend. I owe him the benefit of an interview. Like I said, I'll make my choice in the morning. Good night, Mr. Reeves."

Leaning against the side of the wagon, Luke hooked his thumbs into his gun belt. "I've made you and Tommie a bed out here. Don't sleep in there. Whoever ransacked the place might come back. I can keep watch out here so you'll be safe."

"I don't think it would be prop—"

"Proper?" Luke finished for her. A bitter laugh echoed into the night. "Then it won't be proper every night you're on the trail with any male guide. What do you want, Tess, safety or propriety?''

Perhaps she had lived so long with her own secrets that she now suspected everyone else of harboring them. ''Can I trust you?'' she asked aloud, unaware her suspicion took voice. Though innocent, the question needed an answer for so much more.

''That's for you to decide.'' His voice was low, evasive in its huskiness. Clouds drifted over the moon, cloaking his expression.

Tiny prickles of heat erupted along her spine and spread into rivulets of warmth in her lower abdomen. The sultry night reminded Tess that wherever she sought slumber, it would be alongside Tommie or alone. It wasn't Clifton's caress she suddenly missed, but that of a stronger embrace which she had experienced earlier that morning.

Luke tipped his hat as he sauntered into the shadows, leaving her to wonder whether she should even consider him at all.

Chapter Four

"Are you sure you won't change your mind, Mrs. Harper?" The post commander of Fort Smith scowled at Tess from behind his desk. A serious man in his mid-forties, General Hunt wore his gray hair long in the style most frontiersmen preferred. His drooping mustache resembled Ulysses S. Grant's. "I believe the stage is due in tomorrow. Surely you'll find more comfort back East."

Tess fanned away the intense morning heat, grateful for the action which hid the nervousness of her hands. Bringing her gaze to the general's, she insisted, "Colorado is my destination, sir."

"Then I can be of no help." The officer pierced her with hard-eyed irritation. "Fort Smith is to be vacated and the garrison's troops stationed at Little Rock in the next few months. I haven't the time or the men to spare for your request." Picking up the papers on his desk, he tossed them at her. "Read for yourself."

"That won't be necessary, General. I'll accommodate the lady."

"Mr. Daggert." General Hunt waved the well-dressed man permission to enter. As Jim casually crossed the room and took

47

a seat next to Tess, he doffed the hat which matched the dove-gray vest worn beneath his frock coat. "I don't usually accommodate an interruption when I'm conducting private interviews,"—Hunt's words stabbed with disapproval—"but in this case, your timing is justified."

The gambler extended a hand and the general shook it.

"There you are, Mrs. Harper"—the general's gaze slanted toward Jim—"an answer to your needs."

Taking a cheroot from his coat pocket, the gambler bit off the end, then lit it. Rolling the cheroot to one corner of his teeth, he flashed a broad smile through the smoke. "To *any* of them, Tess."

Tess didn't appreciate the way his attention lingered on her bodice. "I'm sure Clifton would appreciate your interest."

General Hunt cleared his throat and shuffled papers while the gambler gave her the dubious honor of meeting her gaze directly. "Then it's settled. I presume you and the boy are packed and ready to travel?"

She could deal with Jim's other presumptions away from the general's inquiring gaze. "Yes, we are. But I do have one other offer. I wanted to talk terms with you before making my choice."

Hunt frowned. "I thought you said you were without means?"

Tess noted the veins in the general's face and the muscles along his jawline tighten. She suspected the battle that surged through him. His wife undoubtedly nagged at him concerning the matter, and he wanted to see an end to it. To discover that she had attempted to coerce him into helping struck a death knell to Tess's hopes of obtaining any military escort.

"I've taken up enough of your time." Tess gathered her parasol and stood.

Both men rose. The officer half-bowed, offering a smile that didn't reach his eyes. "A speedy journey to you and your young son, Mrs. Harper. Please accept my condolences in the death of Sergeant Harper." Picking up a pencil and blank paper on the desk, the general asked, "May I post a letter to your parents for you? Or would you like to leave a forwarding address where we can send Sergeant Harper's final wages?''

Tess lifted her chin a notch higher. As badly as she needed those wages, the fewer who knew her whereabouts, the better. ''No, thank you, General. I'm not sure of my final destination. My parents and I haven't seen each other since my wedding day. I'm sure they've no wish to hear from me, nor I, them.''

Sympathy softened his tone. ''Then may God speed you on your journey, madam.''

An urge to shed herself of false amenities forced Tess out of the office. Without a glance, she swept past the orderly. As she stepped into the bright June sunlight, a hand at her elbow stopped her from calling out to Tommie. The three-year-old was splashing water at his friend Zachariah near the horses' drinking trough.

''What's your hurry, Contessa? Turn around here and let me look at you.''

Jim's brown gaze darkened to near black as she faced him.

''God, woman, you get more beautiful every time I see you. How are you?''

''How do you expect me to be?'' Never quite knowing how to take Jim's compliments, Tess finally gave way to the belligerence engulfing her. ''Does everyone know? Poor Tess Harper. Stupid, beautiful Tess Harper. A product of parents who swindled people.'' It was too much, finding herself a widow only to learn that what little respect she'd built these past four years was suddenly buried with her husband. Must she start over? Was a woman's worth only to be gauged by the father who sired her or the man she wed?

''The general and Clifton were poker partners. You know Clif,'' Jim reminded her, ''he never could keep his mouth shut if he had one too many whiskeys. No harm done or Hunt would've already had you arrested. The point is, are you going to be all right on your own now?'' Genuine concern filled Jim's hawk-like features. ''I wish I would have been there to change matters, Contessa. Clifton was never good with a gun.''

Luke had never mentioned that Clifton had drawn his gun. He merely said her husband had gotten into the line of fire. Tess wasn't sure of the path her thoughts were taking since Luke Reeves's visit. "Where were you when it happened?" she demanded. "I thought the two of you were supposed to be together."

Jim ignored her question, staring up the street at a group of women coming out of the mercantile. "Looks like services are over. Wonder who they condemned to hell this morning."

"I've got a pretty good idea," Tess muttered and opened her parasol. She turned her back to the church-goers. If he had anything to hide, he was a master of disguise. "You didn't answer my question."

"We rode together as far as Pencil Bluff, but Clif said he had some business to take care of." Jim ran a hand through the chestnut hair at his temple before settling his hat back on his head. "I sat through an all-night poker game and a couple of bottles of whiskey before I heard he'd been shot. Rode here soon as I sobered up enough to sit a saddle. Just barely made it to the burial in time. Clif was my best friend, Contessa. Let me help you." He reached out and tucked a stray wisp of hair back into her bonnet. "I care about you . . . and Tommie."

Brawny shoulders and the sincerity in his brown eyes offered a tempting haven for the doubts spreading through her, but Tess refused to surrender. How would she ever know whether she could make decisions for herself, live by her own creed, if there was always someone to lean on or throw herself into his arms?

Jim's fingers lingered a little too long against her cheek, and she turned away from his touch only to find one of the ladies staring at her. As the group strolled near, Zachariah's mother whispered something to the others, and each chin lifted higher as they passed.

"Good day, ladies," Jim crooned, doffing his hat.

"Mr. Daggert." The general's wife spoke for them all. In a decidedly more condemning tone, she declared her disapproval. "*Mrs.* Harper."

"Ladies," Tess muttered as they passed, wondering if she would ever fit into such a circle of women or if she even cared to do so. The thought was so totally disgusting, she couldn't resist the urge to make the pedestals they placed themselves on teeter a bit. "Sometimes it's not bad being the odd piece out of a jigsaw puzzle."

When their bustles were little more than colorful bobs in the distance, Jim laughed. "What does it matter whether or not you fit in with them? You'll be gone within hours, and they'll be making someone else miserable."

"It doesn't matter," Tess argued, although she realized it did. She might scoff at the women but never at the respectability and acceptance they enjoyed. Jim couldn't understand her need of these things. A man's gun hand always earned him the necessary respect. The quality of a woman's reputation was everything.

"Yeah, it doesn't matter," he teased. "Like snakes don't rattle?"

She begrudgingly linked her arm through the one he offered and allowed him to escort her away from headquarters.

"Didn't know you knew Luke Reeves so well," Jim commented in a tone she couldn't define. "Seems to me a woman oughtn't make a habit of feeding the man who shot her husband, much less consider him for the job you posted."

Tess unthreaded her arm and halted where she stood. "Seems to me, Jim Daggert, you shouldn't be presuming so much. That's no one's business but my own."

"Now, Contessa, I was only trying to spare you from any further gossip, and you know it." Chestnut lashes widened over his eyes in exaggerated disappointment as his lips drew together in a childish pout.

Shading herself with the parasol, Tess ignored his explanation and resumed her walk. "I've lived with gossip all my life, Jim. You know that better than anybody. You've been a fine friend to Clifton and me, but I won't have you or anyone else spying on me, good intentions or not."

He quickly caught up with her. "Spying on you, Contessa?

Watching out for you is more like it. Don't you notice how men look at you? Have always wanted you? Reeves would have to be a blind man if he didn't try to seduce you.''

"That's the silliest thing I've ever heard. Seduce me by killing my husband? I may have been foolish in the past, but do you really think I'm so naïve?'' Determination strengthened her stride. "I know he isn't simply trying to make amends. You forgot, I've been used by the best. I know when I'm being manipulated.''

"Now, Contessa. I know how you feel—'' A loud wail interrupted the gambler's apology.

"Take 'at back, you hear! I do it again if you don't take 'at back!''

Tess gasped as she saw Tommie dunking Zachariah's head in the water trough. The red-headed boy struggled for air, then came up screaming, "Ma-a-ama, Mama!''

Flinging down her parasol, Tess ran and pulled her son off Zach, trying to dodge the small feet and hands still kicking out at his near-drowned friend. "Stop it, son. Stop it! Why would you want to hurt Zach? He's your friend.''

Huge tears welled in Tommie's eyes and trickled down his dust-smeared face. "No more, he ain't!''

As Tess held him back, Tommie spat. The wad missed Zach's feet by inches, but Tommie's adversary acted as if it hit him in the face. He launched himself into the three-year-old, wrestling both Tommie and Tess to the ground.

The ferocity of the impact caught her off guard and nearly knocked the breath from Tess. When she finally found words, the yell she'd intended exhaled in a feeble, "Let me up, boys!'' A whirlwind of three-year-old fists and legs kicked and punched hard until, with regained strength, Tess ordered, "Stop this instant and let me up!''

A strong pair of hands pulled one of the screaming wildcats off her, then roughly tore the other from her grasp. Luke seemed to appear out of the dust and swung Tommie up on his shoulders so Zachariah couldn't reach him.

"Yet me down!" Tommie shouted, struggling to unperch himself. "He's gotta take 'at back."

"Settle down, Tom. There are other ways to handle this." Luke's command was soft yet given in an authoritative tone which instantly stilled Tommie's squirming protest.

"He oughta let them go after it," Jim grumbled as he offered a hand to Tess and helped her stand. "Only way the boy's gonna learn to take up for himself."

"Luke's right." Tess brushed the dust from her skirt. Jim's hands shot out to help her, but she quickly pushed them aside. "Fighting's not the answer."

"Only meant to help." Jim's grin enhanced a suggestive glint in his eyes. "With the boy, I mean."

"Are you all right, Tess?" Luke asked. Gripping Zach by the scruff of his collar, he kept a careful watch on Tommie as the three-year-old made faces at Zach.

Tommie spat again and met his mark. Zach let out another bellow, drowning out Tess's reply that she would be fine.

Like an enraged goose defending her offspring, Zachariah's mother ran squawking from her quarters and grabbed her son, crushing him to her ample bosom. He seemed more in peril of smothering now than he had ever been at the trough. Darting an incriminating glance at Luke, the woman kissed the boy all over his face.

"Did this man hurt you?" Daggers of blue targeted Luke. "If he did, I'll see to it . . . why are you so wet?"

The freckles on Zachariah's face wrinkled into one spotted blotch as he accused Tommie of trying to drown him.

Tess denied the charge against her son. "Tommie would never do such a thing without being provoked. And Mr. Reeves was merely trying to keep the boys from hurting each other any further."

"After all I did for you, Mrs. Harper! Allowing my son to play with yours and befriending you when no one else would." Delilah Wainwright shook a finger at Tess, thought better of it, then pointed it at Tommie. "You need to learn a few manners, young man."

Tess took a step closer.

The woman must have caught the warning in Tess's eyes, for Delilah immediately curled the accusing finger back into her palm.

"I'll deal with my son's part in this, Delilah." Tess's expression hardened. "You deal with yours."

"Everyone told me you were no good." Delilah's brows arched over a look of self-righteousness. "But I felt it was my Christian duty to offer you a hand of friendship. The Lord said when you've tried your best and it doesn't work, to 'dust thy feet and walk from among them.' I shall keep you in my prayers."

Disgusted with the holier-than-thou attitude, Tess did a little poking of her own, in the woman's chest, punctuating her words as she uttered them low and deadly. "Pray for yourself first, Delilah Wainwright. Perhaps someday, if you're lucky and a lot less sanctimonious, you might discover what real friendship is."

"Well, I never!" Delilah backed away, moving far enough to have plenty of running room. Grabbing her son's arm, she puffed and sputtered about the indecency and coarseness of it all. "Come, Zachariah," she demanded, then nearly dragged her son toward her apartment on officers' row.

"She's right. I don't suppose she ever will." Luke's comment met with silence.

Finally Tess began to giggle. Jim's mustache lifted above a silent grin.

Tommie's brows knitted together as he looked up at his elders and asked, "What's so funny?"

Laughter barreled out of Luke's mouth like a roll of thunder. Onlookers stared out curtained windows, and doors stood ajar along the row.

"You know, I once vowed I'd never put another woman's reputation in jeopardy," Tess informed them as her laughter ended. She could easily do just that to Delilah's. But she wasn't Delilah Wainwright, who, if their roles were reversed, would announce to the eavesdroppers some of her adversary's imperfections. Though Tommie's birth had come a few weeks past nine months into her marriage to Clifton, Zachariah's birth was not so full-termed. If it hadn't been for the boys' presence, Tess might have allowed herself the temptation to gossip . . . just this once.

"So?" Jim urged.

"So, why break it now?" Common sense prevailed.

"Or ever." Luke agreed.

It seemed as if the bounty hunter knew Tess was testing herself and was proud that she had passed muster.

"Yet me down, Yuke." Tommie squirmed on Luke's shoulders. When the bounty hunter deposited him in the dirt, Tommie ran to Tess and hugged her skirt. "Mommie, it's not true, is it?"

She hugged him and lowered herself to her knees so she could meet him face to face. "What's not true?"

"Zach, he said . . ." Tears filled Tommie's voice and eyes. Grown-up concern aged the youthful face that began to hiccup. "He said you no good and 'at make me no good too."

"No, son. It's not true. You're all that's good in this world." Tess hugged him fiercely. Damn that woman and her mouth! Had Delilah told Zach more? If so, how many others at the fort knew? The general was a man accustomed to keeping his counsel, but Delilah Wainwright's spiteful tongue knew no honor. If the woman decided to tell everyone about Tess's past, the news would travel like wildfire.

Tess had known from the first time one of the soldiers tried to kiss her and been reprimanded, that she would never be accepted. No one believed she hadn't teased him, not even Clifton.

A beauty like you does something to a man. The words from that horrible night in the Hot Springs bathhouse echoed in her brain now as if the man were standing next to her. Tess shivered as the nightmare of the attacker's foul touch shot remembered pain through her. Wiping at the dirt from the scuffle, Tess knew she could never remove the unclean feeling left by the man who had compromised her. How many times did Tess ask herself if things would have been different if she had told her father she would not lure men to the baths so he could rob them? Probably just as many times, she reminded herself, that he convinced her he would hurt Mother if she didn't obey.

"We must leave today, this very hour." Tess looked first at Luke, then at Jim. *Before someone says even more to Tommie,* she wanted to add. He mustn't learn his way. Not until he's older. Not until he can understand that she might have once followed her father's commands and was as no good as Delilah claimed. But she had paid a dear and irretrievable price for her failings and the respectability she sought so desperately now.

"Let's get outa here." Jim offered her the parasol she'd dropped several yards away. "I noticed you've got a wagon ready. I'll just put my gear with yours and we'll head on out."

Tommie held his arms up for Tess to lift him. Wrapping his legs around her waist, he held on as a frightened baby cub would to its mother. "I wanna go with Yuke, Mommie."

"Now, boy"—Jim's tone implied an anger hidden from his features—"your mother's got enough to worry about without you causing more. Your daddy would want you to act like a little man."

"Mrs. Harper's already got her belongings loaded in my wagon," Luke broke in, stating fact rather than challenge. "It might take you a while to make similar arrangements."

Between sniffles, Tommie whispered into his mother's ear, "I don't yike Jim, Mommie. He's mean."

The beginnings of a headache stabbed at Tess's temples, making her grimace. The trip would be hard enough on Tommie without fear of the man they'd have to count on for their safety. She disliked Jim's attitude almost as much as she hated the idea of entrusting her son's life with the very man who'd killed his father. In the end, Tommie's needs determined her choice.

"Luke's right," she said. "My decision is made. Though I appreciate your offer, Jim, he's the most prepared to take us. I must hire him."

The two men exchanged glances. An undercurrent of words and silent promises . . . warnings . . . passed between them.

Tess felt drained. The sun bore down on her face and neck, exhausting any remaining strength she possessed. It was a long time before nightfall and she meant to camp many miles from here. Let them preen and prattle about their qualifications; her decision had been made.

As she began to walk away, Jim reached out and gripped her forearm. "Wait, Contessa! This is unnecessary. Why not have the benefit of two scouts? I'm heading to Colorado anyway. Got some business in Denver and thought I'd try my hand at mining. Why not travel with you and help out? I can ride shotgun with the wagon while Reeves scouts ahead for danger."

"I have no money to pay you for your trouble."

"I didn't ask for any, did I?"

The idea of two scouts appealed to her. If Jim tried to overstep any boundaries, Luke would set him straight. When Luke revealed his real reason for watching out for her and Tommie, Jim might prove handy. Tess looked to see if the bounty hunter offered any objections. "Luke?"

Though his features were noncommittal, Luke's dark gaze bore into her. "You're the boss."

His cocky stance and tone brought their argument of last night to mind, and she remembered how she had made it clear who would make the choices. Having the distinct impression that he had never said those words to any man, Tess felt a sense of security for the journey ahead and a feeling of uneasiness, as well. She could easily push this dangerous man too far. Sarcasm tingled her reply. "I'm asking your opinion."

His stance widened, though sooty lashes narrowed over his piercing look. "Makes sense. Two scouts would be safer."

From his taut jawline and the twitch in Luke's cheek, she knew Jim wouldn't have been his choice for a second scout had there been another, but the bounty hunter seemed willing to overcome his own prejudice in favor of good sense. She liked that about him. "It's settled then. Tommie and I will meet you two within the hour.'' Juggling her son higher on her hip, Tess breathed an inward sigh of relief and headed for her apartment.

"No objections as long as you get one thing clear, Daggert.'' Luke thumbed up the tip of his hat. His gaze met the curiosity in Jim's sullen brown eyes.

"What's that?'' Full of male bravado, the question challenged.

"Tommie's a three-year-old *boy,* no matter what you or his daddy might have expected of him. Don't be trying to make a man out of him when you haven't completed the job on yourself.''

Both men were noted gunhands, but the blink in Jim's eyes hinted he thought Luke the better.

"You'd like that, wouldn't you?'' Jim taunted Luke, motioning toward Tess's fading figure. "Rile me so we shoot it out and only one of us gets to take her wherever she wants. Makes you look good in the widow's eyes shining up to the boy, doesn't it, Mr. Bounty Hunter? But those better looking than you have tried that little trick and it got 'em nowhere. Hers is a marrying bed and, frankly, mister, you don't strike me as a man with much use for a mattress.''

Luke grabbed Jim's high-starched cravat, drew and triggered his pistol before the gambler could go for his gun. Poking the barrel under Daggert's chin, Luke used the cold steel to assure his sincerity. "Keep your filthy conjecture to yourself, and stay clear of the boy. He hollers or cries one time and you're anywhere near him, I'm gonna rip you apart with my bare hands and feed the pieces to the coyotes. Then you'll wish I'd done you the favor of shooting you. Do I make myself understood?''

Jerking away from Luke's grip and the gun, Jim garnered more courage than most who stared down the barrel of Luke's Colt. The gambler straightened his shirt and vest, adjusting his cravat.

"More than happy to oblige, Reeves. But his mother's a different matter."

Wiping his hand on the butternut-colored buckskins as if he had touched something foul, Luke sheathed the revolver and pulled his hat low on his forehead. "The widow's old enough to make her own choices."

But was she? Did she know Daggert wanted more than a quick straddle? The man was marriage-minded. "Makes a man wonder how much choice her husband had, doesn't it?" Luke taunted Jim. "A pretty lady like that must've had plenty of men wanting to steal her away from him. Even a best friend might take a shine to such a fine-looking lady."

"What are you implying?" Jim's hand wavered near his holster.

Luke never flinched, his gun ready if the stupid man went for his gun. "That maybe I'll be watching you two a bit more careful than I would have. Could be more to those rumors about Harper's dealing with Hoot Hill and a third member of their gang than I suspected. I might have been a bit too hasty in judgment. The plug I pulled out of her husband is the same caliber as mine, but that doesn't necessarily prove I did the killing."

"Watch all you want, bounty man. All you've got are notions." Jim's Custer-style mustache lifted to one side, creasing the sharp planes of his broad face as he snarled, "Proof is what you need."

The jagged white scar on Luke's right cheek and brow twitched at the challenge. He hoped like hell Tess hadn't agreed for Daggert to tag along so the two of them could go on with their schemes while he provided safety. There seemed only one way to settle the doubt gnawing at him and to knock that gloating grin off the bastard's face.

Luke hoped for Tommie's sake that he was wrong. Letting Daggert think he bested him for the moment, Luke moved his left hand clear of the Colt. "Like I said, I'll be watching."

Chapter Five

The mules plodded on a winding path through the foothills, following a northbound course parallel to the Arkansas River. Tess fought to hold the reins as the jacks and jennies nipped and kicked each other, pulling in opposite directions.

Glaring furiously at them from below the brim of her brown bonnet, she slapped the broad leather straps down hard and shouted, "Hyaw!" for the hundredth time that morning, calling encouragement to the working team. Drenched in perspiration, Tess's arms felt as if they were being wrenched from her shoulder sockets. Her fingers vised around the reins that pulled and released as the mules stopped and started.

Oh, to be three years old again, she complained silently and gritted against the pain of the splintery driver's seat. Tommie had stripped to only his trousers, which he hitched up as high as the pant legs would allow. He now slept in the back of the wagon where the horseshoe-shaped tarpaulin kept the searing sun from beating down. With no one but her son near, Tess pushed modesty aside and unfastened her buttons from collar to mid-bosom. She fought to hold the leather straps and fan the linsey homespun to get relief from the stifling heat. Beads of perspiration ran down her throat to pool in the valley between her breasts. The first stop they made she would forfeit the corset. The scalding hot stays were tight enough to suffocate.

Dust raised by the mules' hooves billowed into Tess's face, blasting her with shards of cacti and blackjack leaves. Wisps of hair which had escaped from her bonnet no longer looked blonde but matched the butternut brown-gray of rebel uniforms. While she was licking at the grit that coated her teeth despite Luke's bandana, a spell of sneezes racked her body. When her eyes threatened to swell shut from stinging, Tess decided she should have taken Jim up on the offer to drive the team. But her pride had not allowed that. Determined to prove she could take care of Tommie and herself, Tess had sent the gambler out to scout with Luke.

Not that her decision met with the bounty hunter's approval. He hadn't much liked the idea of Jim not being near the wagon. Then again, at lunch he seemed displeased that the gambler chose to sit next to her on the wagon bed while they ate. Did Luke harbor the same suspicions she did about Jim?

Endless questions poured through Tess's mind as scrubby trees and prickly pears filled the horizon. What she would not give for a few answers concerning the gambler. Had he been a party to selling rifles to the Indians? Had he involved Clifton, or was her husband truly an innocent bystander? Tess wanted to believe Jim innocent, as well. Wanted to put aside her uneasiness and accept, without hesitation, the friendship he offered.

But Jim had no real profession to speak of. He said he kept himself in such fine attire and income by extraordinary good fortune at the gaming tables. When luck ran a bit lean, he took on scouting duties for General Hunt or rode posse for the territorial marshal. Still, those jobs were not frequent enough to set aside the suspicion in her own mind that he earned money another way. A way that was not so law-abiding.

Once Tess had trusted men far too much, and that gullibility had nearly destroyed her. Might still, if she didn't play her cards carefully around Luke Reeves. He was up to something more than guiding her to Colorado, and until she discovered his intent, it seemed wise to keep up her guard.

"This place needs a splash of color," she said aloud, putting aside her disturbing thoughts and brooding mood. "A splash of anything," she added with a quirk of her lips. Green eyes narrowed as a bead of perspiration chose that moment to sting her eye. "Well, not anything."

The thought of striking camp in a few hours spurred her on, adding energy to Tess's tired, aching shoulders and hips. A bath in the Arkansas and a place to stretch out in the wagon alongside Tommie would be wonderful.

A flash of yellow buzzed around her face, and she shooed it with one elbow, trying not to let go of the reins. "Scaaat!" she yelled as she swatted at the yellow jacket that impaled itself just above her right breast. "Ouch!"

Her shout of pain awoke Tommie and startled the mules into a gallop. Suddenly a dark cloud whirled in front of her, droning the danger into which she'd driven. She yanked back on the reins, but too late. More hornet-like insects swarmed the mules' ears and flanks, attacking her and infiltrating the wagon.

"Wake up, Tommie. Wake up! Yellow jackets!" she screamed. "Help, somebody! Help us!"

She leaned back, stiffening her legs to brace herself against a possible stampede of the team. Slapping at her shoulders and face while maintaining control of the frightened mules seemed impossible. The pestilence reached her son, and his wails pierced the air.

The mules bolted into a full-out run, jerking the reins from her hands. Tess fell back into the wagon and landed nearly on top of Tommie. Seconds seemed like eternity as she fought to stand, her grip a vise around Tommie's arm so he wouldn't be out of her reach. With all the force of her fear, she screamed, "Runaway!"

Praying that Luke or Jim heard her scream, Tess shouted, "Hang on, Tommie! Hang on to Mommie and don't let go!"

Fighting the wild rocking of the wagon, she tried to regain

her position on the driver's box. Splinters pierced her gloves as her hands gripped the back of the wooden seat, but she flinched away the pain. When one foot finally settled over the edge and promised to steady her balance, a rut in the road toppled her backward, yanking away Tommie's grasp on her waist.

"Reach for me, Tommie!" she commanded and thrust her arm out, hoping it would be enough to stop his plunge toward the back of the wagon. If he hurtled out at this speed, he would be killed.

"Mommie, Mommie! Catch me, Mommie!"

Tommie clutched for her hand and in a moment of gut-clenching terror their fingers threaded, then slipped. With no thought of anything but her child, Tess gave up the only chance she had of regaining the reins and groped for Tommie.

"God, help me," she pleaded and flung herself to the back just as his legs slid past the end of the wagon. Her fingers grasped, finding nothing. "Please, God!"

A finger. Two. Tess clutched at the precious treasure of that small hand. With every ounce of outrage that filled her heart, Tess yanked. A primeval yell of conquest echoed from the depth of her lungs as the touch caught and held.

The tiny, trembling body fell against her own. Tess clung and prayed, cried and shouted shrieks of relief, of distress. Their danger was long from being over. The wagon jostled and bumped, throwing them from side to side. Tess's heart thundered to the rhythm of the pounding hooves. Leather and reins snapped their uselessness, jingling as the osage orange wheels shuddered beneath the onslaught of hooves and rutted roadway.

Could she make it to the straps again? Struggling to her knees, Tess clasped Tommie protectively. The sight before her knotted her stomach with dread. The reins were tangled in two of the mules' harnesses. In order to reach them, she would have to jump clear of the schooner's tongue and mount one of them as they ran. She faced certain death if she didn't leap

63

far enough and landed amid the grinding hooves. But face it she must . . . if she expected Tommie to live.

One of the jacks went down and the Conestoga veered, tilting dangerously to one side. The terrified scream of its team blended with Tess's own as the wagon threatened to overturn.

Shouts penetrated her terror. Human voices! Hope lifted Tess's spirits even as reality plunged her into crippling doubt. *Could they stop the team in time?*

Luke spurred Talon alongside the mules and grabbed the reins. With a mighty jerk, he pulled the team toward him. The schooner shuddered and righted itself. At the same instant, Jim barreled through the back flap, stretching two firm arms across the width of the Conestoga to prevent Tess and Tommie from being thrown out.

"Whoa there, jennies! Easy there, jacks!" Luke's commands eased the frightened creatures from a gallop to a trot, then finally a breath-relieving canter. Only his powerful control kept the mules from fighting their harnesses and stumbling over the downed mule.

Sweat poured down Luke's back from the supreme effort it took to stop the runaway animals, but never, never had Tess seen anything more appealing. Though Jim's arms held her secure, Luke's bravery had saved her son's life . . . and her own. Not even a day out of Fort Smith, she knew that choosing Luke was the first right decision she had ever made.

When the team came to a lopsided halt, Tess accepted Jim's help out of the wagon. Holding Tommie at arm's length, she inspected the welts he suffered from the insect attack.

"What in the devil did you run into?" Jim gave her no time to pull back her bonnet, but did so himself.

"Yellow jackets. A swarm of them." Tess's hands shot to her red-blotched cheeks to feel the painful bumps. Tears welled in her eyes, but she refused to add hers to Tommie's.

"Well, don't just stand there gawking, Daggert. Unharness that mule and take the team upwind of it. I'll grab some mud and doctor the boy. When you're through, help Tess."

Tess fixed her gaze on Luke as he walked toward the river

and cupped a handful of wet mud. Grateful for his quick thinking, she ran to grab some mud to ease the stinging. Later they
could bathe and rub the welts with baking soda. As she
watched Luke dab Tommie's welts, her gaze was drawn to the
man's magnificent form. Dark hair curled along the base of
his neck while perspiration molded his shirt to the muscles of
his broad back. A gunbelt emphasized his narrow hips and
nestled the Colt against one well-muscled thigh.

Closing her eyes to break the fascination, Tess reopened
them only to discover an even stronger attraction. As he
moved to gather more mud, sleek muscular elegance powered
Luke's every step. When he suddenly became aware of her
regard, danger lurked in his deep blue gaze. The indigo darkened into a fathomless, knowing look that acknowledged and
challenged the flush of desire flooding her senses.

Suddenly Tess felt everything—the dirt in her hair, the grit
on her teeth, the stinging welts all over her body. But more
than anything else, she felt something unleashed inside. A
wild, unmanageable, dangerous infatuation for the bounty
hunter which ebbed into an ache deep within. She willed herself to concentrate on doctoring the bites.

"Do you feel all right?" Jim asked, moving up beside her.
"You look a bit faint."

Tess's hands cupped her cheeks, feeling the hot flush of her
skin. She had actually blushed just thinking of the bounty
hunter. Had she stood there gawking at Luke long enough for
Jim to finish his task? "I'm fine," she muttered, turning from
the gambler's intense inspection. "A bit shaken by the wild
ride, I'm afraid."

Watching Luke apply the mud to Tommie's face and hands,
dabbing wherever the insects left their mark, she was grateful
when he drew Jim's attention to her son.

"How's that, folks? That mud ought to scare off the next
swarm of stingers, don't you think?"

Jim laughed. "It would scare me for sure."

"You missed some, Mista Yuke. Right here." Tommie

pulled down his trousers and revealed several welts on his bottom.

Tess stifled a giggle behind her palms. "Excuse him, gentlemen. He's just a—"

"Boy," Luke finished for her. "That's reason enough."

Tess became all too aware of the intense look Jim gave her. Knowing the way his mind worked, she suspected that he wanted to help dab her unseen bites. "I'll suffer the ones I can't reach, thank you."

Jim's brown eyes widened in exaggerated disappointment. "Oh, but I do so enjoy administering to the sick. It gives a man a good feeling knowing how he's helped."

Tess laughed despite the suggestiveness of the remark. The laughter felt good after such a frightful moment. But a quick glance at Luke found a scowl on his face. Curiosity spurred Tess's thoughts. *Why is he so serious? What would those lips look like curved into a smile?* Deciding she might like to view such a sight, she silently vowed to help him find a better humor.

The first shades of evening spread across the horizon and with them came a reminder of how long and difficult the day had been. Now they had a mule to butcher. "Will we camp here?" Tess asked.

"This is as good a place as any." Luke surveyed all directions. "Besides, all that whooping and yelling would have brought in marauders, if there were any. We're fairly safe."

Should I take that as criticism? Tess almost spoke the question aloud, but he was right. Their screams could have brought in much more trouble than insects. The opportunity to see if he would laugh had proven too irresistible. "We might have scared off the marauders anyway, looking like this. Small pox, you know."

"Mommie, you'd scare 'em, too, and you a big pox."

Luke laughed, a deep full-throated baritone erupting without restraint. While he dabbed the last welt on Tommie's bottom, the bounty hunter continued to chuckle. Tess smiled. The sound might just be worth the painful itch she suffered.

Seeing the companionable look shared by Contessa and Luke stirred Jim's anger. His brows angled in disapproval. "You let your guard down, Contessa. You can laugh at it now, but what if Indians instead of insects waited to ambush you? Or a cougar perched on an overhang? Would it seem so humorous then?"

Luke walked to the bank, cleansed his hands and shook them dry. "It's true that sound carries out here for miles, Tess. That will either save us from trouble or bring it." He stripped off the buckskin shirt, pulled it over a broad muscular chest and flung it onto a blackjack branch. His grin faded as he challenged Jim's glare. "But if we do our job, she won't have to worry about it, will she, Daggert?"

"You saying I'm not pulling my share?" Jim countered.

"I'm saying I circled to the rear twice today and you weren't anywhere to be found."

"Anyone who plans on attacking us would find the same thing, wouldn't he, Reeves? If you happen to get your butt in trouble, the scalawag would think the wagon only had one scout. I could come in and rescue you. Seems I'm pulling my share pretty damn well."

Trying to ward off the confrontation that narrowed both men's gazes to hard glints, Tess touched Jim's arm. The last thing she needed was a fight. They might kill each other, leaving her and Tommie without a guide. "I'll be more careful. My son's safety is too precious to take such chances, despite the fine job you both are doing."

A look of something close to respect passed between herself and Luke. A warm glow of satisfaction filled Tess, and she discovered that pleasing him had somehow become important. Caution spread through her, and Tess swayed as if struck by a blast of heat. Her whole life had been to please a man rather than herself. She refused to fall into that habit again.

"Are you all right?" Luke reached out to steady her.

Tess waved away his hand. Twice in the last few minutes, she allowed herself to appear in need. She was stronger than this and didn't want to be read so easily. "I'll be fine. I just need to wash off some dirt before I put any more back on.''

Luke's brows furrowed as his palm jerked away. ''Then let's set up camp. Daggert, you stake the schooner. I'll do the butchering.'' Walking past the boy, Luke ruffled Tommie's hair. ''Looks like we're having mule for supper.''

''And one demanding ass,'' Jim grumbled into Tess's ear.

Chapter Six

After supper dishes were cleaned and put away, Tess longed to bathe. The quick cleansing she did before cooking merely took away the first layer of dust and perspiration. Now that camp chores were completed, she could give Tommie and herself a good scrubbing.

With a basket of clean clothes in hand, Tess walked alongside Tommie. Jim led his mahogany-colored roan through a stand of dogwood that banked an offshoot stream flowing from the Arkansas River. Luke took first watch and scouted the area. Jim should have stayed back at camp, but he insisted upon escorting them so he'd know their whereabouts in the event of trouble.

Tess caught herself admiring Jim's moonlit profile. He was tall and solid-shouldered, much like his horse. Thick waves of chestnut hair fell well past the collar of his gray morning coat, and the reddish-brown mustache added a daring look. A handsome man to most and always considerate of her, so Tess couldn't fathom what it was about Jim Daggert that put her off.

Upon approaching a bed in the stream which formed a secluded inlet, she halted her steps. Jim and Tommie did the same. "This looks like a good place." Smiling her appreciation, she thanked him for his trouble.

Jim thumbed the brim of his hat. "Anything for you, Contessa. You know that."

His soft-drawl sent a wave of shivers across her shoulders and down her back. There was no doubt he cared for her, wanted her, and the woman in Tess responded to that sincere attraction and his thoughtfulness.

"I need time, Jim." She turned away from the desire shining in his moonlit eyes. "You can understand that, can't you?"

A hand at her elbow gently persuaded her to turn around. When she complied, he drew Tess closer. "A man can only understand for so long, Contessa, then he has to force an answer to the issue."

Thankfully, Tommie chose that moment to tug on her skirts, saving Tess from reminding Jim that her husband had been dead less than a week.

"Mommie, yet's go swimming. I inna hurry." He wobbled off toward the stream.

"Wait, son! Don't go in without me." Not wanting to leave Jim's statement unchallenged, yet knowing the three-year-old would be too excited at the thought of swimming to obey her command, she quickly apologized. "We'll talk more later. He'll plunge right in if I don't get there before him." Gathering her skirt, she sprinted down the path Tommie had taken, not waiting for Jim's answer.

The bank sloped to a sandy shore where a long beam of moonlight illuminated the surface. The stream sparkled with its silvery gleam. Cattails and switchgrass along the curve of the waterway hummed with a chorus of crickets and croaking frogs.

Tommie jumped up and down at the bank. "Come on, Mommie. Yet's go!"

The water looked inviting, and Tess suddenly felt Tommie's compulsion to be free of the perspiration, dust and hard work of the journey. To do nothing but frolic in the water.

"Let Mama change. Take everything off but your flannels. I brought some fresh things for us to wear." Tess found an outcropping of bushes where she hooked the basket on the tip of a branch, then turned to see if he was undressing.

"That's a good boy," Tess complimented as he quickly shucked his clothing, then piled mud from the bank to build a dugout of sorts. Tommie had obeyed her instructions much better in the last two days than in the past few weeks. With Clifton gone so much of the time, Tommie's mood had swung from impishness to impossible. She half expected him to rebel as a reaction to his father's death, but he hadn't. Perhaps it was his friendship with Luke. Tommie hung on every word the bounty hunter uttered. He showed her several things Luke had taught him just today. How would her son be affected when he learned the truth of Clifton's death?

Undoing her corsets and crinoline proved more difficult than usual. Her arms and hands were weakened by the first day at the reins and trembled as she unhooked the metal latches. For a moment she wondered whether she really should leave off the undergarments except for the cotton chemise and pantalets when she completed her bath. But packing away the rest of the undergarments seemed practical. She could sit the driver's box easier and wouldn't have to worry about her legs accidentally touching one of the hot bands that gave her skirts width.

Though she tried to comply to the fashion edicts of the day, common sense told her to leave the corset off as well. Tess unbuttoned her high-topped shoes and set them in the overhanging tree branch so no scavengers would come along and steal them. Raccoons were notorious robbers, and even branches offered little protection. "Might as well make them work for it," she said into the night.

The insect chorus halted at the sound of her voice, and Tess listened to the silence. The wind in the dogwood blossoms, the rustle of switchgrass and cattails, and the lapping of water at the shore were muffled by the deep, endless silence of the night. Without the brief relief of nature's voice, the quiet

71

would be a bit frightening and utterly lonely. A cloud passed over the moon and shadowed the stream for a moment, spreading disquiet and loneliness within Tess.

"Enough of this," she scolded herself. Loneliness was something she had lived with long before Clifton's death; she would not let her spirit decay from it now. Splaying her toes in the warm sand, Tess felt the earth shift between them. "Are you ready, son?" she asked, grabbing Tommie's small hand as they splashed into the stream.

They both squealed in delight at the cleansing coolness of the river water on their skin. Moving in closer to the bank, she set her son down in front of her, careful to make certain the water hit him belly-high.

"Now, shall we wash you first?" She caressed the treasured bar of lavender-scented soap. Would the fragrant soap cause the welts to itch more than they did now? Steeling herself against the unpleasant possibility, Tess decided the pain would be worth it to feel clean again.

"Ahh, Mommie, do I have to?" Tommie complained, jumping up and down.

"Yes, I'm afraid so." This was the Tommie she knew—all boy, protector of dirt, hater of freshly scrubbed skin. "Now what's first—your hair or your face?"

His hands dipped inside the breast pocket of his red flannels and pulled out a lizard. "How 'bout him first?"

Tess yelped as Tommie thrust the reptile toward her face. "Good heavens!"

Tommie giggled. "He won't hurt you, Mommie. He wants to kiss you."

The lizard's tongue darted out as if on cue and she cringed from its slithery contact. Trying to quell her revulsion, Tess reminded herself that this could really be quite laughable if it wasn't so revolting. How she hated slimy, slithery creatures! "Uhh, I don't think a kiss is quite appropriate, son. We haven't been properly introduced, you see."

"His name is Thammy."

"You mean Sammy?"

The lizard's tongue darted out, making Tommie squeal. "See there. He said it again. Thammy . . . not Sammy."

"Well, why don't I break off a piece of this soap?" Tess dug her fingernail into one end of the bar and offered it to him. "You can wash Sam—Thammy while I clean my hair. By that time, maybe you'll be ready for me to wash you."

"You mean I can keep 'im?" Tommie's lashes widened over his green eyes.

Tess laughed. "As long as I know where he's at, at all times. Ooohh!" She shivered with the thought of coming across the creature unexpectedly. But the reptile would fill Tommie's time in the long journey ahead and give him something to play with.

"Oh boy, Mommie. You a tophand."

She laughed. "Where did you hear that?"

"Mista Yuke."

"Did he tell you what that means?" What topic had they discussed which would introduce the word to her son?

"He said you's a tophand of a mama."

A blush of pleasure tightened Tess's cheeks as if the man were there to see it. Realizing she needed to urge Tommie into action, she returned the compliment. "Well, it's easy to be a good mother when I've got a tophand of a son. I'll just bet Thammy could be a better salamander if you'd clean him up a bit too."

Tommie took the bit of soap and began to scrub, informing Sammy he was not a lizard after all but something his mama called a salamander.

Removing the hairpins that held her severely knotted blond coil in place, Tess shook the thick mass from its binds and let it cascade past her shoulders. Fastening her hairpins to the bodice of her chemise so she wouldn't lose them, she lowered herself into the water and dipped her head backward to rinse the dirt from her hair.

Luke scraped the back of his hand across his mouth and wiped away the dust that gathered at its corners. Reaching the slope of the bank curving into the Arkansas earth, he heard Tess's and Tommie's voices. *Damn!* Didn't they realize they were making so much noise, that anyone could creep up on them and they'd never hear a thing?

Carefully dismounting the dun, he threaded the horse's reins over a limb, leaving them unknotted. Stealthily he crept closer and skirted the crackling blackjack leaves so he would be able to prove how silently an attacker could move. The switchgrass grew shoulder high at the bank, and the cattail stems provided an air funnel that anyone could use to move closer underwater.

Tommie squealed as he splashed Tess, and she joined in his laughter, splashing back.

"Quiet, boy. . . ." Criticism died in Luke's throat as he caught sight of Tess's hands delving into the wet mass of thick curls that were piled on top of her head and threatening to spill at any moment. Her slim shoulders and arms were as luminous as the slivers of moonlight fanning the surface around her. Watching her long, slim neck arc backwards made his lips press tighter together. Would the velvet of her skin taste as enticing as it looked?

His hunger grew as his gaze lowered to the wet chemise and he noticed how exquisitely the undergarment revealed firm, round breasts and a healthy portion of a stunning full figure.

Luke watched her massaging strokes and wondered what she would say if he waded in to wash her hair or rub away the soreness inflicted by a day at the reins. He'd observed her at supper and seen her slow movements as she ladled beans. Bending to clean the dishes appeared a bit more difficult than she admitted. Tess denied any discomfort when he asked, and he admired her for it. She meant to take charge of her life as she had claimed, and revealing discomfort meant confessing a lack of strength.

Leaning back into the water, she washed the soap from her hair. As the water ran in tiny rivulets from her hands to her torso, Luke imagined his own body sliding down the same length, tasting her sweet freshness.

The Beholding

Get hold of yourself, man. Luke grimaced as he fought the desire racing through him. He was no longer seventeen years old and preparing to make love for the first time to Laoni.

Gentle Rain. How much like her name Laoni had been. But the Chiricahua maiden believed the Thunder People had come to her during the night before her marriage to Luke, wreaking havoc in the heavens and to his young heart. The Voices of Thunder, Wind and White Fire had warned that the scars on his face bore the mark of lightning—an omen that he would one day tear Laoni from her people.

Luke had vowed to forsake his heritage for her own—an easily given oath. He could no longer endure the white world. Though born Anglo, wealthy and the son of socialites, he'd received little love from his parents. Excelling in horsemanship, studies and law at West Point had barely rated a nod of approval from Olivia and Marsten Reeves. After deciding that nothing he would accomplish would ever make his parents forget they'd produced less than a perfectly sculpted Adonis, Luke dropped out of West Point and headed west.

He had suffered a snake bite while passing through Chiricahua hunting grounds, finding himself recovering due to the generosity of Running Horse, Laoni's father. The months spent with Cochise's war chief and daughter seemed like a long-ago dream. Yet it was a dream which caused Laoni's love to falter. Running Horse, the father Marsten had never been, took Luke aside and said he must deny the marriage rites. If Laoni faltered then, how would she withstand the harsher trials all marriages suffer?

Ten years had passed since Luke walked away from the only two people in his life who cared for him as he had them. Days became weeks, weeks stretched into months, months faded into years. Loneliness mortared the broken pieces of his heart, turning it to stone. The War Between the States provided a battleground to vent his anger, while cathouses pacified his physical needs. The yearning for something more remained long after he gave up the nightly visits to those veteran seducers. A yearning to experience the first touch of genuine love. Love so strongly bound that no dream, no omen, nothing but God Himself could loosen it.

Why such remembrances now? Luke wondered, wishing he could dispel the past as easily as Tess shook the water from her hair. The woman stirred his senses. Long-denied senses, at that. No man could stare at such beauty and not wonder how she would feel beneath him, her eyes soft and hooded with passion while her long legs wrapped around his, allowing a satisfying closeness. Yet Luke wondered if it was more than mere physical attraction he felt. He admired her spunk, and the way she saw to Tommie's needs before her own.

Tess took Tommie by the hand and led him toward the bank. Luke tried not to watch anymore, but the spell she wove held him. The breath-stopping sight of her soft wet curves in the clinging white chemise and pantalets, made transparent by the moonlight, allowed him every alluring detail.

God, she's beautiful—from her bare feet to the crown of those lovely golden curls. A bitter truth sunk in his stomach. With such comeliness, she could have easily seduced the men who patronized the bathhouse her father managed. With such a figure, no wonder men and women alike believed her father's advertisement that he'd found the fountain of youth.

Luke understood the age discrepancy now. Though she was probably fourteen or fifteen at the time, Tess's father must have boasted that she was forty. Those who wanted to believe would easily have been fooled. Whether or not the hot springs offered any real prevention to aging, the disbelievers were intrigued enough by Tess's beauty to want a closer look. With the right clothing, she might be even more beautiful.

As Tess moved behind a bush, blocking his view of all but her head and neck, Luke felt a twinge of disgust. He wasn't any better than an urchin peeping under the batwing doors at the local saloon girls. Disgruntled with himself by how long he'd lingered watching, Luke started to turn away. But the sight of Tommie bending to put something on the ground and turning to cover each ear with a palm revealed the imp was up to no good.

The Beholding

What the devil? A feminine shriek pierced the night, answering Luke's unvoiced question and assuring that everyone in the territory would know the Harpers' whereabouts. Tess hopped from around the bush, one shoe on, the other off.

"I told you to keep him where I'd know where he was." Irritation hardened Tess's voice.

"He jist got away, Mommie. Jist plumb got away."

Luke chuckled at the boy's deliberate innocence. The child was the best fun he'd enjoyed in ages, and Luke looked forward to those hours of the day when he rode scout with the wagon and Daggert spotted ahead. Tommie's unique way of looking at ordinary, daily tasks made Luke enjoy them all the more.

Tess's chin lifted and she cocked her head as if listening.

Luke's chuckle died in the glove that shot instantly to cover his mouth. What if she caught him here? She would never believe he wasn't spying on her. Hell, wasn't he doing just that?

"What's wrong, Mommie?" Tommie stared in the direction her gaze had turned.

"I thought I heard something."

Tommie ran behind the bush and came back carrying something in his hands that had a long tail and legs. A lizard?

"Just hear Thammy, Mommie," he informed her, holding the creature toward his mother.

Tess backed away and stared as if she glanced straight at Luke. "Not unless salamanders know how to chuckle."

Chapter Seven

Three hours later an impatient hand shook Tess from a sound sleep. She froze alongside Tommie. "Who is it?" she asked, pausing as her lashes finally opened to the dark confines of the Conestoga. Her right hand shot to the top buttons of her shirtwaist while the other wrapped protectively around her son. The outline of a man formed.

The breadth of shoulders and the appealing blend of man, butternut leather and tobacco revealed his identity before the compelling masculine voice was heard.

"It's Luke. Get up. Dress the boy in heavy clothes. It's about to drop buckets and we've gotta move out. Don't want him catching cold."

A tiny shiver which had nothing to do with the approaching cold uncurled in the pit of Tess's stomach. The sensation surprised her, for she knew it also did not spawn from fear. Tess wasn't really afraid of Luke, although she suspected that his purpose in escorting her to Colorado had something to do with unfinished business concerning Clifton. But Luke seemed unlike any man she'd ever known. Instead of evoking past humiliations suffered at Hot Springs, he inspired reactions within her she had never experienced. Not even with Clifton. Luke's ability to make butterflies flutter in her stomach simply by the tone of his voice disconcerted her.

"We'll be dressed and out in a few minutes." Her voice sounded unusually husky even to herself.

"You'll be on that driver's box in *one* minute or leave your belongings behind. Gotta get this team up and out of the wash if you want it to live."

"There's no need to—"

Tess's complaint faded as his dark form turned and exited through the horseshoe-shaped opening. She heard Luke telling Jim to tie the extra mule to the back and prepare to drive the team. Irritation sprouted. "I'm not dressed yet!"

"Forty seconds, lady."

Wasting no more time, she shook Tommie awake and ignored his sleepy whimpering. By the time she dressed him, the wagon jarred into motion, and Jim Daggert shouted at the mules from the driver's box. Ignoring any more clothes for herself, Tess checked the knottings of the rope strung from each side of the schooner and told Tommie to grab it. With great effort, she scooted around two trunks until both formed a barrier to the back flap. She would not take the chance of Tommie almost falling out again.

"Thammy's thafe too, Mommie. I got him in that jar Mr. Luke gave me. He punched holes in the top and put a little water in it. Said it would make a safe place for him to ride."

"That's wonderful, son. We wouldn't want him falling out, would we?" After kissing her son quickly on the cheek, Tess crawled onto the driver's box to sit alongside the gambler. "I'll take over now."

"Let her," Luke ordered as his dun moved up alongside the team. He thumbed up his hat and wiped an arm across his brow, quickly surveying her clothes. "Thought I told you to dress warm. When those skirts get wet, they'll soak you to the bone."

"I did as you *ordered,* Mr. Reeves." Tess took the reins from Jim and concentrated on the roadway ahead. The moon cast a shadowed light across the land, making visibility nearly impossible. A spatter of rain hit the top of the Conestoga. Another struck Tess's cheeks. "My son is taken care of, and that's what matters."

Jim lowered his hat to shield his face from the droplets. "Let the lady be. She's been wet before."

Luke moved back to untie Jim's horse from the back of the wagon. Surprised by the bounty hunter's quick accomplishment of the task, Tess wondered if it was merely caution over the storm that had spurred Luke's compliance or whether the bounty hunter had reason not to challenge Jim.

Like a cougar long practiced in hurdling to the next ledge, the gambler bridged the distance between driver's box and horse. Reining the animal into a quick trot alongside the team, Jim opted to safeguard the wagon while Luke rode ahead to set the pace, as the rain started to come down heavier.

After they traveled a couple of miles, Tess's skirts were soaked. She wished now she had not packed away the layers of petticoats, for every jostle of the schooner made the wet cloth burn her thighs.

The team transported them through the night and the recurrent rain. Luke guided them further into the blackjack trees and away from the chance of flood at the Arkansas. After the first several hours, Tess no longer peered into the dark to seek Luke's tall form on the dun. The mules followed his horse, and though she could not see him, both the animals' and the gambler's trust in the bounty hunter calmed her own turbulent premonitions of trouble.

That Luke could see at all through the driving downpour astounded Tess. With the dense thicket providing an endless barricade, how he manage to find a safe pathway through the unforgiving countryside seemed miraculous.

Despite the brambles and pelting storm, he rode on. Tess shivered and wondered how they could possibly endure more. The only reprieve from the cold came when the mules' hooves blasted her with steam rising from the water mixing with the warmed underside of overturned earth.

Moisture from her soaked skirts seeped into her high-topped

shoes, leadening Tess's legs beneath the heavy layers of homespun. If their journey continued much longer in this driving rain, her legs would be numb by the time he called a halt.

Tess knew before she began this ride to Colorado it would be difficult, but that didn't keep her from feeling every ache and pain. She willed her thoughts to better times. To the new beginning she and Tommie would have. If she had the strength to defy her father and refused to be his lure any longer, surely she could suffer this cold and discomfort.

As the team pressed on through the night, the storm gradually slackened. Lightning speared the distance, followed by grumbles of thunder, but their heavenly quarrel moved on to drier ground. The downpour eased into a drizzle. Wind gusted the spatters away, threatening to rip off Tess's bonnet.

"A little bit further, Jenny. Keep up with her, Jack!" She coaxed the mules, hoping Luke would soon find safe ground.

The tall jack at the lead picked up the pace. Added speed surged through the reins, making Tess's hands and arms tighten in response. She bit back a groan. Pressing one shoe a bit higher on the wooden footboard, she braced herself for the jarring trot.

"Hold on, Tommie," Tess instructed him, casting a glance over her shoulders.

"This is fun, Mommie," Tommie squealed, the sound of his voice a soothing balm to the cold that chilled her skin.

"Hang on to that rope, son," Tess commanded, "so Mama can hang on to these mules."

Tommie giggled and began talking like a mute who had just been given voice. His chatter lightened her sense of impending doom, and Tess welcomed the memories as Tommie reminded her of the time he had played monkey across the clothesline she'd strung between two dogwoods near officers' row.

By the time the wind drove several storm clouds into the distance, the cleansing of the land washed away night shadows and replaced them with the silver-gray promise of dawn.

"When will Luke give the mules a rest?" she shouted to Jim. Luke's dun could not be seen, and she wondered how far afield he had ridden. Better yet, how long might it take him to circle back and call a halt to this misery?

As though Luke sensed her exhaustion, the dun trotted into view. Tess exhaled a sigh of relief and resumed a normal position on the driver's box, relaxing the braced stance she had taken to commandeer the team. Her body ached from the constant pull of the reins and bone-jarring roll of the schooner. The thought of resting a few moments on motionless ground and changing into something warm and dry filled her with anticipation.

When Luke signaled Jim to stop, Tess didn't wait for an invitation and reined in the mules. A quick peek at Tommie assured her he was no worse for wear. The heavy tarpaulin had managed to hold out most of the rain. Hoisting him to her hip, she slid from the driver's box in a tangle of wet skirts. Her feet touched the ground, tensing her aching muscles with such force that Tess bit back a groan.

Since there was no way of knowing how long they would stop to rest, certain necessities needed to be dealt with. "Behind one of those," she gently urged the three-year-old toward a copse of dogwood, "and don't linger." *Something might jump out at you from nowhere,* she warned inwardly, keeping her own fear silent so as not to frighten Tommie or, worse . . . give him any ideas.

"Don't pick up anything that crawls, either," she insisted, trying to make light of her thoughts. A shiver rippled down her spine as she thought of the salamander. Tommie collected whatever struck his fancy. In these thickets, no telling what manner of hairy-legged crawler might attract his attention.

Tess eyed the switchgrass closely and bent to pull a handful. With a fearful motion, she yanked it quickly, grateful when her hand returned clutching no surprises. Hurrying to one mule, she began rubbing its flanks with the grass. The animal shivered as her efforts warmed its back.

"Makes you wish you had someone to do that to you, doesn't it?" Luke asked, walking up behind her.

"Don't do that." Tess's pulse caught in her throat. She had

heard no warning of his approach and was forced to take several breaths before she could calm her racing heart.

"I'm sorry, Tess. I didn't mean to frighten you."

His gaze bore into her, and she quickly turned from his curiosity. The man saw things too easily. He might sense that her fear came from something more frightening than having someone walk up on her unannounced.

Tess rubbed down the next mule to keep her mind and hands busy from the disturbing memory Luke evoked. A lock of hair fell down into her face. Before she could wipe it away, he reached out and tucked the strand behind her ear, forcing her bonnet higher. Despite the shadow made by his hat, she became aware of his dark, piercing gaze that held a hint of question.

His hand clamped over hers as she worked. A sliver of warmth snaked up her arm, ending in a coil of tension in the pit of her abdomen.

"Jim and I will take care of the stock."

Tess heard the subtle change in Luke's voice. The hat now shielded whatever she thought she recognized in his gaze.

"Walk around while you can," he instructed. "Don't want you to get stove-up on us. You can put some dry clothes on if you like, but it's gonna rain again. If you want to stay dry, you can ride it out in the back with your boy."

"I'll drive the wagon." The schooner might belong to him, but she meant to pull her share of duty.

"Got any trousers?" He glanced at the way the homespun clung to her.

The wet material revealed her figure far too intimately, and Tess fidgeted beneath his inspection. Though trousers might prove just as provocative, the suggestion seemed practical. "Trousers?"

Luke's lips lifted in a grin as the first rays of dawn danced in his eyes. "Yeah, you know, the things you insisted on wearing this journey . . . *Boss*."

The taunt sunk in as quickly as the question evaporated. She didn't know whether to laugh at his joke or be insulted.

Tess opted for the former. "That's one for you, Mr. Reeves."

Luke thumbed up his hat, revealing more of the merriment warming his eyes. "We keeping score, then?"

Liking his playful side far more than the stern-faced counterpart, Tess decided to join his good humor. "If the game calls for it."

His mouth shifted into a true smile that challenged the hard lines of his face, making Tess's breath catch. When he smiled, his face became the most handsome she had ever seen. The seductive curve of his lips sent a stab of desire through her. Her body's response strained against the homespun's bodice, reminding Tess of the material's mourning colors.

She ought to be ashamed of herself, but wasn't. How could she find wrong in feelings she'd never shared with Clifton?

As if he sensed her inner battle, Luke's mouth straightened into a thin, hard slash. "I don't play unless I mean to win, Tessa."

The warning in his voice chilled Tess, despite the way it softened at her name and warmed into an endearment. "Then you better count your chips now, 'cause I don't intend to lose either," she replied before turning away and walking toward Jim Daggert.

"Will we be able to make a fire?" she asked while the gambler gathered kindling. "A cup of coffee sounds wonderful. With all this rain, is there a dry piece of wood from here to Kansas?"

Jim motioned toward a small pile of willow he'd collected. "If we put them on slow, one at a time, it'll make a small fire. Not enough to dry out your clothes, but maybe enough to heat up some grub and make coffee."

"Sounds good," Tess said, thinking of the fire Luke had ignited—a low-burning lust that threatened to become a blazing passion.

"Grab your canteen and we'll fill it with coffee too." Jim dusted his hat on a pant leg, then settled it back over his chestnut hair. "Reeves'll want to pull out soon as we're done eating."

84

Tess gathered the soggy folds of her skirts and walked around, warming her cold-stiffened muscles. Her thighs burned so painfully she decided she shouldn't disregard Luke's advice about the trousers. Something to keep her thighs from chafing each other would help.

Fortunately, she had stowed a pair of Clifton's red flannels, trousers and shirt, in the trunk. In the cold of winter, she often wore them beneath her outer attire, enjoying the warmth they gave without anyone's knowledge. The flannels would ease the soreness.

Tommie now helped Luke with the remaining mules. She knew the trio expected her to prepare the meal as soon as Jim finished making coffee, so she headed for the schooner to quickly gather dry clothing.

Rather than take a chance that one of the men might need something from the wagon, Tess headed for the denser part of the blackjack thicket. She carefully pushed aside low-hanging limbs and bushes and walked a good way before turning to look back. A dim curl of smoke was all that was visible rising from the fire now. Tess draped the fresh clothing on a tree branch and began to undress.

When her leather kid gloves proved obstinate, she bit the tips to force the material away from her cold, throbbing fingers. The many buttons on her shirtwaist offered just as much struggle as the gloves. Finally, Tess unfastened the last button at her waist and peeled away the wet skirt from her legs.

As the garment gave, a rush of cold beaded Tess's flesh with goose bumps. A deep shiver set her teeth to chattering. She needed no urging to strip off the wet camisole and pantalets and replace them with a chemise and the flannel longjohns. Blessed warmth settled against her skin.

In the same instant, an arm whipped around her and jerked her against a hard, male body. A rough hand cut off her cry of surprise.

"Don't move."

Tess couldn't. Every muscle in her body tensed. Blood surged through her veins. She waited to breathe. To blink.

Please, dear God. Not again! The prayer became vocal against the hand cupped over her mouth.

"What if I had been an Indian?" the low voice threatened softly.

No real marauder would be concerned with what could happen; he would do the damage, then leave. "Jim?" she objected as fear left her and anger arrived in its place. Tess twisted to break his hold, but an iron-muscled arm whirled her around to face him. "You?" she gasped.

"Yeah, me. Sorry to disappoint you." The heat of Luke's eyes raked over her, making Tess's insides quiver from the passion burning in their depths.

"I told you never to sneak up on me again!" Anger increased her struggle in his arms. The movement only pressed her more closely against him. Thigh against thigh, Luke's heat scorched through the flannel from neck to ankle.

Tess's eyes widened as the desire the bounty hunter had aroused from the moment she met him could no longer be denied.

"You needed to be reminded of the danger, Tessa." He glared down at her with eyes that promised the pleasures of midnight. His voice lowered to match the seductive look. "Next time you might not be so fortunate."

Tess tried to jerk free, but he held tight. "Let me go! No man will ever force me again!" She stilled instantly, realizing how much she had revealed.

Luke loosened his hold but held her by one wrist, allowing her distance but not complete release. His other hand shot out and gently cupped her chin, urging her to meet his gaze.

"Again?" The word shook the stone foundation of his heart. *God, no wonder she fought like a hell-cat.* Cold rage iced his veins. "Who forced you? When?"

Tears of fury brimmed her lashes, making Tess turn from the concern etched in the deep lines of his face. Could he understand the shame she'd hidden for so many years, the fear that *she* had somehow caused the horrible act?

He nudged her chin again and she faced him, challenging

him to accuse. Daring him to blame. Luke no longer restrained her wrist, offered no resistance. She could run from his question if she chose, but for the courtesy the man extended her, he deserved an answer . . . the truth.

Folding her arms protectively beneath her breasts, she gathered her courage to tell Luke what she'd never shared with anyone—not even Clifton. It had been easy to play the virgin. A few drops of sherry strategically dripped on the sheets after he rolled over and slept off his lovemaking had satisfied her husband's pride the morning after their wedding. But Clifton proved equally proficient at hiding secrets, easing the shame she had felt in deceiving him.

Realizing that it mattered a great deal what the bounty hunter thought, Tess hesitated. Though unafraid of his disapproval, she suspected he would take the burden on himself. To right the wrong committed. Was it fair to ask that of anyone when she had run from it and done nothing?

"Tell me."

He sensed her hesitation, and something in his eyes asked her to trust. *Believe in him.* "I was compromised almost four years ago," Tess began. "I never saw the man. I wouldn't be able to identify him even if I stared him straight in the face."

She expected revulsion, maybe even pity, from Luke. Instead, his features hardened into an unreadable mask.

"That about the time Tommie come along?" His voice sliced through the night.

Was his anger aimed at her? Tess fought to understand this reaction from the man she'd grown to admire. "Clifton married me within two days of the m-molesting. A few months later, I discovered I was with child. Since Tommie's birth came a few more days than nine months from my wedding day, I have no way of knowing if Clifton was his father or whether the other man is."

Silence enfolded them as Luke looked past her, staring into the distance. A single raindrop—or was it a tear?—beaded in the corner of one eye and slid down his cheek, seeping into the crease defining his scars. Slowly he held one palm out to her, his eyes asking her to take it.

"God, Tess, I'm sorry. Sorry I frightened you. Sorry you ever suffered such pain."

"I've n-never told anyone before," she whispered. Her heart tightened as a dam of tears broke loose and flooded her cheeks. Was it possible that one man in this world could understand all she regretted, all she had suffered, all she desired, and still be her friend? One man who could help her forget the past and find happiness?

With an effort born of hope, she placed one hand in his. With the gentlest of touches, Luke threaded his fingers through hers and simply held them. Asking no more, offering all she needed.

"What if I caused it?" Tess whispered, trembling as she watched the emotion shift in his eyes.

I can't, Luke told himself. *Not now. This is no time to seek answers that would help the investigation. She needs compassion, man, not interrogation.* "You didn't flaunt yourself at the man."

It wasn't a question. Tess blinked at his unconditional belief in her. "No, I didn't. I never even s-saw him." She couldn't look at Luke now. "He grabbed me from behind. I f-fought, but he knocked me out."

He held her close, taking in the misery trembling her body as if it were his own. "Dear God, Tess." As she clung to him, he buried his face in her hair, wishing to offer more, find words appropriate enough to soothe her and take away the years of hurt she suffered.

"No one will ever hurt you again. I promise." The vow echoed from the depths of his heart, and Luke knew beyond all doubt that he meant them. "There are good men out there. Someone who will love you and cherish the wonderful woman that you are."

Their gazes met, locked. Desire twisted through the pain, replacing the cold with a warm rush of sensations. Luke's mouth lowered to hers, his eyes questioning, reassuring.

Stopping a fraction away from fulfillment, he whispered, "Are you certain, Tess?"

She nodded slowly, so full of his presence that she couldn't speak or deny the touch she needed so desperately.

The delicate caress of his breath whispered against her lips, "I'll never force you. Believe me?"

"Yes." The word was a hiss, expelling the tension that filled her.

Instantly the kiss deepened, and she lowered her lashes, engrossed in this new aspect of Luke. He tasted of every craving she'd ever been denied. Imported tobacco. The finest bourbon. Passion.

The tip of his tongue urged open her lips as his fingers slid deep into Tess's hair. She sighed with pleasure, and he caught the soft rush of her breath, making desire leap within her. Slowly, intimately, his tongue traced the sensitive edge of her mouth.

She trembled and gripped the hard strength of his forearms but didn't withdraw.

"Honey," Luke whispered.

Passion hardened him, though his mouth rained exquisitely soft kisses on her lips.

"I'll never think of honey without remembering you. God, I love the taste of you."

"Fine Kentucky bourbon," Tess whispered. Her lashes hooded the intoxicating effect his kiss had upon her. "You taste the way I thought bourbon would."

His hand flexed, and his fingertips slid to cup her buttocks and pull her even closer to his muscular length, revealing the hard shaft of desire the kiss evoked. "You feel better than in my dreams. I've wanted to touch you, Tessa. Make love to you."

"No, Luke. It's too soon. *No!*"

For an instant, Luke just stared at her, and Tess realized the futility of her struggles against his greater strength. The temptation to yield to the passion throbbing in her blood was overwhelming. She had given her body to one man who had desired her and cared enough to offer the respectability of his name. But Clifton's interest had grown cold. Without love between them, the marriage bed had become a duty.

It was her time for happiness. Her time to receive love as equally as she gave it. The next man she shared such intimacy with must forgive her past and bless her with his genuine love.

Staring into Luke's savage blue eyes, she prayed he was a man of his word, the man she longed for. "Luke, we can't. You promised."

Abruptly he pushed away and ran a hand through his hair, furious with himself for wanting her so much. Even as he clenched his teeth to utter the thought stirring his anger, he knew he would regret it once spoken. "Is it no to every man or just to me?"

Her hand shot out and slapped him, the impact echoing into the night and shattering the last remnants of seduction that still pulsed through her.

Saffron rays of dawn revealed the imprint of her hand along his right cheek, highlighting the scars. She inwardly flinched, regretting that she had struck the injury.

Luke noticed the object of her gaze and turned away so she could no longer see his face, unable to endure the first look of pity she'd ever given him. "I'll never force you, Tessa," he repeated the vow, "but some day you'll ask for my touch. You'll beg me not to stop."

He walked away, leaving her to wonder if it had been easy for him to keep his original promise. But she didn't dare challenge the second one.

Chapter Eight

After Tess dressed and emerged from the thicket, Luke bent at his knees, flipping over the long strips of fryback sizzling in the skillet. A half-moon of cornbread rose in the other half of the cast iron. A coffee pot hung from a tripod of branches braced over the fire. Tommie stood beside the bounty hunter, his palms warming themselves over the skillet.

"Sorry I took so long." Tess focused on the cup of coffee Luke offered rather than meeting his gaze. Her fingers brushed his, and for a moment his hand lingered, refusing to let go of the cup. She'd left off her gloves, hoping they'd dry before she needed them again. The minute touch evoked the memory of his body pressed against hers.

Tess almost decided to do without the coffee, but he let go. Steam rose from the cup's rim, making her nostrils flare in appreciation of the coming warmth and taste. Her throat constricted, and she gave in to the temptation. The first sip gratified her tongue, and she sighed with pleasure.

"That good?" The rough velvet of Luke's voice brushed over her like a warm summer breeze.

Tess took another swallow, deeper this time, prepared for the heat. "The best."

His look was piercing as he raised his cup to his lips and drank equally as deeply. She could almost taste him once again, as if they'd shared the same cup rim.

Luke's gaze slanted to a canteen near the fire. "There's more for later. Thought we'd keep one canteen for coffee and the others for water. Maybe we'll find some bourbon somewhere along the way."

She licked her lips and swallowed back the reminder of his kiss.

"We'll need something warm when it starts raining again."

The thought of sharing anything with this man sent a tempest of emotions storming through Tess. Images flooded her mind, and she quickly dammed them. "Don't you mean *if* it starts?"

Luke glanced up sharply. Her voice trembled with desire, but she could only hope he thought it husky and unsteady from the hours spent in the downpour.

"Gonna rain again, have no doubt. You best get some more coffee while this is cooking. Soon as we've eaten, we're pulling out."

Lack of sleep and the bitter cold felt like an anchor tugging Tess to the ground. She sat down, caring little that the earth beneath her was wet and cold. At least it offered a blessed reprieve from the bounce and jostle of the wagon.

The pleasant smell of cornbread browning lulled her into a half-dozing state. Male voices blended with the small pitch of her son's. They talked of plans for the day and answered Tommie's unrelenting questions about the possibility of attack. Despite the many silent questions that Luke's kiss had aroused, Tess's lashes blinked over her eyes, shutting out the disturbing answers. Before she exhaled the next breath, sleep engulfed her.

When Luke looked up from forking fryback into Tommie's tin, he smiled. The sight of Tess sound asleep stirred something inside him that he would have considered affection had she been a small child. He walked over and knelt at her side, touching to make certain she slept out of exhaustion rather than illness. The skin of her throat felt cool beneath his fingers, and her pulse thrummed steadily. Her breath eased into the deep rhythm of slumber, not anything fever-ridden.

"You're a thoroughbred," he muttered in admiration, offering her the highest compliment he had ever paid a woman. As a man raised to spot a champion among the finest, he respected endurance most of all.

"Better wake her up if she intends to eat," Jim demanded as he spooned up his own portion and sat an adequate distance from the fire to avoid the smoke but close enough to enjoy its warmth. As interested in Contessa Harper as Daggert acted, the gambler now seemed more consumed with eating.

"Let her sleep." Luke gently took the coffee cup from her hand and set it aside. She needed some drying time. When the rains started again, even the longjohns beneath her fresh clothing wouldn't be enough to keep out the chill. "Finish your grub. We need higher ground. Keep a lookout for an overhang where we can build a larger fire. We'll save the food, and when the widow wakes up, she can eat."

Glancing at Tommie as the boy alternated stuffing fryback in his mouth and yawning, Luke realized he had no other course of action. Mother and son would fall off the schooner from exhaustion if he didn't allow them time to sleep. "I'm gonna make a bed for the Harpers in the wagon. You can scout ahead while I drive the team. They've suffered enough today."

Jim scooped more into his tin, leaving less than Luke thought fair. He almost said so, but the effort would only sour Daggert's disposition more and make the gambler think of ways to strike back instead of keeping his attention on the trail. Good thing they had packed plenty of jerky and hardtack. Luke stuffed the remaining fryback between the cornbread and wrapped them in a fresh bandanna for Tess. Maybe later in the day there would be better fare for all of them.

From the dense thicket surrounding them, he cut more willow canes and peeled the bark from each. Gathering the stack, he headed for the wagon, then entered the shadowed confines beneath the tarpaulin. New respect for the sleeping woman surged through him. The position of the trunks spoke of the care she extended to her son. The rope strung across the schooner seemed clever and practical. Like the early rays of dawn filtering through the canvas, envy invaded the shutters of his past, opening them to reveal the painful memory of his own mother's uncaring ways.

Setting the canes on the trunks for the moment, Luke shuffled the luggage around until he reached one of the blankets Tommie had used to sit on during the journey. After stretching it across the wagon bed, he piled the willows on the woolen surface, then flung another blanket atop the cane. *Plenty,* he decided, testing the bed for comfort. The Harpers should sleep restfully, considering the conditions.

Tess stirred as Luke lifted her and headed for the Conestoga. Cradling her in his arms, once again he felt the softness that was Tess alone. She tensed at his touch, her eyes fluttering open. Passion gripped him as the fathoms of green softened in recognition.

"It's only Luke," he whispered as his body recoiled against a painful shaft of raw desire. The temptation to pull her closer and kiss the drowsiness from her eyes seemed unbearable, but he'd spent a lifetime learning the control needed to drive away the hurt, the pain and loneliness of being a man whom women wouldn't touch. Yet this woman had pierced that control, as surely as if she'd strung a bow and aimed an arrow at him. She moved him. And for a moment when he had kissed her and she kissed him back, he forgot that her closeness was born of misery.

"Go back to sleep," he whispered. The lowering of her lashes and easing of her body revealed Tess's trust. A sense of satisfaction engulfed Luke. This woman trusted no one yet believed in him. Valued his word. And because of it, he would deny his own needs to ease hers.

As he sat at the back of the wagon and scooted around to lift his feet from the ground, she stirred again. Glad now that he had moved the trunks out of his way, Luke managed to lay her down on the makeshift bed.

"Luke? Jim?" she whispered, reaching up to touch his face. But her lashes dipped against her cheeks again, revealing she wasn't truly awake.

Luke's embrace hardened when she spoke the gambler's name, but he allowed her fingers to find their mark. For a moment, he thought to wake her and put her through the misery of handling the team again, exhausted or not. But the glow of sunlight upon her ivory beauty revealed the exhaustion she suffered. Common sense and the need to hold her once more within his embrace abolished the envy. If it meant pretending to be the gambler for this moment, then so be it.

While admiring the slim column of her neck, Luke unlaced the ribbon beneath her chin. Golden curls cascaded to her breasts, urging his attention to the attractive peaks. As he tied the bonnet to the rope to dry, he remembered the press of her body against his own. She could easily have practiced the profession indicated in the report.

If the report proved true, maybe it was a good thing he was looking for easier assignments and wanted to put his bounty-hunting days to an end. When he couldn't trust his instincts anymore, he wouldn't have the right edge to stay alive. If the report was false, the name of the man who started the hellish lie about her would be added to the molester's. Once Luke discovered both identities, they were dead men.

"Gotta kill the bastard. That's all there is to it," Jim mumbled as earth rolled under hoof and the sky stretched into forever with no hint of danger. The sun burned brightly overhead, so hot his saddle creaked loud enough to give away his position. But it was no good. None of it was any good. Nothing would take away the stirring sickness he felt deep inside. Nothing but Luke Reeves's death.

Did the bounty hunter think he was too stupid to see the way the bastard admired Contessa? Or the fact she stared back with just as much interest! Jim's stomach soured as he remembered how her eyes looked as if they would melt into her lashes every time she met Reeves's gaze.

Tess belonged to *him.* To hell with Harper Hall. Maybe he'd started this journey to persuade her into selling it to him before they got there, but Reeves changed the game. Enduring the thought of Clifton sharing Contessa's bed had been one thing. Jim had known that the foolish soldier couldn't stay alive long. The possibility had urged him to help the blowhard sink so deeply in trouble, there was no way out.

But Luke Reeves was another kind of man. Once in Tess's bed, he wasn't the sort to let anything keep him out.

Gotta stop Reeves now, before she falls in love with him, Jim pledged, scanning the countryside. They were heading into Blue Hawk's territory. The renegade half-breed owed him more than gold for that last load of rifles. He had saved the Comanche and several warriors at Pencil Bluff. By using Hoot and Clifton as lures, Jim had accomplished three things: allowing Blue Hawk and his men time to get away with the rifles, keeping the gold that belonged to them, and ridding himself of Contessa's husband.

Lying to her had been necessary. If she knew he'd been there and hadn't tried to help Clifton, Contessa would never come willingly to his bed, wedding ring or otherwise. He preferred willingness from the woman who'd stolen his heart.

Good thing Reeves suggested he scout ahead. The time spent in searching out Blue Hawk wouldn't seem so suspicious if it took longer than he hoped.

Day stretched into evening as the dun followed Daggert's lead along a strip of the Arkansas River known as Hell's Borderland. The wagon rolled minutes behind. Tess woke and insisted on taking over. It felt good to Luke being back in the saddle where he'd spent the better part of his days since leaving his parents in Austin. Wagons and surreys were meant for folks tied to a home, not a wanderer such as himself.

The forests of blackjack and post-oak mixed with occasional patches of prickly pear. White blossoms of dogwood and dark magenta-colored clusters of redbud provided a relief to the arduous landscape. What would Tess think if he plucked a handful and took them back to her?

Peering into the sun-baked countryside, he shooed away the thought, same as he did the pesky fly that trailed him for yards. She sure knew how to get under a man's skin.

Perched on a branch not far ahead, a cardinal's attention focused on something in the grass. Someone had been following Luke for over an hour. He couldn't take the chance of circling back if the culprit didn't know about the wagon and meant only to rustle a horse.

A man learned to pay strict attention to the warnings that bird and animals gave in the wilderness. Snaking his Winchester from the scabbard and checking the readiness of his Colt, Luke waited uneasily. Bees droned nearby in the still air. Sweat trickled down his face, itchy with dust. He listened, squinting against the salty sting of sweat.

From where he sat his horse, the situation looked bad. He could go in only one direction without turning—straight ahead. The blackjack thicket was too dense for the wagon to pass through.

The fly buzzed annoyingly around his face, and Luke unconsciously lifted a hand to brush it away. Instantly a bullet slammed into a tree trunk, spattering his face with a hail of tiny fragments. Luke fell from the saddle, momentarily blinded.

With long practice, he hit the ground and rolled over, coming up to a bent knee, his gun ready. Though he managed to keep the rifle in his grip, he put it on the ground and pawed at the splinters with one hand.

The enemy had to be close. Couldn't see thirty or forty yards at most, and taking a shot was chancy. The intermingled branches might easily deflect a bullet.

Still feeling a few tiny particles in his eyes, Luke took up his Winchester and scanned the countryside to better situate himself. He'd fallen into a shallow depression only inches below the forest floor, where dead brown blackjack leaves crackled with every movement. Before him rose the tree trunk which had showered him with bark. To his left lay the stark white skeleton of a deadfall.

Trained to be patient, he sensed that whoever shot at him was equally inclined. As the sun beat hot upon his back, Luke wondered if his adversary had worked his way into position to kill him. Wasn't much he could do about it. Moving silently among the leaves would be virtually impossible . . . or was it?

Off to his right, something worried a bluejay. Luke slid his rifle forward a bit and, easing it over his left shoulder, he looked up into the tree above him. The limbs hung low. If he climbed up there, he might get a bead on the killer. His clothing blended well with the limbs and scattered leaves, adding to the possibility of non-detection. Luke studied the branches. A grasp here, a foot there, then climb the rest of the way.

Carefully he rose to his knees, cringing against the half-expected impact of a bullet. He grabbed and pulled. Planting his boot on a low branch, Luke moved up again.

Searching the trees, the grass and brush, he took note of brown grass springing back into position only a few yards away. He fired instinctively at the faint stir, instantly realizing he'd been suckered into a trap.

Another bullet spattered bark and something struck his leg, knocking him from his perch. As Luke fell, the sound of rifle fire echoed in his ears. A branch broke as his body hit it, then he struck the ground with a thud.

Having lost his grip on the rifle during the fall, Luke clawed wildly for his Colt, coming up with it just as a Comanche broke through the brush, knife in hand, eyes widened with bloodlust.

Luke fired, his bullet planting a bloody blossom in the Indian's chest. Something metallic burned Luke's cheek, and he whirled, shooting blindly at a leaping shadow. A second Indian broke stride and fell.

How many? Luke wondered and twisted around, finding his rifle and pulling himself to it. His leg no longer tingled; the pain faded into numbness. When he touched his cheek, his fingertips came away bloody.

Easing himself back into a better defensive position, he reached out with the Winchester to draw the last Comanche's rifle closer. The forest became silent again.

Slow minutes passed. A dizzying weakness engulfed him. His leg throbbed. Luke reached to touch it and discovered that a bullet had cut through the muscle of the right thigh. Blood soaked his pants leg, attracting flies. He would have to get the wound bandaged or pass out from blood loss.

Was that all the shooter waited for?

Trying to make no sound, Luke struggled to remove his boot, hoping he could roll up the legging. Didn't want to take the chance of being caught with his pants down. When the boot gave, he bit back the pain and took off the blood-soaked sock. But the legging was too snug to roll past his calf. Luke put his boot back on and unlaced the buckskin at his waist. With a painful jerk, he pushed the leather past his hips to the wound.

God almighty, I'm in trouble! Luke cursed as blood spread into an ever-enlarging stain with every beat of his heart. Packing grass into the wound, he tied his bandanna around his thigh, then pulled the buckskin up over his hips.

Luke's eyes misted over when he moved, and the weakness worsened. Suppose he passed out. If he did, he would be killed for certain. Only one thing to do . . . hide. But what of Tessa and Tommie? Had they heard the shots? He couldn't let them ride into this hell. *Where was Daggert?*

Gotta take my chances. Luke eased from the tree and inched his way through the grass. Though he expected the dragging of his leg to give away his position, he made little noise at all. Continually searching the ground, the trees, the shrubs, his gaze froze at the sound of a chuckle.

"So we meet again, white man."

Luke could not see him but knew the harsh, ugly voice. *Blue Hawk! The half-breed must be where he can keep an eye on me.* Pulling himself a little further along, Luke sorted the places in his mind. When the Comanche spoke again, the bounty hunter threw his rifle around and fired at the sound.

From a few feet away, Blue Hawk laughed. A bullet tore a furrow in the grass just ahead of Luke, almost burning his fingers. A gully stretched only a few feet ahead and to Luke's right. Though only inches deep, it offered him shelter.

A rush of feet in the grass forced Luke to wheel around, taking aim again. As the warrior sprang into sight and swung a gun muzzle down on him to count coup, Luke fired. At the same instant, from off to the left, another gunshot rang out.

The warrior's body jerked in mid-air as the bullets struck. Still, he tried to bring his gun down on Luke. Two more bullets ripped into the warrior. Blue Hawk fell into the bottom of the gully, landing only inches from Luke, the half-breed's blue eyes opened in disbelief for all eternity.

A strawberry-colored roan appeared at the edge of the shallow, and Luke looked up into Jim Dagger's bearded face. Suspicion made Luke get up cautiously. Had the gambler meant to save his life or was there the chance that he had chosen to come in slow?

Jim cradled a rifle in the crook of his arm, leaning forward over the cantle. Something more ridiculing than mockery hardened his gaze even before the sarcastic words were uttered. "Looks like I came just in time."

As Jim reined the roan half-quarter, he allowed room for the wagon he'd spotted a second before he finished off Blue Hawk. *Damn her pretty hide!* Instead of killing Luke, he'd been forced to save the bastard's life by Contessa's appearance at the edge of the gully.

Now Jim wondered if maybe it wasn't all for the best. Reeves owed him, and the man would honor such a debt. Then there was Contessa. She might express her gratitude as well. That thought alone was worth waiting to kill Luke at another time. Watching the bounty hunter struggle painfully to his feet, Jim signaled to the widow. "He's been shot. Better see to him."

When the prettiest face this side of Fort Smith looked down at Luke, he flashed her an I'm-all-right grin . . . then passed out.

Chapter Nine

Jim Daggert dismounted as Tess brought the wagon to a halt and jumped from the driver's box in a flurry of skirts. Concern etched her features into a mask of worry as she gently removed Luke's hat and cradled the bounty hunter's head in her lap. When her hands began to search the leggings for the exact location of his wound, Jim cleared his throat to stop further exploration. "I meant I'd better see to him. He's hit in a delicate place."

Irritation pricked Tess. "He's losing blood and all you can worry about are my so-called tender sensibilities!" Her voice became curt as anger replaced the fear for Luke's life. "Are you forgetting we've just been attacked by Indians? What if there are more? You can handle the team much better than I. Don't forget I've been a second-hand nurse to the men at the post. I've dealt with more than you could ever imagine." She arched a brow at the gambler. "If you truly want to help, then drive this team to safety."

Jim noticed Tess's quick perusal of the area before giving all her attention to Luke. She had no way of knowing the immediate danger was over, at least until some of Blue Hawk's braves found the bodies. The Comanche would be

101

considerably unhappy without at least one white scalp to justify the killing of their leader. Wouldn't particularly matter to the band of renegades if it was his, either. Perhaps he should pacify her. "I'll help load him in the wagon."

Reluctance stabbed at Tess as she helped lift the unconscious scout. Despite her claim, she preferred to hoist Luke by the shoulders rather than the feet, putting off the sight of the wound until absolutely necessary. As her arms laced through his armpits and the back of his head rested against her breasts, beads of pain moistened the grim line of his upper lip. Ignoring the dark, curled hair at the edge of the buckskin covering his chest, Tess worried over the paleness of his skin.

"Mista Yuke going to Heaven with Daddy, Mommie?" Tommie asked as Jim struggled to lift Luke into the back of the schooner. The boy's voice trembled with dread as his eyes widened and tears welled.

"No, son," she promised, though her grip threatened to slip at any moment and drop the bounty hunter on his head. Tommie had accepted the explanation she gave about his father going to Heaven, and it seemed to have eased her son's loss. But to watch Luke die might be too much for the boy. She needed to convince him that if they fought hard enough, long enough, they could overcome . . . even the clutches of the grim reaper. "I won't let him die."

"Better he faces reality, Contessa." Jim wrangled half of Luke's body onto the wagon bed. He took the remaining weight from Tess by linking one arm under Luke's left shoulder and scooting him sideways into the Conestoga. "The man's bleeding like a stuck hog."

"I've seen worse." Tess climbed into the wagon behind him. But the stain of blood kept darkening, revealing the continual blood loss.

Jim wiped the perspiration from his brow with a sleeve. He hoped that if he were ever in such condition, Tess would fight just as hard to pull him through. "If you can get him to raise that thigh and bend the knee, you can stanch the flow of blood a bit easier than keeping it flat."

"I think I may have some alum in my trunk." Tess gave Tommie a reassuring look. "You'll help me find it, won't you, son?" The boy struggled to unbuckle the lid to the biggest trunk even before she finished the question.

"Not much we can do for his pain unless you packed some whiskey."

Tess didn't like Jim's tone, thinking the gambler a bit unfeeling. "Don't you think you should be rounding up his horse so we can get under way? Tommie and I have Mr. Reeves under control."

As he nudged his hat low over his eyes, Jim's gaze lingered on the beautiful lady he wanted for his own. *Just make damn certain you don't comfort him too much,* he wanted to say, but kept the warning silent. Instead, Jim nodded and exhaled a sigh of resignation. "You take care of the bounty hunter, Contessa, and I'll see to it we get to Wichita safely."

Tess thanked Jim, then quickly studied Luke more closely. A sheen of sweat dampened his face. Pressing the back of her hand against his forehead, she found his body radiating an inner heat.

"Fetch me a bowl of water, Tom." She pointed to the small bucket of drinking water covered and roped in a corner for convenience. Tommie dipped a bowl into the bucket and handed it, along with a washcloth, to his mother.

Sponging Luke's grazed cheek, neck and as much chest as the taut buckskin would allow, she left the cool compress on his brow in an effort to bring down the fever. The shirt would have to be removed if the fever didn't slacken, and the thought of undressing Luke reminded Tess that the buckskin trousers would have to come off first.

She checked the wound and noted that his powerful calves were too muscular for her to roll up the fringed leggings to tend to the wound. The only thing left to do was to unlace the buckskin and pull off the dusty, blood-soaked trousers. Her palms dampened. *This is silly,* she told herself. *His life depends on you.*

"You scared, Mommie? I help you." Tommie patted her trembling hands with his own.

With unsteady fingers she squeezed his palms reassuringly. "Thank you, son. I am a bit frightened because I don't want to hurt Luke. But knowing you can help makes me feel much better." She smiled gently, then began her task. While loosening the lace of Luke's buckskin trousers, she purposely ignored how closely her hands worked near the intimate portion of his body, concentrating instead on making him well.

Jim took control of the team, and the prairie schooner jarred to a roll. A soft moan permeated the air.

"Help me." Tess waved Tommie to the other side of Luke. "We've got to get his pants down and over his hips, so Mommie can doctor the wound."

Tommie tugged on one side while she pulled at the other. With the bounce and jostle of the Conestoga as it rolled over the rutted road, they managed to lower the buckskin over his hips, painful inches at a time.

Luke continued to moan, instigating prayers that he would remain unconscious until she finished the bandaging. Finally the leggings dislodged from the obstinate curve of his buttocks and the buckskin slid past his knees and to his boots. Removing the boots would have to wait until she stemmed the blood flow.

Tess's breath caught in her throat at the sight of his nakedness, and she quickly grabbed a towel from the trunk to cover Luke. When Tommie glanced up at her, she hoped her expression revealed none of the emotions rampaging within. Her son must learn that one should offer comfort and medical aid to the injured, whether it be man or woman, no matter where the injury was.

Quickly unknotting the bandanna tied very high on his inner thigh displayed a seeping wound plastered with dry grass. Gently peeling the grass away, Tess noted where the bullet had entered and then exited out the outer side. The few rags she had wouldn't be enough to stop this kind of bleeding. Glad now that she had washed her pantalets and replaced them with

Clifton's longjohns, Tess hoped they would provide enough material to make a bandage for the poultice.

She applied pressure against the wound while she waited, then nodded at the trunk. "Tom, fetch me my pantalets and the alum powder. The blue jar."

The towel deepened in color as Tommie hunted for the needed materials.

"I can't find 'em, Mommie."

"Yes you can, darling. Just look hard. Maybe they're playing hide-and-seek with you." Tess prayed as his small hands riffled through her carefully stored belongings.

"Here they are!" Tommie flung the pantalets toward her in triumph. Taking a step closer, he stumbled in his haste. The bottle of alum hit the planked wagon bed with a loud crack. Tess's lashes closed instantly over her eyes in a plea that he had not broken pieces of glass into the soft, white powder.

"I'm sorry, Mommie. I din't mean to."

Tommie's eyes stared up at her in sincere remorse. She carefully lifted the bottle of alum, examined it, and offered her son a forgiving smile. "It's only cracked. You did fine, darling."

Relief flooded his face as he stepped back out of her way and folded to his knees to keep watch.

Tess attempted to rip the pantalets into pieces, but the cotton proved difficult and would not give. As she once again applied pressure, Tess's gaze frantically searched the interior of the Conestoga for something to cut the pantalets. Her mind ran through a list of belongings in the trunk. Dare she entrust Tommie with handing her a knife? Her son needed her trust now, and Luke couldn't afford to lose more blood.

"Tom, get a knife," she instructed him, nodding toward the trunk once again. "We have to cut the pantalets. Be very careful, darling. Pick it up at the handle, not the blade. If the wagon bumps or the knife jars loose, just let go and jump back. Don't try to catch it."

"I be careful, Mommie."

To her surprise, he didn't open the trunk again but delved

one hand into Luke's right boot. When his hand appeared again, it gripped the handle of a large Bowie knife. Luke Reeves was full of surprises even when unconscious.

"Mommie's going to let go of the wound so I can take that from you. Put your other hand here where I have mine, sweetheart, and press hard. You won't hurt Mr. Luke even though it'll seem like you are. You'll have to keep the blood stopped while I prepare the medicine. And when I take the knife, you'll need to use both hands. Understood?"

"Oooh, it yooks uggleyee." Tommie's voice cracked with uncertainty though his expression held a mixture of dread, hope and fascination.

Tess waited until one of the small palms pressed tightly against Luke's thigh, before taking the knife from Tommie. She made certain the boy applied enough pressure, then stripped the pantalets into pieces and sprinkled the alum onto them. When she applied the poultice to the gaping wound, she hoped the makeshift medicine would do. The powder should have been cooked until burnt to be truly effective, but they couldn't take the time to stop and make a fire.

Luke lay still as death, no moans uttered within the last few minutes. She pressed one hand against his forehead, then his cheek, and found that the fever raged even stronger. Wishing they could dig up herbs and make a tea which might fight the fever, Tess faced the reality of the situation. Water would have to suffice. Water and her prayers.

"We've got to get him to drink something," she told Tommie. Her son's gaze seemed glued to the bandage on Luke's thigh. "Do you think you can get Mommie a tin?"

"Yes, ma'am." Scrambling away to do her bidding, he quickly handed her the cup and returned to his careful watch.

Tess dipped the tin into the water bucket and tried to force a sip into Luke's mouth. Luke coughed and the water dribbled from his lips, running down his neck. Several more times she tried, but the fever gripped him too deeply.

"Drink up, Mista Yuke!" Tommie urged, taking a big gulp himself. He rubbed his tummy and pretended the water was the most delicious thing he had ever tasted. "Hmmmm-hmm. Gooder'n everythang."

When Luke stirred but didn't obey, the boy batted the tin against Luke's mouth. Tess flinched at the sound of metal against enamel, afraid Tommie would crack the man's teeth. But the childish insistence worked. A white slash of teeth opened, and Luke's mouth formed an O of protest wide enough to let the child pour the entire contents of the cup into it.

Luke gagged and his arm shot out unexpectedly, backhanding the boy from reach. The three-year-old wailed and scooted out of harm's way, wrapping his arms around his raised knees.

"Mista Yuke's mean, Mommie. Yike Jim. I jist tried to help."

"No, darling." Tess gave her son a quick hug. "He's not mean. Mr. Luke's terribly, terribly sick. And when he wakes up"—she couldn't bring herself to say *if* he wakes up—"he won't even know he struck you. If you tell him, he'll be terribly sorry and will apologize, I'm certain."

Tommie did not unthread his arms, making Tess worry all the more. The boy had grown to care for Luke, and this regrettable moment might end his trust in the bounty hunter. Noticing that the movement caused Luke to roll over on his leg again, staining the cotton a deeper crimson, Tess prepared herself for the task of rebandaging the wound. As she worked, Tommie refused to help again.

She stripped the bloodied bandage from the thigh and kept a close watch on Luke's powerful arms, not wanting to be another victim of his fevered fisticuffs. She would worry about how he and the boy would repair their friendship later. For now, she had to concentrate on keeping the man alive.

Slowly . . . hazily, Luke discovered he still lived. If being alive meant burning with the heat of a thousand hells, that is. Pain shot through him, and his lashes jerked open as it concentrated in his right leg. No . . . *thigh*. The thigh felt as if someone had taken a knife, plunged it full hilt into the bone and was twisting it back and forth, back and forth.

As the hard surface where Luke lay jostled and he became aware of movement, his world spun and a curse screamed through his mind. Luke's eyes shuttered closed and he willed himself to sink into the blissful oblivion from which he had just awakened. Heat and pain scorched him, denying the return to the haven of sleep.

Dear Jesus, he thought, praying this was some God-awful nightmare he could dispel. His eyes grated open but all he could see was the shadowed confines of a tent. A moving tent. *Where am I?*

Concentrating on his last conscious moment, he remembered Tess's face filled with concern as she brought the schooner to a halt. *Blue Hawk! Daggert! I've been shot!*

The images faded in and out as Luke tried to recall the moments after the Conestoga rolled into view. The sense of being carried invaded the haze. Someone's hand had touched his brow. A soft, gentle hand. Burning pressure at his thigh. Pain against his teeth but batted away. All fleeting images. Half dream, half nightmare.

Only one vision took substance. Tess's lovely face etched in worry and caring. Not once or twice, but time and time again. Always followed by the touch of a gentle hand. *Her hand.* Willing himself to delve through the fever-ridden memories, Luke recalled every press of her palm against his forehead, every nudge of her fingertip against his lip to feed him the liquid which cooled the raging fire within. Even when the pain at his thigh became unbearable, her gentle touch soon eased the anguish, leaving something tight and binding and blessedly soothing in its wake.

Luke's nostrils flared as lavender invaded his senses. She had been close enough for him to smell the scented soap she used to wash her hair. But this was real. The fragrance was too pleasant to be the remnant of a dream.

Raising his head with painful effort, Luke discovered he was naked from head to waist with a mass of sun-golden hair lying against his left side and blocking the full view of his lower half. Tess's body stretched out next to his. Her head rested on his stomach while one hand lay across his hip. *She slept!*

Admiring the golden harvest of hair that curled almost to her waist, his gaze lingered at the slight curve of her shoulders and the enticing way her waist flared into a becoming span of hips. Though the pain he suffered made her weight seem heavier than he knew it to be, Luke wanted to satisfy his curiosity. Trying not to waken her, he managed to lift his left leg enough to reveal a thin sheet draped over him. The sight of his bare feet made him wonder how she had been able to dislodge his boots.

The sudden realization he was completely naked beneath the sheet contracted Luke's muscles. The stiffening twisted pain through him, and he uttered an oath. Tess stirred against his abdomen, and he instantly shut his eyes, opening them only enough to enjoy the pleasure of watching her awaken. If she knew he no longer slept, she would be all business and fuss. He wanted these few moments to admire her.

"Ohh, such a long night," she sighed, her arms rising to bracket her head as she yawned and arched the stiffness from her body.

The stretching defined the generous swell of her bosom, kindling a new kind of heat through Luke. God, whether or not she looked at his eyes, she would know soon enough that he had roused. The awakening of his manhood beneath the sheet would be difficult to miss.

"Sweet baby," she crooned, "sleep while you can."

Luke thought for a moment that the endearment was meant for him but then noted the direction of her gaze. Tommie was curled up in one corner of the schooner and dozed fitfully. The tone of her endearment spread through Luke like warm honey, and he was reminded of the kiss they had shared. Pain and pleasure fought to seize him, but the memory was too powerful to concede its hold on his senses.

"You're awake!"

Tess's declaration made his lashes open despite an effort to feign sleep. He had wanted to watch her forever, imprinting the morning sight of her in his memory to ease the loneliness of his nights.

Crimson stained her cheeks, and her eyes loomed large and luminous. The palm that had reached out to check the bandage hovered inches below the considerable swell of his manhood. She was frozen in surprise.

Luke attempted to sit up, but Tess instantly forgot her embarrassment and pressed her cool hands on his chest to stay him.

"Don't move, Luke," she insisted. "You're in no condition yet."

He reveled in the closeness afforded him. It had been some time since he'd been able to gaze at her completely. Even when he kissed her, it had been during the first rays of dawn. Usually shielded by a bonnet, now her stark beauty nearly took his breath away. Haloed with hair the color of sunshine, her feathered brows winged into golden arches. Harvest gold lashes forested the deepest sea-green eyes he had ever seen. Though her almond-shaped eyes could darken to emerald when angered, they looked a bit smoky and utterly innocent above her high cheekbones. But it was the moist swell of her lips that intrigued him most. With half-heart shaped crescents forming the upper portion of her mouth, he couldn't decide which he would enjoy tasting first—top or bottom.

Licking his lips, Luke's tongue ran over his teeth in anticipation and stopped suddenly. A frown wrinkled his brow as a memory darted across his mind's eye. "Did somebody hit me?" He could barely talk, his voice sounding like someone grating a rock over a rub board.

"No," Tess assured him and helped Luke lie back. "I tried to give you water and it wouldn't go down." She nodded toward Tommie. "He tapped your teeth to make them open and it worked. But I'm afraid, because of your fever, you thought someone was hurting you. You backhanded him."

"Is he hurt?" Luke attempted to raise his head again to take a closer look at the child.

110

She pressed her hands firmly against Luke's shoulders to offer resistance. "Physically he's fine. But he thought you were being mean. I assured him you were ill and didn't know what you'd done. You might want to explain it to him when he wakes up. He's grown to care about you, Luke, and his feelings are terribly hurt."

"I would never intentionally harm him," Luke vowed, but the words sounded jumbled even to himself.

Tess nodded. "Don't try to talk. I know you'd hurt yourself before you ever injured Tommie. You've been asleep for a couple of days now—"

"Days? Where?"

"Don't worry. Jim's driving the team. He's doing a fine job. We haven't had any trouble since you got shot. After you've rested, we'll talk more. All I've been able to do is get water and a bit of mint tea down your throat. We'll be stopping in an hour or two. I'll make you some broth and you'll feel better."

With as much effort as he could muster, Luke lifted his hand and touched one finger to his forehead. "H-hot," he whispered and licked his lips. "Will you wipe?"

"Of course." Tess grabbed the cloth soaking in the fresh bowl of water she had scooped just before falling asleep. After ringing it out, she mopped his forehead and face, gently cleansing the sleep from his lashes. Ringing it out again, she dabbed the moisture from the top of his lips and chin.

Her hand smelled like soap and lavender and Tess. Luke didn't want the touching to end. He pressed her hand to the dark thatch of hair covering the muscles of his chest. When she hesitated, his brows triangled into a plea. She bit back a smile, but did as he asked. Closing his eyes to the pleasure of the small circular swipes of the cloth, he let the coolness of her touch sink in and ease the last remnants of fever.

When she moistened the cloth again and began to cleanse one sweat-dampened arm, then the other, Luke braced himself for the pleasurable experience. Another rinse and she traced his ribs. Luke thought he had surely died and gone to Heaven.

Yet he had a thing or two to teach the preachers who said Heaven was made of white clouds and pearly gates. Heaven offered a fire fiercer than ten purgatories.

Wings of desire ascended from the tips of his toes, flew over the hell of his injury and peaked again in his most private place. Luke's eyes flashed open. The rapid rise and fall of her breasts seemed born of more than just effort, for it matched his own in rhythm. He knew she felt the beat of his heart, for her hand instantly jerked away.

"More?" he whispered, his gaze slanting to the sheet and that part of him hidden below its thin shelter.

Transfixed, she followed his gaze, then slowly turned back to discover he insisted upon an answer. Her head shook slowly as she sighed, "Noooo."

But Luke would not accept her decree. She wanted him as much as he wanted her. Not now, for he would be of little good. But later. When they made love, he wanted it to be memorable. Better than good. The best either of them would ever experience.

Reaching for her hand, his fingertips touched her own. Though he had told her she would beg for him to make love to her, he knew now he had become the beggar. "I need your touch."

Tess's eyes closed. When she reopened them, Luke noted with satisfaction the passion she failed to conceal. From the moment she had touched his cheek in Fort Smith and forgiven him for doing his duty, he wanted to know every fiber and bone that crafted this special lady. Wanted to feel the beat of such a generous heart against his chest and touch every curve and swell that made her woman. Didn't she sense what he already knew as fact? One day their passion would break the bonds of duty which held him in check and would cut the web of respectability she thought necessary since Hot Springs.

With a large intake of breath, Tess looked as if she were steeling herself against the inevitable. For one disappointing moment, Luke feared that her will would be equally as strong in fighting her desire as it was in ignoring commands. But this

112

had been a plea, not a demand. And as he vowed, he would never force her.

Tess wrung the cloth out again, this time wiping the moisture from her own neck. "Perhaps later," she whispered and dropped the cloth into the bowl.

Like a drowning man grasping for a lifeline, his fingers thrust out to test her resolve. The moment her fingers threaded and clung, Luke sensed he was about to live as never before.

Chapter Ten

Tess awakened and shivered as a cool breeze buffeted the canvas. She stretched her neck and yawned, wondering how long ago Jim had called a halt and made camp. A quick glance at Tommie bundled up inside two woolen blankets assured her he slept soundly and seemed warm enough. The silence of deep night enveloped Tess, and she was grateful for the reprieve from the jangle of reins and the protest of wheels against sod. Still, something other than the chill had roused her.

"Tess . . ."

The hoarse whisper of her name crossed the small space that divided her and Tom's sleeping mats from Luke's.

"Tessa?" Luke whispered again.

Hearing need in his tone, she hurried to his side.

"Are you awake, Tess?" he rasped weakly.

"Yes. I'm here, Luke."

"My leg. It feels like it's on fire. Can you do something?"

"Let me have a look." Something told her to be quick. She groped for the lamp and attempted to light it, but the wind kept blowing out the flame. With each attempt, a moment of flickering light revealed that his eyes were closed and clenched in pain. Another flicker highlighted a fresh stain of blood where the sheet touched the bandage over his thigh.

Sheltering the wick with her hand, Tess whispered a fervent prayer as the flame caught, then held. She replaced the glass cover and held the lamp high to get a better look.

"Dear Heavens," Tess objected as the stench of infection nearly knocked her off her knees. She set the lamp nearby and made quick work of removing the bindings and poultice. Though she forced herself not to turn away from the foul odor, the layer of skin bordering the open wound had turned ashen and oozed a yellow pus. Tess forced back the urge to gag. Worry sprouted and gripped her insides with tension. "You need a doctor."

She jolted to her feet and called loudly for the gambler. When he didn't answer, she jerked open the flap at the front of the tarpaulin and discovered that he had chosen somewhere other than the driver's box to sleep.

Ignoring her bare feet, Tess gathered her skirts and leapt from the back of the wagon. Midnight surrounded her as she peered into the shadows and attempted to define Jim's sleeping form.

Trees and bushes crouched together in sharp-edged shapes that made Tess's pulse quicken and her ears attune themselves to even the most minute sound. *Get hold of yourself,* she silently scolded and purposely strode away from the safety of the wagon. Jim had to be here somewhere. The man was exhausted from three days without sleep; he wouldn't have gone very far.

As if in answer to the calming influence of her common sense, a deep sigh sliced through the shadows and revealed the gambler's resting place. Tess turned toward the sound and retraced her steps. She waited and was awarded with a second sigh that made her stoop and peer beneath the Conestoga.

Resting his head against his saddle, Jim turned in his sleep and muttered something incoherent.

Heedless of the dew-covered dirt, Tess sank to her knees and crawled beneath the wagon. "Jim. Wake up, Jim!" she whispered, then realized the tone might not rouse him in his state of exhaustion. And if it did, would he draw his gun? The gambler might think she was someone trying to ambush him. Cautiously, she raised her voice. "It's me, Jim. Contessa. You must get up. Luke's leg is worse. We've got to get him to a real doctor."

Jim wouldn't rouse. It was a good thing the Indians no longer posed a threat, for he'd be of little help. Anger speared through Tess. Though he'd signed on without expecting pay, the man knew there was Tommie to consider. But her anger quickly subsided into a nagging fear. Where were they, and how close to the next settlement? What if they couldn't get help?

You've got to do something . . . now, Tess demanded of herself. *Don't waste time.* She backed out from under the wagon and rubbed her hands to rid herself of the dirt. Spurred by worry, she climbed back into the wagon and sank to her knees at Luke's side.

For one terrifying moment, Tess didn't see his chest rise. Panic whipped through her, forcing her to lean one ear against his nose and mouth. Her fingers spread across his chest to touch and reassure herself that he still breathed. His breath came shallow, uneven.

Images of Fort Smith and the many times she had doctored the soldiers darted across her mind. The list of herbs and medicines she had packed away in the trunk seemed suddenly useless. *Calm down,* she told herself. *Think about what you know.* Surely there was *something* that could help. If only she had brought more alum.

"Gotta get some salve," Luke whispered hoarsely, moaning as he attempted to sit.

"Lie down," she demanded, her tone harsh with frustration. Casting her trunk a doubtful glance, she willed herself to mentally inventory the meager household medicines. *Camomile and yeast!* The combination shouted through the fog of concern. Or was it charcoal and yeast? Uncertainty taunted Tess until she began to recite the facts aloud: "Charcoal for inflammation. Camomile for gangrene. Yeast to make the infection rise to the surface." She had saved camomile for her favorite tea. She would just have to take a chance . . . a chance that could very well mean Luke's death.

Luke's eyes closed, and she hoped that perhaps he had lost consciousness for a short while. At least it would give him some relief from pain until she could prepare the new poultice. Opening a tin, she pinched a corner off the yeast cake, then added camomile and water to it. When the mixture softened into a gooey substance, she patted it into an oblong shape.

Tess quickly ripped the remainder of her petticoats into strips and dipped the makeshift bandages into the water and rinsed. With the gentlest of pressure, she attempted to clean the wound.

"Ouch!" Luke complained.

"You must be still," she insisted, "or it will hurt worse." He reached down to swat her hand away.

"Don't do that." Tess used her forearm to block the blow while she continued to work. "You're only making this more difficult."

He groaned, bunching the sheets in both fists to keep himself in control.

Swallowing back the bile erupting in her throat, Tess carefully removed the dead flesh that peeled away in damp, gray shreds. The wound gaped. It would have to be sewn together, but the thread in her trunk would need to be sterilized first.

The tallow! She'd read once that a lady had used wax to seal a poultice; perhaps it was the truth and not merely the work of a good storyteller. Tess fetched the lamp and removed the glass shelter. A quick touch of one fingertip informed her the melted tallow along the candle's base would not be hot enough to blister but was warm enough to seal.

"Now this may burn a little," she warned as she smeared the wax along one edge of the bandage. Tess placed the poultice over the wound and pressed down the waxed edge.

"Damn!" The curse rushed through gritted teeth.

"I know it's hot but it won't scald you. This will hold in

the medicine until your leg's better, and I can take time to sterilize everything and stitch it closed.'' She pushed on both sides of his thigh and closed the gap of flesh by several inches. A few more drops of tallow on the opposite edge completed the seal.

"Almost done.'' Her eyes began to burn as she studied her handiwork intensely. Tears formed but she wiped them away.

His hand reached up and groped for her face. For a moment, in his pain, Tess thought Luke might attempt to hit her again. Instead, his rough palm caressed her cheek.

"You're crying.''

She gently pushed his hand away. "From staring so long.''

"Oh.''

Why did he sound so disappointed?

"My leg . . . smells better. *Feels* better.''

"Camomile and yeast.'' She sighed, exhaling some of the tension keeping her body coiled like a taut spring.

"Are you planning to cure me or roast me?''

Despite the pain, he smiled before drifting into an oblivion she knew they both welcomed. His touch slackened as his lips straightened and stilled.

Tess vowed to make him well. If only she really knew the secret to eternal life her father had boasted about in his schemes . . . maybe then she could save Luke's leg. For the remainder of the night she bathed his face, checked the wound for seepage, gauged the healthiness of his breathing, and changed the poultice as often as the discoloration seeped through the bandages. Each time he stirred beneath her administrations, she offered encouragement.

"Come on, Luke,'' she urged fiercely, "you have a job to finish . . . remember? You've got to get us to Colorado. You can't do it lying here on your back.''

Wild with delirium, he fought, but she struggled equally as hard to keep him flat on his back. "Don't you die on me, Luke Reeves,'' she insisted, praying his will to live was stronger than the pain he suffered. "You beat those Indians, and that little boy over there thinks you're a fighter. You can't

118

let him down." *You can't let me down.* "Fight with me, Luke!"

Soon the first rays of dawn filtered through the canvas. Mental and physical exhaustion jumbled her words into non-syllables as her lashes blinked once, twice, then finally closed. Reluctantly, Tess gave way to the oblivion of sleep, hoping, praying the battle had not been lost.

Chapter Eleven

With a night's rest under his belt, Jim Daggert decided to surprise Contessa by making breakfast. Although dawn was more than an hour gone, no one stirred in the Conestoga. He detested the thought of her sleeping under the same tarpaulin with the bounty hunter but found pleasure in the fact that Luke Reeves was too injured to pursue any amorous notions. Blue Hawk might have bungled the original plans, but at least he had proven helpful in another way.

Crawling from beneath the wagon, Jim stood and stretched the soreness from his limbs. A quick scan of the countryside assured him that nothing would hinder a leisurely breakfast, so he headed for the back of the wagon to get the skillet and coffee tin. He stuck his head inside the tarpaulin and the shocking sight that greeted him felt like a blow from a cast-iron fist.

A slim strip of sheet draped the bounty hunter to keep him from being stark naked. Not a stitch of clothing covered him from hip to head and thighs to toes. Only the bandage on his right thigh offered a barrier to the leg that rode the curve of Tess's breasts. With her arm flung just above his knees, one long slim leg completed the sleep-hold her body lavished upon the injured man.

Damn her! Why did she have to be such a helpful Hannah? The bastard might die if that thigh rotted. From the looks of the soiled bandages piled near the wash bucket, she had done her best to see that didn't happen. Contessa's hair fell in curls below her shoulders, and Jim wished he was the one she had bathed and coddled through the night. Having her lush body flung over his in such wanton repose would almost make it worth shooting himself to get her attention.

Luke moved restlessly and mumbled something incoherent. Tess's lashes opened, and Jim couldn't tell if she was fully awake as she groped for the bandage.

"Be still, Luke," she demanded. Her fingers gently touched, then fell limply away as she snuggled closer against his bare leg. One of the bounty hunter's hands delved into her hair. In seconds, his rhythmic breathing blended with Tess's.

Jim turned soundlessly away and grumbled, "To hell with breakfast."

Hours later, Luke awoke, weak but hungry and amazed to find himself feeling better. He flexed his muscles and found them stiff and sore from the bumpy wagon ride. Though his thigh felt tight and hurt like thunder, it no longer burned. Voices outside the Conestoga informed him that Daggert and Tess were securing the camp. Twilight filtered through the canvas, and he wondered how far they had traveled since his last real moment of consciousness. The gambler must think they were out of immediate danger or he wouldn't have camped.

The sound of her voice as Tess approached the wagon sent an unexpected anticipation through Luke. He marveled that she had such an effect on him in so short a time. Was this one of the ways she lured her victims at Hot Springs?

She saved your life, Reeves, he reminded himself as he glanced up and saw her standing at the edge of the wagon bed, watching him. Tess looked refreshed in her nankeen skirt and white-lawn blouse. Knotted in a coil at the crown, her hair shone like harvest gold, haloing fresh, peachy skin. Tess smiled and it warmed him to the core.

"You made it," she said quietly.

He studied her and grinned. "Thanks to you."

They looked at each other for an indefinable moment. No words were necessary. Each knew what had been offered, what had been exchanged.

"Will you come here?" he asked softly.

She paused uncertainly, then lifted herself into the Conestoga and sank to her knees by his side.

He offered his hand. "I owe you my life, Tessa. I'd like to thank you."

"Yes, you do." Amusement softened her reply and she accepted the handshake.

His pulse felt strong now, beating amidst the callus and bone that gripped her palm. Her own pulse seemed to skip a beat, then raced to match the rhythm his had taken.

"How can I repay you?"

He pulled her closer. She found herself drawn to the depth of his eyes. Her lips tingled with the anticipated kiss, but at the last moment before their mouths touched, Luke raised his chin and planted a kiss across her forehead.

"Like this?"

The touch was sweet, endearing, and more devastating than the thrill she'd expected at her lips. Tess's heart tightened with something stronger than affection, more powerful than the attraction she began to feel toward him. Something life-changing.

"Well . . . what have we here . . . obviously a grateful patient?"

It was just her luck that Jim Daggert chose that moment to interrupt. Tess jerked away, uncomfortable beneath the gambler's intense disapproval.

Luke continued to hold her hand, unwilling to let the moment slip away so easily. "A real shame I was the one who got shot, don't you think? But for every bullet, there is a justice."

Storm clouds rumbled over Jim's face. "Just remember you're here to take care of the lady, not the opposite."

Undaunted, Luke grinned at Tess when she attempted to slide her hand away. "Tessa doesn't seem to mind."

"Tessa, is it?" Outrage gripped Jim while she managed to struggle out of Luke's hold. "Since when did it become Tessa? Last night?"

"Both of you, stop it!" Tess whirled on Luke, her anger building. "I'm nobody's Contessa or Tessa. Just plain Tess. And if the both of you don't like it, then keep the fact to yourself until we reach Colorado!"

Jim gave them a scathing look. "Then quit curling up beside him with your hands all over him." His mouth pursed into a straight line.

Tess's hand shot to her hips. "I don't think that's any of your business, Mr. Daggert. And besides, I've never—"

"I saw you, Contessa. You were close enough to rub more than noses."

"Liar!"

"Now, Tess," Luke interjected, "you've got to give the man his due. There was that time last night when—"

Indignation narrowed her eyes. "I'll thank you to quit grinning, Luke Reeves. You know I did nothing but wash and rebandage your injury. I should have taken soap to your mouth!"

Jim's expression hardened into disgust. "Once you finished, you should've rolled over on your own sleeping mat instead of wrapping yourself around him like a spare blanket."

Tess remembered all too clearly now. Though she had fallen asleep in exhaustion, the feel of Luke's hard physique had filtered through her dreams. The press of his flesh against her fingertips had lulled her into a sense of peace. She could imagine the way their sleeping arrangement looked to the gambler.

"I think you better stop now, Jim." Her voice trembled with fury.

A muscle worked in his jaw as the gambler stared back at her sitting so still and erect beside Luke. "Now, don't get riled, Contessa. You know why I'm even bringing this to your attention, but perhaps I overstepped our friendship."

"There isn't any perhaps to it. You did. So let's leave it at that." She tossed Luke his buckskin pants. "If you feel up to dressing yourself, I have things to attend to. Be careful and don't loosen the bandage."

Luke reached out to stop her from rising, but she shrank away from his touch. He lowered his hand slowly to his side. "Sure, I can manage."

The undercurrent of emotions left things unsaid, and he felt an invisible wall form between him and Tess.

In clipped tones, she told the gambler to finish seeing to the stock while she prepared supper. And suddenly in the men's eyes there was no question as to whose expedition this was.

Tess arrived later carrying a tin. "Are you ready to eat?" Luke motioned her in. "I figured you'd let me starve or make me wait on myself after Daggert's comments."

"I should have. You took exceptional delight in making him angry."

His hand spread across his chest in mock dismay. "Me? I was only speaking the truth. You did touch me all the places he said, and if I remember correctly—"

"If you're hungry, eat." She set the tin down beside him with a clatter of utensils.

It didn't help her to recall those same touches and know that he, indeed, spoke the truth. Tess eyed the pillow boosting his head and thought he'd enjoy his meal better if he propped his back against the trunk. "Can you sit up?"

He obeyed and she grabbed one of the blankets, placing it behind him. "Now that's better. Do you think you can manage on your own, or do I need to feed you?"

A look of distaste glinted in his eyes and snarled his upper lip. "Stew?"

She grabbed a cloth and draped it over his chest. "It's good for you."

"My thigh's injured, not my stomach." He grimaced.

"Your body was full of fever and infection. Your stomach may not be as fit as you think. Now lift your spoon and eat, Mr. Reeves."

Luke scooped, making certain to include a hunk of potato and beef. The broth slid down easily, warming his throat and tasting finer than a side of buffalo steak. "It's good," he complimented and took another scoop. "Did you make it?"

A light flush rose to her cheeks. Her previous attempts at cooking on the trail had not been the best. She was accustomed to cooking indoors on a stove, not from fires built over an open flame or fueled by animal dung. "Believe it or not, even I can't mess up stew."

He grabbed her wrist. "I didn't mean to insult you." Luke's tone was sincere. "It really is good and I wanted to thank whoever made it. And Tessa . . ." he spoke her name softly, insisting upon the softer version despite her earlier objection. "I meant what I said. I appreciate you saving my life."

Tess shrugged. "There wasn't anybody else to do it."

"So I gathered. I'm glad you were so eager to help."

One brow arched and she chided, "I didn't think you wanted Jim to do the doctoring."

He chuckled and accidentally dropped some of the broth. "Seems like I owe you a second thanks."

Wiping the stew from his chin, Tess's hand halted as his gaze locked with her own. When his tongue licked a corner of his mouth, a lump caught in her throat. "You owe me nothing, Luke," she whispered. Realizing how husky her voice sounded, she deliberately spoke louder. "Just don't get hurt again. The next time I might not be here to fix it."

The next time I get hurt, Luke thought, *it will be because some blond miss-fix-it has gone and broken my heart.*

Chapter Twelve

"Ready?" Impatient to mount his horse after days in the schooner, Luke lifted one finger to his mouth to warn Tommie not to let Tess in on their adventure. She drove the team now while Jim resumed scouting ahead.

"Soon as I get Thammy settled in my pocket." Within seconds Tommie's fingers gripped the reins Luke had untied from the end of the wagon. Both pairs of hands tugged and pulled the dun closer.

The boy looked up earnestly, his eyes wide with concern as Luke stood precariously at the wagon gate waiting for Talon to half turn. "Can you ride, Mista Yuke?"

"Got to. Can't stand another minute in this rolling tent."

"What if you fall?"

"It'll hurt like a sonofa . . . like a by-gosh."

The freckles on Tommie's nose wrinkled into a grin. A giggle filled his eyes with light and stretched his mouth from ear to ear.

"Sorry about that."

"Want me to go tell Mommie so she can wash your mouth out with soap?"

About the cursing or mounting Talon? Luke wondered be-

126

fore deciding he didn't want her to know about either. Tess had made it plain there would be no slip of the tongue around her boy, and Luke admired her for that. But the pain of the past couple of days often caused him to forget, and the oaths had a way of barreling out when he least expected them. She would mutter a few choice words of her own if she knew he intended on riding Talon the remainder of this journey. Though the wound healed nicely, it was still tender. Luke knew he took a chance riding so soon again, but another day in the wagon would drive him insane.

The three-year-old still hadn't forgiven him completely for the backhand and, on occasion, took a notion to disobey Luke. The boy might choose this time to do the opposite of his instructions, so Luke shrugged off the secrecy. "If you want to tell her, it's all right with me."

Tommie looked a bit disappointed, telling Luke that his ploy had worked. The boy had meant to snitch on him for sure. Shaking off Tommie's orneriness as merely a childish impulse, Luke urged Talon as close to the wagon as possible. "Want to ride?"

"Yeah!" Tommie squealed, then muffled his joy as he glanced at his mother's back through the front flap to see if she had heard. "Can we put a banket up here so I kin surprise Mommie?"

"Don't see any harm in *surprising* her." Luke strung a blanket across the rope Tess had tied across the wagon, all the while trying to maintain his balance and hold on to the horse's reins.

"What are you two up to?" Tess called over her shoulder.

Did the woman have an extra pair of eyes? Luke decided that if forts were commandeered by mothers, there would never be an Indian attack. Mothers always seemed to know when anyone within miles was up to no good. "We're planning a surprise for you, that's all," he answered truthfully, suspecting she had probably already guessed.

"Yeah, Mommie. Me and Yuke and Thammy is," Tommie confirmed.

"Just remember, son. Mama doesn't like surprises that slither."

Tommie's giggle mixed with Luke's chuckle as she concentrated on the team once again and left them to their antics. Luke held his finger to his lips and whispered low in case Tess still listened. "Let me mount, then I'll swing around and help you saddle up."

Having taught Talon to let him mount from the left, Luke worried that the horse would shy when this time he straddled right-legged. "I haven't lost my mind, just the use of my leg," he reassured the animal with a swift pat to the neck. Incredible pain coursed from hip to toe as Luke settled deep into the saddle and gritted his teeth. His legs bowed over Talon, and Luke felt like a wishbone being pulled at both ends.

"Now me and Thammy, Mista Yuke!" Tommie stood with his hands outstretched.

The wagon rolled along at a steady clip. The loud swish of wheels cutting through waist-high prairie grass dulled the heavier clop of hoof against earth. Bumping over a clump of loam, the schooner sent Tommie careening to one side.

Luke's heart seemed to leap into his throat as an image of the boy trampled under Talon's hooves filled his mind. This was a foolish idea. A dangerous one. "Hold on, Tom."

With concentrated effort, Tommie stood.

"Thank God. Now back up so you don't get hurt."

"No, I wanna ride. You said I could and I want to."

Luke noted how much misery the wagon had dealt the boy. Perhaps if he taught Tommie to ride and ride well, the three-year-old wouldn't have to feel every bump and rut in the road. The tot's limp seemed more prominent the past few days, and he had tossed and turned endlessly in his sleep. The constant jarring couldn't be any less painful to Tommie's leg than it was his own injury.

"Grab my arm when I lean into you," Luke informed him as Talon sidled up to the Conestoga. Tommie took hold and thrust himself into Luke's arms, as if born to the saddle.

"Be careful, Thammy wanna ride too." The salamander's tail curled out of Tommie's back pocket.

"Tell Thammy to sit still. If he spooks this horse, none of us will hang on."

Laundry hung across the rope strung from the Conestoga to a cottonwood at the edge of the stream. Tess scrubbed one of the last dirty garments. Now that Luke could ride alongside the wagon, Jim scouted hours to a day ahead. As touchy as the gambler's temper had been lately, she was glad for his distance. Though Jim never failed to profess his love for her, Tess couldn't warm to him.

Perhaps he had been around for so long she couldn't think of him as anything more than a friend. Though he told her he was willing to wait until she changed her mind, the gambler didn't seem as patient a man as he claimed. Did he see the rising attraction she felt for Luke?

How far off were the bounty hunter and Tommie fishing? As if in answer, her son ran into camp, raising a spattering of dust as he climbed into the Conestoga.

"Watch my laundry!" Tess warned. Seeing his haste, she was filled with curiosity as she boosted him into the wagon bed. "You look like someone with a mission."

"Mista Yuke need a mirror. We gonna shave."

"Shave?" Tess laughed. The bounty hunter hadn't shaved in days and she rather missed the scarred face hidden beneath the mustache and beard. Searching through a trunk, Tess found the dressing mirror and handed it to Tommie. "Take it to Mr. Reeves but don't run," she warned. "You might stumble and cut yourself."

Setting him down on the ground, Tess bent over the washboard and began to scrub again.

Tommie kissed her on the cheek, then shouted over his shoulder, "I be weal careful, Mommie. I be widing."

Intent on her cleaning, she only half heard his remark and began rubbing two ends of the camisole together to remove a stain. Her hands stopped in mid-scrub. She dropped the soapy garment into the washtub and flung the suds from her hands. *He said he would be riding, not he would be right back.*

Everything fell into place. The blanket strung across the back of the wagon. The intended surprise. Though she'd suspected the reason for the change in wagon weight, Tess had soon discovered Luke mounting his horse and testing the injury. She had not considered the possibility that he included her son in his daily escape.

Tess stood and marched in the direction her son hurried. Grass crumpled beneath her pounding feet, her skirts swished through the blue-stem. Then she saw him. Tommie, sitting shoulder high on Talon. The sight tore breath from her throat as his soles, which could not reach the stirrups, nudged the dun into a trot. *He'll be killed!*

"Wai—" The command to stop him died in her throat. What if she yelled and spooked the horse? Tom would be thrown or trampled.

Straining her eyes to see Tommie's destination, she knew for certain her suspicion was justified. This was not his first ride. Despite the misfit riggings, the boy handled Talon well . . . or else the horse handled her son well. She couldn't decide who mastered whom. All she could do was follow and pray that nothing happened.

Tess nearly collided with Luke, who stood near the trunk of a cottonwood along the bank. Lathered with soap, the hard planes of his face and chin awaited the mirror Tommie brought.

"Is something wrong, Tessa?" he asked, taking in the features which faced him squarely, wanting to touch the lock of loose hair brushing her cheek as her hands clenched defiantly against her sides. "Looks like somebody's ruffled your feathers. What's Tommie done now?"

The bounty hunter's innocent expression exasperated Tess even further. Her fists shot to her hips, her eyes narrowing. "Don't call me that."

"What?"

"Tessa! And you know very well what's wrong."

"Pardon me, but I didn't know mind-reading was one of the requirements for this job."

"Very funny, Mr. Reeves. It's bad enough that *you* ride when I've told you plainly you can tear that wound open by doing so. But what gives you the right to put my son in such danger?"

A cord in his neck jerked, instigating a tightening in his jaw. "Look, Tess—lady. As far as my leg's concerned, you let me worry about whether or not I'm ready to ride. I'd rather it split down the middle than be cooped up in that wagon from Hell again." His eyes narrowed to match hers, and he leaned closer.

The smell of freshly washed man and lather engulfed her, making Tess all too aware of the danger he presented.

"Maybe I had no call teaching your boy without permission, but it doesn't take a Gypsy's eye to see *you* would never teach him. If you would come down off your pedestal, you'd see the boy takes to riding like you do to bourbon. When he's riding, Tom isn't limping . . . and, lady, that means more to him than anyone as pretty-headed as you seem to understand. To me, that's worth all the sour faces you can make from now till Armageddon. You keep that dove-tailed jackass of a gambler at your beck and call, but don't wag your bustle at me!"

Tess's teeth grated against each other. *Of all the ungrateful* . . . her mind refused to complete the thought. "I wouldn't count on you for anything, Mr. Bandy-leg Bounty Hunter."

"Bandy-leg, is it?" He took a long stride and instantly regretted it, yet would die and spend eternity in Hell before admitting it pained him.

Her chin thrust upward. "Yes, bandy-leg and grizzly cheeks."

Luke grumbled and rubbed his stubbled chin.

"You sound yike an ol' bear." Tommie giggled from atop the dun.

"Yeah, and he's foaming at the mouth," Tess taunted, her gaze rebuking the face caked with drying soap.

Luke bent at the water's edge and moistened his chin. "You

mean this?'' He took a few steps closer to Tess.

She took two steps backward. "What are you going to do?"

"Watch out, Mommie!" Tommie squealed but kept the safety of his perch.

"I'm foaming at the mouth, right? A stark raving lunatic who probably will do something crazy . . . outrageous?"

"Now, Luke, I didn't mean anything by it." Tess backed even further, raising her palms in front of her to hold him at bay.

Luke rubbed his chin, letting the lather stain his left hand. His fingers darted toward her and she shrieked, but he instantly brought them back. He could have easily touched her but didn't. Let her wonder what he intended.

"Where I come from, things that foam at the mouth . . . bite." Luke flashed her a span of white teeth.

"You wouldn't dare!"

"Mommie bites real good, Mista Yuke. I bit Zach once. Mommie bit me back."

Luke feigned a look of admonishment as he took the mirror from the boy. "Spare the teeth, spoil the child?"

Tess laughed, unable to resist the temptation. The lather on his face added to the flashing grin and his repartee was simply too engaging for her to remain angry. "I was trying to teach him not to bite. By doing the same to him every time he bit someone else, he soon learned not to do it. It was for his own good."

"Like teaching him to ride is for his own good?"

Now understanding why the bounty hunter felt the need to keep Tommie's secret, and grateful for the pride the lessons instilled within her son, Tess conceded and nodded. "What do the duelists say . . . touché?"

"Exactly. And now I've got one more lesson to teach." He grabbed a shaving rag he had hung on a limb and wiped the soap from his face. Nodding in the direction of the schooner, he told Tommie to go back to camp. "Keep watch for us, would you? I'd like to talk to your mama alone."

The boy looked to Tess for permission. Wariness choked

off her chuckle. "Well . . . I don't know if he should go
alone."

Luke silenced her objections. "If you need us, you just
shout."

Talon nickered and headed for camp with little urging from
Tommie. As her son disappeared from view, Tess stood in
silence. Her heart pulsed at her throat, deep in her chest and
at the back of her knees. One of Luke's hands gently gripped
her waist while the other opened wide and firm against the
middle of her back, pulling her near. She froze, staring at him
in wonder. "What are you doing?"

"Kiss me, Tessa."

"No."

"You want to."

"Yes . . . no!"

Warm, confident lips pressed sweetly against her denial and
lingered. She never knew the precise moment her lips opened
to the light pressure of his tongue, but heard the whimper of
satisfaction echo in her throat as he took complete possession.
He explored her with meticulous care, flicking the sensitive
inner lining of her lips and tickling the roof of her mouth.

Her hands delved into the still-damp strands of ebony brushing his collar, pulling him closer. Weeks of longing, of dream-
ing, of burning for Luke deepened the kiss. It felt so wonderful
to hold and be held.

"Tessa, sweet God," Luke whispered against her mouth,
"how I've wanted to kiss you." Realizing they neared the
point beyond which neither of them could turn back, Luke
forced himself to think clearly. She would worry about the
boy being alone. And he might have to one day separate
mother from son.

"Feel like walking back?" he asked, duty reminding him
of all that couldn't be. He offered her his arm.

"Yes, thank you." Tess breathed a sigh of pent-up tension
as she allowed him to escort her back, marveling at his control.
He could have taken her but didn't. She wanted to surrender
to his attraction, to make love to him, even looked forward to

it. But he kept his promise, and Tess didn't know if she was glad or disappointed.

Luke studied her as they walked, noting the fine curve of her hips, the firm step that said she was willing to meet life head-on. "Do you know what I thought when you let me into your home, heard me tell you that I killed your husband, and then touched my face?"

She shook her head, afraid to speak, afraid to reveal how easily he could persuade her to succumb to the desire he had kindled within her.

He bargained with his heart by owing her the truth. "I thought you were the kindest woman I'd ever met."

Tess faced him, glad he hadn't said *the most beautiful.* How many times in her life had her beauty scarred her soul? Her gaze locked with his. "And I thought you the most honorable man I'd ever met."

"Not the most handsome?"

She knew what he asked, though his tone revealed none of the emotion he must be feeling. The man spent a lifetime hiding the hurt. She suspected how hard it had been for him to ask and how much what she said would mean to him. For her own son fought the scorn and contempt offered those who suffered any handicap.

"Like the old saying goes, beauty and handsomeness are in the eyes of the beholder. When I look at you, Luke, I don't see scars. I see an honorable man who cared enough to escort us to a safe place. Someone whose heart is so tender, he takes the time to offer a three-year-old a sense of pride that will see him through tough years of scorn and ridicule. I see someone who could have taken advantage of our walk a few minutes ago yet didn't. For the first time in my life, Luke, I feel like a woman cared for, not just lusted after. I can't tell you what that means to me. But I can tell you I'll never behold any man more handsome than you are to me at this moment."

Tess struggled with the words to express the emotion his care inspired within her. Her lips parted in a wordless invitation which was swiftly answered as he moaned and his arms went about her, folding her into his embrace once again, bringing her up against the hard bareness of his chest. His mouth touched hers, testing her willingness, playing, warming, rousing until her arms crept up around his neck. She gasped as his lips traced a molten path to an earlobe and beyond, the hot peaks of her breasts pressing against his chest.

Luke's hands moved to her waist as he clutched her like a man long denied life-sustaining water. Though his mind begged, *Don't do this. You'll only end up hurt,* his heart hoped that for once in his life his instincts were wrong. That something stronger than his word could be trusted to guide him. "Walk with me again . . . later?"

Luke's a drifter, a bounty hunter who knows no home, the voice of reason warned Tess. *Even the small amount of time spent in the wagon rattled his sense of freedom. He leapt at the first chance for escape, just like he would leave you the first time you tried to bind him to you. You'll never hold him.*

But the thunder of desire coursing through her muffled the voice of reason. Just this once she would follow her own heart. Just this once she would travel the path *she* chose and not the one chosen for her by others. Just this once she would believe that true love awaited her, if she dared believe in it.

"Luke," she whispered against his lips, knowing full well where tonight might lead. "I'll meet you here."

"Promise?"

"After I've seen Tommie to bed."

Chapter Thirteen

The moon hung low and skimmed the treetops, penetrating the cottonwood canopies that bordered the stream. Though the night and its shadows beckoned to Luke, uneasiness filled him as he wandered through the tall trees. Tommie should be well asleep by now and still no sign of Tess. The wagon drew him, its canvas as forbidding as it was familiar. *Like Tess.* She fit him like a favorite hat, yet seemed a mystery he couldn't solve.

Stars rose over the Kansas prairie, blanketing the schooner with a sense of peace and safety. The familiar opening in the tarpaulin at the back called to him, but the darkened corridor offered a threshold which might ultimately carry him through past hurts, faded dreams and vanished hopes.

Luke feared nothing, no one. Yet the thought of being denied her company, even if merely to walk along the bank, made him tremble. He leaned a shoulder against the schooner and stared upward into the dark that marked her sleeping quarters.

His mind wandered until it touched on the scene of their first kiss, then the night he woke from the injury to watch her sleep, her hair spreading in golden cascades across his abdomen. Her lips had puckered into a sigh as she stretched and allowed the silken curls to frame her breasts, igniting a flame deep within his already fevered body. The burning inside Luke grew hot at the memory until it spewed out her name in a fervid rush, ''Tessa?''

A dream? The voice sounds real. Tess floated between the nether world of sleep and wishes. Reality faded and she returned to the gentle flow of her dream, swimming in the stream where they had first stopped. Water softly lapped against her body. Moonlight sparkled on the surface, offering a curious indigo beam. Panic slowly washed over her as she realized that Tommie no longer swam near her, ebbing quickly as he waved to her from shore. When she tried to reach her son, Tess discovered she didn't know how to swim. She had never waded this far out, never allowed herself a complete immersion.

From below the surface a man emerged. Like some god of the deep, he rose in front of her, foam lingering at his cheek. The god turned and offered his back, urging Tess to thread her arms around his neck. When she did, he swam. As he stroked, the powerful play of muscles eased her misgivings and she pleasured in the gentle lapping of the waves. Nearing the shore, he let go and turned toward her. A bit farther, she thought.

As if she had spoken, he shook his head. *Swim with me:* his lips moved in a voiceless plea. Only then did she see the light in his eyes. Indigo. The color that filled the night and sparkled in a million stars upon the water's surface. This was Luke's kingdom . . . Luke's realm.

With a laugh of joy she dove with him below the surface, shutting out the world above and releasing the anchor of fear that beckoned her to shore. Something fished Tess from the sweet slumber. A sound . . . near. Erotic as her dream. *Luke!*

She blinked, trying to banish the ecstasy not easily forsaken, only to discover it in human form at the wagon gate, silhouetted against the night.

"Come walk with me."

"Where's Jim?"

"He took watch about a mile out. Said he was tired of playing nursemaid to a boy and a salamander. I told him not to trouble himself; we'd take care of ourselves."

Pushing back the blanket, she stood fully clothed. Naked passion drew her to him. Luke's hands reached through the darkness and wrapped gently, possessively around her waist. Instead of setting her down, he swung her up into his arms, cradling her as if she were a babe.

Encircling his neck with her arms, she gloried in the strength of his embrace. Her fingers tangled softly in the thick ebony strands at his shoulders. "So soft. Like silk," she sighed.

The sound of pleasure purring in her throat sent a faint shudder through Luke. He leaned forward, brushing his lips across her own. "You taste like honey."

She shivered with anticipation as his teeth closed on her lower lip in a caress that was both sensuous demand and ardent plea. The slow, gentle thrust and parry of his tongue enticed her, but her own hunger needed sating. She countered, savoring the sweet intoxicant that was only Luke.

He broke the embrace and stared at her with raw hunger. "Sweet God, why didn't you meet me?"

"I told Tommie his bedtime story and ended up falling asleep beside him. I didn't mean to break my promise."

Luke closed his eyes against the picture she made, her lips moistened by the passionate kiss, hair cascading over her shoulders, and her breasts peaking beneath the homespun bodice. "A man could drown in you."

Her breath caught in her throat as his gaze charted every nuance of her face, mapping the flush of desire that rose in its wake. His control continued to amaze her.

He was a man of his word. *I'll never force you.*

With sweet anticipation of discovery, she began her own exploration. Tracing his brow and the slope of his nose, softly caressing each hooded eye, she followed the tantalizing trail of her fingers with a kiss. Tess cradled the rough texture of his scarred cheek, then stared into his eyes. "A woman could worship you."

He groaned as her lips parted in unconscious invitation.

"Let me down," she implored, thinking her weight bore too heavily upon his injury. But he continued to carry her toward the bank of the stream despite the noticeable limp that hindered his usual fluid movements.

Tess marveled he could see where he walked, for his gaze never left hers. Secluded by trees but only a short distance from the schooner, she noticed a blanket stretched across the grass. Primroses lined one side of the blanket, scenting the air with their wild fragrance. He lowered her to the soft mattress of prairie grass and willow reeds.

Like a warrior he stood over her, his stance wide and imprinted with arousal.

Their eyes met . . . stared.

Luke was afraid for the first time in his life.

Tess knew a desperation unlike any she had ever known.

Then all his inadequacies, all her past wrongs fell away, leaving only the uncertainty of acceptance.

"Stay with me?" A thousand questions he uttered in this simple one.

Was it possible that someone so beautiful within, so handsome outwardly, could care for her? At long last, the loneliness of her life stopped hurting. She thought his name over and over, wondering if this Luke was real or the product of her dream. She knew too well how one could be fooled by believing too easily.

Slowly he stretched his full length, hovering above her, bearing his weight on both elbows. Still he resisted, not wanting to hurt, keeping his promise not to force her.

She beckoned him to her, drawing his heart closer until she felt it hammering with a rhythm to match her own. His lips rained soft kisses on her brows, earlobes, the curve of her neck. Her lips pouted, yearning for his return.

But Luke denied the pleas whispered in his ear, needing to

say the things he had dreamed of telling her. "I was scared of you."

"Scared? Why?"

"I thought you could never care for the man who killed your husband."

"I have my own shortcomings."

He pulled back to see her face. "None that I can see."

"In here," she pointed first to her temple, then to her heart, "and here."

He nudged her chin with the curve of one knuckle and made her look at him. "Not since I've known you."

"Before. A long time ago."

"We all have pasts. Though we can't change them, we can sure try to make now right for us."

Her heart felt too small to contain the promise she read in his eyes. Was this her future staring back? With a will of their own, her hands molded the hard slope of his shoulders.

He closed his eyes as her fingers delved into his hair and caressed the back of his neck. If he lived to be a hundred, he would never tire of her touch.

"You feel so good. Not like . . ."

"Clifton?" Unreasonable jealousy opened Luke's eyes as he took his fill of her incredible beauty. "Do you still miss him?"

"No."

"It's only been weeks. Didn't you love him?" Somehow her answer seemed important. More important than knowing if she was Harper's accomplice in crime.

"I wanted to protect him, nurture him, provide a nice home for him."

Luke braced on one elbow and stared at her. "Sounds like you're talking about your son, not your husband. Were you trying to be Clifton's parent or his wife?"

Sensing his underlying need, she found the courage to admit the truth. "I never wanted him like I want you."

Luke's heart clenched as if a huge vise locked around it. His eyes spoke the shout of joy filling his soul, though his words still questioned, "How can you care for me? No one else in this world bothers to."

"No other woman?"

"Not even my mother."

She pulled him close, wrapping her arms around him. "How very much we need each other."

She had not said she loved him. Had no idea how desperately he needed the words of forever. The sting of tears hitting his eyes made him bury his face in the crook of her neck while his hands held her fast.

As she felt the moisture of his tears, rage surged within her. What gave anyone the right to make him feel unloved? What kind of woman denied the goodness that was Luke? What kind of mother denied her son? Was there only hurt in his life? At least she had Tommie's love. The absence of any love at all seemed a terrifying prospect. No wonder he had built a wall of ice around his heart and traveled the lonely path of a bounty hunter.

She couldn't yet promise him love, but Tess had to let Luke know how much he had come to mean to her. If it meant being a bit forthright in her actions, then so be it. He needed this, and God knew she wanted him. "Show me what you want. Teach me."

The harsh lines of his face tightened to match the tension drawing his body taut. "You don't know what you're asking."

"I know I want to learn everything. The way only you can show me."

With a groan he pulled her closer and kissed her, teaching Tess how much she sought, learning how little he knew. Her nails raked his back as pleasure purred in her throat.

Threads of passion wove through him, knotting deep within as he unfastened the many buttons of her homespun. When the garment fell away, he caressed the velvet ivory of one shoulder, then the other. Her hands delved into his hair, and he thought he would scream as the movement brought the arch of her back, thrusting the rose-crested nipples peaking beneath the camisole closer to his lips.

He was a man too long denied satisfaction, and the temptation nearly exceeded his will. But to rush now after waiting all this time to experience Heaven seemed ludicrous. Carefully unlacing the camisole, he lowered it over the generous swell of her bosom, past her waist and the becoming flare of her hips. He nipped and tugged on one perfectly pebbled nipple, allowing his tongue to taste the erotic essence of Tess.

Salvos of passion sizzled through him and struck with such blinding force, white-hot desire sent the world careening behind his closed lashes. His lips released the taut pinnacle only to capture the other in its stead. His need quickened, demanding fulfillment.

She gasped as her fingers sought to bring him closer, reaching for the buttons of the material that kept him from her boldest touch.

"Let me help you," he offered huskily.

His hands rested over hers as she eased each button loose. The buckskin proved difficult, but the anticipation of filling her hands with rough velvet was too intense for him to let the moment pass awkwardly. Anticipation became approval, sending a shiver over her skin.

His breath hissed between his teeth.

"Did I hurt you?" she asked, removing her hand. "I forgot about your thigh."

With a deep exhale of breath, he attempted to still the currents bolting through him. "I'd say my thigh is safe. I ache in other places."

"Then show me where you hurt." Her hands rested on his hips. "Here?"

His fierce smile matched the dark twinkle of his eyes. "Huh-uh."

Her fingertips traced the hair beginning at his navel, plunging much lower. His skin was supple and warm, the muscled flat plane of his abdomen wonderfully hard. Dare she? "Here?"

"No." His voice thickened with desire.

Her eyes widened in playful sensuality as her fingers cupped the hard reality of his male flesh.

"There." Luke's legs tightened as his breath drew in raggedly. A wave of insane pleasure crashed against the mindless ecstasy felt beneath her touch. Her name became a prayer. "Tessa. . . ."

With an anguished sound, she arched her hips and pressed her aching flesh against him. A granite-hard shaft of hot velvet sank deeply into her, filling Tess so completely she almost wept with need and the perfect complement of their bodies. All her life she had longed for this moment, knowing she wanted it but afraid she could never give as equally.

Passion transformed his face as the power of his thrusts moved in her, increasing the tempo of her desire. His name tore from her throat as their gazes met and locked while long, slow strokes carried him deeper, brought him back, only to delve in again.

He whisked her off to a place beyond consciousness, beyond awareness. Crying for release, she soared up, up, up, until the pressure within mounted and coiled, stretching to a point of near bursting. Suddenly, her head arched backward. His body tensed. A shuddering spasm unraveled the slim thread of sanity left. In ecstasy she cried out his name over and over, weeping as their release came and he silenced his own shout with a desperate kiss.

Luke held her, relishing the feel of Tess beneath him, letting his heart slow to a normal rhythm. Her skin glowed, tasting of the essence their lovemaking evoked. Though his passion was spent, he couldn't resist cupping her breasts once more and paying homage to each. She moaned and he recognized the difference in tone. Rolling over and taking his weight off her, Luke was unwilling to completely relinquish their closeness. He urged her to move atop him and marveled at the lush beauty pressing wantonly against him.

"Will you stay with me in Colorado?" she asked, bracing her chin with her hands and resting her elbows on his chest.

Studying her face, he didn't know how to say what he must.

Tess wiggled for a better position, kissing his throat, nibbling at his ear. She noticed the sudden tensing beneath her touch. Sensing something terribly wrong, she unlinked her legs and moved to one side. Was it possible he had not been awed by the miracle of their lovemaking? "What is it? Didn't I satisfy you?"

Luke drew back, his eyes revealing half anguish, half anger. "Satisfy me? Dear God, Tessa, you're more woman than I've ever known. More than I want to know." And therein lay his anguish. How could he tell her about the jealousy spawning deep inside now that he had been touched by her passion? Luke prayed that Clifton had been the lover who helped her master the bewitching art of lovemaking she seemed so expert at.

The possibility that she might be guilty of seducing the patrons of the Hot Springs Bathhouse seemed more likely now that he knew her skill. And the likelihood cut Luke to the bone. *Damn,* but he wanted to believe her innocent. He knew she didn't lie about being molested; her pain had been too real. She'd saved his life. A deed simply to ensure her and Tommie's safety across Indian territory? If only this indecision would go away.

Luke never let anything but duty rule his judgment, and it scared the hell out of him that all he could think of now was to forget his assignment. Forget the nagging questions that scarred the most beautiful night of his life. Forget that he had nothing else but his word to live by . . . to count on.

Take just this one small moment in time for yourself, his heart whispered. *You've waited for someone to hold you this way, to touch you and fill you with all you've been denied.* He bit her lips; Tess bit back. He pressed the center of his need hard against her. She opened to accommodate his desire.

"I want to know one thing," he demanded.

"What?" she teased.

"Why should I stay with you in Colorado?"

"You know."

"No, tell me."

"Because I care for you."

"More."

"Because I want you."

"Is that all?"

"I need you, Luke."

"Nothing else?"

Once again their bodies melded into one. A seed of warmth planted itself in the pit of Tess's abdomen, sprouting into furrows of desire. Needing no further encouragement, she nourished his movements until she was arching to meet Luke's thrusts. Tess twisted her head from side to side, begging him as he'd once predicted she would, "Please . . ." but not knowing what she asked for. When she reaped the rapture of his touch, a scream tore from her throat.

Instantly Luke captured the sound with his lips but not before experiencing his own shuddering cataclysm. For upon Tess's lips he tasted the words, "*I love you.*"

Chapter Fourteen

Luke's right arm ached from being in one position too long. He started to flex it before his eyes opened to see and identify the pressure upon it. A minimum price for such a memorable night. Tess's lips nestled just beneath the hollow of his neck. Her golden hair cascaded in soft disarray over his arm as velvet curves molded perfectly to his length.

Watching her quietly, Luke noticed the becoming widow's peak above her brow, studied the pattern of freckles lightly dotting her nose. He admired each breath lifting her breasts.

Her nose wiggled, adding a comical tilt to full lips, making Luke chuckle despite his effort to refrain. She tossed the blanket off and stretched long bare limbs. Her toes curled and she raised one knee until it rested against his right hip and thigh. The weight added a mixture of pain and pleasure to his already aroused senses.

The scent of her hair blended with the primroses he had strewn about to please her, but none of the blossoms matched the fragrance that was Tess. Unable to resist the temptation, he stroked the silken curve of her waist, softly caressing the flare of her hip and admiring the essence that was soft, warm woman.

The Beholding

A hand, feathery in its touch, smoothed the ebony wisps of hair that curled along his broad chest. Her lashes fluttered and a smile darted across her lips, then vanished. *Was she pretending to sleep?*

A shudder passed through him as he wondered if she studied him as intimately as he admired her. *How did he compare to the others?*

His hair was unkempt by most standards. He preferred the wilderness style adopted by Custer. Luke sported no beard or mustache as was the custom even here in the West, but most women he had known said they preferred clean-shaven men. His eyes, full-lashed and midnight blue, contrasted sharply with his dark hair and caused many a fight when he was younger. *Pretty as a lady's.* How many times had he been told that? About as many times as he nailed someone's hide over it.

The rest of him could be cut from just about any slab of rock. Lean and chiseled to hard edges, he had earned every scar and callus except the one on his cheek. When he wasn't hunting a man down, he found jobs that challenged him physically so he didn't have time to analyze the wrongs of his life. Couldn't do anything about his face. Hell had wanted him so badly, it marked him while he was still in the womb. Wasn't much to offer a woman who could choose just about any man she set her mind on.

Luke's hand moved away from her hip as if she had already rejected him.

Tess woke. She glanced at his face, her nudity, then sat and reached for clothes and the blanket, all in one motion.

She began to dress with her back turned to him, so he did the same. When she had fastened the last button on the homespun and he yanked on the second boot, they met each other's gaze.

"Morning," he offered, thinking she was the prettiest sight he had ever woken up to.

"Good morning."

"How'd you sleep?"

"Wonderfu . . . I mean, fine, thank you. And you?"

"The best ever. Do you always wake up like you're shot at?"

"No. It's just that it's dawn, and I didn't mean to fall asleep in your . . . I mean I didn't mean to leave Tommie alone so long."

"I checked on him a couple'a times. He's snoring like a bear cub tucked in for the winter."

"Any sign of Jim?"

"No, but I figure he'll be in soon. He's due for supplies."

"Then we ought to be heading back."

A practical end to the night they shared. What had he expected? Luke felt momentarily awkward and groped for something to say, but words failed him. He offered his arm, and she linked hers through it, falling into step beside him.

"Tess, about last night," he paused. "It can't happen again."

She felt confused, not by Luke, but by her own emotions. Had she allowed him to play her for a fool? Tess walked ahead of him.

He reached for her arm. "Are you just going to walk away? Not say anything?"

She was confused. Her steps halted as she faced him. "What's there to say? Last night was obviously nothing more than two people who desperately needed each other."

"It *can't* be more than that, Tessa. I'm assigned to a job that might keep me from you for a long time. Maybe even years. It's better we stop this now before either of us get hurt."

"It's too late for that, don't you think? There are other jobs. Give us time to be together."

"I can't, Tessa. I've given my word." He stared off into the distance, unable to meet her gaze.

"And your word is what you live by . . . right? Everything else be damned." She flung her arms out in frustration, knowing he was right, despising herself for her anger, yet unable to stay in his presence a moment longer. Tess returned to camp alone.

148

The Beholding

* * *

Three hours later, Luke stood in the stirrups and shielded the Kansas sun from his eyes. Talon's ears twitched and his head bobbed, urging Luke to peer closer. A horseman. Half a mile out. *Daggert.* For the first time since he had met the man, Luke was glad to see him. Luke met the gambler halfway and reined to a halt.

"Looks like you're up to some scouting." Jim dusted his hat on one leg, then set it back on his sweat-soaked hair. "That's good, 'cause I could use some sleep."

"Trouble?" Luke checked the horizon for something he might have missed.

Jim wiped his mouth on a sleeve, then thumbed in the direction he had come. "Don't reckon so. There's some kind of herd coming this way. Darndest thing I've ever seen. The drovers are mostly Osage and Cheyenne warriors. The trail boss is a fellow named Jesse Chisholm. Said he was hired by an agent in Wichita to take the herd to New Mexico territory."

"Any way we can pass them by?"

"Sure. If you wanna paddle up the Arkansas. The herd numbers near three thousand and, from the looks of it, stretches from here to Colorado."

"Chisholm know we got a woman and a boy along for the ride?"

"Said he heard about the white woman before he headed out of Wichita. The menfolk are hoping we get there in time for their Fourth of July celebration. Must be planning something special for her and the boy."

"What about the Cheyenne and the Osage? Are they settled enough to let us pass?"

"Chisholm gave his word that if we'd give him the honor of meeting Tess and the boy, he'd personally guarantee their safety. One of his white drovers said the trail boss speaks fourteen dialects and is trusted like a chief among the civilized tribes. If Chisholm gives his word, the Indians working for him will honor it."

"Then it would do us good to accept his hospitality. Maybe

149

an hour or two of visiting will save us days of watching for trouble. How far afield are they?''

"About five hours out at most," Jim informed. "Chisholm's riding point, so you'll see him first. Can't miss him. He's a half-breed with a handlebar mustache. Says he's heard of you. I hope you haven't got reason to know him. Saw him deal with a couple of rustlers, and I'd say you two were an even match.''

"When did you ever see me shoot?" Suspicion gnawed at Luke. The gambler had only two opportunities to witness his gunplay since going to Fort Smith—once at Pencil Bluff during the exchange of rifles, and second, when he'd suffered the injury at Blue Hawk's hand. If Daggert chose the incident with Blue Hawk, then he must have been on the scene sooner than indicated. No bullets had been exchanged between Luke and Blue Hawk after the gambler's supposed ''just-in-the-nick-of-time'' arrival.

"Saw you take care of those Comanche. Blue Hawk took one of your slugs before I got him.''

Just what I suspected. Daggert was up to no good. The time for confrontation with the gambler would have to wait till Luke had all the details and not just suspicions.

"Watch the wagon. I'll meet with Chisholm. If I'm not back by nightfall, you'll know something's happened to sidetrack the herd." Luke spurred Talon into a trot and rode in the direction Daggert had come from. His troubled mind wandered. He couldn't forget how Tess filled him with a sense of belonging. A prospect of home, family . . . happiness.

He had grown to care for Tommie, as well. Like he'd never cared for anything or anyone in his life. Smiling at the image of the three-year-old mimicking his own toss of a lasso, watching the pride in the boy's face and set of his shoulders as he became more familiar with handling Talon were all memories Luke intended to carry with him to quiet the discontent that would fill him for days to come.

What future did his word leave him but a cold, lonely existence that knew no happiness? Yet could he call this happiness? A pain the size of Texas clutched his heart every time he thought about turning Tess in. A heat the degree of ten prairie fires scorched every place Tess's hands touched every time he thought of her, much less looked at her. If this was happiness, it should be easy to go back to his previous hellish life. But it wouldn't be.

Luke knew there was no returning. His destiny changed forever last night. For the first time in his life, he wanted to be wrong. He wanted to break his word. He wanted to believe the allegations were false. Tess had branded him as surely as if she held a running iron to his hide. An omen had taken his first love from him, and now keeping his own oath threatened to do the same to what might become the love of his life.

Tess had little time to worry whether Luke needed to put distance between them or if he simply relieved Jim from a sense of duty. When she returned to camp, she found Tommie crying in his sleep, clutching his leg as if it pained him greatly. A touch of her hand to his forehead warned he had taken on a fever. When she followed her suspicions and checked his hip and leg, she discovered both inflamed.

I should have been here, she berated herself. What kind of mother left her son alone and traipsed off to the woods? Taking the liniment from her trunk, Tess scooped a glob into her hands and began to massage his leg, working out the pain that made the tiny limb draw up.

How many more days until they reached Denver? Idaho Springs was only a day and a half from there. If she could ward off this current threat to her son's health, the healing water of the hot springs might relieve him.

Though Jim was obviously tired and needing his sleep, he begrudgingly agreed to drive the wagon while she remained in the back with Tommie. The wind began to stir in mid-afternoon, blowing hard over the waist-high prairie grass until it bowed in submission. The unbuffered gale shook the schooner's canvas bows and made an unearthly sound as it passed from one opening in the tarpaulin through another.

Tess stared with dread at the little patch of sky she could see from the back opening, wondering if it brought another week-long shower. Anticipating the storm drained her strength. When Tommie's leg swelled and pained him so, rain only made it worse.

Late afternoon closed in on them, tightening like a vise. Hot air swirled under the canvas, bringing with it a suffocating grip to the lungs and throat. Dust and grass billowed behind the wagon and danced as the wind whipped dust devils skyward. The mules balked.

Tommie's eyes took on an unhealthy shine. A paleness settled around his mouth as he began to shiver even in the overwhelming heat. Tess called to Jim, "We have to stop. Tommie's ill. I've got to heat the liniment and wrap him. I need a fire."

"You see the sky?" Jim hollered back over his shoulder. "With this much wind, we can't keep a fire going even if there was anything to burn."

Tess peered over the unforgiving prairie. The day's journey took them deep into the grasslands. Hours away from even the precious willow which could sustain a fire in wetness. It was too dangerous for Jim to leave them and search for wood, and she couldn't commandeer the team and care for Tommie. "I've got to try. Stop . . . please."

The wind shrieked as if laughing at her predicament, but Tess steeled her resolve to defeat it. She searched the interior of the schooner for anything that might burn until her gaze locked on the butter churn. It wouldn't provide much of a fire, but she had no choice but to try.

Jim pulled back on the reins, instructing the mules to halt. "I'll unhitch the team so they can graze. Guess I'd better hobble 'em or we'll lose the lot if that storm acts up."

Tess dug through her trunk and found an extra cotton chemise. She tore it into one long strip of cloth. Gathering the churn, liniment, one of the blankets and a skillet, she exited out the back of the wagon. Tying two ends of the blanket to the wagon wheel and angling the cloth into a half tent, she formed a barrier to the wind. She set the churn below it and began the difficult task of raising a fire in the swirling wind.

The wood seemed only to darken. Tess's pulse raced as she willed the image of a reddish blue flare to ignite, enabling her to cook. Moments ticked by, stretching into eternity. Only a thin trail of ash revealed the fire's birth within the churn. Finally a puff. The blaze flared. The wind challenged, causing the red-blue light to flicker. Another and another flame, and the fire caught and stayed.

"I've got it!" she shouted in triumph. Grabbing the skillet, she rested it on the top of the churn and quickly scooped the liniment into it. "Cook fast," she prayed aloud, her gaze darting between the opening in the tarpaulin and the task at hand. As she strained to hear if Tommie was still moaning, the howl of the wind prevented her from doing so.

The afternoon grew dark as midnight. Flashes of lightning signaled a coming rain. Glimpses of daylight blinked behind ominous clouds spiraling up over the prairie.

"Please don't pour before this gets hot," she pleaded. The rain itself would make the healing more difficult. Without the medicinal plaster, Tommie's fever might rage even more.

In a battle for time, Tess scattered the liniment across the surface of the skillet and hoped thinning the globs would help it warm faster. She felt the heavy oppression of gloomy clouds press down upon her.

"Rider coming!" Jim hollered from inside the wagon.

Tess stole a quick glance and exhaled a sigh of relief. *Luke!* He would help. Having him near sent a wave of reassurance through her. She stood abruptly to wave him in. Her foot bumped the edge of the churn. Flames licked against the blanket and caught. Tess screamed, grabbing the precious skillet without thinking. As pain seared her hands, she dropped the cast iron in the grass. Some of the liniment splattered onto the ground.

"Fire!" she screamed, stalled by a moment of indecision. Should she protect the liniment or put out the blaze already consuming the blanket and now threatening the wagon? She clutched full skirts with her badly burned palms. Tess gritted her teeth against the pain and tried to pat the fire out with them. "Get Tommie out of there!" she yelled. "The wagon's on fire."

Jim appeared at the opening, saw her terror and rushed to help her.

"No, get Tommie!" She fought off his helping hands.

Tess pushed the gambler aside, letting him worry over the wagon. She rushed to the wagon gate, prepared to climb in and get the boy. But before she could put one foot up, Luke appeared over the threshold, cradling Tommie in his arms. The canvas burst into flames above them, beside them, flaring with a heat that made Luke stumble back.

"Nooo!" Tess wailed, groping for them. "Jim, help me. They're still in there!"

Batting away the flames with one hand, Luke strained for the opening again.

Tess ignored the darting tentacles of fire as she attempted to climb. "Hurry, Luke!" she pleaded. "Hurry!"

Luke lowered the boy into her awaiting arms as the gambler reached up and locked his hands about Tess's waist, helping her to come aground. She cradled her son and ran from the wagon, far into the prairie. As she turned, the fire consumed the wagon bed.

"Luke!" She watched in horror as he jumped and a long red tongue of flame licked out at his back.

"You're safe!" Tess whispered, remembering to breathe again. *You saved my son.* Silently she thanked the bounty hunter limping toward her. Then she remembered the liniment. Tommie was far from safety. "The liniment," she yelled at Jim, but the gambler kept running for safety. "I forgot the liniment!"

Luke was closer, but could he make it in time? "Tommie needs the liniment, Luke." She pointed. "In the skillet. By the wheel. Be careful, it's hot."

Luke halted and looked back, as if gauging the possibility. He turned and sprinted toward the skillet, his limp making the dash awkward. Just as he reached the place where she had dropped the cast iron, the wagon burst into a horrendous ball of flame, barreling out at him.

Tess screamed as he dove to the ground, and all she saw was a blinding flash of red.

Chapter Fifteen

"Luke!" Tess placed her son gently on the grass and ran as hard as she could toward the bounty hunter. "Don't die, Luke. Don't die!"

Raising her hand to shield her face, she approached the leaping flames and peered through the wind-driven smoke. Leaning into the gale, she thought she saw his dark form. He moved! As she struggled closer, Tess's cheeks stretched taut against the heat. One palm pressed against her mouth to ward off the instant parching of her throat.

"Grab his feet!" the voice behind her commanded.

Jim. "Help me, Jim. I don't know how badly he's hurt."

Each took a legging and yanked as hard as they could. Though he was not heavy, Luke's weight made the going slow. Tess felt the blood rush to her burned palms as her shoulders strained to keep up with the gambler's easier effort. A drop of rain spattered her face. Thunder rumbled.

"Pour buckets, damn you," she cursed the sky, gritting her teeth against the burning pain that weakened her grip. Lightning flashed seconds behind the rumble. Nothing she did would stop the inevitability of a downpour. She could only soothe Tommie. But the rain would drown out the flames and prevent the chance of starting a prairie fire from which none of them could escape. Another raindrop fell and another, moistening the skin stretched tight by the fire. "Rain!" she demanded again.

Despite the groans emitting from Luke as they dragged him across the grass, every pain he suffered was one less from death. At last they reached a distance far enough away to exchange feet for shoulders. When Tess lowered his leg and rushed to help Jim who already threaded his arms through Luke's, she discovered the bounty hunter still gripped the skillet in his hands.

"Take that ointment and see to the boy," Jim instructed her. "I've got Reeves."

Tess checked to make certain the band was still in the pocket of her skirt where she had stuffed it. If in all the commotion she dropped it, the bandaging would be difficult. A quick pat told her the wrapping remained. The rain fell now in sheets. She gathered her skirt hem and used it to reach for the cast iron. Taking the skillet from Luke's gloved hands, she carefully but swiftly walked to where Tommie lay and placed it beside him. Separating the homespun from the layers of petticoat, Tess tore several pieces of her undergarments and covered the ointment.

As Jim dragged Luke alongside the boy, the bounty hunter shuddered, opened his eyes and sat up. "Is the boy all right?"

"For now." Tess bent beside Luke, staring at him in wide-eyed concern. Her hands touched him everywhere, checking, reassuring herself he was whole. "Where do you hurt?"

Luke gulped back the words racing to his throat. The swallow felt like thousands of razor strops speeding down his throat and landing in a piercing heap at his chest. "Here." Panic filled his eyes as he fought to stand.

"Lie down a minute. You'll be fine." She took him by the arms and forced him back. "You took in too much smoke."

"But Tommie—"

"The boy's not burned. He's got a fever in his hip and leg. Here now, you lie back like I said."

Wilting back to the earth, Luke quit resisting and closed his eyes to the memory of heat streaming past him, scorching his hair and brows. Rain spattered his face as Tess and the gambler worked. He opened his mouth to let the moisture soothe his parched throat. Suddenly callused hands cupped both sides of his face. The smallness of the palms revealed they were Tess's, but why were they so rough? His eyes flashed open and his hands pushed hers back. Blisters formed along the inner folds, blood streamed where the rain hit them. He sat up. "My God, what happened?"

"I burned them," Tess stated the obvious as she blinked away the tears threatening to reveal how much her hands hurt. "Will you be all right? Jim's going to round up the mules while I look after Tommie."

"Not until I doctor your hands, you aren't." Luke slowly got to his feet, but a wave of dizziness made him unsteady.

Tess clutched to hold him still, gasping from the pain of contact.

"Will you quit being so damned helpful?" Luke pushed her hand away. But seeing the pain well in her eyes, he knew he'd been too abrupt with her. "Look, I just mean to quit worrying about taking care of me. We need to see to your hands before you can help any of us. Here, take this."

Luke shucked his buckskin shirt and offered it to Tess. The effort made his breath come uneasily. "Must've sucked in a lot of smoke, but it's easing already. Take this and let me have the boy."

"What are you going to do?" Her brows angled in puzzlement.

"Keep the underside of that bottom down and the rain won't soak through the top. When we saddle up, I'll carry the boy with me and we'll drape the buckskin over him. That ought to keep out the rain or a bunch of it." Gratitude rounded the sea-green eyes staring back at him.

"Thank you, Luke. For . . . everything."

"Don't thank me till we've got you both well." He took her arm and urged Tess toward the boy. Lifting the pieces of undergarments protecting the liniment, he found the ointment still warm. He cupped as much as he could and demanded, "Lift your hands."

"Don't use too much," Tess warned. "I've wasted so much already."

The ointment soothed and warmed, not nearly as hot as it needed to be to comfort Tommie. "Hurry, Luke. It's getting cold."

Luke's fingers circled her palms, bringing ease to the blistered skin, sending heat of another kind up her arm to settle into every pore. "Enough." She pulled away from his comfort and the impulse to give in to his touch. Tommie's good health depended on her.

Like a sinner being chased by the hounds of purgatory, Tess stripped her son of the rain-soaked nankeens. She cupped the barely warm salve in her hands and let it stream over his hip and leg. Despairing at the cold white chill that beaded the surface of his skin, she began to rub his leg briskly only to discover the fever beneath.

"My y-yeg," he sobbed. "You h-hurt my yeg. It hurts, Mommie. It hurts real bad."

"It'll be better soon, darling," she crooned, but he pulled away.

"No, I want Yuke. Mista Yuuuuke!"

"Luke's here, but he's sick too."

"Yeave me ayone."

In spite of his fevered anger, Tess forced his hands down. He began to sniffle and cry for Luke. Her heart felt pierced to the core. Jealousy urged her to awkwardly touch his hair, but Tommie shied away even from that tentative touch.

"Tommie?" Luke stood beside her now, looking large and protective. No wonder her son had called to him. Didn't she rely on that same strength? Didn't he always manage to see them through? She envied her son in that moment, for the unequivocal love he and the bounty hunter shared.

"He wants you." Fighting the struggle within more than

the effort to lift her child into Luke's arms, Tess lost the battle to keep the jealousy from her tone.

Luke gladly accepted the boy as Tommie clung to him and buried his face into the bounty hunter's neck. "Don't cry, Tommie. It's all right, son. Hush now." Terror filled Luke. The heat beneath his touch assured him that if they didn't get the boy dry and out of this rain, everything would not be fine.

Tommie clung to Luke's neck like a lifeline, weighing next to nothing. Luke swallowed hard against the emotion building in his sore throat, but the lump refused to budge. He tried to clear it as Tommie began to shudder. "Shh! Shh now. I've got you, son. Don't cry anymore."

His hand pressed over the small back, feeling each heaving sob. Looking helplessly past the blond head at Tess, he noticed a glint of tears shimmering in her eyes. "Give me that buckskin and help Daggert get those mules. Tell him to hurry!"

She handed Luke the shirt, then turned. Luke watched as she raced over the slick grass, nearly stumbled, found her footing, then raced on. If Olivia had been half the mother Tess Harper was, maybe . . . Luke refused to finish the thought, shaking it off as a product of the emotional turn of events.

Time crept by as the rain continued to pour. But as he had hoped, the buckskin kept the child fairly dry. Luke stuck the injured leg into one of the sleeves so the liniment would remain dry and threaded one arm through the other. The rest of the shirt wrapped around Tommie like a cocoon. Luke had dropped his hat somewhere near the wagon when he had first seen Tess beating out the flames on the blanket. Maybe when they rounded up the mules, Tess or Daggert would find the hat, and then he could shield the rain from Tommie's face.

As Luke peered into the distance, ignoring the cold that tightened his bare torso and shoulders, a shot rang out. From the same direction Tess had taken. *Don't let there be trouble,* he hoped reverently. *Not now.* Luke raced toward the schooner's burned-out hull. At least it offered some protection from the stark prairie. Through the graying shadows, two mules emerged ridden by Tess and Daggert. But where were the horses? "Did you hear the shot?"

"One of the mules broke its leg trying to run," Daggert informed him. "Had to put it out of its misery."

"The other?"

"Couldn't find hide nor hair of it. Seems kind of strange— there's no place for it to go. Couldn't catch the horses." Jim pushed his hat down over his eyes, letting the rain drizzle from its brim.

"Mule's probably down somewhere. Couldn't find it in this high grass unless you know exactly where it fell. My guess is the horses will hitch up with Chisholm's remuda. We'll make do with Jack and Jenny till we find the herd."

Luke's gaze locked onto Jim's hat. "We need to shield the boy's face from the rain. He's fairly dry otherwise. I'd be obliged if you'd give me your hat."

Jim hesitated, making Luke wonder if the man had any common decency inside him. Finally the gambler relented and handed over his hat. "He gonna be all right?"

Luke nodded. "Soon as I saddle up and we can get him to Chisholm's camp. Hope they got a dry spot, 'cause the boy's gonna need it."

He started to hand Tommie to Tess, but the child complained. "Guess you better ride with Jim." Luke patted the child. "Your mama's going to hold you until I get mounted, then she can hand you back to me. Won't you, Mom?"

"Of course," she assured her son, hiding her feelings behind a smile.

In that one unselfish moment, Luke fell in love with Tess Harper. It didn't matter what she felt. Tommie's well-being came first. As rain streaked down his face and dropped to his bare torso, Luke thought he would burst with pride for Tess and weep with pity for the love he had offered his own mother which she'd chosen to ignore.

Settling into the saddle, Luke accepted Tommie and the trust Tess showed. "Don't worry, I'll watch him like he were my own."

"I know, Luke. I know."

Before he could question her tone, she turned and accepted Daggert's hand to mount. The sight of her threading her arms around the gambler's waist was unsettling to Luke. He almost felt her doing the same to him now, pressing her breasts comfortably against his back.

But he needed to put his mind to other things . . . to the boy's health. "Chisholm's not far out. Ride north and listen for the bawl of cattle. Just keep your ears pinned for a constant rumble."

"Stampede?"

Jim voiced the question rising in Tess's mind.

"A herd spooks easy. You saw what happened to the mules." He looked at Daggert, then at Tess. "If that happens, ride like there's range selling for a penny a pasture."

"Can we outrun a stampede?" Tess's gaze searched the prairie. Where could they run?

"Anything's possible as long as one of these mules don't balk."

"And if it does?" Caution filled Tess's tone.

Jim patted her hand reassuringly. "Then hope to hell it ain't the one under us."

Chapter Sixteen

"Did you hear that?"

"The coyotes?" Tess listened to a lobo bay at the now visible stars. The rain had stopped a half hour ago as the wind drove the storm clouds south.

Tess strained to separate the night sounds and finally heard not only the mournful bay but a low singing. A good singing voice crooned "Beyond the Heather Morn," a song from the Scottish Highlands about star-crossed lovers.

A faint breeze stirred, bringing the unmistakable odor of cattle and upturned prairie beneath their hooves. In the distance, dark forms took shape on the horizon. The coyote stilled, silenced by the cowboy's song and the answering bawl of cattle.

Suddenly a big longhorn trotted into sight. Then another and another. The lead steer halted, lifting his head sharply.

"Don't move," Luke warned, reining the mule to an abrupt halt in front of Daggert's mount.

Tess felt Jim's arms tighten on the reins and his stomach clench against possible danger. She strengthened her hold around the gambler's waist in the event they must run. "Is it a stampede?" she asked innocently.

Luke's voice cracked in a half-joking, half-warning tone. "Not yet. And we don't want to give them reason." The longhorn walked a step or two toward them.

Tess watched Jim's right hand slide slowly to his gun, lift it and ease back on the hammer. The click echoed into the night. The big steer twitched an ear at them but kept his eyes trained on Luke's mule.

"That's not a smart thing to do, Daggert," Luke condemned Jim's action. "You shoot and we'll all be trampled."

A man in a yellow rain slicker rode into view, still singing below his broad-brimmed hat. He took a look at them, wiped a sleeve across his handlebar mustache and kept right on singing. But the words no longer followed the Scottish tune.

"The herd's uneasy; speak low and confident," he crooned. "Ol' Get-Me-There's full of sass and a bit skittish tonight."

The big steer ducked his head as he moved up a step. Tess almost saw his nostrils flare. *Well, Get-Me-There, old fella, I'd like nothing better than to get me out of here.*

"It's the woman," the drover sang. "They're used to the wild smell of my drovers. Osage, Cheyenne, Creek. Hardly get nervous 'bout a bear or cat anymore 'cause the men wear skins. But they've had no dealings with a lady and her scents. So just bring the mules in slow and sit powerfully still, ma'am. A rustle of skirts and you'll set off the whole lot of 'em. They'll run you clear into Tuesday."

"We need your help, sir," Tess insisted, careful to keep her voice calm. "My son is ill."

Luke spoke in an equally low tone. "Jesse Chisholm, this is Mrs. Contessa Harper, the woman you asked about." He nodded toward the gambler. "You've met Daggert. Now, if you will, this boy's burning with fever and he needs to get dry or he's gonna be powerful sick."

Jim had said their trek across Indian territory made news in Wichita, but she thought he meant to flatter her in some odd way. "Is there any chance we can build a fire to heat up medicine for my son?" she asked. "I don't know if I'll be able to find the right herbs this late at night, but something will turn up. If you or your men have salve to spare, I could crush the herbs into it and make him a plaster. Our . . . Mr. Reeves's wagon burned a few miles back and we've lost everything, you see.''

''A dun and sorrel skirted the left flank of the herd a while back,'' Chisholm informed them. ''Recognized the dun from this afternoon. Told the Cheyenne riding swing to rope and put 'em with the change-outs. Figured something unfortunate had happened to you folks. Glad to see you're still sporting scalps.''

Tess reached up to smooth her hair.

''Eaaasy, ma'am. Never know what'll set off a herd. No need to worry about my drovers, if you're thinking it won't be safe in camp. They're plenty glad to be working for the North. We're taking these cows to forts out in Indian territory and on to others in New Mexico.''

She realized that he prattled in a low monotone to soothe the beasts after her abrupt movement.

''A boy, you say?'' Chisholm reined half-quarter, slow and precise. ''Just keep on talking, ma'am, and follow me. Seems Ol Get-Me-There's took a liking to you. We like to think we decide where the herd's gonna bed down for the night, but Get-Me-There takes a notion to differ with us now and again. The herd will follow his lead.''

''Bless you,'' Tess whispered at the lead steer as Jim followed the trail boss through the divided sea of hide and hoof.

As the second mule fell into step behind the first, Luke clutched Tommie a bit closer. The boy stirred. Luke patted him reassuringly. Couldn't waste time letting the skittish longhorn make up its mind whether or not he liked the boy. ''You sure have a way with malefolk, Mrs. Harper,'' Luke praised.

Tess chuckled, rich and low, daring to strike the tune Chisholm had left off, ''Only the bull-headed ones.''

A grin curved Luke's mouth even as his shoulders balked from the constant pressure of cradling the child, but watching Tessa ride ahead of him made Luke forget the discomfort. The Kansas moon outlined all the reasons she attracted him, but it was the hidden Tess he liked the most. The gentle laugh. The flare of anger. The touch of reassurance that showed she cared.

The strange sight of a woman riding up to the camp forced the men to concentrate on the beans in their tins. Two of the buckskinned drovers got on their horses and started for the herd strung out to the west of camp.

Their departure drew Luke's ire. "They got something against the widow?"

"Against any woman riding into a man's job." Chisholm reined up short. He dismounted and a boy of no more than fourteen sauntered up and took the leather straps from his boss. "See to the mules as well, Garth. The dun and sorrel that came in today belong to these two gentlemen. Make sure their stock is rubbed down good and fed an extra helping of grain."

"Yessir, Mr. Chisholm."

Tess thanked the tow-headed lad as he helped her dismount, then lifted Tommie from Luke's arm so he could do the same.

"Looks like Cookie already has a fire going. I'll see what kind of salve he's got put back." Chisholm tipped his hat to Tess. "Give me a few minutes and we'll clear a place in the chuck wagon for the boy. Sorry I don't have better accommodations, ma'am, but we're used to sleeping out here rain or shine."

Offering a sincere smile, Tess quickly looked back at her son's wan face. "We appreciate your trouble. Thank you most kindly."

"Pleasure to have someone so good to look at in our midst. Cook's over here."

As Tess followed the man's jingle of spurs toward the cook-fire, each Indian drover kept his attention on other matters. The Anglo cowboys touched their hats but didn't say anything. Those who had lounged now stood stiffly as if they were being scrutinized for entry into Heaven.

"Ahh, Mrs. Harper. So good to have you with us." A thin, crane-necked man wiped flour from his hands onto the apron strung around his waist, offered his palm, then thought better of it. "Charles Peabody. Cookie, to these ruffians all. So happy to make your acquaintance."

The booming tone and British accent were startling in comparison to the man's waifish physique. Beneath his beak of a nose and flaming red mustache, and above his fiery beard, the most beautiful span of white teeth flashed her a genuine welcome.

"How do you do, Mr. Peabody."

Jim walked past his host and stood next to the skillet of beans. "Can introductions wait until later? I'm sure we're all hungry."

"Mr. Daggert, is it?" Peabody's nose lifted in disdain. "Would you be so kind as to allow the lady first honor?"

Tess jostled Tommie as her arms began to tremble from holding him so long. "Please let him go ahead. I must see to my son."

"Your son? This dear little thing?" Peabody rushed to look. "May I?" Receiving her nod, he unwrapped the buckskin and peered closer. "Dear me, but he's simply stunning. Oh, and quite ill, the poor fellow." Looking at Chisholm, Peabody furrowed his brows. "Now why wasn't I told about this?"

"You didn't give me time, Cookie."

Peabody waved a hand as if to dismiss the trail boss. "Well, yes, yes, of course. You men serve yourselves. I intend to help this fine lady with her darling child. May I, Mrs. Harper?" He took Tommie from her arms before she could answer. "My, but this fever is a regular conflagration, isn't it? Don't you worry for a moment, though. I have just the thing to cure him."

Tommie began to whimper softly. "Y-Yuuke."

"Puke, did you say?" Peabody nearly shrieked and held Tommie out away from him.

Luke walked up to the aproned man and took the child from the cook's outstretched arms. "He said *Luke*. That's me. The boy has trouble saying his L's. Got a problem with that?"

The firelight revealed Peabody's large Adam's apple as it dipped, held as if he had a hard time swallowing, then rose again slowly. "Not a solitary one, Mr. Luke."

"Reeves."

"Mr. Reeves."

Unable to endure seeing the delightful Englishman so flustered, Tess gently touched his arm. "Thank you, Mr. Peabody . . . Charles. It was kind of you to offer. But Tommie's become such close friends with Luke, he rarely wants me to help him. In this state of discomfort, I think it's best we let Luke see to him, don't you?"

"Of course, my dear," Peabody replied, regaining his sense of self-assurance. "As his mother, you know best." His mouth twisted to one side in a conspiratorial whisper, "This Reeves is rather imposing, isn't he?"

"To be sure," she answered. Let the man discover Luke's better humor for himself. "Mr. Chisholm said you would allow us the use of the chuck wagon for my son."

"I'd be honored, madam. Wait here and I'll arrange everything." Armed with a mission, Peabody forgot his leeriness of Luke and set to work. A lantern flared behind the canvas covering the chuck wagon.

"Do bring him here, Mr. Reeves."

Tess followed quickly behind, watching as Luke lifted Tommie into the cook's care.

"Now get some water, will you, Mr. Reeves? The bucket is hanging near the front wheel and the water barrel is strapped next to it."

"He doesn't need more water. He's soaked."

Peabody sighed impatiently. "I don't mean to argue, but it is necessary. Now if you'll just—"

"I'll get it," Tess said, trying to run interference between the two men. Luke wouldn't let the boy out of his sight with Tommie calling his name over and over. "Let Mr. Reeves calm Tommie. I'll fetch whatever you need."

Tess headed for the barrel. Finding the bucket, she filled it to a manageable level and bit back pain as her hands gripped the handle and several blisters popped. Putting her mind on other things, she wondered how a man such as Charles Peabody ever got involved with a herd of cattle being driven by a mixed group of Indians headed to New Mexico. Better yet, did he happen to have a pair of ladies' gloves in his possession?

When she returned, Tommie was much calmer. Luke quietly talked to him. Tess set the bucket by Peabody and asked about the salve. Taking the jar he handed to her, she added, "Do you have any cayenne pepper and sarsaparilla?"

"Completely out of sarsaparilla, but I gathered some wild sorrel and hops. Either one are good substitutes to add to the pepper. So young." Pity etched his features. "Rheumatism?"

"Inflammation of the joints, and one leg is a bit shorter than the other."

"Then we'll use them all. I have plenty and this should reduce the inflammation."

Luke bent on the other side of Tommie, staring down at the small blond head and narrow shoulders. Tommie looked pale and tiny in comparison with Luke's dark hair and broad bare expanse.

Tess knew how comforting it was to be cradled in that strong embrace. The bounty hunter chose that moment to look up and she suspected he knew what she was thinking.

"I'll dip the cloth and keep it on his forehead, if one of you can rub in the mixture." She held up her palms as if reluctant to show them, but thought it necessary. "I don't think I'll be able to apply enough pressure."

Taking the cloth and bucket, Luke motioned to Peabody. "You see to her hands and get her to eat something. I'll take care of the boy. Got any dry wrapping I can use to replace this?" He set the bucket down and began to unwrap the cloth binding Tommie's leg.

Peabody slid open a drawer built into the chuck wagon and pulled out a skein of cotton binding. "Use all you need. There's plenty more."

"Now go on, Tess, and quit your worrying," Luke said. "I've got everything under control. He's not burning with fever. We'll have this puny fever out of him in no time."

She allowed Peabody to take her elbow and guide her out of the wagon, but not before glancing back in uncertainty. "Mop his head with a cold rag. Wipe off the old liniment before I bring you the new and—"

"Peabody, get her out of here."

"With pleasure, Mr. Reeves." Charles exited the wagon and anticipated the thrill of sharing some gossip with the woman. Oh, the stories he had to tell. "My pleasure, indeed."

"He's *my* son." Tess's temper flared because she was so tired. She sounded petty, even to herself, but Tommie was all she had.

"What do you want me to do, Tess?" Luke demanded. He had expected the anger long before now and admired her restraint. Even the thought of Tommie having loved Clifton first struck an arrow of envy through Luke's own heart every time he thought about it.

Tess relented, overcoming her jealous thoughts. "He wants you. Forget what I said. I'm tired." She accepted Peabody's hand helping her down. "Just remember, he's little."

For such a small mite, the boy possessed a wail of a banshee.

"I know it hurts, Tom. I'll be gentler."

Tommie's wail died into whimpers. Sobs shook the small body until Luke stopped what he did to make certain he hadn't accidentally hurt the boy in some unseen manner. The bounty hunter checked him over thoroughly but didn't see anything. The hip and leg were well massaged, newly linimented and wrapped. The binding wasn't too tight. From the press of Luke's hand against the boy's forehead, the fever seemed well under control.

"What's wrong, son? Why are you crying?"

"Thammy!"

"What about Thammy?" *Oh God, not that. Tommie didn't need that.*

"He's dead. Burned up."

"I'm sorry, son. I didn't see your critter when I was carrying you out of the wagon. I just didn't think to look for him.''

"You reckon he went to Hell?''

Luke stretched out beside the boy so they were eye to eye. "What makes you think Thammy went to Hell?''

Tommie gulped. "Preacher at the fort said if you go to Hell, you burn up.''

Luke muttered an oath. His God didn't send disciples to preach fear. His God promised forgiveness of wrongdoings if one sincerely hadn't mean the harm. His God offered love and the courage to be wrong so a soul could find the strength to be right. "Thammy was a good salamander, wasn't he?'' Luke asked.

A tear trickled down Tommie's cheek, and Luke wiped it off with one thumb.

"The bestest.''

"Then he went to Heaven.''

"With Daddy?'' The three-year-old's voice rose an octave in hope.

Is that what his mother told him? "Yes, with your father. Don't you think that would be nice for Thammy to meet your pa and your pa to have something of yours to play with?''

What else had she told him? For a reason Luke couldn't fathom he felt a deep desire to tell Tommie the truth. Maybe it was the boy's trust in him. Maybe it was his own need to be able to look the child in the eye and not have this one secret always hounding him. But fear of losing Tommie's respect and friendship made Luke hesitate and reconsider. Was cleansing his conscience worth the possible loss?

"Mista Yuke . . . was my daddy good?''

The expression on Tommie's face looked years wiser. "Why do you ask, Tom?''

"If Daddy was mean, how did he get to Heaven?''

How was he supposed to explain such things to a three-year-old, when his own opinion of good and bad differed so much from other folks' views? Like a gift from Heaven, an idea sprung to mind which might help him resolve both his and Tommie's troubled questions. "You know how you accidentally left Thammy in the wagon and he died?''

''Yessir.'' Tommie's tone was meek and repenting.

Luke nudged the boy's chin up with his knuckle. ''Well, a few folks might call that bad or mean. Others would call it an accident—the wisest choice. So everyone has their own idea of good and mean.''

''What 'bout God? What do He think?''

''Well, I can't speak for Him, but if He's as fair a judge as the Bible says, then I'd say He figures whatever you feel in your heart ought to persuade His decision. Did you mean to leave Thammy and burn him up?''

Tommie's head shook emphatically. ''No sir, Mista Yuke.''

''Then there you have it!'' Luke tapped Tommie's shoulder. ''The Lord knows that and doesn't consider you mean. Now if you left your salamander in there on purpose—''

''No sir, I din't.''

''Then it was just a plain old mistake. And God allows mistakes. There's only ten rules you've got to follow for certain. The rest of them you can break once in a while, as long as you don't mean to.''

''Whew!'' Tommie breathed a sigh of relief that left him looking like a sack of half-packed flour. Luke hadn't realized how tense the boy had been over the matter.

''You know, Tommie. That goes for us big folks too.'' Luke felt scared facing the child with the truth. More frightened than when he had looked down the barrel of the fastest gun he'd ever drawn against or faced that slew of Chiricahuas in Apache Pass. Dreaded it even more than Olivia's looks of disapproval. ''We make mistakes.''

''You, Mista Yuke?''

''Yes, me, Tom. I made an awful one and it hurt some people I really care about.''

''You din't mean to, did you, Mista Yuke?''

''God knows I didn't, son.''

''I tell 'em for ya. I tell 'em you a good man.''

Luke had often heard the old expression ''taking your heart in your hands'' but never understood what it meant until now.

For so many years he had no heart to speak of. Locked behind a wall of stone, he only recently learned that it could be loved and broken within the blinking of an eye. In the telling of a truth.

With my heart in my hands, Luke thought and uttered the words that might forever rip it from his chest. "It's you I hurt, Tom. You and your mother."

Puzzlement etched Tommie's fair features.

Sweat beaded along Luke's hairline and upper lip. "There's no easy way to tell you, Tom. But I made a mistake and I'll be sorry for it the rest of my life. Though that won't bring your daddy back, will it? Forgive me, Tommie . . . I killed your father." The facts of the incident came out in a slow confession but seemed hollow justification.

The green eyes staring back at him first denied Luke's words, then widened, filled with shock, anger and hurt. It was the hurt worst of all that gripped Luke's heart like a fist and threatened to make it stop beating.

A thousand questions raced across Tommie's expression as the boy fought to decipher all that Luke had said. The bounty hunter saw the child remembering, rejecting, analyzing their conversation in his own limited capabilities, then finally drawing some conclusion.

The muscles of Luke's body grew taut as he steeled himself against the boy's fury, as surely as if he faced a hanging judge's verdict.

"You tell my Mommie?" Tommie sniffled.

"She knows."

"Her don't think you meant to?"

"She says she believes I didn't do it on purpose." Luke met him eye to eye. "You ask her yourself. Don't take my word."

Tommie cupped his palm against Luke's scars in the same manner his mother had on that fateful day in June. "I don't think you did neither, Mista Yuke."

Luke crushed the boy to him.

Chapter Seventeen

The smell of fryback and coffee wafting through the hole in the canvas greeted Tess as she woke. Her eyes fluttered open to a more delicious smell . . . cinnamon! Mr. Peabody promised something special to celebrate the boy's recovery and he had kept his word. Cinnamon *anything* was Tommie's favorite.

Tommie's eyes opened and he sat up quickly. Though movement was awkward, he managed to stand. "You smell it, Mommie? Can I have some?"

Tess's heart melted as pain darted across his small face, but he ignored it in favor of Peabody's confection. "Of course you can, darling. Just let Mama straighten her hair."

Hearing the two voices from the wagon, Luke stepped up to the back with a tin in his hand. A twist of steaming sourdough, sprinkled with cinnamon and sugar, nearly filled his plate, and he had already eaten three. "Peabody said to take as many as I wanted, but gave me a what-for look when I went back this last time. I told him I was bringing them to you." He set the plate down. "Morning. How'd you sleep?"

When Tess roused, Luke thought he'd trade his soul for the sight of watching her wake morning after morning.

174

"Mista Luke!" Tommie hobbled across the wagon to the bounty hunter and lifted his arms.

Luke opened his arms and the three-year-old clasped his neck without restraint.

"My leg feels better." Tommie pulled back to face him. "You scratched me, Mista Luke. We better shave again."

The rapt look softening the hard lines of Luke's face caused Tess's heart to tighten in her chest. There was no denying the love the bounty hunter felt for Tommie, nor that Tommie returned it. Why did she feel so envious when all she had ever wanted was a man to love both her and her boy? She suddenly realized that Tommie had said every L correctly. "You said Luke and leg! Tommie, you said them correctly."

God, this feels good. Luke marveled at how such a little hug could make a man's heart swell with so much pride. "He's been practicing hard, haven't you, little man?"

Tess started for Luke, then as she reached him she realized what she had intended to do. They stood inches apart, face to face, studying Tommie. Meeting each other's gaze. A closeness stole over them, binding them in some indefinable way. "Thank you," was all she could manage, but wanted to say so much more. *Thank you for teaching my boy, for loving him. Thank you for coming into my life.*

"It's fun and he taughted me everything. Sometimes I git mixed up, but sometimes I don't!"

Gathering her wayward curls, Tess tried to brush them upward with her fingers. The mass was too unruly without the strict bristles of a brush to master it. "What else has he taught you?" she asked, finding the morning too pleasant to be disgusted about her hair.

"Leave it down. It looks pretty in the sunlight." Luke shared a conspiratorial glance with Tommie. "Should we tell her?"

"Sure." Tommie rocked back on his heels. "I teached Mr. Yu—Luke how to fish for spiders."

"Spiders!" Tess grimaced. "Where? How? Are there any

175

here? Whatever for? Don't you dare get one anywhere near me . . . either of you!''

Luke and Tommie laughed together. The bounty hunter stared at the boy. ''I guess that just about covers it all, don't you?''

''Mommie hates spiders, Mista Luke. I know . . . 'cause I catched one and put it in her bonnet. She scweamed and scweamed and scweamed. Then she whooped my bottom and I scweamed and scweamed and sweamed too.''

Tess wagged a finger at her son. ''And you remember that, young man.'' One look at Luke and the finger changed directions, aiming at the older of the fishermen. ''Don't go getting any ideas, Lucas Reeves. I may be faint of heart where spiders are concerned, but I have my methods for vindication.''

Luke spread a hand across his chest in feigned innocence. ''You suggest I would do anything so devious?''

''If you thought you could get away with it.''

''You know me better than I thought you did.''

''Well enough.''

The teasing took on a serious tone. ''Not as much as I'd like you to.''

''You're the one who says there's not enough time for such matters. I seem to recall you saying something about a job that would keep you away.''

''Ouch, the lady has claws!''

''And feelings, too, Mr. Reeves.''

''Now, Tessa, I told you why.''

''Yes, you told me, but I don't have to agree with you nor like your decision.'' She suddenly insisted the wayward curls do her bidding. When he looked like that, as if he would devour her slowly piece by piece, she could not remember why they argued or what to use as her defense.

''Why, Mrs. Harper, you certainly look ravishing this morning!'' Charles Peabody sidled up to the opening in the back of the chuck wagon, nudging Luke over with a tin. Piled atop its rounded surface, cinnamon confections were stacked three layers deep. ''This big galoot tried to eat me out of pot and

176

pantry, but I see he kept his word and brought you one of my little doings.''

"Oh, he's good at keeping his word,'' Tess taunted.

Luke grinned. "The second best thing I'm good at.''

Peabody blushed before Tess did. "Well, yes, of course. We all have our talents, don't we? Are you hungry, small one?''

Tommie squealed with delight and hurriedly asked his mother if he might have one.

"Be sure to thank Mr. Peabody.''

Though he had to scoot it out from one of the lower rows, Tommie grabbed the biggest roll on the tin. He yelled as his hand jerked back instantly, "Hot damn!''

"Thomas James Harper! You apologize this minute.''

His brows veed together in rebellion. "It's hot, Mommie.''

"Apologize this moment.''

The boy turned around. "I'm sorry, Mista Pea Potty. But you made it hot as Hell.''

"Thomas!'' Tess reprimanded again.

"Well, 'at's what Brace Williams said—not me!''

Luke chuckled and shook his head. "You better stop while you're ahead, boy. Here, take mine. It's cooled off. When these aren't so damned . . . blamed hot, I'll bring you another.''

"Can I eat 'em up on Talon?''

Luke glanced in the direction of the remuda. "Ask Jim if he'll bring over the dun. But don't go wandering off. This isn't our camp, and you could easily get lost.''

"I be careful. Yet me down, Yuke.''

Luke lifted him up, then lowered him to the ground.

"Yook at all 'em cows. Must be hunnerds of 'em!''

"Keep your distance. They need to figure you out first before you take a closer look.''

Tess watched as Luke disappeared from view to introduce Tommie to the drovers still in camp.

"Indians!''

Her son's declaration made Tess wonder how everything

could be so exciting to him. Nothing ever seemed uninteresting to Tom. But then she supposed the world was new to him and everything held a challenge. She hoped that age and experience would never take that from him. Just as nothing or no one would ever take him from her.

"Take your time, Mrs. Harper. The men just came in off the watch and I've gotta get this bunch fed. We won't be striking camp for another half hour at least." Peabody stood there, watching her rise and stretch. He seemed enamored.

Tess began to feel uncomfortable under his blatant adoration and thought she would be less a spectacle out in the open where she could move about. She suspected he was the sort of man who did not pursue women. "Would you have a comb or brush, Mr. Peabody? I'm afraid I've lost everything but the clothes on my back."

Peabody jolted into action. "Oh, but of course. How stupid of me. I have better than a comb or brush. I have an entire vanity tucked away in here. May I?" He pointed to one of the drawers.

"Certainly."

The thin man wore a yellow vest with green-striped suspenders and a dove gray shirt. His red hair had been parted down the middle and was slicked back over two ears that put Jack and Jenny to shame. Blue-gray eyes contrasted sharply to his carroty-red hair. Peabody looked like a plume, dipped in various colors. He reminded Tess of those strange-looking ostriches from Africa she'd once seen being transported up the Mississippi. Peabody looked just as gangly . . . long-necked, long-legged, plumes and a beak of a nose.

Tess hid a smile behind her hand as he turned around.

"Here it is!" he proclaimed with satisfaction.

A small ornately carved box opened to reveal a mirror, comb, hair brush and hairpins, clothes brush and a bar of soap. "Thank you so much, Mr. Peabody."

"*Charles,*" he insisted. "Please. And do consider letting

178

me arrange your hair. I dressed some of the finest ladies in England.''

As the expression on Tess's face must have warned him about the uncomfortable feeling his statement had stirred within her, he raised a palm to his mouth. "How uncouth of me. You Americans say things so differently. What I meant was that I'm long accustomed to styling women's hair. In fact, I'm quite proficient at it. The only reason I no longer conduct the practice is that some brute of an oaf insinuated I needed a more masculine profession. That's why I've resorted to this.'' He waved a hand at the chuck wagon. "I wanted to show everyone I could do a man's job as well as the next. I simply *prefer* hairdressing. Such artistic satisfaction, you know.''

"Think you could do something with this disaster?''

"Of course, my dear. I would love the challenge. But first come meet the men. If I keep them too long, Chisholm will have my fry pan, as they say.''

As Tess stepped out from the wagon, a flood of drovers descended near the cookfire. Before her stood a tall, lanky Anglo. From the stance he took and the swell of his chest, he too considered himself something special.

"Ethan Payne,'' Charles introduced Tess to the man, "bid good day to Mrs. Contessa Harper.''

Tess resisted the urge to curtsey. Instead, she nodded politely and offered a quick smile.

"So this is Tess Harper.'' The slur in Payne's drawl said he approved too well. "Pretty as they claim.''

She was puzzled at the man's manners. Uneasiness crept through her. Could he be someone from her past? There were so many. It was so long ago. Was he the one who had compromised her? If only she had seen the attacker's face!

Needing to back away from the fretful questions darting through her mind, Tess asked the identity of the young wrangler who took care of their mounts.

"Brace Williams,'' Charles informed her. "Fourteen and feisty as General Sherman.''

"You sure are beautiful!" Brace complimented. "Do all women from Fort Smith look so pretty? Will any more be along soon? How do you manage to pin up all that hair? It didn't look so long last night."

"Brace!" Charles placed a restraining arm about the boy. "Ask Mrs. Harper one question at a time . . . later. After she's eaten."

Several of the men offered her a place to sit, but Tess took her meal near the wheel of the chuck wagon. All eyes seemed to watch her every move, and she found it difficult to lift the spoon to her mouth without feeling someone's attention following the path from tin to lips.

"I'm not hungry now." She offered the half-eaten meal to Peabody. "Perhaps I can save a biscuit for later."

"Then if you'd like, I'll tend to your hair while the others finish their meal."

Luke's breakfast churned in his stomach as he watched the Englishman scoop up the brush and move behind Tess to tend to her hair. The man's hands were big for such a small fellow and worked the snarls from Tess's long, sun-kissed curls with ease. When Tess sighed with pleasure and relaxed beneath Peabody's efforts, Luke felt his own muscles grow taut and strung like a bow.

His eyes narrowed as he watched her accept the man's intimacy and let the stranger draw the brush delicately through her strands, easing out the tangles.

"You're as good as you say," Tess complimented.

Luke wondered what else he was good at and when the hell they had time to discuss such things.

"I'm recommended highly by the ladies of the court."

"You did it for them?"

"Each and every one."

Luke grumbled. When Tess opened her eyes to stare at him, he glared back with a sour face. "Excuse me."

"It must be very difficult being away from them." She

softly touched Peabody's hand in sympathy, stopping the brush on a downward stroke.

Anger crept through Luke. He knew that touch well. Did she offer it so easily to everyone? As the Englishman lifted a fistful of her thick hair and let it cascade into a golden waterfall, desire twisted through Luke. He could almost smell the fresh lavender fragrance, feel its silken thickness. His fingertips itched to touch her.

Tess shivered visibly as the man swept her hair up off her neck and bared the nape.

"Rapunzel had hair like this," Peabody informed her, brushing strands of gold upward and pinning them. "The color of sunrise. Soft as down. Rarely have I touched anything quite so beautiful."

Fighting the temptation to cram that brush down the Briton's throat, Luke reminded himself that Peabody was only brushing her hair, not making love to Tess. But as the Englishman's long fingers eased beneath the heavy strands and skimmed over the curve of her neck, they seemed to trace the hairline with a caress.

Jealousy, green and raging, reared its head. *There's only one way to stop this. To hell with what the others think.* Luke strode over to the small man and deliberately looked imposing, placing both fists on his hips and willing himself to tower even more than he already did.

"Do you n-need something, Mr. Reeves?" Peabody stared up at the foreboding man. The cook swallowed hard and his Adam's apple felt as if it stuck.

"Show me how to do what you're doing." Luke's voice was so low that few others could hear, yet it held a definite growl.

Without breaking the rhythm, Luke took the brush and completed the stroke Peabody had started. As he brushed with slow, gentle movements, a sense of satisfaction spread through him when Tess sighed and relaxed.

"That feels good."

Running his hand lightly through her hair, Luke leaned close. "Sure does."

Tess sat up straight, suddenly aware of Luke's closeness. A rush of sensation radiated from the pit of her stomach. Her breath lodged in her throat as a longing, piercing and sweet, claimed her.

Luke's body responded when she sucked in her breath, disclosing the desire stirring within her. She looked up and her eyes warmed like glazed emeralds. *Dangerous. She was just too damned dangerous. She knows how to make a man lose his mind . . . forget his word.*

"Get ready to ride," Luke commanded roughly. "We'll move out when the herd does. We leave in twenty minutes."

She glanced at him in surprise, wondering what had irritated him. "But Mr. Peabody said he had some buckskins that might fit me. I don't think I can stand this"—she touched the hem of her dress—"another moment longer."

Luke handed her the brush and gave the Englishman a go-to-Hell-in-a-channel-boat glare. "Better get to fitting into them, because we're moving out . . . now."

Tess knew better than to waste seconds arguing. Even so, she barely had time to change clothes. When she stepped out of the wagon dressed in the buckskins, she thought perhaps she had forgotten to put something on.

Luke stood there gawking as her hands smoothed down the supple deerhide that fit her like a tailor-made skin. The leggings were just as snug as the top, enhancing every detail of her fine figure.

She felt conspicuous and elated all in the same instant. In the Hot Springs bathhouse, she had not worn garments this revealing, so the buckskin felt a bit scandalous even though it covered everything her dress had. On the other hand, if it made Luke look at her like that, she might just wear it from now till Armageddon. Perhaps now he wouldn't leave her for that job which seemed so important.

"I'm ready. Shall I take the mule or one of the horses?"

"Take Talon," Luke grumbled, mounting behind Tommie

on one of the mules. "Daggert's packing the supplies Chisholm sold us on Jenny. Tom and I will share Jack. This ought to see us into Wichita where I can purchase some more supplies."

And a change of dresses, he added silently as she mounted. He refused to watch that pretty little buckskin bounce against the saddle from here to Colorado. The remaining distance to Wichita would be long enough to endure the distraction.

Chapter Eighteen

Topping the rise overlooking the junction of the Big and Little Arkansas Rivers, Tess witnessed a scene of such lush natural abundance she knew that the settlement was destined to become an important city.

Buffalo, fat and sleek, grazed and lay in the warm sun. Tipis and grass huts stretched for a mile along the river. Wichita served as a center of trade among several tribes. Luke had told her a bit of history about the area, saying he needed to prepare her for the unusual sight of so many friendly Indians. Wichita Indians loyal to the Union during the recent War Between the States took up residency here on the Osage Trail for protection from the Confederate tribes who were in dire straits now.

It was a new town, born overnight to meet the demands of white and red men alike who traveled the local trails and freighting routes. And from all Tess had learned, it promised to become one of the fastest growing settlements in Kansas.

A sprawling hodgepodge of structures rose in the distance. On the outskirts of town, a barrel-chested mule skinner took notice of the incoming party and shaded his eyes to peer closer at Tess. He started running down the center of the street yelling at the top of his lungs, "Here she comes! She's here! The white woman's here!"

Traders and mule skinners, Indians of every shape, size and tribe, began to gather and stopped conducting their business along the avenue to watch Tess ride in. An appreciative murmur rippled through the gang of men who doffed their hats in respect. Several took to spit-polishing their hair, dusting their vests and buckskins and wiping tobacco stains from their mouths. As she passed, Tess offered the briefest smile for the courtesy extended her, but did not meet anyone's gaze directly for fear they would think she favored one over the other.

"I'd say you'll have no trouble getting a room tonight." Jim's face lit with approval at the sight of several saloons in which he could ply his long-unused trade. An extended game of poker was just the sport he needed to wear off the trail dust.

"Look at all 'em Indians, Mommie." Tommie pointed to the rows of triangled lodges extending well into the horizon. "You ever seen so many tipis in the whole wide world?"

Absorbing the sights and sounds wholly foreign to one who had spent most of her married life avoiding this race of people, Tess answered honestly, "No, son. I haven't. But it's nice to see everyone getting along so well."

"That's because it's big profit for the traders to stay friends with these tribes," Luke informed her.

A large, strong-looking man with crow-black hair and clear blue eyes shouldered his way through the crowd. A wave of people parted to allow him room, displaying the respect he had apparently earned from the community. The man approached, waving them toward a hitching post. "Mrs. Contessa Harper?"

Tess glanced at Luke for approval. When he nodded consent, she acknowledged her identity. "Yes, I'm Tess Harper."

"I'd like to introduce myself. James Meade's my name. Got a trading ranch east of here at Towanda." The handsome man doffed his hat. "Welcome to Wichita. To you and your friends."

Luke reined up short where the man stood near a low-roofed

building. Bold painted letters advertised the establishment as
Don Carlos's Trading Post. Rough, blustering men crowded
along the avenue, watching Tess dismount. Luke cursed the
flex and give of the buckskin she wore, defining the lush wom-
anhood beneath.

The ant hill of activity in the public marketplace, carpeted
in a finely ground layer of dust, halted. Tradesmen quit hawk-
ing their wares, Indians stopped bartering blankets and pottery.
Shell-game operators, medicine showmen and black soft shoe
dancers momentarily lost their curious and gullible audiences
to the unusual attraction of Tess.

Uneasy about the intense attention given her, Tess wished
now she had stopped along the trail and changed her dress. A
quick glance at Don Carlos's shop window revealed two fashionable dresses she would give almost anything to purchase.
But the finery cost more than she could spare. Blinking away
her disappointment, she gave one last look at the white-
bordered muslin with the pattern of roses sewn into the
flounces. She would simply have to make do and endure the
buckskins despite the attention they drew.

Waving at Tess's retinue, now completely encircled by grinning, raw-boned men, Meade invited her to go with him and
see how the good people of Wichita would make her feel at
home.

To the townsmen he shouted, "Now you heard that. I don't
want any of you gentlemen sneaking a pinch for free. This is
a respectable lady, and I'll bust any man's head who tries to
worsen her!"

Ignoring a grumble from the disenchanted, he offered his
arm to Tess. She happened to glance at Luke and noticed his
face close into an unreadable mask. Could he be jealous?

Her gaze shifted to Jim. The gambler's expression seemed
rapt as he stared longingly toward the plentiful saloons. He
was finally in his element. Perhaps he would leave their company and forgo traveling on to Georgetown. Surprised that she
felt no disappointment at the prospect of losing Jim's added
security as scout, Tess knew without a doubt she would not

have the same reaction if Luke chose to abandon them.

It might do the bounty hunter good to think she could get along without him, however. He had brooded every since leaving Chisholm's camp.

Meade looked like a gladiator ready to bust a few lions' heads. Tommie gawked at the town's leader. Tess accepted Meade's arm, deciding he would suit her purpose just fine. "Thank you for your kind welcome, Mr. Meade."

"My pleasure, ma'am." He led them down Douglas Avenue at a fast clip. Turning into Main Street, the town's business center, Meade pointed out various establishments and described the horde of trail hands and Indians who used Wichita for trade.

Every storefront in town seemed dedicated to separating the visitor from his money. Red, white and blue banners hung across each door and window, reminding Tess that today was the nation's birthday . . . and Tommie's as well. She had forgotten! How could she afford a gift when every penny must see them to Georgetown?

She was given no time to mull, as the crowd and Meade urged her along. With the exception of a boardinghouse-hotel, a mercantile emporium, and a bank that Meade said wasn't full-throttled yet, the entire business community of Wichita was devoted to imbibing or to Indian trade. As the procession passed each establishment, more and more men began leaving the saloons to join the trailing crowd. Shouting and laughing, they ogled Tess, filling the air with verbal approval.

Bringing up the rear, Luke was hard pressed to keep them from rushing in to challenge Meade's warning. But the scowl on Luke's face forced them to back off a few paces.

Abruptly, Meade halted before a pleasant frame house with a covered front porch. Unlike any of the surrounding buildings, it was set back off the street and bordered by a low picket fence. The throng of trail hands and mule skinners crowded closer, watching her face expectantly.

"Used to be the sheriff's. We cleaned it up and painted it 'specially for you." Looking around the crowd, Meade's eyes lit with pride. "Nothing else like it in Wichita, maybe in the whole of Kansas!"

Tess tried not to gawk, searched desperately for something to say.

"What's the matter, Mrs. Harper?" Meade lowered his voice almost to a whisper as the men edged closer, straining to hear every word. "Don't you like it?"

"Like it? Oh, it's magnificent." She blinked, thinking maybe her vision was clouded from too much trail dust, too many nights of praying she was home and in her own bed. Too many nights of wanting a home of her own and not a borrowed one.

"Magnificent, she said!" he shouted. As he faced the enthralled audience, Meade's chest seemed to burst the seams of the shirt he wore. "Isn't that just about the finest word we ever heard, men? I knew we were doing a mighty fine job fixing it up, just didn't know it was magnificent." He turned to Tess. "Magnificent enough to call Wichita your home, Mrs. Harper?"

My home? Possibility filled Tess. Images of what could be. But wasn't Harper Hall waiting on them in Colorado? "Please don't be disappointed," she began, unwilling to let the man become too exuberant in his expectations, all the while disbelieving she was actually turning down the offer. "I love the house. Really I do. It's just that I can't accept your gift. I couldn't deprive the sheriff of his home, nor am I planning to stay."

"Tell her, Meade. Tell her how much we want her to stay!" one of the trail hands yelled from the edge of the crowd. "Unless you want me to hog-tie her and make the little lady's mind up for her."

"Shut your mouth, mister." Luke jabbed his finger at the man who spoke, then glared around at the rest of the crowd. "Mrs. Harper has a mind of her own and you'd do well not to butt in." Flushed with anger, he knotted his left hand into a fist. He couldn't take them all on, but he could bust a few jaws as he went down.

188

"Enough!" Meade roared. "This is no way to welcome folks to our fair city. Let's show them some hospitality and maybe she'll change her mind." Opening the gate, he waited until she, Tommie, Luke and Jim passed through before shutting it off to others. To the crowd he announced, "Now you all get the fixings underway and rouse up Professor Kettle. Tell him Mrs. Harper's arrived and we're ready for the festivities to begin."

"What sort of festivities?" Tess asked in unison with Luke.

Meade glanced at Luke, paused, seemed to remember something, then scratched his temple. "You're Reeves . . . the bounty hunter."

"So?"

Meade waved them toward the front door of the house. "So . . . I'd like a word with you before you get busy with some of the other finer . . . er . . . offerings of Wichita."

"I'm already committed to a job. Not looking for another."

"I appreciate a man who finishes what he starts. I'm talking later. I'd like to buy you a drink, but for now let me get Mrs. Harper settled."

An ominous feeling swept over Tess. Meade didn't look like the kind of man who just chitchatted. So that meant some sort of official business was to transpire, and she didn't like the sound of that, at all. Something stirred in the wind, and intuitively she knew it had nothing to do with goodwill and brotherhood.

As she climbed the steps to the house, a premonition made her wary, and she found herself wishing they could just take the next stage to Colorado.

"Come in, Mrs. Harper . . ."

Meade sounded like the spider inviting the fly. Goose flesh beaded up Tess's neck, pooling in an icy tingle at the top of her head.

". . . Welcome to what I hope is your new home."

Tess followed him into the house, grateful he didn't insist upon showing her anything but the parlor. Luke stood, refusing a seat on one of the chairs that matched the rosewood davenport where Tess and Tommie settled. He chose to look out the nearest window with his back to the wall.

"Come now, don't look so skittish, Mrs. Harper."

Meade's mouth quirked in a small smile, yet Tess couldn't rid herself of the idea that he meant to intimidate Luke. "What is it you want from us?" she asked, making certain she included Luke in her request.

The town leader's smile froze and his eyes narrowed as he inspected her.

Tess suppressed a shudder. The man resembled a snake sizing up its victim to see if she was worth the price of challenging a fiercer predator.

"I admire a woman who prefers to control her own fate, Mrs. Harper," Meade complimented. "Building empires happens to be my game. But last year I've lost three sheriffs, one run out of town and two others murdered. Staring straight down my throat is another trading season. Newspapers all over the East herald my Wichita as the most progressive town in Kansas. In the West, too, for that matter. Wichita will be the hub for all trails west."

"What does that have to do with us?" Tess asked.

"Though it offers the promise of a beef industry that can reach every kitchen in the nation"—Meade's gaze examined Tess, leaving approval in its wake—"Wichita lacks two vital ingredients for success. We need good women to attract the finer elements of a township, like a church and schools. The second is just as important as bringing in women. We're defenseless, stripped of law enforcement like a freshly plucked chicken." Without altering his perusal, Meade addressed his next words to Luke. "Mr. Reeves, your reputation follows you even here. You're the answer I need to contain the traders' and trail hands' . . . shall we say, more destructive urges."

"See anything you like, Meade? Or are you just window shopping?" Luke's stance widened.

Meade blinked, smiling apologetically at Tess, then feigning innocence with Luke. "Sorry. Sometimes I get carried away with the trials and tribulations of being a small-town mayor."

Hitching forward in his chair, he redirected his focus to Tommie. "Which brings me to the reason for this chat. No doubt, Mrs. Harper, you and your son have made plans to go on to Colorado as we've all heard."

"Yes, that's right. We plan to take the first stage to Denver."

"We hoped to persuade you to stay and set up residency here. Good women like yourself will arrive, following your lead. Children for your boy to play with. I know that with the help of my wife, Agnes, the two of you can begin a Lady's Auxiliary League, leading the community to the finer amenities that women are so astute in developing. As I mentioned before . . . such things as churches, schools and, of course, the theater."

Luke relaxed a fraction on learning that the trader was married and not interested in Tess as a future bride for himself. If she was the fortune hunter claimed in the Hot Springs report, a mayor might prove a welcome prospect for remarriage. Still, from the sound of things, Meade expected her to marry someone else. Either prospect didn't sit well with Luke.

"Me?" Tess could not have been more surprised if he had named her President. "You know nothing about me, sir."

"True. But a woman without the reputation experienced by some of the rest of our less fortunate would prove profitable for Wichita."

Tess would not consider the possibility. She wanted no part of a place that accepted her for reputation's sake. She would become no better than General Hunt's wife at Fort Smith. Before she could utter a quick refusal, Luke interrupted.

"Now the truth comes out." The bounty hunter sauntered from the window and stood behind Tess. "You want to use her to attract a better element. Bring more money to your pocketbook."

Jim took Meade's defense. "That's not so awful, is it? She would be respected and pampered. Contessa deserves that."

Luke snarled at the gambler. "And bring in a richer man

191

to sit at your poker tables. That certainly pleases you, doesn't it, Daggert?''

''I won't be used and need no one to take my defense!'' Anger spurred Tess to stand. Her voice crackled with irritation and authority. ''This is a lovely house your community prepared for me, but I really can't accept it. Please use it for a school or church or one of those finer amenities you propose.'' Drawing her son to her side, she straightened her shoulders in the face of the mayor's disapproval. ''Tommie and I are proceeding to Harper Hall in Georgetown because it's the home his father left to us. Surely you can understand the sentimental value of my decision, if nothing else.''

''Please, Mrs. Harper. I'm asking for the sake of what's best for the community.''

''And I'm doing what is best for me and my son. There are other women waiting for such an opportunity, I assure you, Mr. Meade. If I can be safely escorted across Indian territory, why not do as you've done with that cow herd you entrusted to Jesse Chisholm? Hire a group of men to guide willing brides to the area. You don't need *me;* you simply need a better plan.''

Tess urged her son toward the door. ''Come, Tommie.'' Turning at the last moment, she leveled an emphatic gaze at the mayor. ''You can tell the good men of Wichita I appreciate most kindly their efforts, but I won't be staying.''

''There's no need to leave now. Enjoy the house at least until you head for Colorado. We have a bar-be-que planned in your honor, and for the Fourth, of course.'' Meade rubbed his furrowed brow. ''There will be hell to pay if you lope out of here without at least making a show at the buffalo bar-be-que. After all, a lot of effort has gone into the preparations made in your honor. Perhaps allowing us your company for a few hours will soften some of those tight purse strings enough to finance the expedition for brides.''

''I can't and won't make promises, Mayor. But I'll *try.* We really must be on our way.'' Tess held her hand out to her son. "Tommie, let's you and I go freshen up and leave the men to finish their discussion."

When mother and child left the room, Luke sauntered past Meade and grinned. "Doesn't nail to the wall easy, does she?" His mouth curved into a whisper. "I'll see if I can get her to stay a bit longer if you'll bring back that pretty white dress hanging in Carlos's window. The white one with the red roses. Oh, and that fancy lace parasol and gloves that lay next to it too."

Chapter Nineteen

Luke sat in the drawing room and stared out the windows at the gathering crowd. How long did it take to put on fluff and frill, he wondered as he waited for Tess to dress. Seemed as if they were celebrating the Fourth with the President himself instead of picnicking with a slew of traders. He bought a hot bath and shave at the barber shop and dressed both himself and Tommie in the new clothes he'd purchased at the trading post.

The white cotton shirt and denim trousers looked good on the tyke. Red suspenders crisscrossed the small back. Tommie tried to sit still on the davenport for a while, but soon he disappeared as a pair of stubby legs tumbled over the back of the sofa. Two eyes peeked up over the back to see if Luke watched.

Seeing that he'd been caught, Tommie swung around and sat at attention.

Luke laughed and sauntered over, ruffling the child's hair. "Don't blame you, boy. Waiting on a woman to dress could drive a less patient man to drink."

Actually, it already has, Luke mused, remembering how Daggert had snapped his pocket watch shut ten minutes ago and hightailed it for one of the saloons lining Main. The saloon keepers had taken their business outdoors to better service the audience gathering for the day's events.

An upstairs door opened and shut. *About time.* Luke unconsciously checked his appearance. Though unaccustomed to such luxury, he appreciated the good fit and rich material. The black frock coat and black kerseymere trousers felt as if they had been tailor-made. Though he'd wondered if the embroidered satin waistcoat buttoning over the white linen shirt might better suit Daggert, Luke had taken the merchant's suggestion and waited to see the whole effect. He decided this was the best he'd ever looked.

Fidgeting with the string tie at his collar, Luke lifted the new black hat he'd placed beside Tommie. The hat was creased in the crown where Tommie had rolled over on it. "You ready, son?"

"Sorry, Mr. Luke." Tommie grinned sheepishly. "Want me to punch it for ya?"

"No thanks. I can do my own punching." Luke pushed the hat's underside until it popped back into shape.

"My, don't you two look handsome." Tess stood at the parlor door, her eyes shining with appreciation.

Luke's heart paused in its beat at the sight of her. Heat and longing flooded him. She had swept her hair back into curls that haloed her lovely face, then cascaded to one bare shoulder. A fine blush highlighted her cheeks, and her mouth looked plump and lush as a berry. Bare at the shoulders, the white muslin hugged her bosom in a ruffled bertha, tightened to define her youthful waist, then flared to three becoming flounces.

As his gaze rested on the pearl-buttoned silk gloves gripping the lace parasol, his breath finally released. "You are the most beautiful woman I've ever seen."

Her blush deepened to match the light honeyed glow she had acquired from days of driving the wagon.

"It's the dress," she said. "So lovely. And the gloves. Are you sure you didn't buy them?"

"I told you, I didn't do anything." He fidgeted again with

the tie. Which was only a half-truth. He had bought his and Tom's clothing, and a present for the tyke's birthday. But Meade had made good on his promise. Luke was glad now he hadn't paid for her things. He doubted she would have accepted them. A gift from the townsfolk was a different matter.

Silence filled the room as they took pleasure in admiring each other. The fine cut of figure and physique. The special care each had taken to please the other.

"When we gonna eat?" Tommie stood on the davenport. "I'm hungry."

Tess laughed. "As soon as you get your feet off that and I straighten Luke's tie. May I?"

Hang me with the damn thing. I won't move, he agreed silently, loving the way those green eyes stared at him. But aloud, all he could mutter was, "Uh-huh."

A band struck up outside, signaling that the traditional speeches would commence shortly. Tomtoms and reed music joined in. Luke thought they surely matched the thunder of his heart as Tess drew near. Her hands lifted to his throat, shook almost imperceptibly, then began the task. Luke's eyes closed as a scent of lavender flared his nostrils and forced him to breathe in the essence of Tess. The image of her in his arms on a night that now seemed eons ago was not enough to satisfy the hunger for the flesh-and-blood Tess who stood only a breath away. His eyes opened and devoured her beauty as if she were a feast and he, famished.

She lingered, the task complete. Her breath equaled the shallow intake of his own and her lips parted in open invitation. A flicker of green fire kindled in her eyes. He took off his hat as one hand pulled her into his embrace and drew her closer, eager to appease the lure of her lips. He stopped only a moment away before both remembered they were not alone.

"There, all done now." Tess gulped away the attraction, turning and pretending to pat her hair into place.

"That'll do nicely." Luke patted the tie as well.

Tommie jumped off and grumbled. "Shucks. I thought you's gonna kiss her."

The Beholding

As the boy ran out of the parlor ahead of them, Luke offered his arm, Tess accepted it, and both threw back their heads and laughed.

"My feet are aching." Tess half laughed, half complained to Jim. It seemed she had danced with every man there except Luke. She suspected his leg bothered him again when he chose to visit with several traders, then consented to introduce Tommie to a few of the Indians who had joined the strange celebration.

Never before had she seen such people together—frock-coated gentlemen, painted ladies, blanketed Indians. The few children played games and wrestled, regardless of their race. If she did not have the driving purpose of establishing her home at Harper Hall and taking Tommie to the hot springs near Georgetown, Tess might have seriously considered Wichita as the place to settle. But she couldn't count on such easy acceptance. They expected her past to be unflawed, and it was far from so.

The gambler halted and smiled a sincere apology. "I tend to step on a few toes now and then." He nodded toward the tables set up near Don Carlos's trading post. "I couldn't swear by it, but I think there's sarsaparilla being served for those with an objection to liquor. May I escort you there, Mrs. Harper?"

"Certainly, Mr. Daggert," she countered with equal formality.

Tommie ran up and held an Indian girl in tow. "This is Runs-Too-Slow, my friend. This is my mommie, Missus Harper."

Tess smiled at her son's attempt to say each word carefully. She bent and met the lovely brown-eyed child face to face. "I'm very pleased to meet you, Runs-Too-Slow."

The girl looked the same age as Tommie but tripled him in weight. She stood as round as she was tall.

"She hit that big ol' boy for me. I like her."

Tess straightened and looked in the direction Tommie

pointed. One of the boys playing with James Meade's son stood several inches taller than the rest. "Was that necessary?" she asked, a mother's sense of trouble drawing a conclusion even before he verified it.

"Mama, what's a freak? He said they walk funny and talk funny, so I make a real good one. That's when Runs-Too-Slow hit him. Right in the nose."

Tess wanted to hug the Indian child but didn't know the protocol for such things and didn't dare offend her. She chose to smile and nod. "Thank you, dear, for being such a good new friend to my boy."

A grin spread from ear to ear as the girl took Tommie's hand and simply said, "Tom-mee and Runs-Too-Slow ride Talon."

Even the littlest in the crowd had learned to trade, and Tess thought the world itself should celebrate. Runs-Too-Slow had traded a punch for the right to be Tom's friend and ride the horse.

"Do you still want to rest?" Jim asked as the children scrambled off to play.

"I think it would be a good idea." If she could get him anywhere near the rocking chairs sitting next to the punch table, she might persuade Jim to slow up on his consumption.

"Mrs. Harper?" A hand caught her at the elbow.

What now? She turned to face an extremely drunk man wavering none too steadily in front of her. Wasn't he the one in the crowd that Luke had warned? Big and burly, the man smelled as if he hadn't washed in weeks and his clothes looked as if he had laundered them without bothering to take them off. "You'll have to forgive me. I don't know your name."

"Simon Ragmorton. Rag to my friends." He offered his hand for her to shake, then thought better of it and bowed. "May I have the next dance?"

"I was just going for punch. If you'd care to join us?"

"Punch? Not me. I wanna dance, li'l lady. You can get some punch later. Dance with me first."

"My feet hurt. Perhaps later."

"Then give me a kiss." He stumbled toward her and aimed with his lips. When he missed, a scowl wrinkled Rag's thin forehead. "Don't have to use your legs for a kiss, do ya?" He smiled wickedly. "Then again . . . that might be interesting."

"Back off, mister." Luke came from out of nowhere and met the man eye to eye.

The drunk held up his palms. "You gonna gun me down in front of witnesses, bounty hunter? I ain't armed."

Jim guffawed and held his palms up in the same manner, mocking Ragmorton. "Are those fence posts you're mauling the lady with?"

"Stay out of this, Daggert," Luke said.

Jim shrugged out of his frock coat. "Who died and made you Contessa's defender, Reeves? Set aside that Colt and make me stay out of it."

"Jim, you're drunk." Tess tugged at the gambler's sleeve. "There's no need to fight. I'll dance with the man, if it will settle this."

"No you won't. And Reeves has been asking for this for a long time. You're *my* woman."

"I'm nobody's woman, Jim Daggert. Not yours or anyone else's."

Luke turned, unbuckled his holster and let it slide into the grass. He spread the frock coat out and showed there were no more guns. "This is unnecessary, Daggert. But if it's what you want, get after it."

"Damn if I won't." Jim lunged at Luke.

"Stop it . . . both of you!" Tess used her body as a shield between them.

The music halted and the crowd took notice of what was happening. A circle formed around the three men and Tess.

"She rule the roost, Gimpy?" Ragmorton leered at Luke, then backed away from the expression on the bounty hunter's face. "No, don't reckon she can be that sassy." Ragmorton pointed at Jim. "You gonna let that bitch make—"

Luke caught the mule skinner with a smashing blow just

199

below the ear, cutting off Ragmorton's slur. The man dropped to his knees, then fell backward and lay there.

"Takes a real big man to punch out a drunk, doesn't it, Reeves?" Jim took advantage of Tess's surprise and rushed past her, grabbing a handful of Luke's hair. Jerking the bounty hunter's head back, Jim delivered a brutal blow to the jaw.

Luke sagged, falling forward. A knee rose savagely toward Luke's face. A roar escaped his throat as Luke grabbed Jim's leg, twisted, then shoved the gambler backward against the punch table. As the table flipped, Luke's fist pounded Jim's face again and again as if it were a hammer driving in a railroad spike. Each blow landed with a mushy crunch, and the gambler's nose dissolved beneath a pulpy blotch.

Tess desperately tugged at Luke's arm, screaming, "Stop it, Luke! Stop before you kill him!"

Though beaten, Jim was still half-conscious. As Tess once again placed her body between the two, the gambler jammed his arms against the back of the table and pushed himself erect, inch by inch. Standing once more, he stared venomously into Luke's hard, pitiless eyes.

"Let me finish him off," Luke demanded.

"Don't worry, bounty hunter," the gambler croaked. "You'll get another chance. And she'll have to cart you away in a box."

Luke attempted to grab him by the lapels, but Tess interfered. "Anytime, any place, fancy man," Luke challenged.

"Don't you hurt Mista Luke!" Tommie yelled and raced from across the street.

"Tom-mee!" Runs-Too-Slow cried, running to catch up.

The click of a hammer pulling back made Luke whirl. He shouted Tommie's name as Ragmorton took aim and shot. The barrel spewed flame. Red suspenders dove. Runs-Too-Slow followed. In a blink of horror, Luke's knees buckled from the impact of Tommie's body hurtling into him. The bounty hunter stumbled, the momentum of two small bodies propelling him backward . . . one crying in pain, the other bleeding.

Chapter Twenty

Luke rolled instinctively, throwing his body over the two children as a shield to the next bullet he expected at any second.

"Somebody grab him!" a man shouted. "He's getting away!"

Ragmorton ran down the thoroughfare and was about to turn the corner onto Douglas Avenue when another shot rang out. His body jerked, and he fell face down in the dirt.

"Tommie! God in Heaven, let me see him!" Tess pushed at Luke to separate him from the children. Her heart clenched as if someone had stepped on it and ground it into her back. Nothing seemed real. Everything happened in slow motion. The sounds faded into the rhythm of her pulse. "Get up, son. Please God, let him move."

Luke unfolded and turned, cradling a bleeding body in his hands. Tears burst from Tess's eyes as dual emotions of relief and sorrow swamped her. It was Runs-Too-Slow who lay in Luke's arms, blood soaking the back of her deerskin dress, her eyes open and near vacant. Tommie sprawled on the ground, the breath knocked from him but unscathed.

Tess grabbed him, desperately searching his back for a

wound. Finding none, she turned him around and checked the front.

He gasped as his body jerked with hiccups that bubbled into sobs. "Runs-Too-Slow. That mean man hurt Runs-Too-Slow!"

"Shh . . . it's all right, son. We'll help her. It's all right." Sitting on the ground, rocking him back and forth, Tess attempted to soothe his tears but couldn't. Tommie wanted nothing but to follow Luke.

Luke ran toward the sheriff's house, fighting his limp.

"Somebody get Red Kettle, then tell her father and mother!"

As James Meade barked orders to several men following closely behind Luke's determined gait, Tess made Tommie stand. "Are you calm enough to go with me, son?"

"Y-yes," he stammered.

"Then wrap your arms around Mommie and hold tight. We've got to hurry and follow Luke." Tess clutched the boy against one hip and ran.

At the sheriff's house, Meade waved to her from the front porch, holding the curiosity seekers at bay. "Let the lady through."

She pushed through the crowd, accepting the mayor's help onto the porch.

"Told Reeves to put her upstairs on one of the beds," Meade informed Tess.

She hurried into the house after him. "Did someone call for a doctor?"

A knock on the door frame interrupted Meade's answer. Swinging around as if to shout at who chose to defy his orders, the mayor's body immediately eased. "Oh, it's you, Red Kettle. Thought some fool wanted to test his luck."

Shutting away the faces of the other curious onlookers, Meade introduced the visitor. "Contessa Harper, this is Red Kettle, Cherokee medicine man. Wichita's doctor for the moment. Red Kettle, Mrs. Contessa Harper."

A medicine man? Tess regarded the strongest face she had

ever seen. Wrinkles rutted the Indian's face while obsidian eyes stared at her as if he looked and saw nothing. Red Kettle's expression never changed, revealing none of his thoughts. Tess suppressed a shiver of apprehension.

The Cherokee unthreaded a strip of rawhide from his neck and opened a drawstring pouch sewed to the end of it. He took something from its inner lining and pinched it together, throwing it first at the threshold he had entered, then spattered gray dust up the stairs, chanting as he mounted. Upon reaching the landing, he swirled counter-clockwise, raising and then lowering his chin, chanting continuously. Red Kettle stopped and held both hands together high over his head, clutching the medicine bag, emitting a piercing howl that seemed unearthly.

"Is the doctor here?" Luke yelled from the room to the left of the landing. "Dammit, she's bleeding to death!" He ran to the bedroom doorway, his eyes wide, his shirt soaked with blood. "What's keeping him . . . what the devil?"

Red Kettle uttered a guttural mix of English and Cherokee.

Meade hurried upstairs, tugging on Tess's arm to urge her to follow. "This is the tribe's shaman. He must tend the child, and Red Kettle wants Mrs. Harper to put the boy in the same room, then leave while he performs the ritual. He must separate the girl's spirit from her son's or Runs-Too-Slow will not return to her own body."

"No!" Tess gripped Tommie even more closely and backed down the stairs. "What if he does something harmful to Tom? He doesn't need my son."

"Do as he demands," Luke insisted calmly. "I won't let anyone hurt your boy, but it might save the girl."

"I can't leave him."

Meade closed the distance between them and placed a reassuring hand on her shoulder. "He'll be fine, Mrs. Harper. Red Kettle won't harm your son, but he can be a powerful enemy if you don't allow him to do what he believes will save her. Your son's life will be in more danger if you don't do as the Cherokee asks."

"She's dying, Tess." Luke's voice quavered.

Tess stared into Tommie's eyes. "Are you afraid?"

"No, Mommie."

He looked so small, the Indian so fierce. "Well, I won't be either then," she whispered, braver than she felt. "Remember, I'll wait downstairs for you to come tell me Runs-Too-Slow is all right." Giving him a kiss and a hug, Tess reluctantly allowed Luke to take him from her arms.

The men disappeared into the room, then Tess took a seat on the davenport in the parlor. Hours ticked by as she waited, straining for every sound, counting every intricate design in the rosewood settee to keep from worrying.

Booted footsteps made the stairs creak and Tess jolted to her feet, bracing herself for whatever news she was about to receive.

Luke stood in the parlor doorway, his face etched in misery.

"She's not—?"

"Not yet." Luke exhaled a heavy sigh. "Tom's fine. A real champion, that boy. Taking it all as serious as it is. You've done a good job of raising him."

"What's the medicine man doing?" Tess noted the way Luke kept rubbing the butt of the Colt as if something had stained it.

"Practicing some of his cures. Gave her some God-awful-smelling potion. Said it would keep her spirit at ease. If it's anything like what the Apache use, it's probably peyote or tiswin. He altered her state of mind so she didn't feel the pain so much. At least the bullet's out now."

"Did he give any of the medicine to Tommie?"

"I wouldn't let him. I told him that if the two minds were in the same state, it would be hard to make the separation."

"Thank you." Tess watched him stride over to the fireplace, lift the Colt from the holster and place it on the mantel.

"I've got to get out of this shirt." Luke unbuckled the holster and let it slide to the finely polished floor. He began to unbutton the new shirt, his hands trembling as they edged down toward the blood staining the material.

"I'll get a pitcher and some water. You can wash up." Tess

204

hurried out to the kitchen, found the necessities and quickly returned. Luke was bare-chested now, but his hand again stroked the Colt's ivory handle. Back and forth, back and forth, as his eyes looked out the window, seemingly at everything. At nothing.

"Luke?" Worry flared and made her voice hesitant. Tess cleared her throat when he didn't hear her. "Luke, is something wrong?"

He swung around, gripping the Colt. Puzzlement creased his brow. As if the metal burned to touch it, he gingerly set the Colt back on the mantel.

"Nothing for you to fret over," came the quiet reply. "I need some air."

Tess became frightened. She had never seen him act this way. "What are you going to do?"

"Just stay in the house."

"Don't go out there, Luke. We don't know what Runs-Too-Slow's people will do."

"Maybe that's just what I need . . . deserve."

"You're talking wild."

"This is none of your business."

"It is," she insisted. "I care for you!"

"Then don't care, Tess. Just leave me alone."

Silence ensued, filling the room with turbulent emotion. "You wouldn't understand," he finally said, unaware that he handled the weapon once again.

"I'll try." She hurried to his side. With a gentle press of her hand over his, she made him stop the constant rubbing. "At least let me *try*."

Worried over his strange fascination with the Colt, Tess wondered how she might get him away from the gun. Urging his fingers open, she pulled him forward a few steps. "Come to the kitchen with me. We'll make coffee . . . No, leave the gun."

For a moment Luke didn't budge, then finally followed. He looked upstairs as they passed, but Tess felt compelled to draw his mind away from the little girl.

A large table and four chairs stood in one corner of the kitchen while a pot-bellied stove took up the other. Tess motioned Luke into one of the chairs, then set about heating the stove. As she worked, she talked and noted Luke's silence. She asked questions that had little to do with the shooting, hoping her constant prattle might instigate an answer or two and keep him from brooding. But by the time the stove had heated and the coffee percolated, Luke still sat with his elbows on the table and his hands laced through the hair at his temples. Tess seat a cup of coffee in front of him, taking a chair next to his.

Luke's thumb rubbed the rim of his cup, the same as it had polished the gun. Tess's mind sped through words to say, searching for a subject to break his silence, bring life back to his faraway stare. Finally it locked on something trivial but funny in its own way. "Did you know that every time one of us gets upset, we drink a cup of coffee? Remember the first time we met, you—"

"That's all the hell a gun's good for," Luke interrupted. Standing, he bumped the cup and spilled its contents. "Killing innocent people."

Was that what this was about? The shooting had reminded him of killing Clifton? She reached out to touch Luke, but he jerked away. "You said you warned Clifton but he got in the way. That was no more your fault than this girl's death would be."

"I'm not talking about Harper, Tess. Runs-Too-Slow. I as much as pulled the trigger."

Before she could utter another word, he pushed her aside and jerked open the door, disappearing into the backyard.

Chapter Twenty-one

"Luke, you can't blame yourself." Tess followed him into the twilight, grabbing his elbow and demanding that he turn around to face her. No crowd waited in the back, a surprise amid the fear and desperation filling her thoughts.

"Can't I?" He spun. The confident manner, so much a part of him, vanished. Dark with emotion, his eyes looked strangely vulnerable, his expression strained and serious. "Luke Reeves. Hater of bullies. Gunman. My appointment to West Point didn't impress my parents, you see. Nothing I ever did seemed good enough to satisfy Olivia because I would always be less than the perfect son. I didn't have the good sense to be born unscarred, so I headed west. Fell in love, but Laoni decided not to marry me. Then all I wanted to do was hurt as I'd been hurt, so I joined up when the fighting started between the states."

Tess's heart contracted as she fought off dual emotions— fury at a mother who couldn't love her own child and a pang of jealousy over a woman she had never met. *Do I really want to know this?* she asked herself before questioning aloud, "Do you still love this Laoni person?"

"No . . . I thought I did, but I don't think I would know

love if it walked up and struck me in the face.''

Not understanding how all this related to his anguish over Runs-Too-Slow, Tess fought her curiosity and attempted to guide the conversation to less emotional ground. But Luke could not be dissuaded. Once open, the doors to his past fell from old hinges.

''Didn't agree with the Rebs on the issue of slavery, so I sided with the North. I didn't want a commission, but they assigned me one because of the appointment to West Point. One of the lieutenant generals happened to be a fellow classmate and wouldn't let me go in as a foot soldier. You can imagine how the conscripted Yanks felt about one of their officers being a Texan.''

Luke wiped his hands on his neck as if his throat hurt. ''Almost got strung up. We had beaten a patrol of Rebs and they were in retreat. I ordered my company to cease fire and let them alone. The company brought it to the attention of my commanding officer. Said I was a traitor.''

''Did they court-martial you?''

''Nothing as legal as that. I would've been hung, but news that the war was over days before the battle saved my hide. We just hadn't gotten word, so it proved an unnecessary campaign to begin with. But more than that, my commander agreed with me. Like me, he grew tired of killing people whose reasons for fighting had nothing to do with the issue of slavery. People who were defeated long before we ever faced them.'' Luke's fist clenched. ''All I'd learned at West Point didn't apply in those slaughter fields. Learning to salute and guard duty, even trying to put a few slave traders in prison, is little reason to take lives a man knows nothing about.''

Tess placed a hand over his clenched fist. ''Is that why you became a bounty hunter?''

''I didn't fit anywhere else. The solitary life suited me. Just because I'd fought on their side didn't mean the Yanks were willing to change their attitudes about me as a Texan. When I headed South, I wasn't given much of a welcome either. Not only did the defeated hate me, so did the conquerors.''

Luke stared at her with pain and bitterness that wrenched her heart.

"I became cynical and withdrawn from people. Tracking wanted men gave me a sense of accomplishment that nothing else could. I not only got good at it, some say I'm the best. But men always want to challenge a shootist. Men like Ragmorton. Even Daggert. Now because I was stupid enough to let two drunks rile me, that little girl lies up there bleeding to death."

Tess pressed his fist until it softened beneath her touch. "Luke, you aren't to blame. It had nothing to do with you."

Pulling away his hand, he flung back harsh words. "Would you be so understanding if it was Tommie's life slipping away up there? Would it be so easy to forgive my temper that stirred up this whole mess if the bullet hole was in your boy and not Runs-Too-Slow?"

Anger flared as she met his hard gaze. "I don't know, Luke. I'm as human as anyone else. But no amount of soul-searching or cutting yourself to the core like this is going to help that little girl or change destiny."

"I know that." He flung his arms out in exasperation. "I just can't deny what I feel anymore. I thought I was dead emotionally until you and Tommie came along. Until that little girl took the bullet meant for me. I've lived too long using the law as an excuse. Too long acting without feeling."

Knowing this was the moment she could have all she hoped for, the moment where he would be hers alone if she chose to make him so, Tess fought the inner battle of doing what she knew was best for him or satisfying her own dreams and desires. But the choice was out of her hands, made uncomplicated by the caring in her heart. Tess gathered her courage and challenged him. "You told me, Luke Reeves, you had to finish whatever job you're doing because it's not done. You can't give up now. You gave your word."

When Luke's hands clutched at her waist, Tess opened her arms and he pulled her desperately against him. His body shook violently as his voice trembled with emotion. "I pray to God I never see another child spread-eagled in the grass, hurting from a bullet meant for me.''

Though not a tear dampened her shoulder, Tess failed to hold back her own. She wept for Luke. For his fear of losing the child. And to mourn the misery that had become his life.

The back door opened, and Meade stood in its threshold. ''The girl's parents are here.''

Tess felt Luke's back stiffen seconds before he let go and turned away. Straightening her hair, she smoothed the bertha and glanced at Luke. ''Are you coming?''

''I've got to get a clean shirt. Can't meet them like this.''

''I'll wait for you in the parlor.'' She hoped he understood all she really promised. *I'll be at your side. I'll help explain. I won't let you go through this alone.*

Tess followed James Meade into the kitchen. ''Did you tell them what happened?''

''Red Kettle has come down now. He'll explain.''

''Is the girl alive?'' She glanced up as they passed the staircase and halted outside the parlor door.

Meade raised a finger to his lips and whispered, ''Red Kettle has told me little. He won't until Screeching Bird and Laughing Wind meet Mr. Reeves.''

For a man who had just learned that his daughter had been shot, the large, blanketed Indian appeared calm. Too calm. Sitting next to him, his wife rocked back and forth with her eyes closed, hugging herself and uttering words that sounded like a chant.

Grim, Red Kettle's face revealed nothing as the Cherokee took a chair opposite Runs-Too-Slow's parents. Tommie scooted over to allow the translator room beside him and laced his fingers through Red Kettle's. The shaman's features lit with a brief smile as he gripped Tommie's hand with the gentleness of a grandparent, but his face quickly resumed its stoic mask.

Tess noted Tommie's tear-streaked cheeks and red-rimmed eyes, but he seemed unafraid of the medicine man. All attention shifted to the parlor door where the bounty hunter stood, drawing Tess from her concern for Tommie to a deeper one for Luke.

Red Kettle started in without preliminaries. "Lucas Reeves, Screeching Bird says if his child dies this night, you must leave Ute-cha-og-gra before the sun rises."

"Wait a minute," Tess protested, rushing to Luke's defense. "Everyone in town knows what happened." She met Screeching Bird's gaze defiantly. "We don't have any supplies gathered and haven't made arrangements for a stage. We can't leave Wichita!"

"Let it go, Tess," Luke ordered quietly, gently pushing her shoulders so she would no longer place her body as a blockade to his. "I'd say the man is being more than fair. I'll see to it that you and Tommie catch the next one. Here." He drew out a small bag from a pocket of his trousers. The jingle of coins hinted what was inside. "Take this and get what you need. Daggert can take you the rest of the way. If I don't meet you along the trail somewhere, I'll catch up in Denver. You'll want to rest there before you go on to Georgetown."

"There's only one stage line from here to Denver. Ragmorton's brother runs it." Meade studied the end of his cigarette, then glanced up at them from his position near the fireplace. He picked up the Colt, eyed it, met Luke's gaze, then quickly replaced the gun on the mantel. When the Colt had left the mantel, Screeching Bird had risen to his feet. "Meant to warn you about that earlier. Guess it just slipped my mind."

"Convenient, isn't it, Meade?" Luke took a step toward the mayor. "Get me out of the way. Convince Mrs. Harper to stay."

"I had no such intentions." Meade backed away as Luke stepped closer.

Luke told Red Kettle what he intended to do. Red Kettle translated. The bounty hunter slid his arm past the mayor and retrieved the gun, slipping it into the holster on the floor.

"Luke did not kill Mr. Ragmorton," Tess defended, grateful that Screeching Bird was a cautious man. Perhaps he would be even more so in reckoning with Luke. "Mr. Reeves struck Ragmorton because the man insulted me and several others. If these kind people are willing to accept Luke's explanation, then surely the Ragmorton family can't condemn him. Are you unwilling to help us, Mayor?"

Meade rocked on his booted heals. "My concern is first and foremost for Wichita."

Tess's eyes glinted with anger. "If you really want the best for this town, then show these people your kindness instead of wasting time trying to plot against Luke. If he has to leave as they've requested, then you can't convince me to stay. May I remind you I can either boast about Wichita to other women interested in settling here, or I can be a hindrance."

The mayor's features wrinkled into a scowl. He didn't like to lose an argument, and he had already done so twice with this particular lady. "Ragmorton owes me a few favors. I'll see what I can do." Meade moved as if he were in no hurry, but kept his word and left.

Luke faced Screeching Bird's fierce countenance. "I don't know if you understand what I'm saying, Screeching Bird. If not, I hope Red Kettle will translate for me."

Red Kettle began to talk in his native language.

Tess heard Luke's breath draw in and exhale slowly as if he were garnering something more than strength.

"I will forever keep the honor your daughter has given me, here."—Luke pressed one palm to his forehead, then to his heart—"and here. Whether she lives or dies, her blood is mine. I owe your people."

Red Kettle translated and frowned. "He knows nothing of *owe*."

Luke searched for the right word. "*Trade,* then. As she helped me, so will I find a way to help her people."

Words passed between interpreter and Screeching Bird, spreading pride through Tess. The steel of Luke's eyes, the tone of voice, even the way his legs locked in a bracing stance, convinced her of the sincerity of his commitment. And as she knew, his word once given became law.

Screeching Bird lifted one hand to his forehead, touched it with his fingertips, then slid the hand out in front of him in a down-turned wave.

Luke glanced at Red Kettle.

"He accepts Luke Reeves's trade."

Luke held out his hand. Red Kettle offered an explanation. Red hand gripped white.

"Now we go. Until the sun rises." Red Kettle and Screeching Bird went upstairs to get Runs-Too-Slow while Laughing Wind shuffled to the door, her eyes opened yet unfocused as she continued to chant.

Tess wanted to say something, touch her, offer sympathy, but the silent shake of Luke's head warned her that she would overstep some indefinable boundary that kept white and red women apart.

Tommie kept equally silent, now clutching at the flounces of Tess's dress. Needing the feel of human contact to calm her own disquieting emotions, Tess pressed him close, finding the weight of his small body against her skirted legs comforting and reassuring. The feeling strengthened at the sight of Screeching Bird carrying his daughter downstairs.

If not for the courage of that little girl, it would be her own son looking so pale and limp. Tess's hug became fierce until Tommie yelped. "Forgive me, love," she whispered, the words barely audible.

Luke held the door open for the family and stepped back. Indian women waited beyond the picket fence. Anglos gathered in force as uncertainty rippled over the gathering. Would the tribe take vengeance if the girl died? If so, Indians outnumbered Anglos four to one.

Screeching Bird stretched out his arms and held his daughter for all to see. His words caused a stir among the whites who understood, but red men and women alike merely parted to allow Screeching Bird and his wife a clear path to their village. All, even to the last toddler, followed the wounded child.

"What did he say?" Tess could hardly believe the swiftness of their departure.

"She lives," Meade informed her.

"Oh, Luke, how wonderful!" Tess wanted to hug him but resisted, instead hugging Tommie.

Luke whistled a long, slow breath, the cords in his neck and the hard sinews of his back easing.

"Oh, boy!" Tommie shouted. "Her can play!"

"Not for a while, son," Tess reminded. "But thank the Almighty, she will play again one day soon."

"Get out of town, Reeves!" an angry yell reverberated from the crowd.

"Yeah, and take 'at swindling cardman with you."

Tess linked her arm through Luke's to lend support. "Leave him alone," she demanded. "Screeching Bird and his people don't blame Luke. Why do you?"

The townsfolk insisted upon carrying out Screeching Bird's demand, taking away Luke's option to stay. Obscenities littered the air as one man took courage from another and lashed out with words.

"Go back to where you came from, bounty man!"

"Do the woman a favor and leave her here with us."

Tommie started sniffling, tugging on Luke's leg. "How come they don't like you, Mista Luke? Runs-Too-Slow ain't gonna die no more."

He patted the boy on the back to reassure him. "Grownups sometimes aren't as forgiving as you children are, son."

"That's right, bounty hunter, so it's best you and that there gambler get on outa Wichita before we show you both how unforgiving we are . . . 'specially if them Injuns get riled and take it out on us."

Though several were brave enough with words, none challenged Luke gun-to-gun . . . no one noticing that he no longer wore it.

Chapter Twenty-two

Cracking his whip, Frank Ragmorton swore at the horses. He deliberately rattled the coach, bouncing along the rutted road at breakneck speed. A damn shame the gambler and the other gent rode in the back with the bitch and her boy who got his brother killed, but that was their misfortune. Frank spit a wad of tobacco into the wind and leered as it flung past him, hoping the stream sluiced through the window the lady had opened for air.

The rapid bob of the hat he'd tied around his neck and hung against his broad back kept time with the coach's gait as it raced into the next stage station. A surge of satisfaction jostled through Frank. He might owe Meade more than this son-of-a-bitching ride, but he sure as hell didn't have to make it easy on the sow. It burned Frank's butt that Reeves rode escort on that big dun instead of hitching his mount to the back like the gambler did.

Frank mulled over the idea of flipping the stage on purpose. It would be worth the trouble to see the bounty hunter's face when he pulled out that gal and her young'un to see if they got stoved up or dead. The idea quickly passed. Reeves's hawk eyes missed nothing, and the bounty hunter would kill Frank

215

if he figured the flip had been planned. Not a gunning man himself, the only thing left to him and Rag was the reputation they had built as owners of a swift stageline. A safe one, at that. Already Terry and Company from back East looked to buy him out for a sum larger than he and Rag ever dreamed. Even Rag wouldn't want to put the future of Ragmorton's Stage and Freight Line in jeopardy by having Reeves seek revenge.

Besides, the idea of his and Rag's company becoming the Kansas Stage Line appealed to Frank's sense of destiny. He didn't particularly care to do the tall-hatted gentleman in the coach any harm, neither. Mr. Wideacre paid him months in advance and frequented the line often enough to be one of Frank's best customers.

Frank imagined Rag starting the whole mess. His brother stayed drunk half the time. The second half, he liked to spend in bed with a comely woman, and the Harper woman was definitely one fine-looking piece of petticoat. Besides, Reeves wasn't the one who plugged Rag. The fact the Indians took no other blood than Rag's testified to the bounty hunter's innocence. Next run down to Wichita, Frank swore to look up Rag's killer. His brother hadn't been aiming at the red devil's papoose on purpose. Since that little squaw lived, Screeching Bird must answer to him now. The red bastard had no call finishing off Rag. Should'a just maimed him, like Rag did his daughter.

There wasn't much he could do now to ease his anger at the Cherokee, but he would rattle this coach a mite and wreak hell on Contessa Harper's rear end.

Rousing from a wobbly sleep beside Tess, Tommie awoke and began to whimper. "I hurt, Mommie."

"I know, son. We should be stopping soon," she assured him. Unable to make out the kaleidoscope of rushing prairie in the gathering dusk, she leaned back and closed her eyes against the oppressive heat captured in such close quarters.

The Beholding

Luke had ridden back and said Fort Hays could be seen in the distance, which meant they would halt soon.

Tess's teeth rattled. Every bone in her body felt jarred from its joint. She had bruises where there should have been enough padding to prevent them from forming. Tess wished now she had taken Luke up on his offer to ride Jim's roan an hour or so ago. But the white muslin dress seemed unsuitable for riding, and she hoped to protect its hem from brambles and burrs stirred up beneath the team's hooves and the wheels. Now she wondered if sitting here cramped and hot was any better. Perspiration dampened her skin in a sheen that threatened to stain the beautiful dress.

"May I?" A gentleman across the seat from Tess took off his fashionably tall hat and offered it to her. "I see you have packed away your fan. Please feel free to use this as you may."

"Thank you, Mr. . . . ?"

"Wideacre. Phinneas T. Wideacre." He offered a card from the pocket of his handsomely tailored coat. "Of Denver formerly. Georgetown of late."

Tess looked at him with interest, then read the card. DEVELOPER. HOTELS. RESORTS. MINING. "Georgetown? How exciting. That's where my son and I are going."

"How lovely." The man's blue eyes offered welcome as he arched one graying brow. "And who may I call upon when you're settled? I'd like to introduce you to our fine townspeople . . . if I may be so bold?"

Extending her hand, Tess ignored Jim's glare as his gaze swept over the man to estimate his worth. "Why, thank you, Mr. Wideacre. It's very kind of you to offer. I'm Contessa Harper and this is my son, Thomas James." Motioning to the gambler, she added, "This is Jim Daggert, a close family friend and Tommie's namesake. He and Luke Reeves, the man riding escort for the stage, were guiding us to Georgetown when our wagon burned."

"How unfortunate, my dear. I do hope your husband is well." The man's face wrinkled in sympathy, revealing the

217

tell-tale lines of age that matched his graying Van Dyke and mustache.

"I'm newly widowed, sir, but my husband has holdings in Georgetown. Tommie and I decided we would make our home there. It's a place called Harper Hall. Do you know of it?" Excitement radiated through Tess.

"I hardly think a man of Mr. Wideacre's . . . experience, would know anything of Harper Hall," Jim quickly interjected.

Tess was puzzled by Jim's sudden declaration. Did he mean to insult Clifton by implying he couldn't possibly match Phinneas Wideacre's station in life, or was the gambler simply being kind and offering the man a gracious way not to answer in the event he disapproved of their home?

"Harper Hall? I'm sorry, I don't believe I've had the pleasure." Seeing her disappointment, Wideacre quickly added, "But then I'm away so much. Business, you know. Hardly a moment for pleasure, my dear."

He's being kind, she feared, *or actually hasn't ever heard of it.* This simple fact assured her that Clifton's holdings weren't in the better part of town. Feeling a stab of disappointment, Tess squared her shoulders. Whatever Clifton left them, she would make it home. She had to.

"Did you say the man riding alongside the stage is Luke Reeves?" Phinneas nudged back the curtain with the handle of his cane. "Seems I've heard that name somewhere."

His face became thoughtful as the gold-handled cane once again rested in front of him, and he crossed his gloved hands on its crest.

With a cape at his shoulders and the fashionable hat, Tess wondered if the cane was for vanity or truly a necessity.

"Does he make his living as a bounty hunter?"

"Yes." Tess's curiosity peaked. "Do you know Luke?" The two men hadn't acknowledged each other when they met at Wichita.

"Know *of* him, my dear. I knew his mother, Olivia, quite well, you see."

Tess looked away. She did see. The admiration in Phinneas Wideacre's eyes she read too easily. Tess had seen it far too often from men hoping to seduce her. It disturbed her that he and Luke's mother may have been lovers in their pasts. *Did Luke suspect?*

Coach springs halted with a scraping of brakes and a great cloud of dust billowed through the open window. Tess gasped and Wideacre moved in front of the window to block any further attack.

"I don't suppose one ever grows accustomed to this mode of travel, does one?" He coughed. "Makes a man want to go out and purchase more railroad stock."

The coach door swung wide and the driver gave them a tobacco-stained smile. "We'll sleep here for the night, Mr. Wideacre, and change out the team. The first cot near the front door has the best mattress. Might want to stake a claim before any of the others."

The leather straps cradling the heavy coach creaked as Wideacre stepped to the ground and turned to help Tess. His nostrils flared in an arrogant snub, as if in sympathy with the steaming, blowing team. "Mrs. Harper and her son should have the choice, Ragmorton. Courtesy in all circumstances is a man's obligation."

"Just wanted to make you feel to home," Frank complained. Figuring Tess Harper had enough willing jackasses, pompous and otherwise, to help her out of the coach, Ragmorton headed into the station.

Tess's legs buckled beneath her as she stepped down. Before she could crumple to the ground, Phinneas's cane thumped to the earth and two strong arms lifted her into his embrace.

"I'm fine," she assured him, staring up into caring blue eyes. "Everything swayed a bit and my stomach turned. I just need some coffee or tea, perhaps. Something to settle my nerves."

"Are you certain, Mrs. Harper? I wouldn't want you to faint."

He lowered her feet to the ground, allowing a test of leg strength. Was she being braver than good sense permitted? "I'm fine, really. Thank you for your trouble."

The men working the station had already unhitched the team. Each station offered a new set of horses, usually harnessed within minutes to keep the coach driver on schedule. But this was the last stop for the night, and the passengers would be given a four-hour reprieve from the coach's rock and sway.

A thin man, split-toothed and stringy-haired, barked orders. He introduced himself as the station manager and gestured toward the building. "Go on in, folks. Supper's awaiting. Rest your bones awhile and I'll bring in some fresh sheets."

Tess knew she must eat something. She had no idea when their next meal might be. But what she wanted most was a walk in the fresh night air. She would get Tommie settled in and take her food outdoors.

The long building was drafty and dusty, but offered a buffer to the wind that seemed to endlessly ripple over the Kansas grasslands. Rancid grease assaulted Tess's nose as she followed Wideacre into the primitive interior. Raising a glove to block the pungent odor, she surveyed six cots lined side by side in the east section of the logged cabin. A large dining table stood at the west end. Jim claimed the cot the driver had mentioned, stretching his long frame out without bothering to shed his boots.

Food boiled and bubbled in a skillet. In the center of the table, the station manager had already served up a tin of fried wild onions and potato patties that swam in dark grease. Baskets of cornbread rested at each end of the table. Tess's stomach churned, dreading the cramps she would suffer in rhythm with the coach wheels tomorrow.

Luke took one look at her and reached for Tommie. "I'll see to the boy. He's so sleepy I doubt he'll eat much anyway. Maybe the station manager can round you up some bath water."

With a wan smile of gratitude, Tess turned and stumbled

through the doorway. Once outside, she sucked in a deep breath to fill her lungs, only to choke on the dust the team had kicked up earlier. Clamping her hand over her mouth, she ran toward a building about fifty yards from the station. Tess reached the back of the spring house and rested against the clapboard wall. She took in deep breaths of fresh night air until her head quit throbbing and the stars stopped blinking in and out before her eyes. Ever so slowly, her stomach steadied.

Drawing a shaky breath, she stepped away from the wall and tested her footing, making certain she no longer felt dizzy. Tension bunched her shoulders. Tess stretched the kinks from them, giving way to a rather loud, unladylike yawn that eased the tension coiled in every muscle. The wind caressed her face. She took the pins from her hair and let the curls fall past her shoulders. As Tess shook the day's dust from their thickness, she wondered where the station manager bathed and if there was someplace private allotted to women passengers.

Tess enjoyed the first moment of solitude she had experienced in days, letting it flood her with a sense of calm. She sighed, knowing she shouldn't linger here too long. The others might worry, and four hours seemed little enough time to rest. But the return to the awful-smelling station house and the inevitability of washing by bowl and pitcher seemed even less appealing.

Suddenly two arms encircled her waist. For a moment she thought it was Luke come to share a moment of solitude with her. But these were not Luke's arms! The difference made her whirl, attempting to break free. To scream.

"Don't say a word, pretty bitch, or I'll make it bad on your son."

Frank Ragmorton laughed into her ear. His hot breath brushed over her neck as one hand cupped off her scream and the other gripped Tess back against his chest.

"I can make the ride easy on the boy or hard. You gotta decide which way you want it."

*   *   *

221

Luke sauntered around the corner of the spring house. He blinked once, twice, disbelieving the sight before him. Fury blazed through him, propelling the bounty hunter into a murderous run toward Tess.

"Get your hands off her, Ragmorton, or I'll gut you!" Luke shouted the warning a moment before his fist smashed into the side of the stagecoach driver's face.

Ragmorton bellowed, flinging Tess away so hard she sprawled on her hands and knees. Instinctively Luke reached for her to make certain she wasn't hurt. "Are you all right?"

Ragmorton took advantage of Luke's distraction and retaliated.

Out of the corner of his eye, Luke glimpsed the massive fist aimed for his jaw. He ducked, jamming a left hook into the driver's stomach. Then he followed with a right to his chin. The driver stumbled and fell.

Luke saw the moment as an opportunity to help Tess stand. Offering his hand, he urged, "Hurry, before he gets up for another round."

Tess swatted away his helpfulness and scrambled to her feet. "Why didn't you let me handle this myself?"

Ragmorton attempted to rise. Tess reacted before Luke could get over his surprise at her irritation. Cupping both hands together, she swung as hard as she could and cuffed Ragmorton in the nose. He shouted, his arm swinging out only to miss and send him off balance again. He landed in the prairie grass with a grunt, gripping his nose.

None too gently, Luke grabbed Tess's arm. "What do you mean, why didn't I let you handle this? That man tried to molest you!"

Anger blazed through Tess as she jerked away from Luke's grasp and balled her fists against her hips. "Do you think I would let that happen—" She started to say *again,* but didn't want to disclose such information to the likes of Ragmorton. "I told you I wanted to take care of myself and I meant it." With a look of disgust, she glared at the driver. "My son and

I will walk to Georgetown before I cower to your threats, mister!"

Luke stepped between the two combatants and glared back at her, equally furious. "Fight with him later. You're arguing with me now. What happened to 'thank you, Luke. That was mighty nice of you to rush to my defense'?"

Her chin lifted indignantly. "Maybe it went with 'Don't do me any favors. You're not going to be around the next time I need you, so I better learn how to handle these things myself.'" She gathered her skirts and marched past the spring house.

He wasn't about to let her get away so easily. Temper fueling his stride, Luke caught up, grabbed Tess's elbow and spun her around. "Did you expect me to stand there and just watch while he mauled you?"

"Did it bother you so much?"

Her breath rose and fell rapidly, distracting him. Challenge sparked in her eyes.

"I suppose it's unthinkable that *I* could handle this without you?" she demanded.

"No. You can be formidable when you want to be. But what if it hadn't worked?" Worry crept into his tone even though he attempted to hide it.

"What does it matter? You're leaving, remember? You have a job to finish."

These were words of hurt, not anger. Maybe he'd been too quick to argue with her. Luke brushed back a wisp of hair and pushed it behind Tess's ear. "So that's what this is all about. You're angry because I said I couldn't stay with you in Georgetown."

"I'm mad, Lucas Reeves," she pushed his hand away, "because you bullied your way into my business when I could have easily taken care of it myself."

"Wait till I get my hands on you, you son-of-a-brother-killing bitch!" Ragmorton shook one fist at Tess as he held his nose and ran toward them.

Luke looked from her to the stagecoach driver, then back

at Tess. "Do you expect me to stand here and let him call you that? Give me a moment or two to kick that bastard's teeth down his throat, *then* we can argue all you want."

"I'm not arguing with you or anyone else anymore." She peered over Luke's shoulders. "But Ragmorton doesn't seem to feel the same way." Tess motioned behind Luke.

"Buzzard piss." The bounty hunter swung around to discover Ragmorton only inches away. Luke's fist shot out, missing Frank's jaw but clipping him on a cheekbone. "This isn't any way to settle our argument, Tessa," Luke complained as he heard her move away.

Ragmorton swung and connected, catching Luke on the jaw. "Are you still here, gnat?" Luke groused, spitting a wad of blood as he shoved Ragmorton away. With a curse of exasperation, he tried to get Tess's attention in the same instant he warded off the next blow. "Woman, will you please wait a minute until I get rid of this pest?" The man must be a glutton for punishment, Luke thought, managing to land two more well-aimed fists.

Ragmorton wouldn't be put off. He meant to draw more blood and lit into Luke again. But Luke was a man bent on setting things straight with his woman. Some jobs he accomplished faster than others. Making quick work of Ragmorton's consciousness proved one of them.

Chapter Twenty-three

The stagecoach reached a sprawling village nestled at the junction of the Platte River and Cherry Creek just as the sun set behind the sawtooth crests of the Rocky Mountains. Though home was only a room at the boardinghouse, Denver had been Luke's base of operations since the war. He felt a sense of pride when he helped Tess down from the coach and saw her eyes light with appreciation at the progress the township had made in the six short years since its founding. Stone houses outnumbered those constructed of clapboard or tent fabric. A city hall, three banks and several fine hotels had been built and got as much business as the saloons and brothels.

"I didn't expect anything so . . . so . . . civilized," she said, moving instantly away as if his touch burned her.

"I always feels like I've come home, thought I reside in Georgetown," Phinneas informed her, greeting several of the people by name who stood in front of Carpenter's store awaiting the stage. He offered a hankie to Tess. "This will allay the dust the team stirred. Later, you'll inhale the cleanest, freshest air in all the country and discover there's no sweeter smell than Colorado's pine forests. Where will you and your party stay the evening, my dear?"

Luke met Tess's gaze. Since their falling out, she had refused to talk to him other than polite conversation. Though amiable, her tone left Luke all too aware she expected him to apologize before she broke the barrier of silence. He knew her funds were stretched far beyond her plans already, but the stubborn woman had too much pride to admit it.

"She'll be taking a room over at the boardinghouse for the night." Luke thumbed up his hat. "I've invited the Harpers to supper at the Hotel Dupree." Though he hoped Wideacre would decline, Luke read the look on Tess's face and knew that if he didn't invite the man to dinner, she would. "Would you care to join us?"

"The Hotel Dupree? I heard it has one of the best faro tables in the Rockies." Jim bent to leave the coach, then stretched his tall frame.

"The best *everything*," Phinneas corrected and held out one gloved hand to Luke. "It's been a pleasure meeting you, Mr. Reeves, but I must decline your kind offer. I've a meeting with my lawyer before tomorrow's stage to Georgetown." He turned and ruffled Tommie's hair. "I wouldn't keep your mother out too late, son. The stage leaves at five thirty. Hi Washburn, the stage driver, keeps his schedule to the minute."

"I hope we meet again, Mr. Wideacre." Tess offered her hand to the older man.

A feeling of disquiet coiled inside Luke's stomach as Wideacre bent and pressed his lips against her knuckles.

"*Phinneas*, remember. And I hope you will allow me to call on you once you're settled in Georgetown, Mrs. Harper."

Phinneas-Plentious. The man drips with money and all the right social graces, Luke silently stewed. Olivia had busted enough rulers over his knuckles to make Luke remember some of the niceties. *Enough to get through tonight?* he wondered, deciding on a plan. A glance at Daggert riled Luke more than the older man's sweet talk. The leer on the gambler's face mocked Luke. *That jackass thinks I haven't got a social bone in my body.* Determination filled him. *Hang on to your hatpin,*

Contessa Harper, this bounty hunter is going to dust off the, old manners and sweep you off your kid boots.

Tess took one last glance at herself in the mirror and pinched her cheeks. Two hours had been little enough time to wash, rest and prepare herself and Tommie for the evening ahead. The white muslin had been exchanged reluctantly for the clean serge travel shirtwaist and skirt, but it must do. If not for Luke's generous insistence to pay the remaining expenses to Georgetown, Tess didn't know how they would complete the journey. Though Luke said the money was part of the reward she'd earlier declined, she intended to pay him back as soon as she made an accounting of all of Clifton's assets.

Tommie fidgeted impatiently as she combed his hair. He looked a bit pale from the long, strenuous coach ride, but he had begun to fuss and pout when she'd suggested they simply take a meal in their room and leave the excitement of Denver until another time. She wondered if the stage would stop in Idaho Springs long enough for him to enjoy the hot springs. She must remember to ask Driver Washburn. If nothing else, perhaps they could linger a day or two before the stage made the return trip.

A knock on the door drew her attention away from Tommie's silken hair.

"Are you ready?"

"Ready."

Two freshly scrubbed faces smiled at Tess as she opened the door—one bearded, the other shaven.

"Contessa, may I have the pleasure?" Daggert offered his arm a second before Luke did.

Though her first impulse shouted to accept Luke's, Tess gripped Jim's. She was still angry with the bounty hunter despite all his helpfulness. He had hurt her, and good manners simply weren't enough to make her forget the pain of rejection. "I believe you asked first, Jim."

"You can have mine, Mista Luke. I queened it real good, 'cept this part."

"Obliged, Tom," Luke growled behind Tess.

She was grateful for the child's chattering as they walked downstairs and stopped to tell the proprietress they would be dining out and would not return until late. Tess was pleased to learn that Luke had arranged for a buggy.

". . . worth getting to know Wideacre," Jim said as he helped her into the buggy waiting at the steps of the boardinghouse.

"I'm sorry, I didn't hear what you said," Tess apologized as she settled into the rear seat. Jim spread a blanket over her skirts to stave off the evening chill.

Luke and Tommie took the front seat. The now four-year-old squealed with delight when Luke allowed him to help grip the reins and flick the team into motion. Tess missed Jim's comment again.

"I said, I think it would be worth getting to know Wideacre. He's obviously a man who knows his business and could possibly help us get established in Georgetown."

"Then you truly mean to stay?" Tess never really believed that Jim intended to make a home in Colorado. He'd had too much good fortune in Arkansas. Yet she supposed the lure of gold was something a gambler didn't easily forsake.

Jim placed a hand over hers. "I can gamble here as easy as anywhere. And as I told you, Contessa, wherever your home is, that's where I'll be. I've made no secret of wanting to care for you." His eyes darkened to coffee brown. "I love you."

She allowed him to claim her fingers, all the while studying Luke's back, wondering if he heard their conversation. "I think you've been a good friend, Jim, but—"

"But?"

Jim's grip tightened momentarily, then eased as she attempted to pull away. "But I don't love you, Jim. As a woman should love a man, I mean. You've always been kind to me . . . and Tommie," she added, though she'd always sensed he resented the boy for some reason. Was it because Tommie was Clifton's son and not his own?

"I've got to make a life for myself and my son, or I'm never going to know if I can provide for us. I've always had someone else to lean on, someone else to make my decisions for me. I don't think I can possibly love you the way you want me to unless I've had a little time to learn to like myself."

"I don't give up easy, Contessa. I've tried to stay in the background on this journey because the road was dangerous and it didn't seem the right timing for such things, but we're almost at the end of our journey. It's time I said what I've wanted to say for hundreds of miles. Be my wife, Contessa. Hell, what's love? You didn't love Clifton, we both know that. But you married him. I have enough love for both of us. You'll never want for anything. I'll build you a home better than Harper Hall, and I won't leave you alone like Clif did. I've always stayed around for you, haven't I? I was there long before Clifton, remember?"

He attempted to pull Tess closer, but the memory of Luke's embrace made her withdraw.

"It's Reeves, isn't it?" Jim's voice took on a harsher tone. "But he isn't right for you, Contessa. He's gonna light out of here as soon as you pay up." Jim nodded toward the bounty hunter. "I'll be here long after he's gone."

"Luke?" *Could he hear the longing in her voice?* She squared her shoulders. "Nothing can hold him. He's already said he's leaving as soon as we're settled. And, frankly, I'm glad of it!" And she was. The sooner he left, the sooner she could harden her heart from wanting him so desperately.

"You terrible mad at somebody, Mista Luke?"

Luke looked up from his plate, stared at the other couples enjoying dinner at the dining tables of the Hotel Dupree's grand ballroom, then back at the boy who sat across from him at a table meant for four. How could the child possibly know how angry he felt? How could he explain that the irritation was aimed more at himself than anyone else? "Why do you ask?"

Tommie pointed his fork at the buffalo steak Luke had sliced into tiny shreds. "Cause it looks like you cutting off somebody's head."

Laughing, Luke lay down the knife and fork. His gaze sought and found the gambler as he held Tess in his arms and waltzed on the dance floor. "I suppose I was, at that."

Spreading his arms wide in question, Tommie frowned. "Why don't you ask Mommie to dance, Mista Luke? Her will."

Luke wiggled a finger at Tommie and leaned in closer. The boy leaned in as well. "Can I tell you a secret?"

"Do I hafta keep it forever?" One blond brow arched over the child's narrowed eyes.

"I'd rather you did. But a man's choice is his own."

Tommie's look of disappointment changed into one of assurance. "You can trust me, Mista Luke."

Lowering his voice, Luke whispered, "You know when I told your mama I better not dance because my leg is paining me?"

"Yeah." Tommie tried to speak low, but couldn't quite achieve the tone.

"The truth is . . . I don't know how to dance."

"Golllleee," Tommie squealed the word. "Even *I* know how to dance, Mista Luke. Mommie taughted me."

"Not so loud, magpie. Don't announce it to everyone." Luke glanced around to see who heard. Several heads turned but, thank the Almighty, Tess and Daggert were on the other side of the dance floor.

"Sorry, Mista Luke." Tommie clamped his hands over his mouth, but his emerald eyes lit with merriment. After he quit giggling, his brows veed together and his features took on a seriousness. "You want me to teach ya how to dance?"

Not a bad idea, Luke mulled, then thought better of it. "It would never work."

"You afraid, Mista Luke? I promise not to step on your toes."

"I do want to dance with your mother." Gathering his courage, Luke stood. He wished to Heaven his own mother had taken time to teach him this one finer social amenity, but she couldn't endure the proximity needed for such lessons. "And never let it be said I let a little thing like not knowing how to dance get the better of me."

Tommie stood and pulled up his pants, straightening the suspenders that held them. "First thing is 'member to hitch up you pants. I always check my butnuns, then my 'spenders."

"Got it." Luke hid his smile from the boy.

"Now, 'member, don't stomp my feet. 'Posed to put one here, like dis," he indicated a spot to the left of his left foot. "Put the other one right here."

Luke placed his left foot near the outside of the boy's right foot.

"Mommie always plays the woman and I play the boy. I might mess this up a minutes. No, yeah. I 'member. Since you want to be the boy, I'll—"

"—the *man*," Luke insisted, surprised he enjoyed the lesson as much as he anticipated dancing with Tess.

Tommie's eyes rolled upward. "I never done it like a man. I only know it the *boy* way."

"All right. So show me how a boy does it."

"The lady 'posed to put her hand on you shoulder and her other hand like dis." Tommie held out his left hand and grabbed Luke's right. "Then, the boy 'posed to put the other hand on her waist. I can't ever reach Mama's waist, but I bet you can."

Aware of the attention they drew from the onlookers at other tables and from the dancers passing by them, Luke ignored the impulse to sit back down. He concentrated on what Tommie said.

"Take one step that way and stand on your tippy-toes. Come back down. Then take one step dis away and stand on your tippy-toes agin. When you do that, swing your arm the same way you step.''

As Luke listened to the rhythm of the waltz, Tommie's instructions became easy to follow. The boy laughed as Luke watched some of the other men and imitated their swirling swing.

"This is fun!" Tommie shouted. "Mommie don't turn me around and around like dis!"

"Quite a couple you two are," remarked a young woman as her partner whirled her past them.

No one made fun of Luke's effort as he feared they might, and he found himself enjoying the dance immensely. When the waltz ended, Luke was reluctant to return to the table, knowing Daggert would seek his advantage for as long as he could and keep Tess on the floor. But to his delight, the crowd was in the mood for waltzing and the band complied.

"Go ask my mommie. She wants to dance with you, I can tell." Tommie pointed at Tess who stood only a few feet away, locked in a dancer's embrace with Daggert.

"I'm not ready."

"Don't worry, I step on Mommie's toes sometimes. Her don't cry."

"She might if I stepped on them." Luke let go of his partner's hands and nudged him toward the table. "You'll stay put and not wander off?"

"I fink so."

"And you won't sip any of the wine?"

"Cross my heart and hope to grow whiskers."

"Drink your milk. It'll make a man of you."

"How come you don't drink milk, Mista Luke? Are you already enough man?"

"How come little boys ask too many questions? Now you better let me get over there while there's still a waltz left. It'll be my luck she'll want to sashay."

After making certain the boy was settled, Luke dodged the dancers until he found Daggert's broad back. Tapping the gambler on the shoulder, he couldn't resist offering a grin when Daggert swung around and frowned at him. "If you'll excuse me, I believe this waltz is mine."

Daggert shrugged a shoulder, then turned back to Tess. "This will give me some time to get to visit with Tommie awhile."

Tess looked pleased. "I'm sure he'll enjoy that, Jim."

I doubt that, Luke thought but didn't say it aloud to Tess. She needed to see for herself that Tommie didn't like the man. Something about the gambler scared the boy. Though he desired more than anything to dance with Tess, Luke decided he'd cut it short if he saw that Tommie was too afraid sitting at the table alone with Jim.

"I thought your leg hurt."

He gathered her in his arms. The touch of her waist sent waves of warmth up Luke's arm. Her soft hand rested in his, and he was overcome with Tess's sweet fragrance. Her breath brushed softly against his neck as he tried to match the rhythm of the waltz. It took several steps before the awkwardness eased into enjoyment. "I thought I might try a few dances."

"Is this a newfound diversion of yours?"

He heard the mirth in her voice and suspected she teased him. Tess knew very well he had only learned tonight. He was glad the anger had vanished and he could joke as well. "Do you mean suffering a hurt leg or dancing?" he evaded.

She giggled. "Neither. Do you make it a habit to anger gamblers?"

"Only when they waltz better than I do."

Tess laughed, and he enjoyed the pure sound. He liked the way she looked at him as if he meant something to her, relished the feel of her hand about his shoulders, the other resting securely in his palm. When their gazes met, he knew she, too, recalled another night, another time when they weren't restrained by the distance the waltz required. Luke almost felt her head resting beneath his cheek, her breasts pressed against his chest. The sway of Tess's hips as he whirled her from one side to the other spread a remembered fire through him.

"I'm sorry, Tess," he offered from the depth of feeling

chiseling at the stone that had once been his heart, "all I meant to do was protect you from Ragmorton."

Tess turned from his gaze. "I want to believe that."

"Good, then I have to say this. I can't count myself as your friend unless I do." When he considered what might have happened if he hadn't decided to take a stroll and see if she was ill or lost, it built white-hot rage inside him. "Don't keep putting yourself in such danger." She would probably be angry with him again, but it was a risk he'd have to take.

She whirled away from him. Instead of a burst of temper, she displayed a calm more frightening than anger. "Oh, you've made it perfectly clear you won't always be around. Like I told you, Luke, I'll find a way to protect myself."

"Good, because not a man alive would pass up the chance you gave Ragmorton. Look at me, dammit!" He ignored where they were, all the people who looked on, and pulled her close until he felt the rise and fall of her breasts. "I want you, Tess. I want to be the one to hold you."

He wanted to kiss her senseless, the way he had that one wondrous night that would haunt the rest of his days. But he could make no such requests of her. Not until he made the choice he must—to honor his word and bring her to justice or cast aside all he held sacred and make her his wife. Luke felt her drawing away, saw caution where he had hoped to instill desire.

Tess's voice trembled as she took a few steps backward. "You warned me you were leaving, Luke. I appreciate honesty more than you'll ever know." She half turned, then looked back. "Just don't expect me to wait forever while you make up your mind if you really meant it."

Chapter Twenty-four

Tess wondered what detained Luke as the barrel-chested Hi Washburn tossed her small carpetbag on the boot of the lumbering old coach and shinnied up to the driver's seat. Hi squinted at her with a where-the-devil-is-he look. She offered him a disarming smile, and he subsided into a muttered rumbling.

"Maybe he decided not to go on," Daggert said, helping her and Tommie into the coach.

"No, he would have at least told Tommie good-bye." Disappointment caused her to sound petulant. She'd given Luke every reason to leave last night. He owed them nothing. Georgetown was less than fifty miles away. He had more than fulfilled his end of the bargain. She supposed she could send his pay to the boardinghouse once she transacted business.

"Better get his hide here in two minutes, cause this coach is moving out on time," Hi informed them.

Eight people shared the interior, while another rode on top with the driver. Jim hitched his roan to the boot.

"Hold that stage," a voice called out.

Luke! He made it. Tess wondered if he planned to ride Talon alongside or take a seat.

The driver grumbled something cheeky about a so-and-so who thought time stood still for a badge, then offered a hearty hello to Luke. "So, it's you again. Thought you got your guns busted in Wichita. Should've known that sack of snake piss was lying. Ragmorton ain't got a truth in his head."

Luke rushed to tie the dun to the boot and squeeze into the seat next to Tess. Washburn barked a sharp command to the horses and flicked the nigh leader to buckjump the others. They were off!

Swinging around the corner at a brisk clip, he headed due west. Tommie waved at the few early risers gazing admiringly from the plank walks. Tess braced against the back of the seat, trying to determine the driver's pattern. The bumps and jostles seemed less difficult if she emulated the rhythm of the coach.

Washburn slowed down for the narrow Platte bridge that shook and trembled as they crossed. There seemed to be a short burst of speed, then they began to climb the highlands. The grade leveled and the driver chirped the team into an easygoing but steady trot. A treeless plain rolled past the windows, covered with sagebrush and buffalo chips. The road began to wind, well defined and rutty.

As they bounced along, the passengers introduced themselves. Tess joined in but quickly lost interest as she concentrated on making Tommie comfortable in such cramped quarters. There was more room if she held him in her arms, leaving a bit of space between herself and Luke.

Luke patted his lap. "He's welcome to stretch out here. He looks a bit sleepy. Awful early to have to get up."

Tess stared out the window. "For all of us, after such a late night." She wanted to add *after such a sleepless night,* but didn't. Too many strangers ready to add their own comments.

Luke pointed out landmarks. "That's Mount Vernon Canyon, then Apex Gulch. Over beyond those flat-topped table mountains is Golden City."

Suddenly the horses began to gallop. "Hi's trying to beat his time." A round of conversation between some of the locals revealed Washburn's reputation of being the fastest driver in the Rockies, who strove to improve his time whenever possible.

Tess thought Luke liked the faster clip because it threw her shoulder against his more often than not.

They didn't so much as slow down at Ten Mile House. Instead a man stood before the building ready with a sack which he tossed on top of the coach with a long swing. A word of salutation passed between the station keeper and driver, then the team swung south.

Washburn cursed so loud it drifted back to the passengers. The team slowed. Luke stuck his head out the window, then darted back in. "An ox train. Slow as molasses."

The driver made a wide sweep around them through the sagebrush, hurled a few condemnations as he passed the oxen. The freight liner hurled a few back to Hi in return.

Tommie looked at Tess. "Mommie, what's a road-stealing son of a—"

Tess clamped one hand over her son's mouth and glanced up apologetically. Every face was drawn to her own. "Nothing, son."

"Now that's not true, Tom." Luke frowned and offered the other passengers a wink. "That's oxen talk. That man was trying to get those oxen to move out of the way."

"Can I learn it?"

Daggert leered at Luke. "You got yourself into that one, Reeves."

Luke nodded. "You surely can, boy. When . . . you get big enough to drive a team of oxen."

Everyone chuckled. Tess smiled despite her anger at the bounty hunter.

Though there were sweeping turns and fresh team hook-ups at the hospital portal of Mount Vernon House, fords to cross, and a tollgate run by young Doc Patrick, the coach traveled no narrow roads until they reached Floyd Hill. Dinner was served at Junction Ranch where Tess chose to wash her face but not to comb her hair, since the community comb hanging on the peg looked like it had something crawling in it. Still, the meal tasted delicious and cost a dollar.

By the time Washburn reached the dried-apple-pie stage of his dinner, the hostlers had hooked up the team. With a grand departure, they turned, then slowed down for the climb up a lengthy incline. A hero-worshiping small boy in tattered trousers, seated on a fence, hailed Washburn.

"Yip—ee!" Washburn yelled, apparently showing off for the boy.

Tess hung tight to her precarious roost on the heavy, leather-slung, swaying old Concord coach. She glanced out the window, gasping at the yawning chasm inches away from the wheels. "Does he have brakes?" she worried aloud.

"Probably not using them," Daggert informed her. "Wouldn't do much good if he was. Lord help us if we throw a wheel or the kingbolt breaks."

"Thanks for reassuring us," Luke complimented sarcastically.

A mile and a half below, they reached level ground. Tess offered a prayer of thankfulness. They passed a swift-flowing cascade where a handful of men worked along the stream. The panners looked up and waved their beaver hats at the stage.

"Clear Creek," Luke announced to all who watched. "About five miles out of Idaho Springs."

Tess straightened and took a closer look, straining to see the land and waters, but too many of the others did the same. The gold findings at Clear Creek had been big news in the paper last year. She would wait until the other passengers' interest waned, hoping to get a better view as they rode closer to the springs.

Five miles passed quickly. Idaho Springs appeared to be an active settlement, but after Washburn's grand entry, all he did was stop long enough to toss off a couple of parcels of express. As the coach moved on, Tess assured Tommie, "We'll come back here as soon as we've settled in."

The last change of horses came at Mill City. Approaching a road junction after the Lawson house, the horses' pace stepped up. The driver took a left-hand fork in the road, and the Concord entered a valley with a stream flowing down the center. As they followed the stream's course, soon cabins and small houses began to appear. Though scattered indiscriminately, each generally followed the water course. There seemed little semblance of order and nothing that could be called streets. The road wound in and out avoiding the evergreen trees and marshy places. The Concord crossed a shaky bridge, then the land inclined sharply.

Washburn cracked his whip. The horses strained at the reins and tugged up a block-long hill. Suddenly the driver yelled, "Whoa!"

The horses came to a stiff-legged halt before a large house. A lean, lantern-jawed man stepped out of the crowd of loungers near the doorway and opened the door to the Concord. A grin spread from one side of his face to the other. "Howdo, folks? My name's Lionel Cramden. Welcome to the Silver Queen city of the Rockies . . . Georgetown!"

Tess's first glimpse of the Barton House made her wonder how her own home compared. The house stood on a knoll which afforded a good view of the valley.

Lionel showed them around the inside of the pretentious two-storied hotel. "Better not take in the town tonight," he warned. "You'll want to get your bearings and know your way around. The streets are hilly, and there aren't any real sidewalks. The only lights we've got are kerosene lamps in the saloons and in a few of the shops. Stores close at ten o'clock, but the saloons stay open till the last man leaves. Got two flossy ones in Upper Town—Barney Harvey's Keg House on one side of the gulch and the Gayosa. This is Saturday, so hell will be popping. Miners flock in from all over the hills with gold or silver in their pockets. Durned if they won't be proud to see your little one, ma'am."

"Tommie?" In a protective instinct, Tess gripped her son by the shoulders.

"A child and a good woman's something we don't see

much around here, ma'am. The men will be right proud to make your acquaintances.''

"Then I don't suppose there's a church or a school established yet?'' Her hopes began to plummet. She had staked so much of her happiness on the idea that a home and school would provide the new life she and Tommie needed.

"Hadn't been no reason till now. But I'll bet we could talk Hansel Andersen who runs the local mercantile into lending you his room overhead, and you could conduct the school or church there, whichever you wish.''

Tess held her hands up in a wave of denial. "I'm not skilled enough to do either, but I'll help in some other way.''

"So, you do plan on staying?''

Tess nodded. "I'll be living at Harper Hall.''

Lionel's lantern jaw sagged. "Surely not?''

Misgiving spread a cold shiver of anxiety through Tess. She had traveled too far, suffered too many obstacles to let a single man's obviously bad opinion of her home get the better of her. "Why not, Mr. Cramden?''

"Well, ma'am. Harper Hall is a mine located in Lower Town. Ain't much more than a shack sitting next to the entrance, and Nugget lives in it. He mines the thing for a man in Arkansas . . . a Clifton Harper.''

"My husband.''

"It's got a cot and a stove. Not much else.''

"A mine?'' Tess said the word slowly as her heart sank. "There's some mistake.'' Yet she knew it wasn't. She should have suspected. The papers Clifton had made her copy when he was teaching her to read and write concerned mines. He'd used her until she had caught on. Did he laugh at her even now from the grave?

Laugh, she told him silently, steeling herself against the disappointment. *You won't get the best of me. I'll take your stupid mine and I'll work it. I'll make Tommie and me a life without you.* "How do we get there?''

"You won't let her stay out there?'' Lionel looked from Daggert to Luke. "It's not fit for a lady or a child to live in.''

240

Luke's brow arched at Tess. "Your decision."

"I want to see it."

"We'll help her get settled, then take a room here." Jim eyed the rest-of the crowd. "Are there good poker tables in town?"

"Plenty, for those good enough to play 'em," Lionel said.

"Have you got a wagon or buggy to take the lady to her place?" Luke lifted Tess's small bag and grabbed Tommie's hand.

"Follow me." Lionel motioned them out to a wagon standing in front of the Barton House. "I keep the team hitched near time for the stage to arrive. Somebody's always coming to Georgetown and the silver fields."

He showed Luke where to store her small bag. "Didn't bring much, did you?" Lionel helped Tess and the boy onto the buckboard. Luke and Jim saddled up and rode behind them.

The wagon lurched and soon rolled past the shacks and shanties, some of the large houses and saloons, then headed up the incline.

"How far from town is Harper Hall?" Tess looked back as the town grew more distant. Tents scattered along the stream offered makeshift homes to the miners.

"Far enough to keep Nugget from civilization, but close enough so you can light a fire and the town could see it if you have Indian troubles."

"Indians!" Tommie bounced on the seat.

"Indians," his mother whispered in a slow exhale of breath. *What have I gotten us into?*

As they bumped their way up the hill, Tess noted the box elders, evergreens and aspens that dotted the landscape for as far as the eye could see. Their beauty became lost in the thoughts of how she could clear enough land of their towering height to plant a garden. The wagon rattled and jolted along the pitted road that snaked toward an appalling shack made of pickets.

When Lionel reined up in front of the ramshackle house,

Tess glanced up the trail, wishing this was all a dream, merely a place he had to make a delivery and not the home she'd come to find.

Cupping hands around his mouth, Lionel hollered, "Hello the mine! Nugget, you in there, man?" He turned to Tess. "Got to always announce yourself if you don't want trouble. Might think you're a claim jumper if you don't."

In a daze, Tess climbed off the wagon, staring open-mouthed at the rough building before her. She helped Tommie down, blinking away the tears of utter disappointment. Behind her, the creak of saddles signaled Luke and Jim were dismounting.

Tess grasped Tommie's hand in her own and retrieved her bag. "Is the man home?" she asked, wondering why Lionel Cramden walked over to the hole in the mountain and hollered the same as before. "Is that the mine?"

"Yeah. Might be down deep enough he can't hear. You go on into the shack and have a look around. I'll see if he's in here."

Tess forced herself to trudge the small path to the shack. She raised the iron latch on the door, found it wasn't locked, then pushed it open. The rusty hinges screeched as she let sunshine into the dark interior. Light from the dirty cracked windows revealed a dirt floor, a table and pot-bellied stove. One cot and a wash bucket. In one corner a chest of drawers stood, missing one drawer.

Her heart pounded so hard Tess heard it drumming at her temples. This was a nightmare. Her chest tightened until she couldn't breathe. She gulped and plowed through the male bodies who had followed her in. "Let me out," she pleaded.

"Mommie, don't cry."

"Does madam not approve?"

Tess turned to find a strange man standing alongside Cramden. With the smudges on his face and the pick in his hand, this could only be Nugget. She had expected an older, grizzled man. At first she thought Nugget's question sarcastic, then she caught the French inflection and wondered if he asked about himself rather than their lodgings.

"You're Nugget?" Luke queried before Tess could speak.

"Oui, monsieur. Louis DuMonde LaTouix. *Nugget* to my friends."

Tess understood how he'd earned his nickname. As the man smiled and offered his hand to Luke, then Jim, the span of white teeth had two imperfections . . . two front teeth glistened with gold.

Two heads shorter than herself, the man strutted as if he were at least a foot taller. His dark mustache and beard looked rail thin and painted on rather than grown.

The stout little Frenchman bent, taking her hand and kissing the tips of her fingers. "Welcome to Harper Hall, madam. Had I known you were coming, I would have"—he gestured exotically—"cleaned the place up a bit, oui?"

He bent before Tommie, offering his hand. "Enchanté. Will you be staying long, monsieur?"

Tess stared at the Frenchman for an extended pause. "We'll be staying forever. I'm afraid, Mr. LaTouix, that *this*,"—she waved to the pitiful shack—"is what my son and I must call home."

Chapter Twenty-five

"This cannot be!" Nugget exclaimed, turning to the lantern-jawed man. "Is this a joke, Lionel?" He laughed and slapped his friend on the back. "*Merde,* you win this time. But I will think of something more devious, oui?"

Lionel twisted his hat around in his gnarled hands. "Ain't a joke, Nugget. This is really Harper's wife. *Widow,* I might say. She's come to Georgetown to stake her husband's portion of the claim."

Luke noticed Tess's distress and thought she looked as if she might fall down if she didn't sit soon. "Let's take this talk inside the shack. I think Mrs. Harper needs to get her bearings."

Nugget hurried inside and apologized as he dusted one of the chairs. "I only sleep here and spend my time mining, madam. I regret this is in such a state."

Reaching to one of the shelves nailed to the wall, he took down three metal tins and a bottle of bourbon. The Frenchman smiled apologetically at the crude drinking utensils. "I do not have much company, but they are clean and the bottle, she is fresh. Enjoy."

He poured for Tess first, then for Luke and Jim. Resting

one finger against his cheek, Nugget appeared to ponder the situation. "Ahh, the bucket will do. Tommie, will you come with me to the creek and we will quench your thirst as well? The water is the coolest and finest in all the Continental Divide."

Tess hesitated. She didn't know this Frenchman from Adam, yet he seemed friendly enough.

The man from the Barton House picked up the bucket. "Allow me, Mrs. Harper?" Lionel's eyes rounded into a plea. "A child's an uncommon sight 'round here. Does a man good to see progress a'coming to Georgetown. I'll look after him while you folks talk business. No need to worry. I'll take care of him like he was my own."

Lionel had been nothing but kind. She could tell by the way the man looked at Tommie with a tinge of awe that he wouldn't harm her son or allow him to get hurt. If Tess had to trust someone in this place she meant to call home, she would start with these two men. "I'm beholden to you, Mr. Cramden."

Tommie shoved his hand into Lionel's and the man's swayed back seemed to straighten considerably. As the two stepped out into the daylight, a loud cheer went up.

Tess bolted to her feet and ran to the door. Luke, Jim and Nugget hurried close behind. Stepping out into the light, she grabbed Tommie's hand instinctively, offering Lionel a quick apologetic glance that said her fear had nothing to do with him.

"Look there. It's a boy!" yelled one of the burly men trudging up the path toward the shack.

"A boy," another said and hollered to the next man running down the western slope of the hill.

Men of all shapes and sizes swarmed the hillside leading up to Harper Hall. The jingle of horse-drawn buggies and the crack of whips announced the wagons headed this way as well. When they came into view, Tess was amazed at the number of masculine bodies each held. Men dressed in high-topped boots waded the stream and climbed the hill to join many

245

others clad in blue trousers and red flannel shirts.

Had every miner in the Continental Divide come to Harper Hall?

"You're awfully pretty, Mrs. Harper," a red-headed giant of a man shouted, stopping in his tracks at a respectful distance. "Any more like you coming?"

"Heard at Barton House she's a widder," announced a toothless man as he stroked the salt-and-pepper beard that hung to his belt. "That true, ma'am?" He doffed his hat, displaying a completely bald head.

Nugget acted as spokesman for Tess's party, stepping in front of her and waving his hands high to get everyone's attention. "Now, gentleman. This is no way to greet the lady. Let us give her and her son a real Georgetown welcome. Mrs. Harper, I give you the townsmen of Georgetown, Silver Queen of the Rockies, and of other parts unknown."

A loud hurrah pierced the air as male voices thundered over the yard and hats flew high into the air, each face eagerly awaiting her response.

Tess stepped forward and stared at the sea of faces. The disappointment at discovering such shabby dwellings was momentarily lost in the genuine, rousing welcome. "And hello to you all. I hope I'll get to meet you each individually soon. My name is Contessa Harper and this is my son, Thomas James. He prefers to be called Tommie." She motioned to Luke and Jim and introduced them as well.

"Is it true you're a widow?" asked a man who looked carved from the bark of a pine tree.

His eyes squinted at her in frank approval. Tess didn't know how safe she would be here alone if her status was common knowledge, but she supposed they would learn soon enough anyway. "Yes, it is."

A handsome, blond Swede stepped forward. "One of them your intended?"

Tess shook her head, though she glanced at Luke to see if he had anything to say in answer to the man's question. Disappointed, she informed the Swede, "They brought me across

246

Indian territory. Mr. Reeves and Mr. Daggert were my guides."

Another shout went up as each man celebrated the availability of a new woman in town. A good-looking one at that.

"Now, you men go on home," Nugget commanded, then noted Tess's tired expression. "Madam is tired from the long trip, oui?"

She nodded.

"Mrs. Harper will visit tomorrow when she's rested. Then we can show her how we welcome a friend."

"How 'bout the boy, ma'am?" One miner pointed toward Tommie. "I'll give you twenty dollars worth'a gold if I can shake his hand."

"Count me in," said another.

"Fifty if he'll let me give him a ride on my shoulders."

Tess gripped Tommie's hand tightly and looked at Luke as the crowd bartered for time with her son.

"I'm here, Tess," Luke stated softly. "I won't let anything happen."

But could he take on this many men if something did occur? He wasn't even wearing his Colt, and the rifle was still sheathed in Talon's saddle.

As if he read her mind, the Frenchman reassured, "If any of them hurt the boy, the others will tear the man to shreds with their bare hands. Tommie is safe, madam, as are you. You and the child are a precious dream shared by all these men who want fortune and a family to share it with."

Tess released her hold on Tommie. "Do you want to meet these men?"

"Yes, ma'am. Look at all the friends I got now!" His face radiated with anticipation.

"Then go say hello." A lump of pride knotted in her throat, drowning out the worry of having just agreed to give a part of her son up to total strangers. He had been her sole stability, and Tess's heart lurched at the thought of him needing her less.

Though his limp was even more noticeable as he ran toward

the crowd, she could hardly keep up with Tommie. A hush swept over the gathering. Face after masculine face took on an expression of undying protection as the boy struggled toward them. In that moment, Tess's heart warmed and blossomed with a newfound friendship toward each of them. Now more than ever she was determined to make Harper Hall and the Georgetown community her home. Finally, she stood among friends and people who did not judge.

"Where would you have me start, Mrs. Harper?" Nugget opened the wood-slatted door before Tess could do it for herself. "I have a broom in the mine and a bucket for wash water."

Tess read compassion in the Frenchman's gray eyes. His sympathy soothed her as she stared at the filthy interior and wondered how she would ever get it clean.

"You will have that drink now, oui?" Nugget pulled the chair out for her.

Jim joined them, leaving Luke and Lionel to safeguard the proceedings taking place outside with Tommie.

"Drink up, Tess. You'll need it." The gambler scooted the tin over to her as she thanked the Frenchman and took a seat in one of the ladder-back chairs.

Tess sipped the warm liquid, surprised that it tasted both good and disgusting. The bourbon burned her throat and she coughed, unaccustomed to its fiery smoothness. Like Luke, she thought. Exhilarating on one hand, destructive on the other. Tess put down the tin and studied Nugget. "Why did my husband hire you to watch his mine?"

The Frenchman's brow arched, his eyes becoming guarded. With the first hit of something other than friendliness, he explained. "I'm his partner. The claim is half mine. He paid for the claim and I work it. I always send his half to Fort Smith."

"Half *yours?*" Color drained from Tess's face. Not only had Clifton left her nothing, he'd given her half of nothing. The Frenchman's story explained the money her husband couldn't have possibly made as a soldier. "Then you intend to remain here?"

"But of course, madam. Who would mine the claim?" His features took on concern. "A woman in the mines is considered courting misfortune. You do not intend to work it?"

"No." She shook her head. "I mean . . . I don't know. I didn't have any idea I was coming to a mine. I thought I would have a place where I could take in boarders, plant a garden, make a home for my son."

"All the more reason you should marry me." Jim pressed Tess's trembling hands with his own, ignoring the frown wrinkling Nugget's brow. "I'll work the mine with LaTouix here. All you have to do is stay home and keep the"—he frowned at the planked walls—"shack."

Tess gripped the cup again, causing Jim's hand to fall away. She took another sip of the fiery liquor, feeling warmth settle into her bones. She had awaited this day far too long to take the easy way out, particularly when she didn't love the man offering it. Tess brushed back a loose tendril of hair and glanced at Jim. "If I accept your offer, I'll never know if I can meet the challenge on my own. I've got to try first. If you love me as much as you say, then the answer will wait awhile."

Suddenly the gambler's smile settled into a grim line, his brown eyes sharpening. "I don't want you spending time alone up here with a man you hardly know."

Nugget stood abruptly, facing the gambler. "Do not insult the lady nor *moi*, monsieur."

Jim met him glare for glare. "Be careful how you draw your dueling pistols, Frenchy, and keep your stubby nose out of my face."

"Gentlemen, please stop." Tess rose and met Jim's aggressive eyes steadily. "I've spent months on the trail with two men I hardly know. Spending time with my partner makes just as much sense. Now if you'll excuse us, Mr. Daggert, Nugget and I have work to do."

A slow smile eased Jim's expression. "Can't blame me for

being jealous, Contessa.'' Staring intently at Nugget, Jim settled his hat on his chestnut hair and held the Frenchman's gaze a moment longer before he turned to leave. ''I'll be around.''

''I'm not going anywhere,'' Nugget assured him.

Tess sank to her chair, feeling completely drained. This was the longest day of her life and far from over. She had to clean this pig sty until it shined. Not only was it a necessity to change the shack into a place where she and Tommie could live, now it was a must. Under no terms would she accept Jim's proposal.

Nugget walked to the door and paused. ''I'll fetch the broom and water, Mrs. Harper. I have some lye soap in one of the chambers I use as a storage room. The cavern is cool and *bon,* good, for keeping food supplies. I'll show you our possessions later, when you've had time to yourself. And, Mrs. Harper—''

''Please, if we're partners, you ought to call me Tess.''

''Tess.'' Nugget smiled. ''Do not fear me as your friend implied. I would never insult a lady in such a manner.'' Without warning, he left and closed the door behind him.

The shabbiness of the room loomed around Tess like a shroud thrown over her hopes. Though made of glass, the windows beneath the burlap curtains would need hours of scrubbing. Evening light seeped in through the cracks of the planked walls, making Tess shiver at the mere thought of the cold she and Tommie would suffer come winter. Iron brackets offered a way to bar the door against marauders. One of the table legs stood at a precarious angle and would give way if it wasn't repaired soon. The stove hadn't been scrubbed in ages, and she vowed not to eat a single bite from anything cooked on or in it until she personally saw to the cleaning.

The cot standing in one corner boasted a clean blanket and pillow which she supposed Nugget would claim for himself. Tears brimmed in Tess's eyes but she refused to shed them. Weeping was for the defeated, she reminded herself, wiping the back of her hand against each eye. Tess sniffled, telling herself it was merely the dust that had caused the reaction, nothing else. Whether it was false courage inspired by the bourbon or simply an act of pure defiance, Tess rolled up her sleeves and jerked down the burlap curtains from the windows. "And I haven't lost yet," she challenged the four filthy walls.

When the door opened, Luke towered above her son as Tommie limped toward her, forming a cloth basket with his shirt.

"Lookie here, Mommie. We got lots'a money. We can fix our house up real good now."

Chapter Twenty-six

Despite his impulse to leave the cleaning to Reeves and the Frenchman, Jim decided to roll up his sleeves and help. This might be the best way to convince Tess he meant business about the marriage proposal. As night and the cleaning progressed, he discovered that being helpful had its benefits. When Luke and Tommie made their frequent trips to the creek to fetch fresh wash water, Jim stole a closer look at Tess, watching her hips wiggle as she scrubbed the stove. The fullness of her breasts as they strained against the homespun while she reached to sweep the cobwebs out of a corner sent a surge of desire through him.

"Why don't you let someone tall do that?" suggested Luke as he followed Tommie into the shack. Instead of taking on the task himself, he set the water bucket down, took the broom from Tess, then thrust it hard against Jim's chest. "That way she won't have to reach so far, will she?"

Jim's jaw clenched as anger heated his face. He could look any way he damned well pleased at his future wife and the bounty hunter better know it, here and now. "Better learn how to do this, hadn't I?" Jim ignored Reeves's glare and smiled

252

at Tess. "Plan on being around a lot." He let the rub sink in. "Unlike some of us."

Luke took the bait. "I won't leave till the work is done."

"And what work is that?" Jim had a good idea that Reeves hadn't hired on just as guide. The man suspected something whether or not he knew anything for certain. Jim's gut instinct told him Reeves hadn't hung on this long because of a guilty conscious over killing Clif. If the facts were known, it might have been Jim's own bullet that had plugged the soldier. He had taken aim clear enough for it not to miss. But the bounty hunter had been quick to decide it was his bullet that did the damage, not Jim's deliberately aimed one.

Could it be possible that Reeves knew about the mine scams? If so, how much did he suspect? The possibility shed a whole new light on the bounty hunter's infatuation with Contessa. If Reeves had seen even one of the documents used in selling the salted mines, he would have noticed that the handwriting matched hers. Could it be the bounty hunter wasn't in love with her and only played her and the boy for fools so he might learn the truth?

The more Jim mulled Reeve's actions, the likelier his suspicions became. Someone here locally had hired the bounty hunter to find out who was behind the scams. He must have traced the trail back to Clifton, except Clifton died. With Contessa's handwriting on the bills of sale, Reeves must think she was a part of Clif's schemes.

Anger filled Jim. At least his own love for her was genuine. He wanted this mine because of what Clifton told him about its value, but not as much as he wanted Tess. The plan to marry her and get the pleasure of the mine and her bed had been the best solution. As her husband, he would control all of Tess's possessions. But he had almost made the mistake of thinking he might be forced to obtain the mine without a marriage contract.

The fact that Reeves didn't want Tess and intended to make her pay for a crime she was involved in but not guilty of, riled Jim to the point of madness. He had to think of a special way to rid Contessa of the bounty hunter's threat. A way worse than death.

"I asked what work was that?" Jim repeated, this time his tone much harsher.

Before Luke could answer, a voice called from the yard, "Hello the shack!"

"*Sacre bleu,* come back at daylight!"

The Frenchman's words echoed into the night as he attempted to prevent the visitor from approaching the door. A furious discussion followed. Nugget promised to tell Mrs. Harper of the visitor's call.

"I'll be back at daylight, ma'am. You can bet on it!" The caller hollered.

"It is I, madam," Nugget announced before opening the door and entering. He held a half sack of flour cradled against one hip, a tin of coffee and a slab of something wrapped in burlap against the other.

"Hello the shack!"

"Enough!" Nugget hurriedly handed Luke the provisions. To Tess, he shrugged elaborately. "Another suitor, I fear. Let me handle this, madam. I will see they do not disturb you the rest of the night."

"What's a suitor?" Tommie glanced up at Luke.

A man who better be worthy of her, Luke started to say, but offered an answer that revealed less of his own feelings about the matter. "A man who wants to court your mother and someday become her husband."

"If he be her husband, he be my new daddy?" Puzzlement etched Tommie's face.

Tess and Luke's gazes met . . . locked. "Yes, Tommie, that's how it works," Luke said softly.

"When did you say you were leaving for Denver, Reeves? Tomorrow?" Jim wanted to make it clear that Luke had no intention of staying around. She and the boy needed to know that the bounty hunter cared more for his job than for them. Maybe they would see that *he,* Jim, wouldn't leave them. That he would be the better husband.

254

"I said when the work is done."

Tommie's eyes rounded in surprise, and Tess clutched her arms together as if forming a barrier between herself and the inevitability of Luke's leaving.

A hammering on the door halted further discussion. Before anyone could take a step, Nugget opened and peaked around the planking. "Nailed up a sign telling everyone to stay clear until dawn. Should keep out all but the ones who don't know how to read. You must sleep, madam, for the men will be back. They wish to admire you, *mais oui*?"

"Smart fellows," Luke commented. "They have every reason to, don't they, Tom?"

The boy nodded and clung to Luke's leg, afraid the bounty hunter might go anywhere without him.

Not that I'd mind, Jim decided. But Contessa would never let the child out of her sight. If he married her, he supposed the boy came with her. How much trouble could the kid be?

The widow quickly turned around, her voice low and full of something Jim couldn't determine.

"I'll make something to eat. I know we're all starving. Thanks, Nugget, for the provisions."

"Tommie and I will go wash off a bit." Luke lifted the boy and nestled him over his broad shoulders. "This time don't push me into the water until *after* I get my boots off," he warned the child teasingly.

If the townsmen could view this, Jim was certain they wouldn't waste their time trudging up here to offer marriage to Contessa. She and her son had only one choice in mind for Clifton's replacement. Contessa might not know her own mind yet, but her body spoke volumes. The way her eyes lit with pleasure when Reeves walked into the room, the way they threatened to shed tears at learning he intended to leave, conveyed how much she loved the bastard. Yes, he needed to get rid of Reeves once and for all. In such a way she would never allow the bounty hunter back into her life.

* * *

By the first rays of dawn, word spread through camp of Tess's eligibility. She found herself swamped with offers of marriage that staggered the imagination. Even Georgetown's elite—judges; doctors, a lawyer or two—joined in the race. Gamblers, drifters, prospectors and gunfighters alike played the fearsome odds of winning her hand. Addicted to the game of chance that had brought them to the silver camp, most staked a claim on her before the sun fully crested the Rockies.

At first, Tess felt flattered and amused. Another knock on the shack door announced a well-dressed stranger who indicated he hoped to visit Tommie Harper. Hair slicked back and smelling of bay rum, the man nodded a greeting to Tess, offered a gift to her son, then accepted one of the ladder-back chairs and stiffly lowered himself into the seat. While Tommie oohed and ahhed over promises of a rocking chair, carved soldier, a horse, or puzzled over dishes, a bolt of calico, a churn, the caller proudly recited his assets and the lavish manner in which he could provide for the boy.

The offers surprised Tess: mining stock, precious gems, a small fortune in gold pieces, all willingly given in exchange for a marriage vow. Without fanfare, or even the slightest attempt at small talk, the men presented their intentions with little delicacy and intense solemnity. Tess ceased being amused by it all and began to resent the endless bartering. Though she had a sleepless night and looked more like a scrub woman, suddenly she felt like a prized brood mare on an auction block, with each man trying to outbid the other. The feelings evoked memories of standing in front of the Hot Springs bathhouse listening to her father lie about her age, convincing men and women alike that his waters provided such healing they restored youth.

Of all who sought her favor this morning, Jim was the only one who asked for her hand without the ruse of visiting Tommie. ''I'd consider your proposal more kindly,'' she told the gambler who bent on one knee before her and gripped her hands in his, ''if you'd give me a bit more time to think.'' Tess's shoulders ached from the long night of cleaning. She yawned. "All I'm interested in right now is a hot bath and a few hours sleep."

Tommie yawned, tired from all the attention and weary of all the men who stood around awaiting his mother's decision. "I sleepy, Mista Luke." He held his arms out for Luke to lift him. The bounty hunter pressed him against a strong shoulder which made Tommie feel warm and protected. His lashes blinked fast, making his eyes feel suddenly so heavy he couldn't keep them open. But Tommie didn't want to go to sleep. Not yet. He had to know just one more thing. "You be here tomorrow, Mista Luke?"

Luke's hand pressed against Tommie's back and snuggled him closer. "I'll be here."

"Gooo-ood." The word escaped Tommie's mouth in a restful sigh that sent away the troublesome thoughts stirred by his daddy's friend Jim. Luke would be here. It was safe to sleep now. *Safe.*

"This little man's gone, Tessa. Where can I lay him down?"

Unconsciously Tess brushed back a wisp of hair and flicked the dust from her skirt. She glanced at Nugget who stood near the stove, devouring one of the sourdough biscuits she had made. "May my son use your cot, Nugget?"

"Manna from Heaven," the French complimented as he licked his fingers. "Oui, madam. I give up the cot gladly for the boy. For the biscuits, I too will propose." He winked.

Tess laughed. "That's the best offer I've had all morning, don't you think, Luke?"

Luke placed the boy on the cot and covered him with the blanket. His gaze lingered on the freshly scrubbed pink cheeks and the wisps of blond hair still damp at the ends. Could he endure the sight of this boy calling any other man Pa?

The bounty hunter stared at the crowd of men, Jim in particular. She wanted an honest answer. He would give her one. "I think Phinneas Wideacre is the best."

"He's not even here to speak his piece," one of the others argued.

"That's true," Luke admitted. "But the note he sent clearly states she can keep her half of the mine without having to hand over control of it to him as her husband. I doubt most of you are willing to make the same concession."

Most in the crowd could not meet his gaze.

"I thought so. Go on back to your diggings," Luke ordered. "Mrs. Harper doesn't need a man looking to court her and the boy for the sake of a fortune."

Jim saw his chance. "How come you know what the mine's worth? You're new-arrived, same as me."

When shamed, the fastest way to get rid of blame is to put it on someone else. This Luke understood as all gazes rested on him. If he told them the truth, he would reveal his cover. Months of work would be lost and those involved in the mine scams would be warned, particularly if Tess was not guilty of the crimes. Despite the hurt he knew it caused and partly because of it, he saw a way to make her forget him and what he might eventually call down upon her head. "Have I ever indicated I wanted her for any other reason? Wideacre is the man she should marry."

"Please, everyone leave." Tess stood and braced her hands against the table to keep from shaking. "I do not intend to make any decision. I haven't even made up my mind to marry again. Now that you've all proven to me you're the kind of men who would use a child"—her gaze locked with Luke's and she forced back tears of fury and the deepest hurt she had ever felt—"to obtain a fortune, I'm not certain Georgetown is meant for homes and families and the *trust* that goes with them."

Men slowly filed out of the shack, each unable to meet her rightful scorn. Jim doffed his hat. "I'll see you later this afternoon. I'll be at the Barton House if you need me. Get some sleep."

"I doubt that will come easily." Tess stared at Luke.

Nugget cleared his throat. "If madam will excuse me, I'll make a bed in the mine and close my eyes. The biscuits were *magnifique*!"

Tess smiled at the Frenchman's effort to lighten the mood, but the smile disappeared as the door closed and only she and Luke were left standing in the room. She glanced at Tommie to make sure he was asleep and did not hear what she needed to say.

"You used me . . . not just me, but *Tommie*." The truth felt as if it ripped her heart. *God, don't ever let Tommie know.*

"That's not true, Tessa. I love Tommie as if he were my own son."

She believed him. Wanted to. "Then you used me. You just wanted me. Never loved me."

"Wanting you is easier than loving you, Tessa." His tone echoed the loneliness engulfing him. He reached to touch her, but she moved away.

"Just leave, Luke. Get out of our lives."

"Tess, don't do this. There are things you don't know about me."

"I don't want to know any more."

Luke started to advance. "Trying to get something through that stubborn head of yours is harder than outrunning a prairie fire. I'm only doing a job, dammit. Just like you're spending all your time being a mother and giving none to being a woman."

She stepped closer, her face hot with anger. "The way I care for my son is *my* business."

Luke frowned. "You don't understand. I'm not condemning you for it. I'm saying you have your priorities, Tess, I have mine." How could he make her understand? He was losing her. Losing the only woman who had ever loved him as equally as he could love her. All for the sake of his word and the past she would not reveal.

"Go. I don't ever want to see you again."

"I promised the boy I wouldn't." How could he live without her? How could he never hear her voice again? Ever sleep without knowing he would awaken and see her lovely face? How would he forget her touch?

Tears rolled down Tess's cheeks as she took a step backward toward the cot. Her heart pounded so fiercely she thought it might break and cease to beat. Luke was right about one thing . . . perhaps if she concentrated long enough, hard enough on raising Tommie, there would be no time to think about the night she'd spent in Luke's arms. No time to miss what she was about to give up forever. No time to worry that she had something within her that Luke couldn't love. "Leave us and don't ever come back," she whispered and turned her back to Luke.

Chapter Twenty-seven

The gambler kept careful watch on the shack, wondering how long he had to search through Reeves's saddlebags. Contessa would keep the bounty hunter a few minutes, but it might not be long enough.

Like a prospector looking for an elusive piece of gold, Jim dug deeply into one bag, found nothing, then tried the other. Still nothing. As he buried his hand beneath the saddle, the dun snorted in objection. "Private men keep private compartments," Jim whispered to the horse, groping to feel anything that might prove his opinion correct. Running his fingers along the aged leather, he searched for any minute difference. A bulge halted his progress. A pocket?

"Easy, Talon. Easy, boy," Jim soothed as the animal moved to one side and nearly jerked Jim's arm from its socket. "Damn you, be still! You'll have Reeves out here plugging me full of lead. Just a bit more and I'll have whatever this is."

With a final tug, the gambler pulled a notebook from the hidden pocket. When he opened the leather-bound volume, Jim's eyes lit with satisfaction. A quick glance showed the two folded documents were telegrams, but the notebook

261

proved to be more incriminating. The written report gave Jim all the ammunition he needed to convince Contessa that Luke Reeves was up to no good.

Talon neighed, jerking against the reins looped in a low-hanging box elder branch. "Shut up!" Jim cursed as the horse continued to object. The hinges on the shack door squeaked as they opened, warning the gambler that Reeves had heard the horse's protest. Not wanting to take the chance of being seen, Jim ran into the mine and took refuge in the first cave, where Nugget housed the supplies.

"Not you too, Talon."

The gambler listened as the bounty hunter complained. Reeves's voice echoed through the tunnel. "What's *your* reason for being so grouchy? At least you got some sleep."

From the grunt the bounty hunter made, it sounded like he had lifted something heavy. Crouching behind a stack of empty crates, Jim noted Reeves's disgruntlement growing louder as he drew nearer. The gambler hid the report and documents between two of the crates. If he was caught, he didn't want to be holding Reeves's possessions.

"Maybe when she gets some sleep, I can talk some sense into her," Luke grumbled, then paused. "Hell, maybe if I get some sleep, I'll *want* to reason with her."

Jim waited until he was certain his adversary had plenty of time to bed down, then edged away from his hiding place, retrieving the report from its haven. Like a lover stealing away from a married woman's bedroom, he moved soundlessly through the tunnel. When he arrived at the opening, the dun looked up from the grass and stared at Jim. Would the animal raise a fuss and give him away now?

Deciding he didn't have time to stick around and find out, the gambler circled around the hill and found the roan where he had left him to graze. Tucking the contraband in his shirt so his hands would be free to rein, Jim mounted and wound his way through the forest. When he arrived at a point about a mile down the path from the mine, he turned around and headed up the path as if he had come straight from town.

Enough miners would see him come up the hill to confirm that he had been to town and had had no time to steal anything Luke Reeves might find missing.

Tess yawned, considering stretching out beside Tommie on the cot. She could easily give in to the sleepiness that threatened to close her eyes, but she needed to wash first. The sun shone brightly over the Rocky Mountains and radiated through the cracks in the planked walls. She wouldn't have the privacy to strip down to her chemise, but she would at least wash her hair and scrub her face and hands.

"Hello the shack!"

Jim's voice forced a perturbed sigh from her lips.

"I must talk to you."

What do you want now? Tess grimaced at the thought of having to deal with one more man this day. But she remembered her manners and put on a polite face. Opening the door, she stepped out into the bright sunlight. As she shielded her gaze, the sun beat down on her hands and prickled them with heat.

Despite her effort not to appear rude, Tess yawned. The long hours of cleaning the shack had taken their toll. "Can we talk some other time, Jim?" she asked. "I'm very tired."

Jim dismounted and hitched the roan to the yard post. "I don't think you'd want me to wait where Tommie's concerned."

Immediately the sleepiness drained away. In its place, a premonition of trouble roused her lagging senses. She waited impatiently as the gambler dusted off his hat. She found it irritable that he took his own good time and she finally said so, "Speak up, man. What's this about Tommie?"

Chestnut brows veed over his brown eyes in a look of momentary anger, then eased. "Is Reeves about? Noticed his horse near the mine."

Tess shrugged. "I suppose he's visiting with Nugget. Now what about Tommie?"

Jim moved toward the shack. Tess realized he didn't intend

to discuss anything until they went inside. She motioned him in ahead of her, followed, then closed the door.

Taking a glimpse of the child asleep on the cot, the gambler turned to Tess. "Reeves means to take your boy away from you."

No matter how much Luke's words had hurt earlier, the accusation seemed ridiculous. "Why do you say such a thing?" she asked, unwilling to believe the claim.

Producing the notebook and documents from his shirt, Jim handed them to her. "Read these, then you'll understand."

As she unfolded each telegram and read, Tess's fingers began to tremble. A sense of having been betrayed, worse than any she had ever felt against her father and Clifton, gripped her heart. With a quick glance at her son, she whispered in a voice made low by heartbreak, "He means to convict me of forging the mine claims, doesn't he?"

She couldn't endure the look of sympathy creasing Jim's features. Tess knew him too well. The brown eyes glinted with grim satisfaction . . . a satisfaction gained by her and Tommie's possible ruin. Yet he cared enough to bring Luke's ruse to her attention.

"If Luke takes me to the sheriff," she worried aloud, "what will happen to Tommie?" Icy fingers of fear crawled up her spine and brushed her neck with a chill that made her shudder. Cold reality gripped her thoughts. Luke meant to separate her from the only good thing in her life.

"Tommie will probably have to be sent to his grandparents," Jim answered. "Since he has no fath . . . since he can't rely on his father."

"Never!" Tess shouted, then cupped one palm over her mouth to hold back the sob of grief that threatened to overcome her. Realizing she might wake her son, she lowered her tone. "They'll never get the opportunity to do to him what they did to me, as long as I have breath left in my body to prevent it. Let's go down to the creek where we can talk more. He needs to sleep, and I have to wash my face."

*   *   *

The Beholding

A ray of sunlight beamed through one of the cracks warming Tommie's face. He woke slowly and sat up. A glance around the shack informed him he was alone. Tommie lowered his legs to the floor. Someone had taken off his shoes and put them in the corner. Limping over, he sat down in the dirt to put them on. *Mommie? Mista Luke?* Maybe they were outside. He decided to look around.

Maybe his dream had come true. Mista Luke and Mommie were fighting in the dream, and Luke left. But the dream couldn't be true ... could it? Talon grazed in the grass near the opening of that dark hole where Mista Nugget lived. Mista Luke wouldn't leave without taking Talon.

Jim's horse stood hitched to the post outside the shack. Maybe the gambler and Mommie were visiting somewhere. Jim liked to visit Mommie too much. Tommie hoped the mean man went back to his own home soon.

He noticed Talon's reins wrapped around the branches of a tree. Everyone must be with Nugget in the hole. If he took Talon away, Mista Luke might hafta stay. Then Luke could be his friend forever.

With determination the four-year-old limped toward the dun, thinking how much fun it was going to be climbing up the tree to loosen Talon's reins. Maybe if he climbed high enough, he could jump down on the horse's back like he saw some of the big Cherokee boys do.

"I'm sorry, Talon." Tommie patted the dun's foreleg as the horse curved his head and bumped his nostrils against Tom. "But I gotta take you away. Don't be mad."

When he got to the tree, Tommie wrapped his arms around the trunk and began to climb to the branch that held the reins. "When Mista Luke stays with me forever, I ask him to find you. Then he be both our daddies."

The bark scraped his palms as Tommie climbed, but he pretended he was a grizzly bear and soon forgot the discomfort. The reins became two poisonous snakes in his vivid imagination. "Get off my tree!" yelled the bear cub as he reached the limb and pulled himself up to sit and rest.

Dia Hunter

As the branch shuddered beneath his weight and cracked, Tommie gripped the slender bark and tried to maintain his balance. For a heart-stopping moment he thought he would fall and get in big trouble with Mommie, but the branch held. "Bears gotta be careful, don't they?" he told the big dun.

The horse raised his head and looked at Tommie as he inched across the branch toward the reins and tested his weight again. Talon bobbed his head as if to agree, causing the reins to shake the branch.

"Hey, be still!" Tommie ordered. Suddenly the tree looked very big and where he sat seemed far away from the trunk. "Better hurry'n get down."

Just as Tommie strained toward the reins, a dark-haired man appeared over the hill bathed in sunlight. Mr. Nugget! With the fear of knowing he would get in trouble, Tommie grabbed for the reins, heard the branch break away from the tree, and felt himself falling, falling, falling.

Chapter Twenty-eight

Luke blinked away the remnants of the dream he didn't want to finish. He had heard someone calling, calling, calling to him . . . at first from a long way off, then closer. But just as Luke reached out, the person's face took form and contorted. Tommie's mouth rounded into a scream. Cold sweat dampened Luke's hairline and brow as he jolted up to a sitting position. The dream seemed too real.

Nugget had already risen. His blanket was rolled and stacked in one corner with a few other belongings. The cavern darkened considerably since Luke had fallen asleep this afternoon, and the air was much cooler. He would take a walk, stretch the soreness from his muscles and decide what his next move would be. Although Tess could make him leave her property, he was determined not to leave Georgetown until he had proven once and for all her innocence.

The passageway leading to the hillside took several minutes to walk. As he drew near the opening, Luke halted in midstride and strained to listen. A sound. Something human. *A childlike whimper!*

Running as fast as his legs would carry him, the bounty hunter burst through the mine opening and saw what his eyes dreaded. Tommie sprawled on the ground at an awkward angle with Talon pawing the earth next to him. A branch had broken away from the tree. *Did he fall?*

"Tommie! Son!" A thousand questions raced through Luke's mind as he ran to the boy. His hands trembled as he checked to see if the child still breathed. Finding Tom alive, Luke tucked the boy under one arm, then mounted Talon. He had no time to make a travois or any other makeshift stretcher, no time to fetch his saddle. In a moment's hesitation he thought to go get Tess, but even that might take too long. With a quick nudge to Talon's flank, the bounty hunter spurred the dun into an all-out gallop toward Georgetown.

Tess and Jim walked back to the shack only to see Luke galloping away with something in his arms. "Guess he decided to go, after all," she muttered, unsure whether or not she was glad about his leaving. She had a few more things to say to the man.

As she noted the breakneck speed at which he traveled, caution crept into her thoughts and made Tess shield her eyes and glare harder. "Good Heavens!" she yelled and began running toward the roan. "He's got Tommie."

"I told you he meant to have your boy, Contessa." Jim ran to keep up. "He's trying to steal him for you. Maybe use him as blackmail to get your mine."

"Hurry," Tess demanded. "We don't have a moment to lose." She didn't allow the gambler time to saddle up in front of her but took possession of the reins and made him sit behind. Flicking the reins, she kicked the roan into a path-eating chase. As she wondered if she might catch Luke in time, Tess prayed with all her heart that her eyes had deceived her.

The going was slow and it seemed that every step forced a moan from Tommie's lips and a prayer from Luke's. The bounty hunter flinched with each whimper, feeling responsible for not having gotten to the child sooner. With each mile toward town, he begged for the boy's life which had come to mean so much to him. Luke offered anything in return if Tommie would only wake and walk again.

When he finally reached town, Luke headed for the Barton House. Lionel rushed out to see what had happened.

"Fetch the doctor! Hurry, man!" Luke did not care that his voice broke and displayed every ounce of fear he felt. He carried the boy in and placed him in one of the downstairs beds. After spreading covers to keep him warm, the bounty hunter heated the stove to boil water and gathered fresh rags for the doctor.

The doctor came quickly. Lionel made swift introductions, then guided Doc Hammond to the boy. Luke and Lionel crowded around the bed as the gray-haired, bespectacled physician examined the boy.

Hammond stared over his glass rims at Luke. "A fall?"

Luke nodded solemnly.

"How far?" Hammond pressed various parts of the small body.

"From a tree. Maybe eight feet." Dread filled Luke's tone.

"This boy crippled?" Hammond examined the bruises on Tommie's hips.

"Yes."

"How long? One hip always been bigger than the other?"

"All his life, I think," Luke answered, recalling everything Tess had ever told him about her son, wishing he knew more.

"Well, you're lucky. Only the big hip's broken. It would be a good time to take out part of the bone."

"Then he's going to live?" Luke's breath hissed out in relief.

"Got a lick in the head, but thank God in His goodness, He planned on little boys being rambunctious."

Luke's shoulders sagged, and he absently wiped his eye.

The doctor placed a comforting hand on Luke's shoulder. "Don't worry, mister. Your son's gonna have a powerful headache, but he'll pull through. It's this hip that's gonna trouble him a lot worse unless you let me break it and set it as it should have been two years ago. He would have a good chance

269

of walking better if you do. Now, I can't promise to rid him of the limp entirely, but it won't be near as noticeable as it's been. Won't swell so much either, if you'll make him do all the exercises I suggest.''

''You can do that?'' Luke blinked. *My* son. The doctor's assumption sunk in. Yes, he loved Tommie Harper as surely as if he were his own.

Hammond nodded solemnly. ''It won't be an easy convalescence. In fact, my suggestion would be to take him, *carefully* mind you, to Idaho Springs so he can use the mineral water to heal faster. The boy would think he's having fun instead of exercising.''

''I'll get him there. You have my word.''

''All I need right now is your approval to correct the bone.'' Impatience carved the doctor's face.

Luke hesitated. He would have hell to pay when Tess found out. ''It will make him walk easier?''

''Much easier.''

''Then do it.'' The boy's health was all that mattered.

Minutes ticked by as Luke waited in the parlor of the Barton House watching Lionel pace up and down the carpet. The front door suddenly opened and a barrel-chested man entered, followed closely by Tess and Jim.

''We saw your horse outside, Reeves. Brought the sheriff with us.'' Jim wiped his feet on the rug. ''Sheriff Mason, this is the man you're looking for.''

''Where's Tommie?'' Tess's eyes blazed in anger.

''In there.'' Luke motioned with one hand, exhaling a long sigh. ''Having his hip reset.''

''Hip reset!'' Tess's face drained of color. ''What happened?''

''He fell from a tree, near as I can tell. I saw a broken branch and can only guess that's what happened.''

Tess waited to hear no further explanations and ran into the room Luke had indicated.

''You sure it was an accident?'' Jim's eyes narrowed suspiciously.

"What are you implying?" Luke moved toward the gambler, but the sheriff instantly blocked both men.

Mason's nostrils flared at the smell of the medicines Doc Hammon steamed on the stove. "Now, I ain't taking sides, but Mr. Daggert here brought up a few questions I'd like to talk to you about."

Luke flashed Daggert a murderous scowl that warned he would take care of him later. To the sheriff, he replied, "Let's discuss this outside."

Mason agreed and noted that the bounty hunter wasn't armed. He knew for a fact the man was a gunsharp. The accusations the gambler had made against Reeves didn't seem likely, but Daggert had talked sense too. Every man from here to Silver Plume would try to string up the bounty hunter if he didn't check out Reeves's story and pass the word around. When they reached the front porch, Mason propped one leg over the railing and crossed his arms.

"Okay, let's have it. What is it you want?" Luke stopped several feet away.

"A few answers."

"Depends on the questions." Luke's gaze met Mason's.

"Did you hurt the boy?"

"No."

Mason had to look away from the bounty hunter's intense regard. "Why does Daggert think you did?"

Luke sized the man up from head to toe and found him lacking. "Ask him."

"I'm asking you."

The sheriff outweighed him a good thirty pounds. He had fists the size of bear paws but was probably just as lumbering. "I don't speak another man's business," Luke answered. "Just my own."

"What were you doing *before* you found Tommie Harper?"

Luke related how he awakened, thinking he had only dreamed about Tommie, realizing now that he had actually heard the boy yell.

Mason stood and uncrossed his arms, firing his next question. "What are you doing at Harper Hall?"

So this was his real concern. Luke knew the kind of man he faced now. Anytime a man of Luke's profession arrived in town, the local sheriff always felt a bit threatened. Well, this particular lawman could lay his worries to rest. Luke no more wanted to make this a permanent home than Tess wanted to be bossed. "I guided Mrs. Harper and her boy from Fort Smith to here."

"Why are you staying now that's done?"

"I got to have a reason to stay?" Luke's hands dipped into his back pockets. How much of this was Mason's curiosity and how much was fueled by Daggert's?

Mason's lips compressed and a muscle ticked in his rounded jaw. "There any truth you're nosing around trying to learn about the salting that's going on around here?"

Luke faced Mason directly. The Denver Stock Exchange did want to know who was behind planting enough gold in the worthless mines to make certain they drew the attention of gullible buyers. "Maybe."

Mason looked surprised by Luke's bluntness. "Then maybe you've got reason to want that lady's mine all for yourself."

Luke's hand snapped away from his pockets, and he remembered he no longer wore a holster. "Am I being accused of something, Sheriff? If so, state your charges or let me go. I've got a little boy in there who needs me to take him somewhere. If you're going to lock me up, then do it. If not, then go about your business and let me go about mine."

"I'll leave you alone for now," Mason warned, hitching his holster higher. "Until the boy gets better and can speak for himself. Wanna reconsider telling me about whatever the hell it is you're hiding?"

Luke noticed Mason observing his weaponless state. Gun or no gun, Luke figured he could take the man if necessary. Mason seemed too interested in the salters. Since the scams had been going on for nearly four years, whoever brought in the culprits would probably become a local hero. Small wonder Mason thought he was trying to grab some of that glory.

He acknowledged the tin star on the lawman's left pocket. "You talk to him all you want, Sheriff, but *after* I take him to Idaho Springs and get him well."

Chapter Twenty-nine

Icy fingers of fear gripped Tess's heart. "What do you mean there's nothing more you can do?"

"Exactly what I said. I'll make him as comfortable as possible, but now it's all up to the boy."

When the bounty hunter walked into the bedroom unannounced, Tess attempted to hide her distress about the doctor's verdict, but Luke's gaze was too piercing, too knowing.

"What's wrong?" he demanded, reaching for her.

She jerked away, moving closer to Tommie's bed. "Dr. Hammond says there's nothing more he can do for Tom."

"What's she babbling about?" Luke's attention shifted to the weary doctor.

Hammond's face paled beneath the bounty hunter's intense regard. "It's just that your boy's color is not good. His body underwent a shock. The bone is set. His hip will heal, but that's an awful nasty bruise on it. It'll take time and some gentle exercise."

Luke scowled. "I meant to ask you. Doesn't that bruise look a bit strange to you?"

"What are you implying?" Tess asked before Hammond could speak.

"That it was awfully long and funny-shaped. Could a fall do that?"

The doctor nodded. "It's possible. My guess is the horse shied and kicked him."

"Not Talon," Tess and Luke said in unison.

Hammond shrugged. "You said the branch had broken loose about eight feet off the trunk?"

"A rough estimate."

"Then it's possible a fall could do it. All I do know is that he's had an awfully bad fall and he's lucky it wasn't worse." Hammond placed his instruments into the black bag, then handed Tess a paper. "Take this list of exercises and follow them religiously when he gets well enough to move. I wouldn't count myself much of a physician if I didn't tell you the truth, little lady. That boy doesn't need to get a fever now; I doubt he could fight it off."

Tess rose. "Stay. I know you're tired, but you can't just leave."

"Ma'am, I've been at Ogden Perigrew's place since yesterday, and setting your boy's bones wasn't a snap of the fingers, by any means."

"Maybe if you have some coffee or rest awhile—"

"Tess, don't do this to yourself." Luke attempted to comfort her, but she wouldn't let him.

"You worked on my son without my permission."

"Your husband said—"

"He's not my husband."

"God in Heaven, lady, I didn't know!" Hammond motioned toward the bounty hunter, braving a direct look at Luke. "He gave me permission. The way he carried on, I thought he was the boy's father."

Hammond gathered a few more things, tossing them into his black bag. "I'll leave you two with the boy. Fetch me if . . . well, Lionel knows where I'll be. Keep the child calm and lying flat."

When the doctor left the room, Lionel stuck his face around the door and asked, "How's the little fella?"

Luke's expression never changed. "Keep fresh water coming."

The lantern jaw lengthened. "Will do," Lionel whispered, then closed the door softly behind him.

"Tessa, look at me." Luke gently pushed her away to demand that she face him. "I did the right thing. Tommie will be better for it. You do want him to walk easier, don't you?"

She blinked back tears, staring into his eyes, wanting to hope, desperately needing to believe. Yet how could she? This man had lied to her. Suddenly she could no longer endure the false comfort of his touch. "You're right," she said, gathering strength from deep within and moving away from Luke's strong arms. "He will, but I'm the one who'll make sure he does. Tommie will never be yours. Get your lawyers and your judge. Take me to trial. I hope this job's worth it to you."

"How did you find out about my investigation?" Luke asked, exasperated because she shrank away from his touch every time he reached out to comfort her. "Are you guilty, Tessa?"

"Does it matter? You've obviously assumed I was, or else why did you help us get here? I thought Clifton and my father used me. At least their reasons were to line their pockets. Yours was only to hurt."

"I never meant you harm, Tessa."

"You didn't think it would hurt me to discover that you were playing me for a fool? It wouldn't hurt to fall in love with you and think I didn't measure up in some way? That I didn't mean enough to give you reason to stay? Or that if you turn me in, my son will have to return to my so-called parents?"

"Your parents?" He never considered the possibility that the boy would have to live with the folks Tess mistrusted so deeply. "I never thought—"

"You didn't care."

Low and piercing as sharp-edged steel, her words cut him to the quick. "You've got every right to feel the way you do," he told her, holding his palms up in front of him as if to surrender to her justice. "When I started this investigation, I intended to turn you in. But I didn't count on one thing, Tess." He stepped closer. "I fell in love with you."

He took hope in the glimmer of longing written in her gaze when it locked and held his own before Tess began to shake her head slowly to deny his words.

"Then I began to realize you were innocent," he continued. "The allegations were just that—allegations. You were loyal and caring. You saved my life when letting me die would have made escape much easier. That alone might have persuaded me, but, Tess, I'd lived by my word so long that it was all I could trust. I was afraid not to take you in. Afraid that if I didn't honor my word, I would no longer have anything to anchor me. Anything to count on."

"And now?" she whispered.

"I found out there's something worth trusting more. Not people, not words, but a feeling so strong nothing on this world can break it." He demanded her gaze and got it. "No matter how many things make you seem guilty, I'm not going to take you in. In fact, I intend to do everything within my power to find the real culprits behind the scams."

She didn't say anything, her silence causing each beat of his heart to drum louder in his ears.

Tommie moaned, attempting to turn on his newly set hip.

"Get Lionel in here with some water," she ordered. "He'll quit tossing and turning if I can keep him cool."

Luke stood there staring, wondering if he should leave but laying all his trust in her hands.

"Well, if you intend to save me, then save my son as well. So get on with it, will you?"

The possibility that Luke had spoken the truth warmed the chill that had gripped Tess's heart since the gambler had showed her the report. Once Tommie's health improved, she would consider telling Luke everything as well. But would he change his mind about turning her in, after he discovered she was truly guilty of the Hot Springs scams? Could he still love her once he knew?

*   *   *

Luke pulled a chair to the edge of Tommie's bed. He propped his elbows on his knees and pressed his fingers together in prayer, his attention never wavering from the child's face.

Light and shallow, Tommie's breathing barely stirred the covers over his chest. Of all the battles Luke had fought in the war and all the gunfights he'd faced, none of those moments scared him as much as sitting here watching the little tyke's pale features. The moaning had stopped three hours ago. Now only an occasional flutter of the boy's eyelashes showed his attempts to awaken.

Laying a callused palm on the small brow, Luke was relieved at the definite coolness beneath his touch. They were doing a good job. A wisp of blond hair hung over the corner of Tess's beautiful mouth, and he carefully tucked it behind her ear, trying not to awaken the beauty whose body curled next to her son's.

Nature's call urged Luke to leave the room for the first time since the drama began. He reluctantly decided there were a few other needs to attend to. Pulling the blanket over the sleeping pair, he bent and kissed the child's brow and softly brushed a knuckle over Tess's cheek. "Sleep tight, you two. I'm going to get us something to eat and see to Talon."

Tess stirred but didn't awaken. Luke trod softly across the room and closed the door quietly behind himself. Running a hand through his hair, he yawned, admitting the exhaustion spreading through his body. Lionel was sleeping upright in one of the parlor chairs, his long, gangly form stretched at an uncomfortable-looking angle.

Shaking him awake, Luke whispered, "Cramden. Wake up, man. I want you to keep an eye on the widow and the boy. I'm going to take my horse to the livery, then round us up some grub. If Daggert asks to see them, tell him they can't be disturbed. I'll be back in a while."

Lionel nodded, stretched his arms and stood. "Count on it. The boy going to be all right?"

"Looks like it." Luke smiled. Relief sent new energy through him.

"I don't care what the gambler says. You love that kid and wouldn't hurt him." Lionel placed a fatherly pat on Luke's shoulder.

Emotion welled in Luke's eyes, and he cleared his throat before attempting to speak. He offered his handshake. "Much obliged.

"Gotta see about Talon," Luke announced after Lionel gripped his hand in friendship. Unaccustomed to having someone accept him so readily, Luke didn't know much else to say or do. "Maybe I can buy you a drink later."

"I'll take you up on that. We'll celebrate the boy's good health."

Luke headed out of the Barton House and gathered Talon's reins. "Hey, fella, you think I'd forgotten about you?" He gave the horse a quick pat before mounting. "I'll get you some oats and give you a quick rub-down."

As Luke worked at his various tasks, he relived every moment since meeting Tess and Tommie Harper. Such pain he'd caused them. All for the sake of keeping his word to a group of men who meant nothing to him but money.

Years ago, he had shut himself off from his emotions because they were too risky. But now he gave them full rein. Olivia, Father and Laoni had all refused his love, and in their own way refused to love him. He had built a wall of stone around his heart, deciding it was better not to love at all. But Tess was different. Not once did she deny caring for him. Even in her anger over his investigation, she admitted loving him.

And all he had done was mock that love. No wonder she hesitated. He didn't deserve her, yet he loved her. All Luke knew was that he would move Heaven and earth to see her proved innocent. And if, God forbid, he failed to convince the Stock Exchange, he would battle the courts clear to Washington to have her sentence stayed. Tess and Tommie wouldn't be separated . . . if Luke had to defy the law himself!

Chapter Thirty

Mommie? Where are you, Mommie? Tommie wondered as he willed his eyes to open. The room looked dark and unfamiliar, frightening. *Is this Heaven?* All he could remember was looking up at the dark-haired man for just an instant, then hearing the branch snap and falling forever. *Am I dead like Papa?* "Papa, where are you?" He tried to whisper aloud, but his mouth tasted as if somebody had stuffed it with cotton.

Gradually his eyes opened and accustomed themselves to the dark, and the footboard took form, a dresser, some other furniture. *Heaven's sure got plain ol' things in it.*

As he attempted to sit up, a throbbing pain in his hip made him collapse back onto the pillow and he muffled a cry of alarm. *Mommie said there's no pain in Heaven. Do Papa still hurt, too?*

"Tommie, how do you feel?"

The boy turned toward the wall and looked at his mother's tired face and rumpled hair. She rested in a chair next to the bed, but immediately moved forward and sat on the bed beside him, clasping his hands. Her gaze moved rapidly over his face as he asked, "I'm not in Heaven?"

"No, thank God. You're with me."

"Am I in trouble?"

Tears brimmed in his mother's eyes. She shook her head and laughed. "Only if you ever scare me like that again. What would Mommie do without you, little man?"

She hugged him, accidentally pressing against the place that hurt.

When he complained, she said, "You've had a serious fall. The doctor had to reset your bone and says when you get well, your hips will finally be the same size. If we do all the exercises, you won't hardly limp at all."

Tommie's eyes widened. Maybe when he fell, he had gone to Heaven and God made him well and sent him back. "Can I tell Mista Luke?" He tried to sit up again, but the injury prevented it.

"He already knows, son. He'll be back in a few minutes. Luke's rustling up grub and feeding Talon."

"Talon hurt?"

"No, he isn't," Tess assured him, brushing hair away from Tommie's forehead. She pressed her palm against his brow. "You want to tell me what happened? How you got hurt?"

Tommie hesitated, afraid she would be angry because he tried to take Talon away. But Mista Luke had said to always tell the truth even if it hurt. Tommie didn't know if he could stand much more. The pain in his hip hurt more than having to eat turnips.

But Mr. Nugget probably already told her. "I thinked if I taked Talon away, Mista Luke would stay wiff us. I din't like all those mens. I love Mista Luke. Why can't he be my new papa?"

Tess looked flustered. "That's difficult to answer, son. Just go on with your story."

She always got red like that when he said something she didn't want to talk about. Tommie didn't know if that would help him this time or hurt him. He quickly told her how he had gotten hurt. ". . . and when Mista Nugget came over the hill, I reached for the reins and the tree broke. I felled."

"Nugget saw the accident?" Tess blinked as her child nodded. She had forgotten all about the Frenchman. If he'd seen the fall, why hadn't he told someone? If Luke's story was true, then the time difference between the fall and Luke finding him remained unexplained. The Frenchman had not once shown his face at Barton House asking about Tommie's welfare. Why would he hesitate to tell anyone about Tom . . . unless there was some reason he didn't want anyone to know? Could it be that this was not an accident? Dr. Hammond blamed Talon, but what if Nugget had wanted Tommie dead? The possibility made no sense.

"Well, if you aren't a sight for tired eyes." Luke entered the room, carrying a tray of food. He placed the meal on the chest of drawers and hurried over to Tommie's side.

The bounty hunter's big hand reached out to Tommie, which he shook real hard. But as Luke started to pull his hand away, Tommie reached out with both hands and pulled him down for a fierce hug.

The big man's shoulders tightened and his whiskered face scratched Tommie's cheeks, but it was about the bestest hug his friend had ever given him.

"Glad to see you feeling better," Luke muttered, his voice sounding kind of low and funny.

Mommie had a silly look on her face too, kind of soft and mushy like a doggie looking at her puppy.

"After you eat, do you feel like a ride?" Luke placed the food tray on his lap. He had arranged the food to look like a face on the plate. Two eggs formed the eyes, a gob of jelly made a nose, and two strips of bacon curved into a smile.

"You mean you'll let me ride Talon"—Tommie's eyes lowered as he confessed—"after I try to take him away?"

Tess explained what her son had told her.

"I won't leave you, Tom," Luke reassured him. "I promised I wouldn't."

The child stared at his friend. "Will you be my papa then?"

Luke grinned. "I suppose that's up to your mother."

Tess avoided a direct answer. "There's a few things to settle first, son. When you get better, we'll discuss this more. Fair enough?''

"No," Tommie complained.

"Fair enough." Luke's hand reached out and hers met it halfway.

Tommie thought maybe Mama liked Mista Luke real good.

"Do you think it's too soon to take him to Idaho Springs?" Tess urged Tom to eat what he could.

"Hammond told me to get him there as soon as possible. Tommie will only get sore laying in bed. But it's your decision, Tess. I'll go along with whatever you want."

Tess stood and straightened her skirts. "I want to do what's best for my son and get on with our lives. I've got questions to ask Nugget, and Jim for that matter, but those can wait until Tommie's better."

"Then let's take the boy swimming."

Tommie saw the look that passed between his mother and Luke. *Yessiree, Mama liked Mista Luke real good and Mista Luke liked Mama too.*

Tess hated the rotten egg odor pervading the air of the mineral springs as she and Luke carried Tommie between them and stepped fully clothed into the waters.

"Buzzard pis—" Luke snapped off the curse escaping his lips and offered a wicked grin. "I mean, isn't this hot!"

Hot hardly described the heat that pierced Tess's bones like a dagger of fire. Tommie squirmed between them and demanded to go back to the ledge. Her skin was flushed with the heat rising above the bubbles.

"Hey, dis don't hurt," Tommie remarked, bobbing up and down in the bubbles. "Look, Mommie, I can bounce."

Tess watched her son's body rise above the bubbling surface, then plunge down until only his head remained above water. Luke followed suit and she did the same. Like trout they frolicked, urging Tommie to twist and turn, bounce and test his leg as Doc Hammond had instructed.

The water revived, soothed, tickled and relaxed them. Like

tiny raindrops that pelted everywhere, the bubbles invigorated them. Air pockets exploded into sound on the surface, gurgling, matching the joyful giggles of Tommie's enjoyment. Of Tess's own and Luke's.

She closed her eyes and gave herself to utter relaxation, experiencing every touch upon her toes, her thighs, the center of her spine, her breasts. With a deep sigh, she watched as Luke helped Tommie float on his back and try a number of movements she would have thought impossible with a mending bone. No wonder her father had earned such money at Hot Springs. Perhaps if he had been truthful about the water's qualities, he could have made an honest living at them.

"They say this cures colic and constipation, arthritis and gout, goiters, dandruff and bad temper." Her voice took on the carnival barker loudness practiced by her father.

Luke spun around. She saw the look in his eyes and knew he questioned her involvement in her father's scams.

"Does it cure lovesickness?" he asked.

A tenderness enveloped her. He cared enough not to insist that she speak of the past in front of Tommie. How could she have ever believed that Luke would wish him harm? "I hope not," she answered, "because if it does, I want my money back."

Luke laughed and headed for the ledge, carrying Tommie in his arms. "What do you say we take you to the attendant and let her give you a hot mineral bath while your mother and I finish our spring bath?"

"Is it a good baff like this one?" Tommie looked both eager and suspicious.

Tess's laughter mixed with Luke's as the bounty hunter chuckled. "Yes. Believe it or not, there are such things as good baths."

Luke returned and sat down on the ledge, then eased into the pool. With a few deft movements, his clothes came off and were flung to the bank.

"W-what are you doing?" Tess lowered herself further into

284

the water as if she were the one totally nude. "Someone might come in. The attendant."

"No, I paid her well to take special care of Tommie," he said calmly, gliding through the water at an alarming rate, drawing closer. "I told her not to disturb us. That we would come get him in a while."

"Oh." Tess's breath caught, then exhaled into a single word. "Luke?" She couldn't remember what it was she was going to ask. The froth bubbled away, offering a tantalizing glimpse of the man beneath. But the currents shifted and left only a view of his shoulders.

"What is it, love?" He moved closer, his eyes darkened to mimic the stark hunger in them.

She became aware of how erotic the water felt bubbling against her, arousing her senses to pinpoints of feelings. But if the water was intoxicating, so much more was Luke's muscular physique, chiseled in granite and sinew, tanned with health and vigor.

"Come here."

Low and husky, his voice compelled her to obey. The currents sprouting from the springs seemed to be at his command, for she felt herself drawn in his direction. To her surprise he spun her around, kneading her shoulders.

"We've got to talk . . . about everything," he encouraged, moving his hands up and down the length of her back, to the top of her buttocks, then back again. Her head lolled to one side, making her hair fall forward over one shoulder.

"Feel good?"

"Yesss," she hissed. Miracle hands increased the massage, erotic as the bubbles.

He leaned forward, his arms encircling Tess's waist as he kissed the back of her neck. "I know you're not guilty of the mine scams. But tell me about the hot springs." His tongue took liberties with her ear. "You're so beautiful."

She felt his nakedness press against her and wished her own clothing were gone. "I was young and stupid . . . no, gullible is more the word. You see, I believed I had to protect my mother from my father.'' The past spilled out in a torrent of words.

''I've been the stupid one.'' Luke's lips pressed light kisses around her neck, up to her cheek, to her mouth. ''I should have listened to my heart all along. Duty's a mightly lonesome word.''

''Then you believe me?'' she whispered.

His gaze lifted to stare longingly into her own. ''From now until forever, love.''

Her lips parted in unconscious invitation, shaping his name. ''Luke—''

But it escaped without a sound as his teeth closed over Tess's lower lip in a caress that sent ripples of pleasure through her. Sensations long denied tingled along every nerve as his tongue plunged to taste her. She met the thrust with her own delicious parry and satisfied her craving of him. Tangling his hair in her fingers, she pulled him closer, the hunger deepening and unsated.

Tiny explosions ignited in the lower part of her body. Rivers of sensation raced through her veins, peaking her breasts. Her heart swelled with love until it overflowed. Slowly her eyes opened to find him studying her. She marveled at the love shining back at her from those indigo depths. Love that accepted all her failings and promised devotion to all her hopes and dreams.

At long last, the loneliness that had been Luke's life ceased. The stone wall crumbled in his chest and left a foundation of trust. Her name echoed over and over in his mind. *Tessa. Tess. Beloved Tess.* His heart hammered with exultation as she moved to allow a closer fit.

''Kiss me again,'' she whispered.

She looked lovelier than anything he had ever viewed. Luke touched her with reverence, with awe. ''May I?'' he asked, unbuttoning her blouse to remove the final barrier between them. Her hands touched his, helping as he knew they would the remainder of their days.

His breath sucked in at the sight of her perfection. Passion burned in the depths of her eyes, making her shiver and arch closer. His control slipped, taking with it long years of hunger for love. His body soared with desire.

With a groan he kissed her again as his hands caressed each welcoming inch of her flesh, possessing, asking, demanding what would forever be his. Lightning thundered through him as her nipples pressed wantonly against his chest. With a moan of delight, he lowered his lips to their rosy pinnacles and granted them equal affection.

She cried out in pleasure, and he could not resist viewing the transformation that passion aroused within her. Flushed with heat, her breasts mirrored the loving caresses of his mouth. The pulse beating in the soft hollow of her throat matched the rapid pace of his heart. Most beautiful of all were the green pools of love, dilated and banked with desire as deep as his own.

She was the most beautiful woman he had ever seen and he wanted her to be his wife.

Luke could not bear to look at Tess a moment longer without making his possession complete. With a thick sound of need, he pressed his aching flesh against her. She parted her thighs, offering the touch of softer flesh. He had to tell her, speak before passion ruled him. "I've waited for you all my life."

His words ended in a soft, low sound of pleasure as Tess claimed his mouth. Despite his urgent need, he cherished the tender, slow kiss of acceptance she gave him before blessing him with the gift of her body.

With each slow movement, Tess watched the face of the man she loved. Anticipation radiated through her as tension gathered and his slow, rocking strokes became faster, deeper. She began to unravel, sending currents of ecstasy spilling through her senses. "Luke," she whispered, "I lov—" Her back arched as pleasure eddied through her.

But it was his voice that uttered the three words which might forever dam the past and flood their future with joy.

"I love you."

Tess held him, crying his name in reverence, unwilling to let this moment be stained with the truth she would reveal all too soon.

Chapter Thirty-one

The invigorating waters stirred the trio's appetite. Luke escorted Tess and Tommie into the inn and waited for the hostess to seat them. He scanned the patrons' faces as was his habit when entering any room. No notorious outlaw here. Only a gray-haired lady's face blocked by her menu prevented him from seeing everyone. Feeling confident that all was as it should be, Luke took a seat with his back to the wall.

After ordering food, he insisted Tess indulge herself in a glass of brandy. For Tommie, he ordered sarsaparilla.

When the brandy was poured, Tess sipped it and smiled at Luke over the rim, teasing him as the tip of her tongue darted out over her lips. "Mmmm. Brandy tastes almost as good as bourbon."

Luke's brow arched, but his lips curved in approval.

Soon a family of great number, painfully thin and modestly dressed, arrived at the table next to them. Luke watched the procession of tow-headed youngsters as their mother guided them to their chairs in quick precision. He guessed the woman's age to be about ten years more than his own, but her face was deeply lined and sallow. Her red, gnarled hands gave signs of a hard life. Though their clothing looked frayed, no buttons were missing, and each of the children had been well scrubbed. A baby rested on one hip, while another refused to take a chair and stood tucked beneath the unused armpit.

Their father followed later. A good deal older than his wife, the man kept staring at Tess as if he knew her. Luke glanced back at her, aware she would not meet the man's gaze. Who was he?

"Begging your pardon, sir . . . ma'am," the fellow interjected, "but don't I know you from somewhere?"

Tess shook her head slowly, clearing her throat. "I don't believe I've had the pleasure."

The stranger's brows veed as he puzzled over her answer. "I could've sworn. You from Arkansas, by chance? Hot Springs?"

Tess gulped the brandy, her hands visibly trembling, but she quickly set the goblet back down. "From *Georgetown*," she insisted. "Sorry."

Was he one of the men she supposedly seduced? Luke felt a strange sense of anger at Tess for lying, yet felt an equal need to protect her from that sad past.

The man continued to stand. "I could've sworn, ma'am. But you wouldn't be that kind of lady, I'm sure. She was the no-good kind. Said the springs could cure just about anything. And it durned well did. Cured me of going anywhere without my Carolina and thinking I could trust folks so readily. Now Carolina holds my savings while I'm a'bathing. Cain't no thief steal my money whilst I'm easing these old bones."

The food arrived. Luke looked at all the hungry eyes staring at his plate and found it difficult to begin eating. Though he had no idea how much the man had lost to Tess's parents, perhaps there was a way to return it. "Please, why don't you and your family join us, Mr.—?"

"Webster Krugg." He motioned his wife over. "This is my missus, Carolina. And that's all right, sir. We just come in for a drink."

"I insist, Mr. Krugg. This is my treat, and it will give Tommie someone to visit.'' Luke stood and nodded his acquaintance to Carolina.

"The Lord's blessings to you, sir. I'm mighty grateful. If you won't be offended, we'll sit here and let you folks talk peaceful. With this big a brood, Carolina and I gotta take turns afeedin' our little'uns. You drank the water yet? It tastes like a by-god, but it sure'll knock anything loose that's latched on where it shouldn't be.''

"Mr. Krugg!" Carolina scolded. "Remember the children.''

Luke rose from his chair as the woman bobbed a curtsey. "How do?''

"Kinda hard to forget nine young'uns, Mrs. Krugg!" Webster grinned from ear to ear, offering his wife a wink. She blushed becomingly.

Luke introduced himself and halted when he nodded toward Tess. What if she didn't want her name revealed?

"Contessa Harper,'' she quickly interjected, "and this is my son, Tommie.''

"Now, I know I was mistaken. The gal I'm thinking of wasn't a Harper, and she didn't have no children.''

"Perhaps it's someone who looks like me.'' Tess visibly relaxed.

"Gosh, I wish I had so many bruvers and sisters,'' Tommie announced, his voice full of awe.

Luke glanced at Tess, watching her blush match their guest's. Carolina Krugg smiled shyly. The woman cast her gaze downward as the baby hid his face in her bosom.

"You have a beautiful family,'' Tess complimented, to put the woman more at ease.

"I'm real proud of each and every one of them.''

"Guess if we stand here jawing, you folks are gonna miss your meal. Sorry about the mistake, Mrs. Harper. Guess my ol' eyes are failing me.''

"That's perfectly all right, Mr. Krugg. Frankly, I'm glad my life has led me away from being that kind of woman.''

When the couple returned to their brood, Tess would not

look Luke in the eye. She became uncommonly quiet and ate her bites slowly. Luke didn't want to talk much in front of Tommie, yet he couldn't let her go on in misery. "Tess, there are going to be times when both of our pasts catch up with us. I haven't been a saint either, you know."

"For better or for worse, you mean?" She lay down the knife and glanced at Tommie. He seemed more interested in staring at the Krugg brood and their antics than anything being discussed at the table. "Believe me, Luke. My past is far worse than you can imagine. I need to tell you so much, but this isn't the place." Her gaze slanted to Tommie.

Luke shook his head. "You don't need to explain anything. You are what you are *now*."

Tess smiled sadly. "I pray you always feel that way, Luke, but I am what I am because of that past. I'm not sure it's all gone. I don't know if it will ever be. There will always be a Krugg who recognizes me. And I hope to God I can gain the strength to face them and the truth about myself."

Placing his hands over hers as they twisted a napkin, he halted her from berating herself. "There's only one in your past who concerns me, and you know which one I'm talking about. When I find him, I intend to kill him."

"I won't have it!" She pushed away his hand and flung the linen napkin down on the table.

"You two fighting?" Tommie asked and sat up straighter.

Tess blushed to the roots of her hair and quickly offered in a calmer tone, "You can't go off trying to right my wrongs."

"That's one wrong committed *against* you, love. That means it was committed against me too."

Tommie grimaced. With a bored sigh, he turned his attention to the family at the next table. One of the boys blew bubbles of sarsaparilla out his nose.

"Who is that woman staring at you?" Tess asked, agitation etching her features. "It's awfully rude of her."

Luke spun around and caught a glimpse of the profile deliberately turning to hide her face as she rose and headed for the restaurant's entrance. He pushed back his chair and slammed his napkin down on his plate. "My past is catching up with me . . . damn her!"

"Olivia, what in God's name are you doing here?" Luke grabbed Olivia's elbow and made her face him.

"Lucas, what a pleasure. I had no idea—" The mask of surprise that graced her high cheekbones and lips could have won her a role on any stage.

"Don't forget who you're dealing with, Olivia. I'm your son, for whatever that means to this world, so I know you. Why were you trying to sneak out of here without being seen if you didn't know I was here?"

"Oh, darling, really . . . don't make such a scene."

Her tone became angry, though her gaze darted around to see if anyone watched. He hated that about her. She couldn't even be upset without thinking of the social considerations.

"I saw you were sitting with the young lady and the child, and I simply didn't want to disturb you."

"You didn't want to disturb me? I haven't seen you since I was eighteen years old, Mother dear. Don't you think I needed a little disturbing after nine years?"

"Well, yes. Yes, of course, dear." Olivia straightened the lace at her high-necked collar. "I meant to . . . visit you later. After your meal."

Luke tugged on her arm. "Join us now, Olivia. I'm busy later. For the rest of my life maybe. Take the opportunity while I feel like giving it."

"That's no way to talk to your mother," Olivia scolded but followed his urging anyway.

"No, it isn't," he whispered into her ear as they walked toward Tess. "But then you never have acted like my mother, have you?"

"Really, Lucas!" she said in exasperation, hurrying her steps to put distance between herself and her son. Seeing the surprised expressions of Luke's company, she realized they had heard her exclamation. "What a darling child," she crooned, attempting to draw attention away from herself. The boy offered his hand to shake, and she shook it, only to discover he had given her a gob of mashed potatoes.

Tommie giggled. Olivia looked horror-stricken.

"Thomas James Harper!" Tess rose to her feet. "Apologize this minute!" But the four-year-old scooped another spoonful and flung it at the Krugg boy who was making faces at him.

Luke laughed, a hearty baritone sound that echoed over the restaurant. Each mother took their child in tow, apologizing profusely to Olivia Reeves.

Tommie fussed and squirmed, causing so much ruckus that Tess pleaded the woman's forgiveness. "I'm terrible sorry, ma'am. He's on the mend from a broken hip and is tired and cranky. Do forgive me for not staying to visit. I'd best get him to bed." She looked at Luke questioningly. "Will I see you later?"

Olivia's eyebrows arched a notch higher.

"Perhaps tomorrow then," Tess conceded.

Luke gave the tyke a playful spank on his bottom as Tess settled Tom on her hip. "You be a good boy and no more potato fights. Understand?"

Tommie held out his hand, and Luke opened his. The last glob of potatoes plopped onto the bounty hunter's palm. "Here, Mista Luke. You can play with it."

Olivia chuckled, then quickly cleared her throat.

Luke returned the glob to Tommie's plate and wiped his hand with a napkin. "Take that kid to bed, tie him up, then beat on him for me, will you?" Luke teased.

"I would," Tess countered, "but I'd be afraid he'd get loose and do the same to me. Think I'll cuddle him up and read him a story instead."

Waiting until the pair were gone, Luke ordered more wine for his mother.

"I see you haven't forgotten some of what I've taught you," Olivia said as he filled her glass, then his own.

"Some things are worth hanging on to," he conceded. "Some aren't." The Kruggs had the good grace to keep their attention upon their own children and not his and Olivia's

294

conversation. Luke decided to have the chef wrap up an extra cake for the children to take with them.

"Such as?" Olivia asked.

"Such as the letters I never got. The visits from you and Father. I guess memories are something not on the Reeves's agenda."

"When did you become such a brash boy?" She sipped the wine.

A cord twitched in Luke's jaw. "When you stopped caring if I ever became a man."

"I never stopped, Luke." Olivia stared at him with sincerity. "I might not have known how to deal with you, but I wanted to."

"Was it the scars, Mother? Were they so terrible even *you* couldn't look at me?"

Olivia's gloved hand reached across to his larger one. Despite the proper upbringing that warned he would be displaying improper manners, Luke shied from her touch. Surprise and something else . . . disappointment? . . . etched her features, then were quickly hidden.

Her skin appeared pallid, wrinkled. She no longer looked the society beauty but had become an aging dowager. How it must hurt to see that time had its own justice for the vain.

"Is that what you thought, Lucas? That I couldn't endure the sight of you?"

"More or less. You never proved differently."

Regret shimmered in her eyes. Tears for him? Was this part of her act or did he dare trust the hope sprouting in his fragile heart? Tess had torn down the stone wall and left his emotions vulnerable, and it scared the hell out of him that he wanted to believe this new Olivia. This Olivia he had never known.

"Lucas . . . *Luke,* darling. I couldn't look at your scars because I blamed myself for them. Not you. Your grandmother told me to take better care of myself during the time I carried you within me. I scoffed at her warnings. Horseback riding, dancing until dawn. Parties and social functions fed my sense

295

of worth, you see. To be shut away for nine months was a custom unthinkable to me.

"Then you decided to be born. The delivery became difficult. The doctor said my bones had actually broken . . . cutting you and blocking your entry into this world. You almost died. But you were a fighter even then. Despite my stubbornness, I might say. When I discovered your scars, I blamed myself. I suppose every time I looked at you, I was reminded of my foolishness . . . my selfishness.

"Now I realize my actions after your birth were more cruel than before it." She touched his face, caressing the scars that had kept them apart physically and emotionally. The scars that could not bring them back together. "Can you forgive me?"

Luke could not speak the words she wanted to hear, but instead made a concentrated effort to get to know her and allow her to know him. When he finally walked Olivia back to her hotel room, he actually felt a reluctance to leave her company. Before him stood no gray-haired dowager, but the woman of incomparable beauty he had adored in his childhood and longed for in the countless, tear-filled nights of loneliness that had been his youth.

He looked back at her now from the eyes of manhood and was astonished that he actually meant the words, "Perhaps one day soon the two of us will forgive each other."

Chapter Thirty-two

Jim Daggert was angrier than Nugget had ever seen him. He paced the floor of the hotel room, lacing the curses with the name of Luke Reeves.

"That fool," Jim thundered, "thinking with her legs instead of her head. I'm sorry for the day I ever asked her to marry me." He turned on Nugget. "You know what Contessa has done? She's gone and forgiven the bastard. No way I'll ever get her to marry me now. We'll just have to take the mine the hard way."

"They will be after me for certain, monsieur," Nugget reminded. "The boy saw me clearly."

"You can deny it. Say he must have been out of his mind with pain."

Sweat trickled down the Frenchman's face. It stung his eyes, but Nugget refused to let them blink, not trusting the piercing gaze of the man who studied him. He and Daggert had managed to keep their partnership quiet until now, but things were going wrong and at a rapid pace. "It would do no good. You know Monsieur Reeves, he will check on such things."

A worry dug at the Frenchman. He thought he knew the gambler. They had been partners in the mine scams for four years. After Clifton and Hoot no longer shared a fourth, Nugget had thought the partnership with just Jim would be better off. He wasn't so certain anymore. The gambler was running scared. What if he started talking? It was his word against Daggert's, but the gambler was a faster draw than he. He needed to keep Jim's confidence.

"You want the widow, oui?" Nugget asked cautiously.

Jim's eyes narrowed. "So?"

"So . . . the bounty hunter, he will not scare. We have found that out. The only way to stop him from getting too close to Madame Tess and our operation is to convince her not to marry him and send the gentleman on his way."

Jim's brow furrowed. "How do you propose we do that? I've tried everything I know, short of killing the boy."

"That did not work either."

The gambler's eyes widened, then quickly masked their surprise. "You caused that accident?"

"Let us say the fall did not hurt him as much as the clubbing of his hip. I tried to hit his head, but the horse got in the way. I only hurt the child's leg. Perhaps what you need do is use the mining claims to force Madame Tess to marry you, oui?"

Nugget found encouragement in the closing of Jim's eyes. The gambler tugged at his chestnut beard, the way he always did when he mulled a problem.

Finally Jim nodded. "I guess there's no other choice." His face brooded. "She isn't going to agree to it any other way."

When Tess answered the knock on the door of her hotel room, she swung back the oak panel in anticipation of greeting Luke. "Hello, darling, I'm almost finished dres—" To her surprise, Jim Daggert stood there with one half-raised fist, the other clutching papers.

"When did you get here?" She looked out in the hallway to see if Luke had shown him to her room. "Let me finish dressing and I'll meet you in the foyer."

"No." Jim barged his way into her room. "I'll talk to you here."

Tess tried to shut the door on him, but his greater strength prevented her from doing so. "Leave!" she demanded. "I'll cause a scene."

Jim laughed. "You don't want that, do you, Contessa? A widow alone with a man in her room. Wouldn't do much good to that fine reputation you've tried so hard to build over the years. Then again, you were considering letting Reeves in here, weren't you? Or is someone else your darling this week?"

Tess glanced at the bed. "All right, come in, but keep your voice down. Tommie's resting." She moved aside, keeping a substantial distance from Jim.

"Here, read these." The gambler thrust the papers toward her.

As Tess scanned the pages, her heart felt as if it were sinking. "Where did you get these?"

"I've had them for quite some time. You know what trouble they can cause, don't you?" The look in his eyes matched his gloating tone.

"They can incriminate me of salting mines." She stared at him in disgust. "What is it you want from me? What have I ever done to hurt you?"

"You didn't love me, Contessa," Jim accused, moving toward her. "That's all I've ever asked of you, and you wouldn't even do that."

She shrank away, refusing his touch. Anger flared within him and he grabbed her. "Don't ever move away from me again, do you hear? If you do, that boy won't have a mama to see him grown."

Tess backed away from his advance. "What do you intend to do?"

Jim's face drew closer until his breath fanned her face. "I'm going to give you a choice, Contessa. Either you marry me and I'll tear up these papers you so unwisely copied for Clifton, or I'll turn them over to Sheriff Mason and let him decide if you were really only learning to read and write when you copied them. But after I tell him about the Hot Springs scams, somehow I don't think he's going to look too favorably on that possibility."

"Why would you want me to marry you when you know how I feel about Luke?" Tess hated the feel of his hands upon her flesh. She struggled in his arms, but he wouldn't let go. His fingers clutched tighter, bruising.

"I should have killed him back on the trail like I'd planned."

"You shot him?"

"Blue Hawk got in the plug, not me. But I could have. Just didn't choose to. Thought you'd think better of me if I looked like a hero. But that wasn't good enough for you. There was no getting you to love me. So I'm going to have to make you do it."

"Why me, Jim? Plenty of others would gladly have you."

"Sure they would. But none of them feel the way you do. Ever since that night I made love to you . . ." He paused, then his grip tightened as her body went rigid with realization.

"Made love to me?" Only three men had ever touched her body—Clifton, Luke and the man who. . . . "Dear God, *you* raped me!" A thousand curses filled her mind as she began to fight, a scream tearing from her lips. Jim attempted to cup Tess's mouth with his palm. The possibility that Jim might be Tommie's father sickened her. She fought harder, jabbing her elbow into his stomach, kicking at his shins.

"You made me second choice even then, Contessa," Jim accused, shoving her toward the bed and warding off her blows.

"Run, Tommie!" she warned. "You're in danger!"

Tommie woke and whimpered, trying to move, but the injury wouldn't let him move fast enough.

"You married Harper when that bastard didn't deserve you. Shouldn't have never gotten the pleasure of what I'm going to take from you now."

"Nooo . . ." she mouthed against the hand that finally closed off her protest. He meant to molest her again, but this time with her son lying next to them. Tess jerked her head to the side. His hand moved with it. Though she hoped the action would free her, it only provided a clear bite at his fingers. Tess bit like a raging lion.

"Son of a bitch!"

"Mista Luke!" Tommie screamed. "Help us!"

Jim backhanded the boy. Tess clawed backward, trying to reach the gambler's eyes, before a mighty blow struck her head. Light turned to darkness as she turned and clutched at Tommie. With an effort born of desperation, she threw her body over his to protect him from the gambler's madness, then crumpled into unconsciousness.

"Tess! Tommie! What's wrong?" Hearing no answer but Tommie's muffled wail, Luke threw his shoulder against the door with all his might. "Open up in there!"

The door held. He hit the oak panel again, but the hinges wouldn't give.

"Get out of here, Reeves. Go back where you belong!"

Daggert! Cold rage coursed through Luke. Why didn't Tess answer? Had the bastard hurt her?

"Let 'em go, Daggert, or I'm coming in, damn you!"

"You aren't calling the shots here, Reeves. I am. You'll get them when and if I'm through with them."

"You touch either one and you're a dead man."

"Too late, Reeves. I've already had her."

Murder, hard as steel, scraped the edges of Luke's sanity as he kicked and pounded the door with the fury of a lunatic. He willed the hinges to loosen.

Jim laughed at the bounty hunter's futile efforts, not noticing the man who slipped like a shadow through the bedroom window. The hinges gave an inch . . . another. The gambler drew his pistol.

"Drop it, Daggert," Nugget's voice sounded deadly. Jim whirled around and stared down the barrel of a two-shot derringer.

A ripping of hinges took Nugget's attention momentarily away.

Jim grabbed Tess up, pointing his gun at her head. "No, you drop it. Unless you'd like to see this little lady's brains splattered all over the room. Then I can tell the law how you wanted her dead so you could get the other half of the richest mine this territory has ever claimed."

Nugget's mouth twisted with rage, but he dropped the gun. Just as the hinges broke, Jim fired the pistol. Nugget went down.

Jim whirled as Luke burst through the door. As Tommie moved beneath her, Tess jerked upright. Her elbow struck Jim's arm. His shot went awry. The gambler cursed.

"Luke!" Tess screamed and threw herself on Jim's back, clawing at his face. The gun aimed again, but Tess pulled Jim's head backward as hard as her strength would allow. A knife left Luke's boot, whizzed through the air and plunged into Jim's chest. He sagged to the floor beneath her.

Untangling herself from the gambler's body, Tess ran across the room and threw herself against Luke. He wrapped his arms around her and held her close, burying his face in her hair. Relief shuddered through her.

"H-he was the one, Luke. Jim was the man who—"

"It's over now, love. He's gone. He can't hurt you . . . ever again."

"Mista Luke?" Tommie struggled to roll on one side.

Luke took him in his arms. "I'm here, son."

"How come Mr. Jim be so mean?"

Luke let out a long sigh. How could he explain this to a child who should never be witness to such ugliness in men's souls? "You've got to cut pretty deep sometimes, Tom, to find a rotten core."

Chapter Thirty-three

During the investigation into Jim's and Nugget's deaths, Tess spent hours thinking about the wrongs of her life and how she blamed everyone but herself. Life was a matter of choices. Good and bad. She had let her father and Clifton manipulate her and had lived in utter hell because of it.

She was tired of running, tired of hiding from her past. Lies and secrets were all she had ever known, and the day to end them was now. She loved Luke Reeves with all her heart and, more than anything, she wanted him to be the man she had fallen in love with. If he was to be that, then there was nothing else to do but turn herself in to Sheriff Mason, tell him the entire story, and help Luke keep his word and his job. But first she needed to talk to Tommie.

Telling Tommie she would be leaving him in Luke's care for an indefinite time turned out to be less difficult than she expected. Her son was attentive to all she told him, grasping as much as a four-year-old could. She held back nothing of her past, confessing it all. The wrongdoing. Agreeing to her father's wishes to save her mother from the beating he would give her if Tess disobeyed. Later on when Tess discovered her mother had lied about the abuse, Tess thought it too late to change. Too many thefts had occurred, and she was too frightened of what her parents might do if she refused to continue. Thankfully, Clifton proposed and the marriage became a way out.

"I'm not telling you to disobey your elders, son." She brushed back a wisp of blond hair so much like her own. "But it's better to trust what you believe is right. You'll know it in here." Tess pressed his heart. "The truth is a voice that's sweet and kind. It hurts sometimes, but it always ends up feeling much better."

"Mista Luke told me the same thing." Tommie squeezed her tightly, clinging.

He sensed that the leaving would be long; Tess could tell it in the way he tried to enfold her in his small embrace. She glanced at the bags which were packed and ready. The thought of leaving him seemed unendurable, yet she knew she must. If he was ever to learn what facing the truth meant, she must become an example. Luke would care for him. Love him . . . until she returned.

"When did Luke talk to you about this?" she asked, more out of a need to hear his voice one more time before she said the final dreaded good-bye.

"On the trail, when he been shot. He told me that you made some mistakes when you was a little girl, but you didn't mean to."

Tess couldn't hide her surprise.

"Don't worry, Mommie. Mista Luke say God don't do bad things to people if you don't mean to be mean."

She hugged him fiercely and whispered a silent prayer of thanks to Luke and the Creator who had brought him into her life. "You listen to Luke always, son. He's one grown-up who's not going to make you do bad things you don't want to."

"You mean I can if I want to?"

Tess laughed and kissed his cheek. "No, I certainly do not." She rumpled his hair. "You're going to be good, for Luke, aren't you?"

"Most certainly will," he promised, mimicking her. "And I'll make Luke be good too."

Tess smiled sadly. "Give him this letter when the sun doesn't shine in the window anymore. Promise me not to do it before then . . . no matter what."

"I promise, Mama. You be back soon?"

Tears flooded her eyes but she pressed them away with the back of her glove. "Very soon, my darling. Before you miss me, I hope."

Tommie flung his arms around his mother. "I miss you already, Mommie."

Tess closed the door of the hotel room behind her, shutting away the sound of her crying so Tommie wouldn't hear it. With a glimpse down the hall at the door to Luke's room, she whispered, "Take care of him, Luke. I trust you with the rest of his life."

She turned, tiptoed down the hall and headed toward uncertainty.

Luke whistled as he entered the hotel, looking forward to the special occasion he planned for Contessa and Tommie. He shifted the packages he carried into one hand and knocked on Tess's door. "You two hungry? I've got quite a night planned."

"Come in, Mista Luke," Tommie called out. "And I'm real hungry."

Luke found the door hadn't been barred and opened it to find Tommie sitting near the window staring out, looking mighty forlorn for such a small little boy. Depositing the packages on the bed, Luke glanced around. "Did your mother have to step out for some reason?"

Tommie nodded, his profile revealing a tear-stained cheek. "Mommie's gone."

Maybe it was the tone of the boy's voice or maybe it was a sense of premonition, but suddenly fear knotted in Luke's empty stomach. "What do you mean, *gone?*"

Tommie turned completely toward Luke, and the bounty

hunter saw the child's red-rimmed eyes. He had been crying for a long time.

"Mommie went away. Her gave me this. The sun is down now so I can give it to you."

Luke took the letter he offered and read the words quickly. "When did she leave?" he asked, glancing up into green eyes that mirrored his own sense of loss.

"While ago. Her coming back, Mista Luke?"

"Yes, boy, she'll come back," Luke promised, taking the small body in his arms and letting the child weep on his shoulder.

"How come I don't feel it right here, Mista Luke?" Tommie placed his palm upon his heart.

Luke's eyes blurred. "Because we're afraid, Tommie. And being afraid of losing someone you love sometimes makes you feel nothing so it won't hurt so bad."

"Do you hurt, Mista Luke?" Tommie said against his shoulder.

"I feel nothing." His voice cracked.

"Are you afraid?"

"More than I've ever been of anything in my life."

Luke decided that he must ask Olivia to come sit with Tommie until he could track Tess and talk some sense into the woman he loved. Gathering his pride, he asked the clerk her room number and carried the boy to Olivia's room. When he knocked, Olivia asked him to identify himself.

"It's Luke, Mother. I must speak with you."

"Luke?" Surprise curved her lips as she opened the door and stared at the smaller boy in his arms. A graying brow rose over her almond-shaped eyes. "Do come in."

"I don't have time for a lot of explaining, but I need your help desperately. You remember Tommie. He's going to be my son very soon—"

"Going to be?" she interrupted. "Lucas, are you in some sort of trouble?"

"I will be if I don't hurry. I can't travel fast if Tom's with me. But if you'll watch him, maybe I can catch Tess and stop her from doing something we'll both regret."

Olivia pointed a long, sculptured nail at the splint Tommie used to help him walk. "Will the boy be much trouble?"

Exasperation filled the bounty hunter. "Mother, what problems do you expect? He can't go anywhere without help."

"I be troubles sometimes, sure enough, lady. I don't want Luke to tell no lie."

"You're a lot of help," Luke groaned, offering his mother a pleading look. "For the most part he lays around, though it would be nice of you to take him swimming in the springs." Luke quickly explained the doctor's exercising orders.

"What is it you plan to do while I'm caring for this sometimes troublesome child?"

"I'm heading to Georgetown. In the meantime, if you can get a message to Phinneas Wideacre, see that he brings district judge Olan Wallace to Georgetown. Tomorrow on the stage, if he can make it."

"You love this woman, don't you?"

"With all my heart."

Olivia motioned Luke to place Tommie on the bed. "Then I'll keep the child until your return."

"Bless you." A compulsion unlike anything he'd ever felt in his mother's presence shot through Luke. The safeguard he had always thrown up to block any feeling toward her rose, but he fought its hold on his emotions. Before he could change his mind, he kissed her on the cheek. "Thank you."

"Oh, my . . . you're welcome, son," she replied in a fluster.

He pointed a finger at Tommie. "You mind and don't go climbing any trees while I'm gone. I'll bring back your mommie, then we'll all get married . . . okay?"

Tommie squealed with delight. "Sure thing, Mista Luke. Will that mean Mrs. Olivia be my grandmaw?"

"I certainly will not, young man!" Olivia gasped, her fingers splaying wide across her throat in distress. "If you intend to be related to me''—she paused, offering the imp an imperial frown—''then I will be your grand*mother!*''

Luke headed for the door, knowing that both Olivia Reeves and Tommie Harper had met their match.

Chapter Thirty-four

Tess managed to hitch a ride into Georgetown with a mule skinner. Though the man talked incessantly, he was friendly and demanded an answer only now and then. She had a good deal of time to consider her actions and decide they were the right ones. Perhaps the judge would be lenient when she turned herself in of her own accord and confessed to her part in the scams.

The mule skinner flicked the team into the last run toward Barton House and yelled, "Whoa, you oat-eating, turd-dropping sonsabitches!" He tipped his hat at Tess and spat out a wad of tobacco. "This where you get off, lady?"

"I do believe it is, Mr. Arbuckle."

The man remained sitting. She gathered her skirt hem and prepared to step from the wagon. The mule skinner hadn't washed in several years, if his clothing and the stains on his fingers were any indication. Tess sighed, grateful he wasn't the courteous sort who felt required to help her down. "Don't trouble yourself, sir. I can make it on my own."

"Oh, yeah? Well, all right, missy. If ya say so." He smiled a grin shy of a few teeth. "Maybe next time I'm thisaway, I'll give you a holler."

Tess returned his smile. "That'll be a day to remember, Mr. Arbuckle. It surely will. Thank you most kindly for the ride."

Arbuckle did her the courtesy of handing down her bag, but shouted the team into a trot before she had cleared the yard. Dust billowed beneath their hooves, coating her with a layer of sand, instigating a cough that nearly made her gag.

Lionel Cramden came around the house at a fast walk. "Why, Mrs. Harper, it's sure good to see you. Where's that little'un of yours? And Mr. Reeves?" A frown wrinkled his brow. "Don't tell me he up and left you, taking the boy?"

"Nothing like that," Tess assured him, allowing the tall, lanky man to take her bag. She told him about all that had transpired in Idaho Springs, leaving out the fact that Luke didn't know she had left.

"Nugget behind all those scams, you say? And that gambler fella in on it too? Don't guess you ever know, do you?" Lionel scratched his head.

Following him into the clean interior of Barton House, Tess gazed at the doorway to the room where Tommie's life had teetered in the balance. If Lionel knew her part in the scams, would he be so willing to extend his hospitality?

"Want a room for the evening, Mrs. Harper? It's pretty slow around here. You probably want to rest up before you go out to the mine. Be kind of lonely out there without Nugget and your boy to keep you company. Won't charge you, ma'am. Bis'ness is slow. Lotsa rooms are empty. Boss'd be pleased a lady such as yourself took a notion to stay the night."

Tess smiled at the considerate man. "How about if I give you my answer later, Mr. Cramden?"

"*Lionel,* please, ma'am. I'd be proud if you'd consider me a friend."

"You've been a fine friend to us already, Lionel. Thank you." Tess untied her bonnet and fluffed her hair. "Would you happen to know where I can find Sheriff Mason this time of evening?"

Lionel rubbed his chin, narrowing his eyes in thought.

"That would be over at Millie's place. He's kind of sweet on the gal that runs the Spittoon Saloon." A blush heightened Lionel's cheeks. "I don't suppose you know her?"

"I haven't had the pleasure . . . yet." Tess wanted to grin at the audacious name the lady had given her establishment, but Lionel might think she laughed at his blush. She wouldn't make him any more miserable than he'd made himself.

"I'll go fetch him and you see yourself to home." Lionel slipped the slouch hat off the peg near the register and plopped it down on his head. "Got some coffee brewing, or if you'd like tea, there's rosemary leaves in the cupboard. You remember where the kitchen is, don'tcha?"

Tess nodded and thanked him, watching as the gangly man hurried out the door. She half hoped he didn't find the lawman, but knew the hope would merely delay what she must do. Perhaps brewing a bit of tea would get her mind off the confession to come.

"A little bit further, Talon," Luke crooned into the horse's ear as the dun ran low and swift through the winding path toward Georgetown. The animal gave it his all, his body lathered with sweat, nostrils snorting in time with his ground-eating gait.

Precious fool, Luke whispered to Tess as if she were the wind blasting his face. *Don't do anything until I get there. Just a few more miles. A few more.*

Olivia opened the door and stared into the face of the man she'd come to love over the past several years. "Phinneas, you came!"

He removed his tall hat and propped his cane against the wall, taking her in his arms and kissing her soundly. "Of course I did, my dear. Your message did say it was urgent."

"Well, hello there, Mista Wideaka! How you been?" Tommie waved at him from the bed.

Phinneas stepped away from Olivia. "Apparently far better

311

than you've fared, Mista Harper.'' He searched Olivia's face. ''What is the meaning of this, my dear?''

Olivia quickly filled him in on the details, and within the hour, her lover had made arrangements for her, Tommie, Judge Wallace and himself to journey to Georgetown.

''What am I supposed to do with her?'' Sheriff Mason asked a surprised-looking Lionel. ''I haven't ever put a woman in jail before . . . much less a decent one.''

Lionel shook his head. ''I don't know, Sheriff. The men'll get pretty riled up if you're asking me.''

''Well, I ain't asking you!'' Mason growled and paced the floor, running a hand through what remained of his balding hair.

''But you just asked—''

''Forget what I asked, Cramden, and think, dammit!''

Tess sighed, sitting in one of the parlor chairs and staring up at the two men as they worried themselves into a frazzle. ''Put me under house arrest if you don't want me to go to jail. You can trust me. I came here on my own; I'm not going to run away.''

''Not *this* house,'' Lionel protested. A look of apology darted across his face. ''Don't mean to be unfriendly, Tess, but the boss would have my scalp. Not to mention, the men-folk around here would never use this place again. Wherever you get put, there's going to be a big problem.''

''Well, I can't say as you're much to blame, given all you told me.'' Why he ever wanted to be the hero who solved the salting scams escaped Mason now. ''If I take you in, Mrs. Harper, I'm going to be branded a bully and a lot of other offensive names I'd rather not be saddled with.''

Tess threw her hands wide in exasperation. ''I can't even give myself up!''

A pounding of hooves skidded to a halt outside in the yard. Tess rose, a sixth sense warning that trouble rode in with her name on it. Whoever it was didn't bother to knock. With a jarring of the door, Luke barreled into the room. Sweat poured from his brow as first relief, then anger clouded his face.

"What the hell do you mean leaving me?"

His voice bore a high and mighty attitude she would have normally taken on, but he didn't look in any mood for an argument.

Tess stepped back until she backed against a chair. Her hands went up in front of her, protesting the body stomping toward her in earnest. "Now, Luke, I mean to see this through."

"Oh, do you now? Well, madam, so do I. In fact, we'll see it through together, like we decided before you took the notion to do things on your own again." He pulled Tess against his chest, pushing her arms behind her. "Got any rope on you, Lionel?"

"Well, sure, but . . . hey, you ain't meaning to tie Mrs. Harper up, are you?" Lionel looked horrified.

"Where's my son?" Tess demanded.

"With my mother," Luke reassured her, then answered Lionel's question. "I'm going to tie the future Mrs. Lucas Reeves to me until Judge Wallace from Denver gets here. Do either of you men have any objections to that?"

Sheriff Mason and Lionel both shook their heads. Mason looked relieved. "What a man does with his intended is his own business, and ain't a fella in the territory gonna bicker with you on it."

Lionel shot a glance at Tess, who stared at Luke with loving eyes.

"It's all right, Lionel. I happen to agree with my future husband on this particular matter."

As the lanky man fetched the rope and tied her hands around her intended's waist, Tess smiled, knowing she could easily maneuver out of the position if she chose to do so. What was Luke up to?

"I think maybe I'll just mosey on back to Millie's place," Sheriff Mason announced. When Lionel stood there gawking at the couple who had eyes only for each other, Mason cleared his throat to get the lank man's attention. "I said, it seems Reeves has everything well in hand."

Lionel blushed a deep crimson at the implication. "Oh, yeah, sure, Sheriff." In a louder voice, he added, "I think I'll mosey on over with you."

As the pair went out the door, Mason argued loudly, "Who the hell you shouting at, man? I was standing right there two feet away from ya."

"I wanted to let them know I was getting out of there."

"You think they heard a word you said?"

"Don't reckon they did," Lionel commented as the door swung shut.

Tess was unaware of anything but the man encircled in her arms. Light tremors spread through her as he stared down with loving eyes.

"Tessa, do you know how hard it was to go to your hotel room and not find you there? Thank God, Olivia agreed to watch Tommie."

She shook her head, then buried her face against his chest. "I'm sorry, I just couldn't run away from my problems anymore or have anyone else resolve them. I had to come tell the sheriff. I didn't want to ever worry about you leaving me because of my past, and I didn't want you to go against your own word."

His gaze searched her face. "I'll always want you, Tessa. You're mine now, and what is mine will remain with me forever."

"I know it was wrong to just up and leave, but you have to understand. I had no choice. If I expected to take on a new life, I need to put the old one completely to rest. Otherwise there were too many old ghosts to haunt me." She willed him to see through her eyes. "If you fell in love with me, I wanted it to be the real me, not the image my father bartered with, nor the role I played as Clifton's wife."

Luke gently lowered his head and kissed her closed eyes.

He traced feather-light kisses along her cheeks, the edges of her earlobes, the soft hollow of her neck.

When Tess's lips parted in open invitation, he pressed his mouth to hers, engulfing her with a kiss that promised forever. As the kiss deepened, Tess swayed against him, and her heart did a wild dance in her breast.

"Tessa," Luke murmured, his voice cracking as he buried his face in her hair. "God, how I love you."

A swell of love filled her, bring with it a surge of warmth and safety and a sense of belonging. "Tell me again, Luke," she whispered against his neck. "Tell me you love me as much as I love you."

"I'll love you until the day life leaves my body and for an eternity more," he said almost savagely, kissing her lightly on the nose. "Touch me, love, the way you did on the very first day we met. Touch my soul the way you have every day that I've known you."

As easily as the bonds had been tied, Luke slipped the rope off, freeing her hands. Moving over him with sure intimacy, her fingers rediscovered all that was Luke. With a fiery possessiveness their bodies merged. Tess luxuriated in the way his meshed so perfectly with her own. Warm tingling sensations seeped into her veins, becoming liquid fire as the velvet sinews hardened beneath her touch.

Each looked at the other, and as one they laughed . . . like two children sharing a delightful secret.

Less than twenty-four hours later, Judge Olan Wallace pronounced judgment on Tess Harper's past crimes.

"In lieu of the evidence which proves you were coerced into forging the mine documents and the fact that you were only a youth who believed she was protecting her mother in the Hot Springs scams, I sentence you, Contessa Harper, for the rest of your life to the jurisprudence of your husband, Lucas Reeves, to be pardoned whenever he takes the notion."

The judge smiled and rapped the gavel three times. "Now let's get on with this life sentence so I can kiss the bride."

Tommie tugged on the judge's robe as his new Daddy and Mommie kissed. "What's a honeymoon, Mista Judge? Can I go too?"

DELANEY'S CROSSING

JEAN BARRETT

Virile, womanizing Cooper J. Delaney is Agatha Pennington's only hope to help lead a group of destitute women to Oregon, where the promise of a new life awaits them. He is a man as harsh and hostile as the vast wilderness—but Agatha senses a gentleness behind his hard-muscled exterior, a tenderness lurking beneath his gruff facade. Though the group battles rainstorms, renegade Indians, and raging rivers, the tall beauty's tenacity never wavers. And with each passing mile, Cooper realizes he is struggling against a maddening attraction for her and that he would journey to the ends of the earth if only to claim her untouched heart.

_4200-2 $5.50 US/$6.50 CAN

Dorchester Publishing Co., Inc.
P.O. Box 6640
Wayne, PA 19087-8640

Please add $1.75 for shipping and handling for the first book and $.50 for each book thereafter. NY, NYC, and PA residents, please add appropriate sales tax. No cash, stamps, or C.O.D.s. All orders shipped within 6 weeks via postal service book rate. Canadian orders require $2.00 extra postage and must be paid in U.S. dollars through a U.S. banking facility.

Name_____
Address_____
City_____ State_____ Zip_____
I have enclosed $_____ in payment for the checked book(s).
Payment <u>must</u> accompany all orders. ☐ Please send a free catalog.

GOLDEN DREAMS

ANNA DeFOREST

After her father's sudden death leaves her penniless, Boston-bred Kate Holden arrives in Cripple Creek anxious to start a new life, her elegant upbringing a distant memory and her dream of going to college and becoming a history professor long-forgotten. But the golden-haired Kate soon finds that the Colorado mining town is no place for a young, single woman to make a living. Then desperate circumstances force her to strike a deal with the only man who was ever able to turn her nose from a book—the dark and brooding Justin Talbott.

As skilled at passion as he is at staking a valuable claim, Justin vows he'll taste the feisty scholar's sweet lips—and teach her unschooled body the meaning of desire. But bitter from past betrayals, the wealthy claimholder wants no part of her heart. He has sworn never to let another woman close enough to hurt him—until the lonely beauty awakens a romantic side he thinks has died along with his ideals. For though bedding her has its pleasures, Justin is soon to realize that only claiming Kate's heart will fulfill their golden dreams.

_4179-0 $4.99 US/$5.99 CAN

Dorchester Publishing Co., Inc.
P.O. Box 6640
Wayne, PA 19087-8640

Please add $1.75 for shipping and handling for the first book and $.50 for each book thereafter. NY, NYC, and PA residents, please add appropriate sales tax. No cash, stamps, or C.O.D.s. All orders shipped within 6 weeks via postal service book rate. Canadian orders require $2.00 extra postage and must be paid in U.S. dollars through a U.S. banking facility.

Name _____

Address _____

City_____ State_____ Zip_____

I have enclosed $_____ in payment for the checked book(s).

Payment <u>must</u> accompany all orders. ❏ Please send a free catalog.

BESTSELLING AUTHOR OF
BLAZE

Kane Roemer heads up into the Wyoming mountains hell-bent on fulfilling his heart's desire. There the rugged horseman falls in love with a white stallion that has no equal anywhere in the West. But Kane has to use his considerable charms to gentle a beautiful spitfire who claims the animal as her own. Jade Farrow will be damned if she'll give up her beloved horse without a fight. But then a sudden blizzard traps Jade with her sworn enemy, and she discovers that the only way to true bliss is to rope, corral, and brand Kane with her unbridled passion.

___4310-6 $5.99 US/$6.99 CAN